OUR DARK MIRROR

BOOK I

JAMES CHANCE

For Darla and Pierce, without whom this story—and all the things that make life worth living—would not exist.

TABLE OF CONTENTS

OUR DARK MIRROR

BOOK I

JAMES CHANCE

CHAPTER 1

THE STRANGER FROM THE EDGE OF THE WORLD

Blood streamed onto the ashen ground, a single color in the thriving dark. A pitiful shape curled against the earth, small only beneath the vast shadow that loomed above it. Three sets of eyes gleamed red in the murk; three heads, three maws, countless teeth, too many claws now slick with wrath.

"Your only task, your very reason for being–forsaken! Desecrated!"

"Please, *please*, Father, I–"

"You have disgraced our kind. You are a defiler, a traitor."

"It was a mistake!" This desperation was so fierce and so desolate that it rivaled the beast's fury. "I looked away for one second, and he slipped past–"

"LIES!" the beast thundered. Grit clattered down from the ceiling, so high above it was veiled in darkness. "Your sister has seen it–how you whisper, how you plot! Together with this filthy mortal, this human–"

The son's life was draining away now, little by little, onto the earth, onto his paws. Oh, it hurt. All of it hurt. But that color was so *bright*.

What could he do? There was only one thing left.

"You're right," he said, closing his eyes, bowing three canine heads. "Father...my Lord Cerberus...you're right. I was foolish, trying to deceive you."

The monster's ears pricked with interest. It was enough–just enough–for a moment's mercy.

"I'm so sorry, Father. I was wrong. I...I saw something in him, in that human. He deceived *me*, because I'm weak, and I'm naive. He made me believe he cared about me, that..."

His despair overflowed and his words choked.

A deep rumble traveled through the beast's body. Satisfaction. "And you see now, do you? That every human is the same at heart. Selfish and treacherous and greedy. Reveling in their free will, until they spend it away and become our charges. And even now, they still bargain!"

"Yes," the son forced out, almost pleading. It was all he could manage.

Any humor the great beast had shown now decayed, leaving those three horrific faces barren.

"And my very own brood...taken in by their guile. Inconceivable. Unprecedented."

"I'm sorry." The words were tiny. He hated himself thoroughly, with every part of him left to hate and be hated. He was pitiful. It was the worst thing to be. But now, it was that or death.

And he had seen too much of death.

The beast drew himself up, a cruel mountain against the dark sky. Those blazing eyes tore the betrayer apart without touching him.

"How could I glimpse even a mote of worth in you now? You are nothing, now that you have defied your purpose. Obedience is your sole path–the only thing we ask of you. And now you have strayed from it. Now you know the horrors in the wilderness beyond. You cannot unknow them. You are lost to us."

No–don't– "But I can find the path!" his son begged. "Please, Father–give me one more chance to prove myself."

It wasn't enough. He could smell it. If he let one single word overtake him, it would be too late.

"The human! The prisoner!" he blustered, before his father could do so much as draw breath. "He's out there now, in the mortal world. He–he has some kind of plan. Something that would defy us even further. I can find him. I can hunt him down, and bring him back. I can make this right."

Cerberus paused, his thoughts flitting through his devil's eyes. His son lay still, bleeding out onto the dead earth, waiting with his heartbeat ticking closer and closer to its end.

At last, the monster's lip curled. "He will not trust you after this."

A pang of outrage found his son, unbidden. *Are you making me beg for my life?* He hated himself again after it passed, ashamed.

"I know his scent better than any of you." His claws dug into the dirt until they ached—a useless anchor. "And I know *him*. I know how to bring him back to Hell without alerting the other mortals. Our Lord wouldn't want us to cause mayhem in the mortal world, would He?"

Again—just enough. A little twitch in the face. The barest glint of hope.

"This will not redeem you."

Dread grasped his stomach with frigid teeth. It wasn't enough after all. He was wrong. And now he was going to pay the final price.

And for what? Was it worth it, you damned mutt? he snarled to himself.

No. He couldn't let this happen. One betrayal was enough. If he let that traitor human get him killed—

"I'll do it anyway," he burst out. "I hate him. I hate *every* human. You were right about them, Father. I'm sorry I didn't see it until now. I'll never stray again. I'll become retribution itself, if it means I get to bring that bastard to justice. Please, let me do it!"

"...I am not your father."

Panic gripped his heart. *No—please—*

"Not anymore. My son was called *Anendotos*, the unyielding. But he has yielded, and thus he is no longer."

Cerberus towered above his pathetic son, little more than a scrap of mangled fur at his feet. All around him stretched the bowels of Hell, the infinite horizon of death itself. His past and future. He was nothing, truly and fully.

And he expected the final blow—a final burst of color in the endless night.

"I name thee now *Ntropi*, for you are disgraced. And this you shall remain until your task is complete."

His son jolted upright. He almost forgot to avert his gaze from his father's might.

As if guessing his next words, Cerberus went on: "Make no mistake—this is not a promise. We shall see what awaits you come your return. But as of this moment, you are banished from the Underworld. Tread not upon this ground until the prisoner writhes in your grasp."

Cool relief shot through his son's veins. He swayed on his feet, unsure if it came from the news or blood loss.

One more chance. He could still redeem himself.

"Thank you, Lord Cerberus, thank you," he sputtered, bowing all three of his heads as he backed away. "I promise, I will restore our honor. I will bring him back."

But that lip curled up again, showing cruel fangs.

"That is not all. No mortal may see your true form. Nor can they know a soul has escaped from Hell. Humans do not know of us—not until they die. These are the laws decreed by our master. If you fail to capture the prisoner without revealing our existence to the mortal world...you know what awaits you."

His son's heart turned to ice. *That's impossible. He must know that! Is he toying with me?* "How? The moment I set foot in the mortal world, they will see what I am!"

"Yes. And so, the greatest disgrace, you have earned. You shall be human, to hide among mortals."

"What?" the word slipped out before he could curb it.

A searing pain sliced across his chest, as if those demon claws had found him again. But when he looked down, there was no blood at all. At least, not on his skin.

Four jagged lines, the flesh now healed and whole beneath. But it was thick and pink. The fur would never grow there again.

And then the familiar weight slipped from his three necks. Before his very eyes his collars fell, clanking onto the ground in a glittering heap of bronze. They seemed to glare up at him, as if they too despised what he had done.

"No..." he breathed, fighting the sick swell of vertigo. "Please, no..."

When he lifted his eyes, his father had turned away. He was no more than a shadow again, receding into every other shadow and the secrets they veiled beneath the earth.

"Fa—Lord Cerberus? What do I—"

"I shan't deign to look at you, now."

And then the pain spread, raging through his bones, his nerves, his fur...
He was...*changing.*

"Now, this is what you must do..."

A hand grasped the damp stone at the edge of a deep, black chasm. Dirty fingers shook as they hauled a nameless man from the depths of the earth itself. He crouched on the precipice, gulping breath, his plain clothes dark with water and clinging to his wiry form. Only feet away a waterfall thundered down into the abyss. It spat on the stranger that stood on its lip, daring him to venture too close so it could swallow him again.

He stared at it as if something held him there, seducing him back into the darkness. But then he pulled away.

Green. He had never seen such green. It seemed to suffuse the very air. Sunlight filtered through leaves, striking them with a brilliance that almost hurt his eyes. What the trees didn't catch beamed onto the forest floor, dappling it with little pools of warmth.

So *this* was bright.

The breeze was cool and damp, brushing his olive skin and ruffling the dark hair that fell around his ears. He realized he had never breathed freely before. Every breath beneath the earth was hot and arid, as if the very air yearned to choke him.

He closed his eyes. A thousand scents filled his senses. The wind brought to him the high drone of unseen insects, the rustle of birds in the high canopy, the crackle of paws in the undergrowth. These were the earth's vitals–its heartbeat, its breath, the tune it whistled to itself as it carried on.

It was...alive. Here, everything was alive.

It was better than he had ever imagined.

This stranger to the world stood at the edge of it, basking in it all, as if sating a starvation that had plagued him since the moment he was born.

But then the guilt began to crawl back inside–that, and another feeling, old as his bloodline:

The hunt.

I have to find Benjamin.

Suddenly, inexplicably...the stranger knew where his prisoner was. A sixth sense. He felt it like a rope had been tied around his ribs and was tugging him through the trees, weak but relentless.

Maybe this won't be so hard, after all.

He climbed carefully down the crag, following the waterfall's runoff towards the wide pool below. Balancing on only two legs made it harder. When he reached solid ground, he winced. Pine needles jutted through the leaf mold, prodding the tender soles of his new feet. He needed shoes, he decided, with a strange sort of relish.

He walked on, weaving between crowds of tall, thin trees and thicker, denser pines, growing like stolid sentinels over the shivering leaves of their brethren. He brushed his fingers across their scaly bark, marveling at how much he could feel on his skin, how each digit could rove on its own. His two legs swished through clumps of ferns crowding the trunks, trying to follow animal trails. This forest was bright, but deep.

Finally the brush began to thin, and then sunlight burst across his vision. He screwed up his eyes against its harsh touch. Between blinks he found himself looking out across a wide field painted with white markings. Beyond, a vast collection of buildings loomed, all straight edges and archways. Several mahogany-colored banners fluttered from its pillars, emblazoned with the letters "UoA" in gold. A matching sign stood out against its white facade: "UNIVERSITY OF ALDERWOOD."

A footpath leading there snaked along the edge of the field, separated by a chain-link fence. As he began to follow it, urged on by his sixth sense, his gaze was drawn to a spot of color in the middle of the field.

His heart quickened. There were humans here.

They were dressed in some kind of uniform with the same colors as the college's banners, and their voices drifted across the clearing. He couldn't make out the words, but it was clear they were having a serious discussion.

Then, one of them looked up.

"Hey there, bud! Are you okay?" the human called. He brushed past his companions, hurrying over to press his hands against the fence.

Shit. The stranger didn't want to look, but he did anyway.

This human was unlike anyone he had ever seen. His face seemed like it was carved of marble, a perfect portrait of concern. He was tall, his shoulders and chest broad, his pale arms well-muscled but their curves soft. His eyes were so bright, they could only be borne of this world—the precise color of shallow seas, his hair their golden sand. Underneath the earthy human scents, he carried distinctive notes of clove and jasmine.

He was pretty, yes, but...it was more than that. Something else shone through. A sunbeam that warmed the man who crawled from the earth.

And then that warmth turned to heat—a surge of hatred that blazed through every nerve.

Every human is the same at heart. Selfish and treacherous and greedy.

He straightened his soaked shirt collar as best he could.

"Of course I'm okay," he said. The human's voice was light and steady and expressive; his own sounded so dark in comparison, tinted by an accent that sharpened his consonants and rounded his vowels.

The human blinked, as if startled by his sharpness. "But...your clothes," he said hesitantly, as if he didn't really want to insult him by pointing them out. "Did you just come out of the woods?"

Stop looking at me like that.

"Henry, who is this guy?" Another of the young men had wandered over. This one was shorter but equally broad, with cropped brown hair and duller blue eyes. He only smelled like human, and a particularly musky one at that. One glance was enough to tell that he lacked the brightness Henry exuded—not just in appearance.

"Not sure," Henry replied as he looked the newcomer up and down. He was obviously trying to be polite, but his curiosity got the better of him. "I've never seen you around before. Are you lost? What's your name?"

Right. What had his father told him? "Vincent Chálkinos." Defiance egged him on. "I'm not a child, I know where I am. I go to this college. I just got here today."

An uncertain smile crossed Henry's face. He had dimples. "Okay, okay! Easy there, bud. I believe you."

No, you don't. This was going to be a problem.

"Nah, dude, no way. You look like a hobo," Henry's friend said. "Why the hell were you coming from the woods? Town's that way." He jabbed a thumb west, past the school's facade.

To Vincent's surprise, Henry shot his companion a look of displeasure. "C'mon, Jake. Ease up."

"But the year started a few weeks ago," Jake argued. "Why would he transfer so early?" His expression darkened. "You trying to score some free food or something? Just beat it, alright?"

Vincent silently cursed himself. He should have lied better. He should have said he had been here the whole time.

"Hey," said Henry suddenly, and turned to fix his friend with such a stern look that even Vincent was caught off guard. That strange charisma he commanded turned so swiftly in the opposite direction. "Knock it off, Jake. He's not hurting anyone."

Jake blinked, incredulous. Then he turned aside. "Let's just get back to practice," he grumbled.

"You guys go ahead without me." Henry began following the fenceline towards the school, gesturing for Vincent to come along.

Shit. Now he was in for it.

"What–why?" Jake said, alarmed. "Where are you–"

"You can handle leading it without me, can't you?"

Jake faltered. Then he snorted and turned back to join the others across the field.

Henry paused in his step, looking at Vincent expectantly. He hadn't moved.

"I told you, I don't need help."

"You might've mentioned it," Henry said, his grin returning as if he thought he was *so* irresistibly funny. "But you're new, right? Do you know where your dorm is?"

"Yes." He didn't. But how else was he supposed to get this guy off his back?

"Oh, okay! Which one is it?"

Vincent hesitated a moment too long. "I'm not telling *you*."

Henry laughed. It was so earnest and boyish that it would have cheered anyone up. It only pissed Vincent off.

"Okay, okay, I get it. I promise I won't stalk you. I just want to make sure you're all set. I'm an R.A., so it's kinda my job anyway."

"A what?" Vincent asked before he could stop himself.

"Oh, sorry—a resident advisor. It's a college thing. I make sure students living on campus are doing alright. Following the rules, feeling welcome, going to bed at a reasonable hour."

Vincent frowned. *Great. Now he's going to be checking up on me. Why did I have to run into* him *of all people, first thing?*

"That last one was a joke, by the way. I guess I'm losing my touch."

Just then they reached the fence's gate. Henry fumbled with the latch, which gave Vincent some headway. Once he was on Vincent's side, he had to jog to catch up.

"Just let me show you around, okay? You don't owe me anything. Not even an answer about the woods."

"Why?" Vincent shot back, more heated than he intended. He knew it would only make him seem more suspicious, but he could hardly stand it—this human acting so *noble*, like he had any right to hand-hold him, to talk down to him, to remind him of the last human who had—

"I just wanna help. That's all, I swear. You look like you need a little."

Vincent stopped suddenly, facing Henry and fixing him with a withering look.

"Don't you *dare* pity me. I know what I'm doing. Just leave me alone."

A tense gravity pulsed between the two of them. Then Henry's face softened.

"Something happened to you out there, didn't it? You don't have any luggage or anything, and you look like you've been through the wringer."

Vincent fought back the urge to bare fangs he no longer had. *You have no idea.*

"I don't pity you. I don't think you're weak or anything for getting mugged, or–or whatever happened. I know it must feel like that. That's how I would feel. But you're *not*. Everyone has a bad moment sometime. And everyone deserves to have someone around to help them get back on their feet."

Something strange panged through Vincent's heart. It was familiar, but only just. And he hated it.

"Well *I* don't, okay?" he spat.

Henry smarted, and Vincent forged ahead. At first he felt a prickle of satisfaction that Henry didn't follow. Then an unwanted thought trailed behind it:

That's it? He gives up on his morals so easily?

This human was nothing like Benjamin. It was probably better that way.

Suddenly, footsteps rushed at his back. He pivoted on instinct, ready to defend himself–

Henry halted paces from him, such a look of ardent determination carved into that marble face.

"Where is it, then? Your dorm? Show me."

The lies had run out. Vincent stood there, silent, seething. But gradually the heat subsided, and cold misery trickled into the space it left. Here he was, alone in a world he didn't understand, a world that didn't understand him, and somehow he was supposed to navigate it to hunt down his mark. Even this encounter told him all he needed to know–he couldn't even set foot outside without arousing suspicion. Finding Benjamin was the easy part, thanks to that sixth sense; but how could he hope to drag him back to Hell without alerting the mortals?

It was becoming clearer and clearer to him now: his father never intended for him to succeed.

Why humiliate me? Why not just kill me already?

"...I can't."

"Can I see your student ID card?"

Vincent gave in. There was nothing else to do now. He fished in his pocket, finding the wallet his father had given him before he left. He flipped through it, but it only contained what his father called a "credit card."

"I ah...don't think I have one."

Henry nodded. Then he smiled. Those charming little dimples returned. Vincent hated them.

"Come on, then. The registrar's office is closed now, but we can take care of that on Monday. For now, you can stay in my dorm."

"What?" Alarm coursed through Vincent's chest. With it came the image of curling up on the floor in Henry's room. Then he realized how strange that would be, because he looked like a human now. Did that mean he was supposed to share his *bed?*

Somehow, that idea was worse.

"I'm a stranger to you," Vincent argued, incredulous. It wasn't smart to point it out, but he couldn't help himself. "You don't even know for sure if I'm a student here. And you would let me sleep in your room?"

"Oh, god, no! My room only has one bed instead of two, because I'm an R.A. But there's an empty room across the hall you can have."

Hot embarrassment crawled up Vincent's neck. "That still doesn't answer my question."

Henry's smile deepened, and so did those contemptible dimples. "You're not a bad guy. I can just tell."

Vincent almost laughed. *Is he really that brainless?* Maybe he was one of those do-gooders his master sent away to Heaven—able to deny their human nature long enough to earn it. One of the lucky few.

Benjamin would despise you.

Or...maybe it was all an act. Why would anyone have faith in him? Especially considering how he was behaving? It was his best weapon—there was no way it wasn't working.

"Just, uh, don't tell anyone I'm doing this, alright?"

Before Vincent could reply, Henry started off.

For a moment, he wondered if he could just...ignore him. Take off in another direction, lose him entirely, follow the sixth sense pulling him towards his duty. It hadn't eased for a moment since he emerged from the chasm beneath the waterfall, like a gnawing hunger he couldn't sate.

But that would only create more trouble. This Henry—brainless or not—was extending him an olive branch, and, knowing humans, the opportunity may not come again. It wouldn't hurt to have someone in his corner who knew this world. Especially someone who navigated it as well as Henry seemed to.

And...knowing Benjamin, he wouldn't be able to simply walk up and collect him. After all, he had played Vincent well enough to escape Hell itself. Vincent would have to be the one to outsmart him this time.

So he followed after Henry.

They entered campus through a corridor supported by elegant archways. Vincent's eyes were grateful for the shade; the sun's glare was beginning to wear on him. They passed several detached buildings that were presumably classrooms. In the gaps between them Vincent could see a courtyard decorated with planters and a large stone fountain. It made a pleasant burble that echoed between the archways. Little bright butterflies flickered over colorful plants and around the water's edge. A few students milled about on benches with books or friends, but fortunately none of them looked up to notice the strange, tattered man and his escort.

Eventually they stepped back out into sunlight, crossing a large, grassy quadrangle dotted with vast, manicured oak trees. Their branches snaked out in all directions, casting dappled shade across the lawn. Henry kept a steady pace along the sidewalk, but Vincent trotted ahead onto the grass, relishing the cool, soft brush of it against his bare feet. He could feel Henry's eyes on him, but he chose to ignore it.

They stopped in front of a building at the far corner of the quad, which mirrored several others beside it. Giant letters affixed to its facade read: "WALDEN HALL."

"Home sweet home," said Henry.

It was cool inside. They passed a front desk area with stained wine-red carpet. Beyond it lay a recess for vending machines, which cast their neon glow on the walls. At the end of the hall was some kind of lobby with various couches, a ping pong table, a fireplace, and a TV. It was empty, almost eerily so.

Vincent could practically feel the building's age in the very air he breathed. Still, it felt...comfortable, somehow. He couldn't put his finger on why.

Henry took a sharp left into a long hallway, its walls lined with doors. They each had a number and one or two names posted on rudimentary signs. Someone had decorated them with random stickers–dinosaurs, glittery stars, funny hats, short motivational phrases.

Finally, just before the back door, they stopped at a room labeled 139. A sign below it read "Percy" in fancy lettering, accompanied by stickers saying "Good job!" and "Be yourself!"

Henry hesitated, staring at the door. Vincent looked up to find his face unusually blank. Puzzled, he tried his key. It opened.

The right side of the room was bland–an empty loft bed, a desk, bare shelves.

The left side of the room, however, was filled with personal effects. The desk and shelves were piled with books, framed pictures, and other clutter.

The colorful bedsheets lay askew as if someone had just gotten up. But they hadn't; the blinds covering the window above it were drawn and dusty.

Vincent walked slowly inside, gazing around. Henry stayed by the door, his hand on the frame. After a moment he seemed to recover, clearing his throat.

"Here we are! This side is all yours," he said, gesturing to the empty half.

Vincent threw him a glare. "Seriously?" *Not that I have any right to complain, but...*

Henry's brightness finally faltered. "Yeah. Um, I'll get you a blanket and a pillow. Need anything else?"

"You said no one lives in this room, right?" It certainly didn't smell occupied.

"Well...yeah."

"Then why don't I just use this side?" Vincent swept a hand towards the furnished half of the room.

"It's not your stuff." Henry almost sounded sharp, which surprised Vincent. Henry seemed to realize it, and relaxed. "Sorry. I'm uh...storing it for someone."

"...Okay." Vincent knew better than to press. Instead he sat on the empty mattress mutinously, making direct eye contact. Henry grimaced.

"So, um...do you have any money?"

"Of course I do."

"Yeah, of course you do...I just thought, maybe since...well, anyway, I've got a night class soon, but how about we go get you some stuff tomorrow? I can drive you into town, they have a Walmart there."

Vincent fought to keep a smirk off his face. *Guilty?* Then he realized what Henry was offering.

"Oh, ah...I guess. Sure."

That seemed to ease Henry's mind. He smiled. "You got it. Well, I'll let you get settled. I'll pop back in before my class starts and bring you some dinner, how's that sound?"

Did he really want to watch him that closely? Did he suspect something after all?

But that was ridiculous. How could some human know anything about what he was? What he was here for? Surely after Vincent got his affairs in order with the college, proved he was supposed to be here, Henry would back off.

Or maybe, despite Vincent's warning, Henry did pity him. He wasn't sure which was worse.

"...Alright."

"Cool! See you soon, then!"

Henry left Vincent alone in the half-empty room.

His clothes weren't so damp now, but they had seen better days in whatever previous life they had before him. He was starting to feel itchy and tired, especially now that he was alone. This exposed, soft skin felt *everything*. He rubbed his throat firmly with his hand, which soothed him a little. His bare neck felt so light, so vulnerable...

Then something thumped at the door. Startled, he peered at it, but nothing else happened. Slowly, he went to open it–

And found no one on the other side. But at his feet lay a blanket, a pillow, a stack of clothes, a towel, and a couple bottles of soap. Everything was neatly folded.

Vincent stuck his head out into the hall, but it was empty. He retreated, narrowing his eyes down at the offerings. Then he picked them up and laid them out on his bed.

The T-shirt was teal and far too big for him, as were the salmon-colored shorts and the pair of matching sandals. It suddenly occurred to him how small he was in comparison to his benefactor. *Thanks for that, Father.*

He tried to remember how big Benjamin was, but it was impossible. Vincent had only ever been around him in his own true form. But he had a sinking feeling that overpowering Benjamin in this new human body was not going to be an option.

Not for the first time, he wondered if his father *wanted* him to fail. He had surely set this up intentionally. He could have given Vincent a more useful body.

Vincent stubbornly shook himself out of his thoughts. He was being ungrateful. Of course his father wanted him to succeed–it was their family's pride on the line. He needed to get back on task, and try to blend in.

He remembered seeing a bathroom down the hall–it would have to do. He put on the shoes, picked up the rest, and started off. He cringed at the sound his feet now made–*flip-flop, flip-flop*. He suddenly no longer wished for shoes.

It took him a minute to figure out how to work the shower. At first he thought the cold water was the extent of the experience, which was good enough for him. Then the water heater kicked in, and he discovered something entirely new. He relaxed against the tiled wall with a deep sigh, and took his time washing.

When he finished his gaze lingered on his clothes. They were so dirty it surprised even him. He could only imagine what he himself had looked like. No wonder Jake had been so perturbed by him. Henry must be too polite to show it.

Vincent's discomfort only grew as he stood in front of the bathroom mirror, his slender frame nearly swallowed by Henry's clothes. He felt far too warm in them, somehow. The subtle scent of clove and jasmine drifted over his senses, contending with that sixth sense that compelled him towards his mark, chewing at the base of his ribs...

He backed away from the mirror, shaking his head to clear it. But the scent lingered, soothing the sharp edges of his mind. He quickly gathered his things and shut himself in his room.

But the air was no better in here–in fact, it was heavier, somehow. The lamp looked dimmer than before. Vincent's head felt like it was filled with cotton. He curled up in Henry's blanket on the bare mattress. He eyed the other bed enviously, but he didn't want to piss off Henry. The thought surprised him at first. Then he decided it was just because he didn't need to cause more trouble for himself. Nothing more.

Unable to relax, Vincent slid off his bed and wandered to the other side of the room. His eyes moved curiously over everything. There were notebooks, a biology textbook, a poster for some movie Vincent didn't know, little pots with succulents in them that were just beginning to wilt...and framed pictures with various people in them, but one in common: a young man with soft, earth-colored features and curly black hair.

In every single photo he wore a large, oval-shaped turquoise pendant on a silver chain. Some of his faces beamed at the camera and others smiled with a crease of worry. The latter stuck out in a well-dressed photo alongside an older man and woman, their hands over his shoulders. Vincent found the boy's true smile in more places–a cerulean pool filled with laughing people, a forest lit only by campfire, a snow-bleached hillside dotted with skiers–each with the young man at their center, surrounded by bright faces, grinning at Vincent's invisible eyes.

The more he looked, the more a strange warmth began to creep over him. He felt almost comforted by it; but at the same time, he felt very small.

He forced the feeling away. His sixth sense burned in his chest. He had a job to do here. He didn't have time for this.

He crept back towards his own bed, willing himself to rest. But sleep did not come.

Instead the room seemed to drift away from him. The walls and floor and ceiling stretched impossibly, taking the other bed and its clutter with them, leaving him alone in his little dark corner of the world.

His stomach lurched. He gasped, struggling to tear himself away from the vertigo. The lamp was still on–but it was barely a glint now. Deep shadow clung to every corner. He could barely see his own bed under him. It felt as if all the air had been sucked out of the room, and his chest grew tighter with each breath. Panic began to rise in his throat–

"You can sleep in my bed, if you want," said a new voice.

CHAPTER 2

THE GHOST OF ROOM 139

Vincent startled. He gripped the collar of Henry's shirt tight against his neck as if it would somehow keep him safe. He looked around wildly, that cold voice still echoing through his very nerves–and then he spotted it. Just a shadow, barely that, silhouetted in the dim lamplight. It looked vaguely like a person, but its edges were distorted. It held a deep gravity, like a hole torn through the very fabric of space. Every instinct cried out against its existence. He couldn't bring himself to look directly at it.

"Wh-who are you?" he demanded, despising the tremor in his voice. "Show yourself!" He didn't want it to, but he refused to cower.

"*I...I can't. I'm sorry.*"

Vincent wasn't sure if the words were spoken aloud, or if he felt them deep in his chest. The voice was garbled, but little bits of it felt almost normal, carrying the tone of someone young and male and...meek. He couldn't find a better word for it. It was a horrible mix, the fearsomeness of this presence with its timid demeanor.

"*But–but I'm Percy. S-since you asked. You're, um, Vincent, right? That's what Henry said...*"

"You know Henry?"

"*I did...he hasn't spoken to me in a long, long time...*" A sudden chill spread throughout the room. "*Though...I don't know how long it's been...*"

Out of the corner of Vincent's eye he saw the shadow drift up the wall towards the ceiling. The cold remained, but the sense of unease slowly lessened, allowing Vincent to breathe fully again.

He glanced over at the pictures on the desk, barely able to make out the silhouette of the young man he found in them. "That's you, isn't it?"

"*Yes...*"

He paused. Was he allowed to say it? He decided it was worth the risk—what could this shadow do to him anyway?

"How did you die?"

The reaction wasn't as turbulent as Vincent expected. The room seemed to lurch all around him, but the answer came with only a tremor of confusion.

"*I don't...remember... Everything has been so dark, lately...*"

"You probably don't even know how long you've been here, do you?"

Again, the *no* came as half-word, half-feeling. But before Vincent could say anything more, the shadow spoke again, its voice and presence intensifying.

"*What am I supposed to do, Vincent? I've been here so very long, and nobody can see me...nobody except you... It feels like I'm dying here, I'm fading away so slowly into s-something...something I...I can't even tell you...I can't...*"

The shadow spread over the walls, creeping closer and closer to him. Alarm rose in his throat. The presence prickled at his senses, as if searching his innards with invisible tendrils for whatever essence it now lacked.

Vincent had felt this before when he walked among the shades of the dead, countless times—but never so intensely. Perhaps it was the oppressive truth of being a lone, lost soul surrounded by those still living, all of them blissfully unaware of his empty misery.

A pang of rogue sympathy struck his heart, catching him by surprise. It *hurt*—like it had found a weak spot, a fresh bruise.

Or a scar.

He shouldn't feel *sympathy*. But he did.

Again? What is wrong with me? he thought savagely, trying not to lose his grip. He could feel it beginning to spin away from him—

So he grabbed onto something else—something he was allowed to feel. Something not altogether different from his sixth sense:

A sense of duty. This ghost did not belong here.

"I can help you move on," Vincent said, steeling himself. "If you just—"

There was a sharp knock at the door. Instantly the dark presence halted, then slipped back into the far corner of the room. Vincent drew a breath of relief, although the hair on his body still stood on end.

"Vincent? You in there?"

"Yes!" Vincent risked a glance towards the shadow, but it was no more than a speck on the ceiling. He took the opportunity and made for the door, yanking it open.

Henry stood there looking just as cheerful as ever. He held two lidded trays of some kind, and through the transparent plastic Vincent saw food inside.

"Surprise!"

"Oh. Is it that late already?"

Henry nodded. His smile faltered as he glanced past Vincent into the dark room. For a moment Vincent wondered if he could see the shadow; but then, he said, "Oh wow, did the light bulb go out? Some welcome that is. I don't have any spares, but we can totally pick one up tomorrow when we go shopping. Hope you're not afraid of the dark!"

"No. No, I'm not."

Henry seemed to miss his tone. He was busy flicking the light switch on and off, as if that would help. After a moment he gave up and said, "Well, let's go eat in my room, then. I hope your shower was good, at least?"

Vincent had to fight the now-familiar warmth creeping up the back of his neck at the memory. "Ah...yeah. It was nice." He didn't know what else to say.

He took the tray Henry offered him and followed him down the hall. Glancing out the glass of the back door, he realized with a start that the sun had in fact already set. He hadn't thought it had been *that* long...

Henry's room was as bright as he was. Football paraphernalia with the school's logo decorated the walls, coupled with the image of a cartoon pheasant. These were joined by posters depicting grandiose landscapes and people, emblazoned with odd titles like "The Lord of the Rings." His shelves housed rows of novels and figures—most of them little people, but a couple model spaceships as well. The room was half the size of Vincent's, and there was only one bed and desk. Everything was impeccably neat and organized, the bedclothes folded perfectly and the pillows fluffed.

"Did you go to...what do they call it...army school?" Vincent asked, sitting at Henry's clean desk.

"You mean military school?" Henry laughed, plopping down on a beanbag chair. "My dad's just very particular. I was always told to keep things spick and span." He shrugged, opening his food tray. "I guess a lot of people take the opportunity to drop everything their parents make them do once they're in college, but I never felt the need. I love my dad."

Vincent copied Henry, looking inside his food container. It held a reddish stew with chunks of meat, beans, and some kind of vegetable in it. In a compartment beside it was a pile of mashed potatoes. He eyed them dubiously.

"It's not poison, promise," Henry said, winking at him. He took a big mouthful of potato, making a very theatrical show of chewing and swallowing it. At the end he pretended to gag and slumped over in his seat, letting his tongue hang out.

Vincent felt a smile tugging at the corners of his mouth. He forced it away, rolling his eyes. He took a bite of the potatoes as well, not expecting much. But as soon as the buttery flavor settled in, a surge of hunger overtook him. His mouth flooded with greed and he barely kept himself from wolfing the rest down, acutely aware of Henry staring at him.

"Go back to dying," said Vincent between bites.

Henry grinned. "Ooh, try the chili. I think it's pretty good, anyway. Ava down the hall always says it's too spicy."

Vincent did, and the sharp tang of spiced tomato and meat delighted him. Soon all of that was gone too, well before Henry had gotten through half of his. He didn't miss this.

"How long were you wandering around in the woods, anyway?" he asked. Vincent could tell he was trying not to seem too interested, which annoyed him.

"Not long."

"Well...do you think your folks will be worried about you, if you haven't called them yet? Do you want to borrow my phone?"

"No, that's alright. I can get my own tomorrow." Yet again he decided to go along with Henry's assumptions–but he didn't want him to get too far, so he said, "You have class soon, yes?"

"Yeah, in about twenty. The theater building isn't far, though. Hey, what are you majoring in, Vincent?"

"Philosophy."

"Wow, really? I didn't think we had much of a program for it... You didn't want to study closer to home?"

"Not really." Vincent gnawed on his spoon, trying to think of a way out of this conversation. No matter what he said, he kept cornering himself.

"Where *is* home, anyway? You um, have a bit of an accent, but I can't quite tell..."

Damn. What kind of accent *did* he have? He supposed it was the same as his father's, and long ago *he* had come from...

"Greece."

"Greece! Why would you come *here* for philosophy? I thought Greece was like, the best place to be for that!"

Again Vincent silently cursed himself. He shrugged. "There's only so much you can learn at home. Better to broaden your horizons."

Henry chewed on his fork thoughtfully. He had finished his own dinner by now. "I s'pose so. Still, strange place to end up. There isn't much all the way out here."

"Where is the food place, by the way?" Vincent asked quickly, casting a longing look at his empty food tray.

"The Commons, you mean?" Henry chuckled. "Well, you probably don't want to go that far, because of your...um, but I have some change, if you want some snacks to tide you over. C'mon."

Vincent followed Henry out into the hallway, towards the front lobby. They passed a couple other students, whom Henry greeted brightly. They all seemed very friendly with him, but their eyes passed over Vincent dubiously. He assumed part of the reason was how odd he must have looked, dressed in Henry's oversized, brightly-colored clothes. He wondered what else they saw to make them uneasy. He tried not to look at them, and acted as dull as possible in a vain attempt to avoid holding their attention.

The little alcove with the vending machines was unlit, apart from the stark bluish glow of the machines themselves. The corner was almost as eerie as Vincent's room, but Henry seemed unfazed as he showed him how to select the snacks he wanted. He noticed Vincent's disquiet, however, and said, "It's kind of creepy back here, isn't it?"

"Not really," said Vincent, piling little bags of chips into his arms with increasing awe as Henry continued handing them over. He was apparently intent on setting him up for several days, at least.

"Well, I think it is." Henry paused, then said, as if reading his thoughts, "What do you think of your room?"

Vincent could sense something charged about this question. He decided to proceed carefully.

"It's fine. I imagine I'll be leaving it soon, though, right?"

"I'm not sure. Depends on if they already assigned you somewhere else." After a pause he added, "I bet you could stay, if you wanted. It's nice not having to deal with a roommate."

Vincent felt a jolt of surprise. *Does he want me to stay?*

But why? Vincent was sure he had been nothing but difficult to deal with. Maybe Henry really did suspect something was wrong with him...

Well, then he would just have to double down.

"I thought the other resident was coming back? You said you were storing their stuff for them."

"Ah..." After a heavy silence, to Vincent's surprise, Henry finally broke. "He's...not coming back. I'm sorry I didn't tell you before. The guy who used to live there was..." He trailed off.

Vincent's curiosity got the better of him. "What happened to him?"

Henry turned his face away, the neon light of the vending machines casting it into deep shadow. "Nobody knows for sure. The police haven't... He was found just outside of campus with...with multiple wounds."

"What kind of wounds?"

Henry cleared his throat sharply and shook his head. "I just can't talk about it. Percy...he was my friend, you know?" He started back down the hall before Vincent could say anything, leaving him no choice but to follow. "I am sorry about putting you in that room. It's just the only one nearby. If you want to move, you can."

Vincent didn't answer. "So you're just going to leave his things there like that?"

"Nobody's come to collect them yet. I don't think his parents want to face it, to be honest. I...I can't say I blame them. It just feels...I dunno, wrong, somehow. Like sweeping it under the rug that he even existed."

Vincent clenched his jaw. "That's how death is. There's no way to keep them around, no matter what you do. Or don't do. At some point, someone *has* to move everything."

"But not yet," Henry said, as sharply as Vincent had ever heard him speak. He decided not to argue. But he had to wonder if all humans were like this—hating and avoiding death so thoroughly.

Minutes later, alone in his dark room, Percy's invitation echoed in his ears: *You can sleep in my bed, if you want.* He couldn't even sense the ghost's presence anymore, although he had a feeling he was still here, somewhere.

Vincent moved across the room and slipped into Percy's bed. Immediately he realized why humans used them. It was nothing at all like finding a scrap of shelter back home, either out on patrol or in the kennels. There he could only hope at most for an ancient rug or a patch of ashen grass to cushion him against the hard ground. Here the blankets were soft and thick, the mattress plush beneath him. They kept the chill of the autumn night at bay, which somehow only made it even cozier. Despite the strangeness of the world around him, everything felt impossibly safe curled up in his little corner.

As he nestled his head into Percy's pillow, he pushed away the unease that wriggled in the back of his mind. Percy was *dead*. And he obviously wasn't upset by this.

Before Vincent even knew it, his thoughts gave way to a deep sleep.

The next morning, after what felt like the best sleep of Vincent's life, Henry led him out to the parking lot at the back of the building, where they hopped into his little sky-blue car (a "Mini Cooper," apparently) and drove off onto the country road towards town. He clicked the radio on and a crescendo of voices filled the cabin. He said the song was called "Mamma Mia" by "ABBA," which was incidentally his favorite band. The sound surprised Vincent; he had never heard anything like it. Henry sang along with it shamelessly.

After a minute or so, Vincent realized he was humming the tune, too. He stopped himself.

He gazed out the window to busy himself. Towering pines flickered past on all sides; then they burst out into a stretch of hills dotted with trees and what rays of sunlight found their way through the cloud cover. Little yellow and pink wildflowers decorated the sides of the road between quaint country houses. Vincent found himself wondering what kinds of lives were lived in there, hidden behind those walls.

Just as they reached the open air, a new song came on that bounced through the airwaves. Each beat seemed to echo with the thud of his heart. It made him feel strange...like it was easy to forget about his reason for being here, everything that mattered. *Is this...what music is supposed to feel like?*

Suddenly his window rolled down and cold air rushed into the cabin, whipping across his face and tousling his hair. It caught the song's synth midair and together they danced around him, tugging at him to join them.

This time, he gave in. He leaned his head against the window frame, squinting against the wind. His mind began to drift, and his heart felt lighter than smoke.

"Y'know, a smile looks good on you, Vinny."

Vincent turned in time to catch a glance from Henry. He was wearing his signature smile, but...softer. That undue warmth crept back up Vincent's neck.

"Vinny? Why call me that?"

"Why not? We're friends now."

"Well, it's–" He paused. "Are we?" he said more quietly.

"Yeah," said Henry, as if it was the most obvious thing in the world.

Suddenly the song ended. It was called "Electric Love" by "Børns," according to the radio host. Vincent couldn't help the disappointment that crept in, and the next song couldn't quite fend it off. He sighed.

By the time his thoughts caught up with him, he had forgotten to reply.

Soon enough little clusters of buildings appeared on the pale horizon, and then they were driving past storefronts. Many of them had porches with hand-painted signs and little window displays–hunting and fishing gear, cold-weather clothes, craft supplies, and so on.

A little ways out of town, a larger, boxy silhouette came into view. A bright blue and yellow sign on its facade proclaimed "WALMART," leering down at them as they parked in the oversized lot. That sense of lightness that had carried Vincent through the forests and fields faded quickly, even before the music switched off.

The place was a labyrinth; Vincent could barely make any sense of anything. He simply trailed after Henry, half-listening to his chit-chat. He kept a wary eye on every person they passed, convinced they were staring at him even if they were obviously looking elsewhere.

Henry led him through the different departments with a big blue cart, helping him choose the items he would need. He tried not to look so fascinated with them all, but he could tell Henry had already caught on. He kept looking at him with something that hovered between delight and pity, and Vincent decided to ignore it for the sake of his own pride. Still, he felt a guilty kind of satisfaction as he chose versions of things he decided he liked—jasmine-scented soap, bedclothes with a sleek red and black pattern, tough leather shoes, a variety of collared shirts, jeans, jackets, and pants in dark colors, and even a phone and laptop (upon Henry's insistence).

I need these things if I'm going to maintain my cover, he told himself, a bit too gleefully.

"Did you really just want collared shirts?" Henry asked. "No T-shirts? They're a lot more comfy."

"I guess..." He had to admit, Henry's shirt was pretty soft.

"Do they wear ties in Greece?" Henry said, wandering over to a nearby display.

"Ah...sometimes." Vincent had no idea.

Henry grabbed one and slung it over Vincent's neck, stepping back to appraise it. Vincent tried not to fidget under his gaze.

"Yep. That's good. You should get some."

Vincent must have looked unsure, because Henry added, "You have no idea how to tie it, do you?"

Indignation flared in Vincent's chest. He snatched up the ends and started wrapping them around each other until the loop closed. Sort of.

When he looked up, Henry's dimples had arrived to shoulder the burden of trying not to laugh. Vincent scowled.

"Um—good try!"

"Stuff it," Vincent growled.

"What? It's—I mean, it's *unique*—"

Vincent started to lift it back over his head, but Henry swiftly stepped closer.

"Oh, here, just..."

Vincent tipped his head back, giving him plenty of space to work. Plus, this way he didn't have to look at him. He was way too close for comfort. Warm breath grazed Vincent's throat, the scent of clove and jasmine filling his senses, dulling his thoughts...

After a minute that lasted forever, Henry retreated. Vincent realized he could breathe again. He hadn't even registered how fast his heart had been beating until it began to settle.

But...the tie did look good. And even better, the steady pressure around his neck was comforting.

"I'll show you how to do it when we get home," said Henry. He looked far too pleased with himself.

"I never got the hang of it, okay?" Vincent lied. But what was he supposed to say? That he had only had hands for the past day and a half? He was lucky he knew how to use them at all.

"There's a trick to it, for sure," Henry replied kindly. "My dad had to show me a lot for me to get it."

"I guess mine had other things to worry about," Vincent muttered, collecting a couple other ties from the display.

"Like what?"

Vincent froze. *Why did I say that?* He pretended not to hear and started off down the aisle.

"Uh, Vinny, the checkout's this way."

When they returned to campus, Henry helped with the laundry. While they waited in the basement laundry room he showed Vincent how to tie a tie a few more times until he managed to copy the knot, albeit messily. He settled for wearing it more loosely around his neck, still appreciating the touch it provided.

When the laundry was finished they took it up to Vincent's room, and Henry opened the blinds for the first time. The half-sun helped brighten the room's air considerably, and although Vincent kept an eye out, he saw no signs of his eerie roommate.

Henry stepped out so Vincent could dress. When he looked into the mirror above the sink, he was startled to see himself looking...normal. Well, normal enough.

He held the brush he had bought like it was some kind of alien technology and tugged it through his dark brown hair, uncaring of the pain, until it passed through smoothly. It still looked a little strange, being longer than what he had seen on most other men so far. He combed it back and made a low ponytail. Now he looked considerably better, despite the shadow that seemed to linger on his features. He didn't look like everyone else, not entirely...but he would be able to blend in now.

When Henry came back in, he too seemed impressed. "You look good, Vinny!" He beamed at him and then his side of the room, now furnished. "And so does everything else!"

Vincent felt a little smile finally cross his face. He turned his head to hide it, forcing out a scoff. "You don't have to humor me so hard."

Henry made a dramatic groan. "Just when I thought we were getting somewhere..."

"What's *that* supposed to mean?"

"Nothing, nothing!" Henry laughed. "You're just so stubborn! Pretending you hate me, but letting me drag you around anyway."

Vincent stopped short. "...I don't *hate* you."

Henry clutched his chest. "You *what?*"

Vincent rolled his eyes. But he realized he was still smiling. "You heard me, jackass."

Suddenly his sixth sense surged back at full force. It pulled him inexplicably towards some point in space—nearby, but not close enough. It felt like his father had reached right into his chest and yanked at his heart. As if to remind him what he was. What *Henry* was.

Cold shame swept over him. He was doing it *again*. He battled hard against the swell of memories. Benjamin had his own charms that had coaxed Vincent to trust him—but he wasn't like Henry. Henry was so forgiving, so warm, so funny, so...unlike anyone Vincent had ever met.

It was too good to be true. It always was–he had learned that. Henry had an agenda, whether or not he was aware of it, because that's what humans did. Even if he really was a do-gooder, it was all for his own reward. Vincent had allowed himself to forget. Allowed himself to trust Henry, to get caught up in this place.

What would his father think? Did he know, somehow? Was that why–

"Well, who do we have here?"

A new voice. He turned to see a young woman leaning against his door frame, arms folded. Her features were pale and carefully manicured, her lips plump and very red. Her hazel eyes looked unnaturally bright against her eyeliner. They lingered on Vincent.

"Oh, hi Melanie!" Henry's tone was pleasant as usual, but Vincent's sharp senses detected a reserved note. "We're just getting Vincent settled in. He transferred here yesterday."

"Really," said Melanie. "In *this* room?"

"Yeah," said Henry, with a shrug. "I mean...it can't just stay empty forever."

"Mm, well it wasn't exactly empty before." Melanie held out a delicate hand to Vincent. "It's good to meet you, Vincent. I'm Melanie."

Vincent grasped her hand and shook it. She smelled strongly of coconut, and little else–not even the normal human scents that usually lingered beneath. He had never met a mortal so perfectly clean. Melanie's head tilted ever so slightly, and he caught a glint of curiosity in her eyes.

"She lives just down the hall," Henry added. "Ava's her roommate."

The moment seemed to last too long before she retracted her hand. "I'm hosting a party Friday night. Kicking off the first big football game of the year. Everyone's going," she added pointedly, whisking herself away. "I'll see you there, I'm sure."

When she had gone, Henry said, "Oh my god, you *have* to go, Vinny! Melanie's parties are the best."

Vincent wondered if being invited was a good thing. It was certainly a surprise. Maybe Melanie was being nice...or maybe she only bothered because of Henry. Either way, he was hardly going to a human party when he had something much more important to do.

"I'll think about it."

When Henry departed, Vincent was left alone again with his sixth sense.

Except he wasn't alone. Not here.

"*It's her...*"

The whisper rose up from a shadow just beginning to stretch across the far wall. Vincent couldn't directly look at it any more than he could before.

"Melanie?" he asked.

A low croon began to vibrate through the walls. He could feel it in his very bones.

"*She did it...she made it happen...*"

"Made what happen, Percy?" Vincent asked, trying not to shiver.

"*She's the reason I'm dead.*"

CHAPTER 3

HUNTERS & HUNTED

V incent's heart skipped a beat. "Are...are you sure?"

"*Yes...*"

"How did it happen? What did she do, exactly?" It felt strange to him, considering how amicable she seemed. Maybe it was an accident...

Then again, she *was* human. He shouldn't be surprised.

"*I–I don't remember. I'm sorry!*" Percy's voice rose in desperation.

The air grew heavier and heavier with each passing moment. Vincent pulled his tie taut around his neck to steady himself.

"*But I know it was her...she did...something...*"

"That's not exactly helpful," Vincent pointed out. "If she's really responsible, we need to be able to prove it."

We? Vincent caught himself. That *sympathy* was creeping back. He shook his head sharply.

"No–I'm not here for this. I have something else to do here, something way more important. I can't get side-tracked trying to help you."

"*Y–you* have *to...Vincent...you're the only one who can hear me...*"

"That can't be true. Someone around here has to have the Sight."

"*N-no one talks to me...*" Percy protested, almost whining. "*They can't...o-or maybe they're just ignoring me...*"

As if called by his sympathy–*no*, his thoughts of duty, he told himself–the tether between Vincent and Benjamin tugged at his senses. This time it *hurt*, as if it was tangled around his heart.

"*You p-promised you'd help me move on...d-didn't you? O-or did I imagine it...*"

Percy sounded genuinely unsure, and something urged Vincent to pounce on the opportunity to mislead him.

But he couldn't do it. This miserable specter had nothing left. And Vincent wasn't about to start breaking his word now, even in this faithless world of mortals. *Why the hell did I tell him that?* he growled silently. But he knew the answer.

Not *sympathy*. Percy didn't belong in this world. His very presence felt wrong, on more levels than Vincent could name. His deepest instincts urged him to correct this, to lead him to his proper place. Wasn't this part of his duty as well? Surely it couldn't take too much longer...

Finally he sighed. "Alright, look...I'll *try* to help you, okay? I only know a bit about these kinds of things. But you're going to have to help me more than just giving me hints, got that? I'm here for my own job, and that's my priority."

At once the room seemed to brighten, and Vincent could almost feel the fervent nod from Percy.

"*Y-yes! I'll do anything...*"

"Then you have to think. Hard," Vincent insisted. "I need something useful. Something to prove Melanie's involvement. Any memories you have of what led up to...to the moment itself. I know it can be...traumatic...but you don't have a choice."

Percy's alarm filled the air. "*B-but...I don't know h-how I'm supposed to do that... W-what if I take too long? How long do I have before you l-leave me?*"

Another pang of sadness coursed through Vincent, countered only by a burst of indignation. He shouldn't be so easily affected by this pitiful creature.

You know what sympathy got you. Forget it.

"I'll give you two weeks," Vincent said flatly. "After that, I'm going to finish my work here and go home."

"*O-okay...*" A moment of heavy silence passed. "*What...are you here to do? Y-you never told me...*"

"I don't owe you any answers," Vincent said, turning away from him and grabbing his jacket. "It has nothing to do with you."

"*M-maybe I can help you back? S-since you're being so nice to me...*"

"I don't need your help. I know where my mark is. You can't do anything, anyway."

"Then...then why are you doing all this? I-if you're just here for a job, why don't you just do it and move on?"

Vincent was already halfway out the door, and he closed it behind himself without another word. He wasn't sure if the ghost could follow him out of the room or not, but he had had enough.

Outside, Vincent's sixth sense pulled even harder, especially now that he was paying attention to it. He started off across the quad with a purpose in his stride. He passed several groups of wandering students, uncaring if they stared or not. Perhaps they wouldn't, now that he looked relatively ordinary.

Finally he came to a large square of storefronts with the same lettering as Walden Hall. Mahogany flags on poles lined the courtyard, each with their gold "UoA." There were more students milling about here than the rest of campus, and Vincent decided this must be the University of Alderwood's central hub.

His sixth sense was pulling him towards the side building marked "THE COMMONS." As he slipped between the pillars at the entrance, he recalled Henry mentioning the name before. He soon realized why. His nose told him the moment he ducked through the doors: *food.*

The inside was immense, filled with various food stations where staff served lines of students behind counters. The rest of the space housed booths and tables, many of them occupied. The entire building echoed with chatter. At first Vincent was overwhelmed, his head swimming with the cacophony of human goings-on. But he tightened his tie and gripped his sixth sense like an anchor's tether.

He was close. He could feel it.

Vincent knew it would look strange to be here without purpose, and he couldn't do anything to Benjamin anyway–not here, not now. Besides, he was hungry. So he stepped into the line closest to him, where line cooks tended small pans. Each was filled with various ingredients students requested for some kind of make-your-own stir fry.

Waiting wore on him quickly. Every passing minute felt like a year to him as his senses tried to drag him in the direction of his target. *So close.* It was a hunger like any other, desperate to be satisfied. He tapped his foot against the tile floor. The line moved up, one by one.

Then, he saw him.

Suddenly none of the noise around him mattered. It was just him and Benjamin.

Benjamin Warwick–deathly pale, mousy-haired, freckled, hunted eyes the color of a winter sky. He was sitting at a booth by himself only a few yards away. He gazed intently down at a book on the tabletop, picking at his lunch. But even if he looked up, he wouldn't see Vincent. A line of students waiting at another station snaked between them, leaving Vincent only a small gap to see through. It was perfect.

Even so, he was surprised Benjamin couldn't sense the darkness of his presence, the heat of his gaze trained on him, a wolf to a wounded rabbit. How could he not? But it was better if Benjamin thought he was safe. Much better.

No more sympathy.

"Hey dude, you're up."

A voice lanced Vincent's concentration. He found a short, raven-haired young woman staring at him from her place in line just behind him. She had her arms crossed, her dark, narrow eyes tight with annoyance.

"Sorry," he muttered, stepping up to the station. He stared blankly at the lineup of raw ingredients through the glass, and the cook grew impatient as he tried and failed to describe what he wanted. Finally he just pointed to whatever looked good, and hoped it would be.

He scooted along the line with the others as the cooks worked, resisting the urge to glance back at Benjamin. *Now you know he's here, for certain. You can't do anything about it now,* he reminded himself, fingering his tie.

At the end of the line, the cashier grabbed his plate from the cook and handed it to him. Then she held a hand out expectantly. Vincent stared.

"Oh, come on, man..." The girl beside him sighed roughly, then reached across to hand the cashier a plastic card–her student ID. Vincent looked at her, equally surprised and puzzled. She scowled back at him.

"I got it. But next time you're on your own, dumbass."

"Ah...thanks," he said, lamely. He took his plate but lingered for a moment.

"What are you waiting for? A doggy bag? Get out of my way."

Vincent awkwardly shuffled aside. She brushed past with her own food. He was fairly sure she would have shouldered him aside if he hadn't moved. Before she could leave, however, he finally mustered some courage.

"Wait–did you pay with your student ID?" he called after her. He hated how helpless he felt, but he had to get his bearings somehow.

The girl stopped. "Are you serious, dude? Have you just been starving to death in your room all semester?" She gave him a once-over, then snorted, "Guess that would explain the look."

Vincent grimaced. "I'm new, alright? I'm not from here."

"You think I care? Figure yourself out, weirdo." She marched off to sit alone with her back to him, only a couple booths down from Benjamin's.

Despite the attitude, Vincent couldn't help his amusement. Her welcome was practically the opposite of Henry's, and she was almost half his size. There were all kinds of unusual people here.

Vincent went to an empty booth, just out of the way but positioned so he could still keep an eye on Benjamin. He started on his food, but realized he was hardly enjoying it at all. His *other* hunger was far more ravenous today.

He was only distracted from it when a familiar voice rose above the din.

"Will you just leave me alone, man? I'm trying to eat my lunch, I don't need you ruining my appetite."

Vincent peered over the booths, picking out the back of his new acquaintance's head. A boy now sat opposite her–tall and wide, with dark shoulder-length hair and glasses too small for his face. He looked more out-of-place than Vincent did, now. His expression hovered somewhere between shock and hurt.

"I–I just thought you might want some company, Casey," he said. "You're all alone over here, aren't you? Or, um, is your boyfriend coming...?" he added, with a dejected note.

"I don't have a boyfriend," Casey snapped, ducking her head to continue eating. "And I don't care."

"What are you watching?" he asked, leaning towards her. She snatched her phone aside.

"*Don't* touch my phone!" Casey snarled. "Are you deaf? I told you to get lost."

The boy's anguish grew on his face, then morphed into something more bitter. "Why? I'm just trying to be nice."

"Do I have to write it down for you, Hunter? Leave. Me. Alone." Casey's tone invited no argument, but Vincent could see one brewing in Hunter's expression regardless.

Instinct flooded him and he stood without a thought, striding towards their booth. He stopped beside Casey and fixed Hunter with a withering look.

"You heard her. Leave," he growled.

Hunter gaped at him. Then he stood. "Who the hell are you? You said you didn't have a boyfriend!" he added, glaring at Casey.

"I *don't*." Casey completed the angry triangle, glowering up at Vincent. "The shit are you doing? I don't need your help."

Vincent ignored her, stepping towards Hunter menacingly. Vincent was slimmer and shorter by more than a head–not much of a threat, ordinarily. But a shadow seemed to sweep over the table, chilling the air between them. He didn't take his eyes off him for a second, and even Hunter couldn't help but take a step backwards.

"*Leave.*"

But Hunter's pride overshadowed his cowardice. "I'm just hanging out with her! You're not her goddamn boyfriend, stop trying to win her over!"

His voice was far louder than Vincent's or Casey's, and suddenly many eyes had turned to face them, curiosity buzzing through the dining hall.

"Will you two shut up and let me eat in *peace?*" Casey slammed her hands down on the tabletop. Nobody flinched.

Vincent's gaze bored into Hunter, cold, relentless. He took another step forward. "Don't argue with me. You heard what she said. It's very simple. You leave now, or I'll make you."

Hunter's fist swung. But Vincent was ready—he ducked aside easily. With a sharp kick to the groin, Hunter fell. He groaned loudly, rolling over on the floor. The onlookers gasped.

Vincent's instincts moved in fast. He had to leave—now. In a moment he had slipped away, using some of the stations' lines as cover. Some eyes followed him, but soon he was out the door. Only then did he risk a glance back through the windows—

—and saw Benjamin, staring straight back at him in horror.

For a moment, Vincent was frozen. *Shit.* Now Benjamin knew he was here. *Why* did he pick that fight? He wasn't a guard in this world—he was a hunter. But his damned instincts kept getting in the way.

There wasn't a trace of sympathy about it. That's what he told himself as he took off through the square and ducked around a corner—only to nearly slam into someone coming the other way.

Both of them stopped short. The girl let out a little *eep*. Then they recognized each other.

"Oh, Vincent...you startled me," Melanie said, tucking a stray strand of hair behind her ear. She offered him that pretty smile of hers, glancing over him again curiously. This time, Percy's words echoed in his mind:

She's the reason I'm dead.

"Where are you off to in such a hurry, hmm?"

"Sorry," Vincent said, skirting her and starting down the walkway. A hand grasped his forearm, and he turned in surprise, barely suppressing the instinct to snap.

"What did you do?" Melanie asked sweetly, the barest hint of a smirk gracing her plump red lips.

"Excuse me?"

"My friend told me there was a fight at the Commons." She dropped her hand from his arm to finger the phone sticking out of her shallow pocket. "And you're running straight from there."

Vincent narrowed his eyes, trying to ignore his heart stuttering. "That got out fast."

"So did you do it?"

"None of your business."

"*Everything* is my business. Oh, but don't worry–I won't tell," Melanie added, her words honeyed.

"How am I supposed to believe that? If 'everything is your business.'"

"You just are," she said. "Then again, I can tell you did it, at this point. Do you know Casey Helliker? Are you into her?"

Vincent tried to relax his shoulders, to no avail. He had underestimated this girl's cunning. Her involvement in Percy's death suddenly didn't feel so far-fetched.

"No. I just met her. Some guy was harassing her, and I didn't like hearing it."

"Hmm, so you're a white knight, then?"

"I wouldn't say that," Vincent replied flatly. He had no idea what she meant. He glanced behind him towards the square, but couldn't see anyone pursuing him–yet. "Look, I need to get out of here."

He started off yet again, and cringed as he heard her footsteps following.

"Oh, they won't find you. I'll make sure of that."

Vincent glanced at her, suspicious.

Her smile twitched slightly. "In exchange, you can be my date for the party on Friday."

Vincent faltered. "What?"

Melanie didn't stop–she snagged his arm again and forced him to keep walking ahead with her. A ripple of anxiety radiated from her grip, traveling through his body.

"I'll even get Ava to fix you up, *properly*. You're almost hot, but you're too weird. Trust me, this will be the best thing for you, starting out at this school."

What's that supposed to mean? His ears grew uncomfortably warm at her words, but he ignored them. He didn't want to give her the satisfaction. "How are you going to keep me out of trouble? A lot of people saw me back there."

"A magician never reveals her secrets," Melanie said smoothly. By this time they had reached Walden Hall, and he ducked inside. He instantly felt better under shelter.

Vincent glared at her, but he could tell he wasn't going to get anything out of her. It was clear she had some kind of sway on campus, between her promises and how quickly the drama had reached her ears. And she was acutely interested in it–and him, apparently. He wasn't sure he liked the implications of that, much less the ones he couldn't guess.

But there was something important about her–not just because she was involved in Percy's murder. He sensed that it would be wise to stay in her good graces.

"Alright. I'll go with you."

Melanie's smile widened slightly. "See you then," she said, and started down the hall.

Vincent lingered until she had gone, wondering just what he had gotten himself into. It seemed he was right after all–reaching Benjamin was going to be *much* harder than he had hoped. Especially now that he knew he was found.

The next few days passed like a fever dream, both agonizingly long and only a blur. On Monday he finally made it to the registrar's office (with Henry's help) and got his own student ID and choice of room. Much as Percy's presence unsettled him, he had gotten used to his current room.

Besides, it was probably better than taking a chance on another, more *lively* roommate. At least this one wasn't going to suspect anything too strange about him.

He also got his class schedule. Apparently he was actually expected to attend the classes he had been mysteriously signed up for, or he wouldn't be able to stay for long. He was thankful for his philosophy major–despite his unfamiliarity with the concept of school, he was surprised to find he enjoyed it.

He listened intently to the lectures, munching on something passionately all the while. He even found himself offering comments now and again, especially during discussion groups. He had no clue there were so many ideas humans created to make sense of the world around them. The best part was the books and stories they used to play them out, as if to prove to one another how it was possible.

When he wasn't in class, he was dodging Henry. The less he got involved, the better. And now that Vincent had proved he definitely belonged here, and was getting the hang of things, he didn't need to appease Henry as much. Vincent hated how nosy he was, how much he laughed at Vincent's jabs and grumblings, how sweet and pretty and perfect he was. He was nice to everyone, and everyone seemed to like him, too. It was unnatural. Impossible. Aggravating. Maybe he didn't just pity Vincent–maybe he pitied *everyone*, for not being Henry Wellfellow.

When he wasn't in class or dodging Henry, he was tailing Benjamin. As he suspected, it was easier said than done. His sixth sense led him straight to him every time, but Benjamin was expertly cautious–always in public places with plenty of eyes around, or otherwise tucked safely indoors where Vincent couldn't reach him. He wasn't stupid enough not to lock his room, and breaking in would draw attention–especially since Benjamin had a roommate. He seemed to have an answer for everything.

Frustrating as it was, Vincent continued following him as often as he could. After all, it was only a matter of time before Benjamin slipped up. He was a loner by nature–sooner or later, Vincent would catch him alone.

At the end of the first week, Vincent found himself sprawled across one end of a sofa in the dorm's common area, idly spooning macaroni and cheese into his mouth as he scoured *Paradise Lost*. People came and went, but Vincent had learned to tune them out. He couldn't concentrate at all in his own room, feeling those unseen eyes trained on him as if starving for his attention.

Presently someone did enter his peripheral vision, and he only glanced up when they spoke.

"Hey–Vincent, right?"

Vincent looked pointedly back to his book. "Yeah. Friend of Henry's?" he assumed, as he often did, and correctly.

The girl laughed. "Of course, who isn't?" She sat down in the armchair across from him, slipping off her sandals and tucking her legs underneath herself. "I'm just waiting for my...well, my date. He lives in this dorm."

Vincent nodded, still reading even as his concentration was slipping. It was a bit annoying.

"I've never seen anyone sit like that. I thought I was the only one."

Vincent lifted his book to glance down, noting how haphazardly he had draped himself over the couch. "Thanks."

"Oh, I'm sorry, I'm not trying to insult you!" the girl exclaimed. "I just always get teased about sitting on my legs and stuff. I thought it was funny."

Vincent finally decided to get a better look at her. She was taller and bulkier than most women he had met so far, with an open and kind face. Her skin was dark and her coiled black hair was tied back into a ponytail not unlike his own. She smelled like warm, clean human, with a bright note of citrus.

"I didn't realize," he replied, not sure what else to say.

"Well, I'm glad no one laughs at you about it," she chuckled. "I'm Sierra, by the way."

"Vincent."

"You said," she pointed out, making Vincent feel a bit foolish. "It's cool. A lot of people know you anyway. You're a bit of a talking point around here, with the late transfer and all. And your room..."

She trailed off, and Vincent grimaced. "Oh, don't worry. I heard all the rumors about that." After an awkward moment he added, not sure if he really wanted the answer, "What about me? What are people saying?"

Sierra laughed nervously. "Nothing bad, I promise! People are just curious, really. I heard that you're from Greece, and you're going to the party tonight with Melanie, so you must be something special."

He relaxed a little. Melanie had kept her promise–no one was talking about his fight with Hunter. He had no idea how she pulled that off.

Of course, that also meant he was stuck going to the party. Having her as an ally was non-negotiable now.

When he tuned back in, Sierra was still talking. "Everyone says you have to be really hot. Or, um..." She broke off, flustered.

Warmth crept up his neck. *Hot?*

"God, sorry! I didn't mean to say that! I'm not trying to hit on you, honest! That's just what people expect since Melanie's interested in you, and she's, like, the queen bee around here. It's all very high school, isn't it?"

That made more sense. There was no way he actually lived up to those expectations–not with the way people looked at him. Like there was definitely something wrong with him. He just wasn't sure what. Maybe they weren't, either.

"Ah, so you don't think I'm hot," Vincent said snidely.

Sierra slumped against the side of the armchair with a little groan. "Nooo, of course not! Wait–I mean–*you* know what I mean, you ass!"

"No, I get it. Mysterious Greek exchange student. I should be hot. That's how the story goes, yeah? Too bad I'm me."

"What's that supposed to mean?" Sierra said hotly.

Startled by her sudden indignation, he shrugged.

"Oh, I am *not* letting you talk shit about yourself. I mean, you're going out with Melanie King, for god's sake! Isn't that proof enough for you?"

Sudden heavy footfalls saved him from having to reply. He turned to see Henry's friend Jake approaching. He was dressed in the same mahogany uniform as when Vincent had first met him, emblazoned with a gold number

"2" on the torso and shoulders. A thundercloud loomed across his face, his gaze lingering on Vincent as he stopped beside Sierra. She looked up at him brightly.

"There you are, Jake!"

"Hey, Sierra," he answered, finally looking at her. He reached down to rest a hand on her back. "Are you ready to go?"

"Sure!" Sierra unfolded her legs and stood up, offering Vincent a smile. "Are you coming to the game?"

"The game?"

"Yeah—the football game? The big one tonight?"

"Oh. No, ah...I have to catch up on some homework."

"You don't like football, huh?" Jake remarked, with an air of judgment. He kept his hand on Sierra's back.

"Oh! They probably don't play it in Greece, do they, Vincent?" Sierra put in.

Vincent decided to take the out. "Not really."

A little smirk twitched onto Jake's face. "Well, ever heard the saying 'When in Rome'? You might want to start."

"I'm from Greece, not Italy," said Vincent coolly.

Sierra snorted a laugh. "Oh, but you're still going to the party afterward, aren't you?" She seemed genuinely concerned about this, which surprised him.

"Well...yeah."

"Wait—you're going to the party, but not the game?" Jake asked him.

"I didn't know there was a prerequisite to parties," said Vincent. He felt very clever, using college terms to make his point. *See, Henry? I don't need you.*

Jake's lip curled, but he ignored the quip. Instead, he seemed to have a better idea of how to corner Vincent. "So, who are you going with?"

"It's not like I *need* someone to go with, do I?" Vincent replied, growing more and more irritated with Jake's little game.

"Oh, not really," Sierra cut in, patting her hand against Jake's broad chest playfully. "It's just a good excuse to ask someone out, right?" Jake shifted uncomfortably. "Besides, Jake, he's actually going with Melanie—you didn't hear?"

Jake blinked at him in surprise. "Oh. How'd you manage that, man?"

Vincent shrugged. "I'm hot, I guess."

Jake frowned, but Sierra laughed.

"C'mon, Jake," she prompted, tugging on his arm as she started off down the hall. "See you later, Vincent!"

Vincent waved her off before settling back into his book. It took him a minute to realize he wasn't really reading it, only thinking of the exchange. He decided he liked Sierra, against all odds. And he didn't like Jake. The feeling was surely mutual. He had no idea why Jake was so close with Sierra—or Henry, for that matter.

Then again...Henry hadn't given up on Vincent yet, either. He just kept showing up with that winning smile everyone else liked so much.

What does he even want from me?

Eventually he returned to reading and demolishing his macaroni and cheese. But the longer he kept at it, the more his thoughts gnawed at his brain. Henry was playing tonight, and everyone else seemed to be going to watch. He had no idea why this was supposedly such a big deal...

"Um, hi...you're Vincent, right?"

Vincent looked up at the second girl to sit across from him that day. This one had startling candy-apple-red hair, matching lipstick, and a girlish face painted ghostly white. She almost looked like a storybook character. Behind her heavy eyeliner, her round blue eyes betrayed little other than curiosity.

Vincent lowered his book slightly. "Yes?"

"Oh," she said, much too brightly.

"You sound disappointed."

"What? Of course not!" Vincent didn't believe her. She moved on: "I'm supposed to be helping you get ready for the party."

"Ah," said Vincent, finally closing his book and straightening up. "You must be Ava, then? Melanie's roommate?" That explained the trace of coconut lingering around her. Her own scent carried more lavender.

The girl smiled, a little too tightly. "That's me. C'mon."

Ava led him to a room a few doors down from his own. He instantly knew which half belonged to whom. Melanie's side was prim and elegant. Nearly all of her belongings were painted pale pink and gold, accented with crisp white curtains and furred tuffets. She had even brought a vanity with her, its mirror outlined with strands of pretty white lights. In comparison, Ava's side was a style Vincent had learned to describe as *goth*–dark colors, strange patterns, shelves filled with hanging plants and crystals, a tapestry along one wall depicting a skull broken by a backdrop of twisting thorns.

Ava stepped up to the vanity and patted the chair in front of it. For a moment, Vincent wondered if he had gotten the room's orientation wrong.

"Isn't that Melanie's?"

"She lets me borrow it. And she wants her date to be the talk of the party, anyway. She'll want me to use all my best tools."

Vincent sat down, gripping the sides of the swivel chair uneasily. Ava bent closer to peer at him, making him feel uncomfortably warm.

"That bad, ah?" he asked, trying to ease his own tension.

Ava snorted, then whisked away to her side of the room. She began rummaging for something and returned with an armful of hair and makeup products.

"What are you going to do?" Vincent pressed. She was acting too mysterious for comfort.

"Oh, you'll be fine. Just trust me–I know what I'm doing."

Vincent tugged at his tie, trying to calm his nerves. Ava began tending to his face and hair, spraying something on his head and brushing something on his cheeks, telling him when to close his eyes or hold still, and he did his best to comply. The worst was trying not to flinch while she painted something across the edge of his eyelids.

He tried to ignore the crawling sensation under his skin. He was wholly unused to this kind of close attention, let alone touch, but he was determined not to show any weakness to this strange girl or, by extension, her formidable roommate. As she worked, he desperately tried to think of anything to talk about as a distraction from his own awkwardness. As he glanced around her side of the room, he spotted a pack of tarot cards on her desk, neatly boxed atop a purple cloth.

"Ah, you read tarot?" he said, trying to sound casual.

"Mhmm," she responded, not pausing in her work.

"Is it like...for real? Or just for fun?"

Ava glanced at him. "It's both."

"I've never had a reading before. Maybe you would give me one sometime?"

"Do you actually believe in that kind of thing, or are you just messing with me?"

"I wouldn't mess with you. Especially when you could ruin my reputation with a bad stroke of whatever it is you have there."

Ava made a thoughtful sound in her throat. After another moment fussing with his hair, she returned to his front. She bit her lower lip, assessing him, until a little smile drew across her face.

"That'll work. Alright, let's get you into something better. What do you have?" Ava said, already starting towards the door.

"What?" Vincent slid out of the chair, rushing to follow her. "Where–"

"Clothes, dumbass. You have to have something party-worthy."

Vincent had no idea what was party-worthy. He let Ava into his room, trying as he always did to ignore the sensation of being watched. The two of them sifted through the clothes he had bought with Henry to pick out a few things Ava insisted were "perfect." He was only glad he actually had something for the occasion after all. He figured disappointing Melanie was the last thing he wanted to do right now.

When Vincent returned to the mirror fully dressed, he was startled to find himself staring at a stranger. Well, almost. He was himself, of course, because he had those same distinct dark eyes and narrow features and dark chin-length hair, but everything was arranged like a living painting. Somehow Ava had accentuated his cheekbones and jawline, and added a sleek wave and shine to his hair that still let it fall effortlessly. She had also emphasized his eyes with eyeliner, adding another layer of darkness to his visage that made his gaze even more piercing than before. Topped off with his leather jacket and loose wine-red tie, he looked like he belonged on an album cover for some kind of music that was far cooler than he would have pegged himself. Probably something Ava herself would listen to.

Ava grinned behind him in the mirror, fluffing the sides of his hair a few times lightly with her fingers. "Good as new. Better, even."

Vincent wasn't so sure–after all, he didn't have a good compass on what was appropriate or not for such a setting as this. But as he looked at himself, his discomfort waned to a tentative pride. He couldn't say he didn't like this look.

"Well, Melanie will be happy at any rate," Ava added with a sigh. She glanced at her phone. "We have a few minutes. Did you still want that tarot reading?"

"Oh–yeah, sure. I've always wondered if it really works..."

"Of course it works," Ava snorted, grabbing her pack of cards. "If you know what you're doing." She laid the purple cloth out on her desk and began shuffling the cards with obvious care. Vincent couldn't help the little stutter of excitement in his chest–there was something about having his very own fortune that pleased him deeply.

Finally Ava glanced up at him. "Is there any question you have in particular, or something you want to know about?"

Vincent thought for a moment, then shook his head. "Just anything, really. Maybe, ah...something important about what I'm doing right now?" He didn't want to divulge his true intentions, as curious as he was, so he kept his words vague.

Ava didn't seem to mind. She picked out three cards and laid them out on the desk face down. "Alright. The first one is your past–where you're coming from. The second is what you are right now. The last one is where you're going."

She flipped over the first card. Its artwork depicted a large man with curved horns sitting atop a throne, clutching chains in both clawed hands. At the end of each chain a man and a woman knelt, bound and collared with blindfolds over their eyes. A chill shot up Vincent's spine.

"This card is The Devil. It's saying that your past was marked by being restrained by something dark, like an addiction or even a person keeping you down."

The next card showed a bloody man collapsed on the ground, swords sticking out of his back, stark against a stormy sky.

"Man...you've got a lot going on, don't you? This is the Ten of Swords. I know it looks gruesome, and I guess it is, but it's not one-for-one, you know? It means endings. Death, failure, sometimes betrayal. It's a warning to keep an eye out for things that would do you harm, especially if you don't expect them."

The room seemed to sway around him as his unease grew.

Ava revealed the final card. This one depicted a tall stone spire crumbling to pieces, struck by lightning. Vincent caught the look of dismay on her face.

"The Tower," she said quietly. "It means...well, in my opinion, it's the worst card you can get. I guess other people have different ideas on it, but...it means upheaval. Disaster. Something that will upend your current life, and force you to build it from the ground up again."

She paused, then added, "Maybe it isn't that severe. Who knows? Sometimes it's talking about something a lot less earth-shattering, and sometimes not. Either way...you should be on your guard. I don't know what's happening with you, but it's not good."

He found himself staring at Ava, his thoughts churning. There was no possible way she could know...could she? No–she didn't seem like she understood the specifics of what he was, and what he was here for. Maybe it was only luck that the cards pinpointed such things. But still...

Vincent watched as Ava slotted the cards back into their box. "Do you read for people often?"

She shrugged. "When I can."

"Do people usually say it's accurate?"

"I've never done a bad reading," she huffed.

"Have you...ever done anything else before, like a seance?"

"That's not really the same thing as tarot," Ava said, annoyed. "But yeah, sure I have. I wouldn't recommend it to an amateur, though. Hasn't anyone ever told you not to play with ouija boards?"

"Are you still talking about all that weird stuff, Ava?"

Ava and Vincent looked up to find Melanie herself stepping through the door. She was completely done up already, her makeup immaculate and her long hair perfectly curled at the ends.

"Always," Ava replied wryly. "Your boy's ready, by the way. You're welcome."

Melanie paused to look Vincent up and down, a pleased smile growing across her face as she did. Somehow, he felt like prey being observed before the chase.

"I knew I could count on you, Ava," she said. "The eyeliner is a nice touch. He almost looks like one of your emo punk band boys. But, like, in a good way. Maybe I'll let you take a turn with him next party," she teased. Ava rolled her eyes.

"Oh yes, nothing I like more than being passed around like a platter of meat," Vincent muttered, resisting the urge to tighten the tie around his neck.

"Don't be such a killjoy, Vincent."

Melanie patted him twice on the butt. He winced. It took every ounce of self-control not to snap at her with fangs he no longer had.

Henry would have just laughed at his quip. Suddenly he found himself wishing he was here. He pushed the thought away angrily.

I can handle this myself.

Melanie grabbed a gold handbag waiting on her bed, then said, "Well, come on, now. We still have a game to catch."

"What?" Vincent said, caught off guard.

"Look, I couldn't care less about football." She flashed him a sly, reproachful smile. "But it's a big deal around here, if you haven't noticed. We have to see the last of it at least. Then we can slip away, don't you worry–I still have some stuff to set up before things get started."

Vincent had a feeling it was going to be a long night.

CHAPTER 4

THE PARTY AT THE DEVIL'S MAW

Floodlights blared all around the football field, illuminating it as if in broad daylight–but a strange sort. Cold and white, with deep black shadows wherever it couldn't penetrate. Vincent yearned to shelter in one of those shadows, feeling entirely out of place here, but he couldn't. Melanie was leading him to the stands erected at the edge of the field, already packed to the brim with excited students.

He couldn't see a single empty seat left, and wondered whether Melanie would really accept standing on the sidelines through the entire game. He was banking on the hope that she might want to leave sooner. But as soon as he thought that, Melanie stopped in the walkway near the front row and bent her head to talk to a couple of the people seated there. The clamor overwhelmed Vincent's ears, keeping him from hearing what she was saying, but in less than a minute the spectators rose, abandoning their seats. Melanie took one of them, beckoning Vincent over to sit in the other. He did, baffled.

He grew even more so at the game itself. It was nearly impossible to understand what was going on, even with the announcer's aid. He didn't dare ask Melanie for explanations, and not only because he wouldn't be able to hear her.

After a while he figured out the basic goal and rhythm of the game; but it was fraught with starting and stopping. Every time someone really got going, something got in their way, and the referee would stop the action so everyone could reorient themselves and begin again. Looking around at the delighted fans, he had no idea why anyone thought this was fun to watch. He couldn't even tell who was who from this distance–all he could see was the numbers on their uniforms.

Then, he remembered: Jake had a number "2" on his uniform. That was something to watch, at least. He seemed to be doing well, as far as Vincent knew–he got his hands on the ball a few times, making some good progress down the field. Once he even managed to twist out of the way of a couple defenders from the other team, running the last few yards to the end of the field with the ball in hand. This made the crowd leap up with a thunderstorm of cheers.

However, the number "1" player was involved in most of the plays that gave the home team a lead. Whenever someone made a good move, he was always right there with a hearty pat on the back or shoulder. Once, when the other team snagged the ball and broke ahead, he called for a huddle and began directing his teammates with gestures this way and that. Afterward, the team managed to reclaim the ball and the trajectory of the game, which sent a wave of excitement through the crowd.

Near the end of the game number "2" broke through the other team's defensive wall and made a mad dash for the end of the field. But he wasn't alone–in an instant he was swarmed, and couldn't avoid the other team's guard this time. The ball spun into the air–

With a mighty leap, number "1" caught it. He landed hard but with perfect balance. He ducked just out of reach of the last two defenders in his way, and all of a sudden he was sprinting to the end of the field completely unfettered.

The entire crowd jumped to its feet as one, and the screams that followed nearly deafened Vincent. He realized he was on his feet too, unable to fight the infectious triumph all around him. It was a strange feeling–like somehow they were all reaching in and lifting his heart into his throat with their own hands.

Finally the crowd began pouring out of the stands, chattering amongst themselves. Melanie urged Vincent out of his own seat and they made their way across the grass towards the field itself. Vincent was apprehensive, unsure what she was up to, but soon found out when they crossed paths with the team themselves. All of them were mingling together, sweaty and smiling with helmets under arms, exchanging congratulations and highlights.

"Amazing game," Melanie said, striding up to the two players talking at the center. They both stopped to face her, still beaming.

That's when Vincent realized—the number "1" player was Henry Wellfellow.

"Thanks, Melanie," he said.

"Perfect start to the season, I'd say," Melanie went on. "And to my party. We'll bring some real energy tonight. You boys aren't too tired to attend, now are you?"

"Of course not," Jake grunted.

"Wouldn't miss it," Henry agreed. "Just give us a minute or two to get cleaned up, would you?" he added with a wink.

Melanie smiled demurely back. "Well, duh."

Just then, Henry noticed Vincent. His smile faltered in a strange way. "O-oh—hey, Vinny! Damn, you look..." His smile redoubled, but he glanced away, breaking eye contact. "Different. *Good*, I mean. For the party?"

Something odd crawled inside Vincent's chest. He didn't quite understand that reaction. He had almost forgotten his own new look. "Yeah. Ava's handiwork."

"Oh! That's so sweet of her." Henry cleared his throat. "Well, uh, I guess you caught the game after all?"

"I barely understood what was going on half the time, but...I guess you did something right," Vincent said, gesturing broadly to the buzzing spectators.

Henry laughed. Vincent cracked a smile—this time, he couldn't help it.

"Good thing *this* game was your first! That could've been awkward. Maybe you're my good luck charm, huh?"

Vincent felt a little warmer. Before he could figure out why, Melanie snorted. "As if you need it. You never play a bad game."

Henry shrugged. "I've had 'em." Then he nudged Jake playfully. "But this guy really brought his A-game too, didn't he? That touchdown was amazing! Thank god we're having a party!"

Jake, however, didn't seem as enthused. His grin faded as he took Henry's praise.

"Sure," said Melanie. "But good thing you were out there to save that last play. I guess nobody can expect perfection unless you're Henry Wellfellow, hm?"

Henry shook his head. "Oh, c'mon, I'm not perfect. And besides, I'm nothing without the team."

"Modest as always." Vincent caught Melanie's gaze flicking to Jake. The shadow seemed to have settled darker across his face. "Anyway, we still have a lot to set up. Come on, Vincent."

She led him out through the gate, starting along the path beside the field that led to the forest beyond. The further they walked towards the trees, the more his unusual good mood sank into dread. His nerves tingled through his body as they drew closer and closer, and then his fears were confirmed:

They were setting up the party near the waterfall–the one he had first emerged from.

At first he was suspicious, but it soon became clear the location was chosen simply for the large pool at the waterfall's base, which served as a perfect swimming hole. The early autumn evening was cool, but not cold enough to deter the fun. They did erect the main party area a few hundred feet away from the waterfall itself, which at least gave Vincent some distance as a buffer–but not enough. He did his best to ignore the crawling beneath his skin, but the waterfall's roar was intent to remind him of its presence.

Fortunately party preparations kept him busy enough to distract from his anxiety. Melanie had him running here and there with various drinks, snacks, and decorations. Finally people began arriving with their dates, still buzzing from the aftermath of the game, and she dragged him off to join the greeting party. She was as sweet as usual, and he did his best to keep up as she introduced him to each of them, little more than a blur of passing faces in the half-light. Still, he didn't miss the social blessings of being introduced as her date. He supposed he should be grateful. He just wondered why she wanted him to go with her so badly in the first place.

Finally Melanie seemed satisfied as the flow of arrivals slowed, allowing him to return to the party proper. He milled about aimlessly, watching as strangers danced and chatted with each other, drinks in hand. He began to feel like little more than a shadow at the edge of the world.

"Oh my god, is that Vincent? Wow, you look incredible!"

A familiar voice broke through his ennui. He turned to find Sierra, armed with a smile. Jake stood close beside her, one arm around her as if he thought she would wander off without him.

Vincent fiddled with his tie. "Thank Ava. It's her fault."

Sierra snorted a laugh. "Somehow, I'm not surprised." She glanced around the venue, beaming. "See, Melanie King parties are something else, aren't they? You having fun?"

Was this supposed to be fun?

"Thank you," Melanie's voice arrived before he could reply. She strolled up behind him, practically glowing. "And thank Henry. It doesn't hurt to have something to celebrate." Vincent noticed Jake's grip on Sierra tighten.

Melanie gestured towards the bar Vincent had helped set up. It was already well-visited, and the rising noise level showed it. Even the music had gotten louder to compensate. "Help yourselves to drinks. There's snacks around, too, if Charlie hasn't snatched them all. There's also swimming at the Devil's Maw, of course."

Vincent's attention snapped back to her. "The Devil's Maw?"

"Yeah. That's what they call the waterfall."

"It's freaky," said Sierra with a little shudder. "If you stand at the top of the rocks, you can see a hole where the top part of the falls just...disappears."

"People say it leads to Hell," Jake said, his stony expression suddenly parting into a mischievous grin.

Vincent's heart missed a beat. *Do they know...?*

"But nobody can say for sure," Jake went on. "Anyone who's ever gone inside never came back out."

Vincent relaxed instantly. As much as he could, anyway.

Sierra shoved her shoulder against Jake's playfully. "Nobody's actually gone in there, Jake! Stop spreading rumors."

"I'm sure someone has," Melanie said. "You know how college kids are."

Sierra turned back to Vincent. "Well, anyway...it's funny how the rest of it just ends up being a nice little swimming hole, huh? People come here all the time. I guess the creepy factor is just as fun, though."

Suddenly, Vincent's sixth sense surged through his body. His chest clenched with a vicious hunger, wrenching his attention towards a silhouette hovering near one of the snack tables.

Sierra immediately followed his gaze, frowning. "What's wrong? Oh—is that Benjamin Warwick?"

"Why did you invite *him*?" Jake asked Melanie.

"I didn't," she said, pursing her lips.

Vincent was making every effort not to succumb to his instincts. They were so powerful, he was perturbed by how close Benjamin was able to get without him noticing. Even if he was preoccupied with the Devil's Maw, it was no excuse. This was a grim reminder: he wasn't focusing hard enough on his duty.

He suddenly wondered if his father had any control over his sixth sense—if he knew Vincent was struggling, and wanted him to feel his displeasure. How much *did* his father know?

Vincent tugged hard at the tie around his neck, but this time the pressure of it didn't soothe him. Instead, it squeezed his throat until he had to let go.

He couldn't pursue Benjamin here, in the middle of the party. Still, this was the closest he had come to catching him so far—unprotected, out in the open in the dark of the woods... Maybe if he kept a close eye on him, he could catch him off guard...

Through the haze of guilt he devised a little plan, and turned back to the others. "What's up with Benjamin Warwick?"

"Oh, he's just kinda creepy," Sierra answered, although she looked hesitant.

"Not just that. He's into some serious shit," Jake put in. "Shrooms, acid, hippie stuff. Even more than you'd think on a college campus. He's like, obsessed. I've heard he's been carted off to the psych ward more than once."

Vincent expected Melanie to add something snide about him, but she didn't.

Instead, Sierra went on, "There's just something really wrong with him, you know? Everyone can feel it. I don't like judging people like that, but..."

Everyone can feel it. Just like they could tell something was off about Vincent. It had lessened since he learned to blend in better, but it wasn't enough. People still watched him a little too closely when he passed by.

"Want me to kick him out, Mel?" Jake said.

"No, no," Melanie said swiftly, with a sigh. "Too much trouble. I'm sure he'll behave in public."

"How about that other guy, Hunter?" Vincent prompted, testing the waters. Maybe he could kill two birds with one stone. "What's wrong with him?"

He felt Melanie's gaze shift to him pointedly.

"I guess he has similar vibes," Sierra mused. "But I don't know..."

"He's just a typical incel," Jake scoffed.

"A what?" said Vincent.

Jake snorted. "You don't–? Never mind."

"I did hear he got in a fight with someone over a girl at the Commons," Sierra said.

"Even I didn't hear who it was," Melanie put in mildly.

Good, thought Vincent, satisfied. They didn't know he was involved–just as Melanie had promised. *You made this stupid night worth it after all.*

"Now *that's* a miracle!" a familiar voice cut in.

Vincent turned, and there was Henry. His hair was now neatly combed back, and he wore a clean button-up and jacket in his favorite pastel colors. Sierra immediately went over to hug him, and Vincent didn't miss the annoyance on Jake's face.

"I hope I'm not too late," Henry said, his dimples deepening as he caught Vincent's eye. Maybe it was just the stark contrast to being around Melanie and Jake for so long, but now that Henry was here the tightness in his chest eased.

"Fashionably," Melanie responded, although Vincent caught a sour note. Nobody else seemed to notice.

"Awesome game, Henry! You were *amazing!*" Sierra exclaimed, beaming at him. "I mean—not like you aren't normally!" she added quickly, earning a chuckle. Vincent noticed that familiar shadow return to Jake's expression, even deeper in the half-light.

"Oh, thanks, Sierra! We've been training hard, huh, Jake?" Henry said, reaching over to grasp his friend's shoulder heartily. Jake only grunted in reply.

They didn't go unnoticed for long—in only a few moments, more people began wedging themselves into the little group to chat about the game. Henry kept his hand on Jake's shoulder as he laughed with them, but most of the attention was obviously focused on Henry.

A familiar feeling returned to Vincent—he was only a shadow again at the edge of it all, completely separate from this spotlight and yet inexplicably, inextricably connected to it. The triumph they all shared tingled in the very air like sunlight. And Henry's smile was the brightest of all. For just a moment, Vincent felt its warmth.

Soon Melanie began encroaching on the small crowd with an air of impatience. Her aura was enough to urge people to wander off, still chatting with one another as if hardly realizing her influence. When she reached Henry, she looked around very pointedly at the stragglers. "Didn't you bring anyone with you, Henry?"

Henry's smile faded considerably as he turned back to Melanie. "Aren't there enough people here already?"

"As a date, silly."

Henry shrugged. "I didn't know I had to?"

Vincent caught the smallest twitch of a smile. "You didn't," she said. "Anyway, we were about to go swimming, actually. Care to join us?"

"Sure! That sounds like a good time." Henry elbowed Vincent playfully. "Ready to freeze your toes off?"

Vincent hesitated. Melanie noticed and said, "You *are* coming, right, Vincent?"

"You didn't tell me I needed a swimsuit." He didn't even own one.

Melanie gave him her best look of sympathy. "Oh, I'm sorry. Well, you don't really need one. Some people just strip." She gazed at him expectantly, giving half the impression of a playful schoolgirl and half something more hungry. Vincent pulled his tie tighter around his neck.

"Ah...I'll skip swimming this time. It is a bit cold."

Vincent didn't miss her air of disappointment. "Suit yourself," she said breezily, and flounced off to join Jake and Sierra.

Jake didn't look back, but Sierra hesitated before following the others. "See you later, Vincent!"

Henry didn't move. "You're not just gonna stay here alone, are you?"

Vincent paused a moment too long. Henry pressed a hand to the small of his back, urging him gently forward. The sudden contact, the closeness of it, made his heart jolt.

"Come on, you can at least put your feet in!"

"I–I really don't–"

"I won't just let you stand here by yourself. That's stupid."

Vincent opened his mouth to protest again, but the words wouldn't come.

Why wouldn't they come?

He should be hunting Benjamin–stalking him, catching him in some dark corner of the party, if he got lucky. Gagging him somehow, finally changing back to his true form, dragging him back to Hell. The Devil's Maw was so close, after all, it would be even easier, as long as he didn't make a commotion...

But instead, he let Henry lead him away. Something strange and warm was incubating deep in the pit of his chest, just outside the reach of his sixth sense. He felt its tether tighten as he walked further away, vengeful, almost painful–more than it had been before. But he fought it, concentrated on that little glowing ember instead.

Not yet, he told himself. There were too many people around. Someone would see, or hear. But when the party died down...that would be his best chance. It was better to lie low with Henry and the others until the time came–pretend he really was just another college student having fun.

The half moon glittered on the dark water, its silvery sheen mingling with the little golden orbs reflecting the lights Melanie had strung up around the edge of the pool. Melanie, Jake, and Sierra had already jumped in, laughing and chattering. Their clothes lay in piles on some towels at the edge of the water. All of them were wearing swimsuits under their party attire, apparently. Vincent suddenly wondered if Melanie had intentionally avoided giving him the memo.

"Oh, hey! You gonna come in after all?" Sierra called over to him from the pool.

Vincent fidgeted with his tie. It took him a moment to notice that Henry was undressing just a few feet away. He tried not to stare as he unbuttoned his shirt, revealing perfectly curved muscles, from his broad chest and shoulders to his strong, lean stomach. It was obvious he worked out regularly–probably because of football. But he didn't boast the chiseled abs of someone intending to flaunt their physique. Rather, his body looked pleasantly thick and soft to the touch.

Not that Vincent would know.

He forced himself to look away as Henry slid his pants down over his swim trunks. Instead he took the opportunity to find himself a nice flat rock at the edge of the pool to sit on. He slipped off his shoes while Henry waded into the water, exclaiming about the cold.

Jake immediately sent a mighty splash in his direction. He returned it with a yelp and a laugh. The whole scene devolved into a splash fight in moments, punctuated with the girls' squealing. More people Vincent didn't know clambered over the rocks at the top of the falls. They took turns jumping down to a clear spot in the pool below, raining water down on everyone nearby.

Vincent wondered if he wouldn't have felt more lonely away from all the ruckus. He tested the frigid water with his toes, shivering. Eventually he slipped his feet in, kicking one absently as he watched the others play around. All the while, the waterfall loomed over him like the shadow of someone he once knew. He could almost feel the mist like breath on the back of his neck, hoarse whispers mingling with the thunderous water, reminding him of the time he was wasting while he should be pursuing his prisoner. Maybe he was missing the perfect opportunity to corner Benjamin right now, out alone in the dark...

"Hey," a familiar voice said, pulling Vincent away from the pressure of his sixth sense sucking at his core. Henry was treading water at the foot of his rock. "Do you know how to swim?"

Vincent nodded. *Not that I've done it before...* It was an instinct, a sureness.

"I don't think anyone would mind if you just kept your pants on."

"You don't have to tell me what I can do."

Henry suddenly giggled. "Aw, no! He's back!"

Vincent blinked at him in confusion. "What?"

"The old Vincent! The mean one, who just hates me *so* much."

Vincent glared at him, but there was no fire behind it. "Oh, shut up."

"Aaaaah! You got me! Man down!" Henry pretended to drown, sinking into the water until his head submerged. Bubbles rose where he vanished.

Vincent fought the smile that clawed its way onto his face. He lost, but he didn't resent it quite as much this time. Moments later, Henry resurfaced with a splutter of a laugh.

"You're not funny," Vincent told him flatly.

"I know..." Henry shrugged, slapping his arms against the water's surface. "But I always gotta try...it's the actor's burden!"

Vincent rolled his eyes. "Will you stop being a nuisance if I get in?"

"Yes!" Henry said eagerly. "I promise!"

Vincent sighed and stood, emptying his pockets and removing everything above his waist. The night air chilled his bare torso, warring with the tingle of his nerves. He didn't look down—he couldn't. He didn't want to see those scars again.

He tried to ignore the gathering stares as he slid into the water, shivering as it shocked his skin and soaked his jeans. It was even colder than he had expected—colder than he had felt in a long time. *Is this supposed to be fun?* the thought came again.

"Whoa...what happened to you, man?"

Jake's voice reached Vincent's ears, and he suddenly felt a lot warmer—and not in a good way. He could feel everyone's eyes on him now—Henry, Sierra, and worst of all, Melanie.

He rose to get out of the pool, crossing his arms over his chest. But before he could leave, he felt a strong hand on his shoulder holding him back.

"Damn. That's a messed up thing to ask, don't you think, Jake?"

Jake's lip curled, but he didn't respond.

Henry wrapped an arm around Vincent's shoulders, steadying him. His first instinct was to thrash, dart away before he was trapped. But before he could, Henry bent close, his breath warm against his ear. A shiver traveled down his neck.

"Don't let it get to you. Nobody's gonna say anything else about it while I'm here, I promise you that."

Vincent's heart missed a beat. With it came a pang of frustration. He almost said it aloud: *I don't need you to protect me.* But something stopped him.

When was the last time someone tried to protect him? He couldn't remember. He wasn't sure there ever was one.

Henry didn't wait for his reply. Instead he resumed the fun with a hefty splash aimed at Jake—a little more aggressive than before. Jake let out an indignant yell and splashed back, forcing Vincent to duck out of the way to avoid it.

Fine. You want me to stay?

Vincent began to swim a wide circle around Jake. Henry seemed to realize what he was doing and redoubled his efforts to keep Jake's attention until Vincent reached his back. He gathered as much water as he could in a wide arc and–

SPLASH!

Henry's laugh rang out as Jake rounded on Vincent, dripping and vengeful. Vincent sneered at him and ducked underwater before he could retaliate. The cold shocked him anew as his head went under.

It was dark underwater, but the moon and the lights above were just enough to make out something strange. A pitch-black hole yawned into the earth at the very center of the pool, disappearing unfathomably deep below. The sight of it sent a shudder through Vincent's body. He quickly resurfaced.

He was immediately met by a hearty splash from Sierra, making him sputter. She laughed in triumph.

"Got him! Corner him, Jake!"

But the hole beneath them had captured Vincent's attention, and he turned to the others. "Hey...how deep does this pool go?"

Even Jake seemed to sense the shift. He stopped his onslaught, shrugging. "Who knows? It's supposed to connect with some cave system or something underground."

"Maybe someone should get some diving equipment and check it out," Sierra suggested.

"What's the point?" Melanie said, unamused. "It's just tunnels down there, if anything."

"What if someone hid some treasure in there?" Sierra said. "It'd be the perfect place!"

"No, it wouldn't," Melanie scoffed. "It would be too hard to retrieve. Besides, it's the first place you'd think of."

"No it isn't!"

"You literally just guessed there would be treasure there."

"Well what if there *is*, because that's what they thought people would think?"

"Dare you to go and check," Jake said to Sierra with a sneer.

Sierra's eyes widened. "Me? No way. I'm not getting trapped down there."

"Chicken." Jake prodded her side with a finger, making her squeak.

"Am not! I'm just *smart*!"

"*You* do it, then, if you're so brave," Melanie urged Jake.

"Uh, I don't think that's a good idea," Henry interjected.

"He's only swimming down far enough to take a look," Melanie argued.

"It's better than jumping from the rocks, anyway," said a new voice.

Everyone looked up to find Ava climbing delicately down into the pool, sporting a black two-piece swimsuit with enough lace to be underwear. She didn't even seem to flinch at the cold as she settled into the water.

"There you are, Ava," Melanie greeted her. "I was beginning to think you were going to ditch us."

"You'd never let me hear the end of it if I missed all the fun," Ava replied dryly.

Henry glanced up at the people crowding near the edge of the rocks at the top. "You think I should ask them to come down?" he said, apparently taking Ava's words to heart.

"People jump from there all the time," Melanie said, touching Henry's arm lightly. "Stop being a goddamn hall monitor for *one* night, will you, Henry?"

Vincent noticed Henry's expression tighten in a way he hadn't seen before. He shrugged Melanie's hand off as casually as possible. "Alright, alright."

"So who's gonna dive first, then?" Sierra said, looking expectantly at Jake.

Jake smirked. "I'll go."

"You'll bring me back any treasure you find down there, won't you?"

"Of course. But then *you* have to go next."

"What! I didn't agree to that!"

"Too bad. Or else I'm not going, and you'll never know what's down there."

"Ugh, fine..."

"Deal."

Jake sucked in a deep breath, then disappeared under the water's surface.

Everyone went silent, waiting for him to emerge. Each second seemed to stretch on and on.

Ava finally broke the tension: "How deep do you think he's going?"

"As deep as he needs to impress Sierra," Melanie said.

Sierra aimed a little splash in her direction, but it didn't reach her. Worry was growing on her face as she eyed the spot where Jake had been.

"I knew this was a bad idea..." Henry muttered. "We should–"

"Oh my god," Melanie sighed. "I swear, I'm not going to invite you next time if you keep bitching, Henry."

Suddenly, in a burst of water, Jake emerged. He gasped for air, and Sierra immediately clung onto his broad shoulders.

"Oh, thank god! What happened? Did you find anything?"

Jake shook his head, still panting. "Just...more tunnel...goes pretty far...it's too dark..."

"Ugh, I wish we had a flashlight or something!"

"Well, you still have to go down there either way," Melanie told her. "You promised."

Sierra frowned at her. "I'm not gonna see anything, though..."

"You guys are impossible," Ava sighed. She climbed out of the pool and pulled her phone from her towel. "Melanie, did you bring any plastic bags?"

"Yeah, there should be some by the snack tables."

"I'll be back. Don't do anything too stupid," Ava said, heading off dripping towards the main party. The noise seemed to be dying down–it must have been getting late. Or, more likely, early.

While they waited, Vincent noticed Henry still looking displeased. The others had resumed fawning over Jake and his feat, much to his apparent enjoyment; so Vincent said to Henry quietly, "Melanie's really got it out for you, ah?"

Henry blew out a puff of a laugh. "Well, she does for you too. Just in a different way."

Vincent grimaced. "I'd rather she didn't."

"Well, she's not my favorite person, either. Don't worry."

Vincent quirked an eyebrow. "I think that's the closest I've seen you come to not liking someone."

Henry laughed. "Maybe publicly. You don't have to put up with her, you know."

"Yeah. But I owed her a favor."

"That's how she gets you," Henry warned.

"Maybe so. It's just hard right now not to take it."

Henry was quiet for a moment, and Vincent tried not to focus on the searching look he gave him.

Breaking the silence, Vincent said, "I'm surprised you couldn't find a date to take with you tonight."

"Oh...well, I didn't really want to settle for the sake of settling. I was...going to ask Sierra, actually," Henry admitted, and Vincent could barely see his face flush in the half-light. "But Jake got to her first. That's okay, though."

Vincent tried to ignore the new discomfort roiling in his chest. He didn't have a name for it. "She's cool." He couldn't find anything else to say.

At that moment, Ava returned. She turned on her phone's flashlight, then zipped it into a plastic sandwich bag. She handed it to Sierra.

"If you lose it, I'll expect the newest model from you."

"Very funny..." Sierra swallowed thickly and pointed the flashlight down into the depths of the pool. Nobody could see much from the surface, other than the rocks at the bottom and the hole itself, filled to the brim with darkness.

"I lived," Jake assured her, shoving her lightly. "Don't be a baby, Sierra."

"You don't have to do it," Henry piped up from beside Vincent. For once, no one paid him any mind—the thrill of the game was too great.

"Well...here goes."

Sierra gulped a deep breath and ducked under the surface.

Everyone watched her silhouette swimming down towards the hole, the bottom of the pool illuminated by Ava's phone. Slowly the hole swallowed the light, and with it, Sierra.

"How far *did* you get?" Ava asked Jake after a moment of tense silence.

"I don't know. A few yards in?"

"She looks like she's going farther..."

"She wants to find her treasure," Melanie said with a smirk.

"I *definitely* went farther. She's not gonna find anything."

Time stretched on. The silence was deafening. The tension seemed to muffle the beat of the music from the party and the gleeful voices atop the waterfall. Everyone watched the dark spot underwater as best they could in the gloom. There was no light from within.

It hadn't been that long, surely. It just felt longer.

No...Sierra was taking too long.

"Where is she?" Henry murmured.

"She should be back by now..." Ava said, and even she looked concerned.

"Well, shit," said Melanie.

"Fuck," said Jake, looking frantically between Henry and Melanie. "What should we do? Should we—"

Henry glanced back at Vincent. Their eyes met, and somehow Vincent understood. He nodded, and together they took a deep breath and plunged beneath the water's surface.

The alarmed voices of their companions were staunched, a final farewell from the surface world. Darkness closed in around them as they swam deeper, down into the hole.

Soon they were in a narrow tunnel. Vincent could barely make out the pale form of Henry in front of him, using his arms and legs against the walls to propel himself further down. He was Vincent's sole comfort. The weight of the water and the earth bore down on him, clamoring to enter his body and fill his lungs with crushing death.

He had never felt this breed of fear before. But he wouldn't leave Henry or Sierra down here alone. He couldn't. His own resolve surprised him at first, but it didn't waver. If they died down here, he would never forgive himself.

The tunnel gradually leveled until it ran diagonally through the earth. It narrowed as they went, until Vincent's shoulders brushed the walls on either side. Even worse, his chest was beginning to tighten and ache. He was losing oxygen. And somehow, they still had to find Sierra–and make it back.

Panic rose like a knife in his throat, and it was all he could do to try and stifle it, knowing it would waste precious oxygen. But the darkness crawled all around him, circling like a wolf, gnawing at the edges of his vision, his body, his mind–

And then, light.

Henry's silhouette moved in front of it. Vincent squinted past him–and there she was. Sierra's body was lodged in the tunnel.

His heart dropped into his stomach. Her eyes were closed.

No. I won't let this happen.

The phone had fallen to the tunnel floor face down, the flashlight illuminating the cave. Vincent rushed to get it, holding it up so they could see better. Stones jutted out of the tunnel walls, trapping Sierra's body towards the top of the opening. Henry grasped her shoulders and began pulling, bubbles billowing from his nose. Vincent hurried to help, yanking on Sierra's arm with his free hand.

It wasn't enough. Her body wouldn't budge, and the tightness in Vincent's lungs was growing by the moment.

He stopped. He searched the opening, desperate to find anything he could use to dislodge her.

There.

He waved a hand at Henry to catch his attention, pointing at the rocks that held her. He left the phone on the tunnel floor and pushed Sierra's body at an angle to try and flip her sideways. Henry caught on and added his own strength to the maneuver.

With a burst of waterlogged dust and gravel, her body was free.

Vincent snatched the phone and hefted one of her arms over his shoulder. Henry took the other, and both of them began walking themselves up the tunnel as fast as they could.

With each passing moment, a hundred more knives seemed to pierce Vincent's chest. He felt his body convulsing as it tried to draw breath, but he fought it, forcing the instinct down–

Just a little longer–

But the darkness was winning. It crept in around the edges of his vision, broken only by little pinpricks of false light in a thousand colors.

He wondered what would happen if he died here. Would his soul return to Hell, condemning him to his failure? Or would he simply cease to be?

It was too late now. He would know soon. The lights were growing brighter and brighter, overtaking everything he could see–

And then, there was no more tunnel. The lights were above him now. Something dragged him upwards, urging him on, and he mustered the last of his strength to kick and swim and follow–

Vincent burst into open air, heaving great, desperate gulps of breath. He struggled to tread water with the weight of Sierra at his back, even with Henry's help. But then the burden lifted. Voices clamored around them. Somehow he found a rock to stand on in the pool, and as he breathed the darkness faded from his eyes.

Relieved, he recognized Henry beside him, panting just as he was. Between them, Jake and Melanie were lifting Sierra–

Suddenly, her eyes shot open. She flailed, coughing up water and then gasping horribly. Vincent noticed something glint around her neck.

"She's okay!"

"Sierra?"

"Stop splashing me, I got you–"

Someone above them screamed.

SPLASH.

Something heavy crashed into the water from high above, sending a tidal wave across the pool. Everyone flinched away from it. They looked around wildly until they spotted a dark shape flat on the water's surface.

"What was that? Did someone jump?"

"Didn't they see what's happening down here?"

Vincent shone the phone's flashlight on the shape. The beam trembled. It was a body, face down in the water.

CHAPTER 5

VIGILANTE

D ark blood had already begun to spread along the water's surface, glistening from a chasm in the back of the body's skull. For a horrible moment, the whole world was frozen.

Then a wail rose from above them, breaking Vincent out of his stupor.

Henry, still panting, splashed towards the body as it began to sink. The handful of remaining partiers began crowding around as well, but Melanie and Jake shouted at them, warding them off. Henry flipped the body over. The tide of blood grew even faster with the wound submerged. That spurred most of the onlookers to back away, scrambling back to shore.

Vincent glimpsed a pallid face, eyes open and bloodshot and unmoving.

Henry bent his head close, listening for breath, then pressed his fingers to its neck with mounting desperation.

"She's dead," he said, his voice cracking.

An uproar answered, fraught with panic and confusion.

"Who is it?" rose over the din.

"That's Mira! Oh my god!"

"Mira?"

"Mira!"

The girl's name became a cacophony. On one hand, Vincent was relieved not to know her personally. *That could have been Sierra. It almost was.* On the other, the sight of the poor girl dead in the water made his stomach churn.

"Did anyone see what happened?" Henry called out, looking around. He cradled her body as if he had forgotten how to move. Even from here, Vincent could see him trembling.

"She hit her head on the rocks–"

"She must have jumped wrong–"

"Maybe she slipped–"

But no one had any answers.

Henry made a growl of frustration, but when he looked back down at the dead girl, his expression quickly melted to misery. He lifted her body, guiding it across the water's surface to the edge of the pool. It left a path of blood in its wake.

Suddenly a hand grabbed Vincent's arm. He whipped his head around, only to meet Sierra's stunned face. He tried to calm his hammering heart.

Wordlessly she held onto him, as if to steady herself. Discomfort tingled through his body. He looked for Jake, wondering why she hadn't gone to him; but he was beside Melanie, who was murmuring something close to his ear. He looked shaken. He didn't even look at Sierra.

So Vincent remained there with her, waist-deep in the bloody water, watching numbly as the others wandered back in the direction of the party that had now gone silent. They left the corpse where it lay, as if no one could muster the courage to even look at it now, let alone touch it.

Finally Vincent waded to the pool's edge, guiding Sierra with him. He only remembered just how cold he was when he climbed out, the chill of the early fall evening biting at his wet skin. He grabbed a towel for Sierra first, wrapping her in it roughly before snagging one for himself. She looked at him gratefully, but something inside him still prickled at her presence. He turned away, searching for Henry.

He found him still shivering in his swim trunks as he directed people away from the pool. "Don't leave yet—not until we can give statements to the police," he was telling them.

Without a word, Vincent flung a towel around his shoulders. Henry turned, startled, but realized who it was and relaxed.

"Vincent..."

"Sierra is okay," Vincent said, looking away. "Come on. You should get your clothes."

"Thank god..." Henry breathed. He clutched the towel around himself as if only now recognizing the cold. He glanced up at the other party-goers, who were gathering among the remnants of the party, murmuring to each other with wide eyes. They seemed to be taking his words to heart, so he said, "Alright."

He followed Vincent back to their makeshift camp, where their friends were already drying off. He went to get his clothes, but Vincent hung back, his sharp ears directing him towards where Jake and Sierra were crowded close nearby.

"What were you thinking?" Jake was saying, glaring at her.

"I thought I could make it!" Sierra looked miserable. "It was right there..."

"I hope it was worth dying for," Jake snapped.

"No...I just wanted to prove it, and I got stuck," Sierra grumbled.

"You're lucky Henry and Vincent were there," Melanie put in airily as she passed, wrapped in her own towel. Apparently she had been eavesdropping, too. Jake scowled.

"Next time, don't put your goddamn pride over your life," he growled, turning away to gather his things.

Sierra watched him for a moment, then turned her back on him. "I *knew* there was treasure down there..." she muttered. She fingered something shiny around her neck as she spoke. Vincent realized he had glimpsed it earlier when she emerged from the water. He wandered closer to get a better look.

"Did you find something?"

Sierra looked up at him with a glint of rebellion in her eyes, but quickly realized he wasn't going to berate her for her decision.

"Yeah..." She held up her necklace so he could see. "I just saw a sparkle down there, and I thought I could get it real fast..."

Vincent's blood ran cold. It was a large, oval-shaped turquoise pendant on a silver chain–the very same necklace he had seen around Percy's neck in every photo on his desk. The only difference was that now a deep, jagged crack snaked through the center of the stone.

"Vincent? Is something wrong?"

"No...it's pretty. I just don't think it was worth it."

Sierra's expression hovered between defiance and anguish, and the latter won. She sighed deeply and hung her head.

"Yeah...you're right." She paused, then touched Vincent's arm again. He didn't move away, even if he wanted to. "Thanks, Vincent. For saving me. I'm really sorry you had to do that."

Vincent softened a little, despite the dread still hanging heavy in his chest. Before he could reply Sierra looked up over his shoulder, and he turned to see Henry joining them. He still looked haunted, but he fashioned his best attempt at a smile for Sierra's sake. She immediately moved to hug him, which he returned wholeheartedly.

"I'm so sorry, Henry," she said, her voice breaking. "You guys almost died for me. I could never thank you enough!"

"It's alright, Sierra. I'm just glad you're safe."

"Hey, um...do you have my phone?"

They all looked to find Ava approaching, looking uncharacteristically awkward. Vincent realized he was still holding her phone, its flashlight blaring. He handed it back to her.

That gave Vincent an idea. He went to get his own phone, safely tucked under his dry clothes. He returned to the others and pulled Sierra aside.

"Let me take a photo of that necklace."

"Oh—why?"

"I think I've at least earned a picture."

Sierra opened her mouth as if to argue, then seemed to think better of it. She held the pendant out for Vincent and he snapped a photo. Then without a word he left her to Henry and went to get his clothes. He had had quite enough of this party.

"We have to get the body back to campus."

Vincent glanced up from his things to find Melanie looming over him.

"We?" he repeated scornfully, buttoning his shirt.

"*We*," Melanie insisted. "You're my date, and it's my party, after all."

"Didn't anyone call an ambulance or something? Isn't that what they're for?"

Melanie leaned closer to him, her gaze hard. "Listen, Vincent. I'm not letting *my* reputation get sullied by this whole affair. If the school finds out someone died because we were partying at the Devil's Maw, we're all going to be royally fucked. Especially after what happened to Percy Quailheart. You feel like getting expelled? Because I don't."

A dark loathing seeped into Vincent's gut. He was beginning to see the girl that somehow had a hand in Percy's death.

"Don't think for a second I won't drag you down with me," she added with a curl of her lip. "You'd be lucky if they don't arrest you. Or deport you. They do that kind of thing for a lot less."

Vincent's stomach clenched. He *couldn't* risk that. If the authorities began looking too closely into his affairs, kept him from Benjamin...everything would unravel.

"What are you planning to do?" he asked grudgingly.

"We're just going to stage a little something," Melanie said. "Make sure it doesn't get back to us."

"Like?" Vincent's patience was thinning.

"You'll see."

It was all he could do to follow Melanie, who had now stopped beside the body with Jake at her side. Just like the others, neither of them looked directly at it.

"The old shed behind the gym," Jake was saying. His voice was stiff, but Vincent noticed a tremor in his hands. "No one ever goes back there."

"Is that secure enough?"

"What's that supposed to accomplish?" Vincent cut in, trying to withhold his disgust.

"We just need to clean everything up here." Melanie began to say something else to Jake, but Vincent broke in again.

"Then there's no reason to move her. What are you planning on doing with her?"

Melanie sighed. "We're going to find a good place to make it look like a suicide, okay?"

"What? Why?"

"It's an easy cover-up. Overstressed college kids—you know how it always goes. All we have to do is get our story straight with everyone who's still here."

Something squirmed deep in Vincent's gut. He swallowed hard, trying to push it down.

"You think everyone is just going to go along with it?"

A little smirk flitted across Melanie's lips. "You really need to ask? It's *me*. Need I remind you about your little problem? No one's hassled you about it, have they?"

Vincent suppressed a growl. She was right. He had no idea how she managed to keep so many people quiet about his fight with Hunter. Even if she was well-liked, it was a tall request...

"You really don't think any of her friends will come clean?"

"Please. She wasn't close enough with anybody for that. Kind of a loner. Even I don't know that much about her. No one will want to stick their neck out for her."

Was life really that cheap? Would Mira be nothing but a sad footnote in the college days of her classmates? Vincent didn't even know her for a single moment. He wondered what she was like, to have so few friends, none of them true. Did she deserve to be forgotten? Was she anything like him?

He recognized it a moment too late, after it had already seeped past his defenses like poison—that damned *sympathy*.

Maybe we both deserve to die alone.

"Why not just leave her here, then?" he said, warring with his own heart. "All the evidence is here, and we can clean up the party stuff so it looks like she was out here on her own."

Melanie sighed. She shared a look with Jake, then said, "I guess that works. But you have to help us round everyone up."

"No. You do it," Vincent growled, this time unwilling to hide his resentment. "Just leave her body to me."

A beat of silence followed. Then Melanie shrugged. "Fine."

Only when he heard their footsteps recede did he return to the girl. He crouched, grasping her arms and hoisting her into his lap. It was eerie how alive she looked, despite the gaping wound in the back of her head. For a moment he felt as if he were cradling a sleeping woman, and a sick warmth spread through his body that he thoroughly hated. This was far too intimate for him. What would she think, a stranger handling her body like this when she could do nothing about it?

But it didn't matter, now. She was dead.

Vincent lifted her torso again, pulling her a few feet across the same damp earth he had first felt between his toes when he emerged from the Devil's Maw. But she would never emerge. The last of her warmth had already faded; she was as cold as the waters of her temporary grave. With just a little push they welcomed her back into their frigid embrace, lapping at her skin and her chestnut hair as she half-sank into the pool. Vincent turned away before he could see her blood blossom again in the moonlit water.

The moment he did, his sixth sense returned–first a dull ache, then a vengeful squeeze around his ribcage. It urged him deeper into the woods. His heart quickened as he realized: Benjamin hadn't gone back to campus. He was still out here. Maybe even alone. This was the chance Vincent had been waiting for.

Maybe tonight wasn't a total loss.

He started off into the trees, following that dark instinct. The shadows closed in swiftly around him, but he didn't mind. He could still see. Nothing would creep up on him.

Or so he thought.

Suddenly, a weight slammed into his back. He thrashed, but it was no use. His assailant dragged him aside and shoved him against a thick tree trunk, an arm across his throat. The unmistakable scent of clove and jasmine struck him.

"What the *hell* was that? Why did you put her back in the water?"

Vincent grasped the arm pinning him, but he didn't have the strength to push it away. Again he silently cursed his father for making his human form so small. No guilt chased the thought this time.

"Henry–let me go, damn it, I'm not–" He choked as the arm pressed harder. He didn't think Henry was capable of looking so menacing.

"Answer me *right now*, Vincent."

Vincent's head spun as his thoughts raced. Of course Henry wasn't going to allow this–why didn't he realize that before?

"Alright, okay! Can you at least let me go so we can talk normally?"

Henry hesitated. Then he released Vincent.

He stepped away from the tree so he couldn't be cornered again, doing his best to scrape together the rest of his composure. His sixth sense still tugged hard at his heart, but he couldn't listen now. He forced it down.

"I–I know what this looks like," he began, trying to steady his breathing. "I didn't want to. But Melanie said we'd be in deep shit if I didn't help her cover up our involvement."

"She's afraid of getting in trouble for the party?" Henry crossed his arms. "I highly doubt they'd pin anything on her, or you for that matter. She should know that."

"Well, I don't know. I just don't want to be arrested."

"You're not going to get arrested, I promise. That's not how things work here." Henry stepped back. "I'm gonna go bring her body somewhere closer to the road. I assume nobody's called the police yet? I guess I'll do that, too," he sighed. "It's always me..."

Vincent wasn't sure if Henry was right, but he didn't want to find out. And it wasn't his only reason for appeasing Melanie, either. "No, wait–please, I really don't want to piss off Melanie."

Henry narrowed his eyes at Vincent. "I know she's a big deal around campus, but honestly, she gives herself too much credit. I can handle her."

Vincent shook his head. He could feel the situation slipping through his fingers–fast. "No, I–" He stopped, gritting his teeth. "I ah...got into a situation a few days ago. Something she covered up for me. It's not just this."

"What? What happened?"

Vincent hesitated, fingering his tie, but he didn't have any other choice at this point.

"I got into a fight with some guy who was heckling a girl at the Commons. His name was Hunter, I think."

Henry stared at him. "Really? You did?"

"He was causing a scene. He deserved to be put in his place. Besides, if I let it continue the girl probably would have done a lot worse to him," he added, recalling Casey's aggressive disposition.

When Henry's stare didn't break, Vincent shifted uncomfortably. "Look, I'm sorry. I know you're not supposed to do things like that around here. That's...not how things are handled where I come from. I wasn't–"

Henry's hand fell firmly on Vincent's shoulder. He winced.

"I get it. Really."

Vincent blinked up at him. "You...do?"

Henry smiled, although it wasn't quite as radiant as usual.

"I'm the same way."

Vincent gazed at him dubiously.

"Yeah, I know what you're thinking. I'm a goody-two-shoes, right? Sure."

"That's not–"

"I don't know what your culture is like, but over here, a lot of people think the best move is always to keep quiet and let the law or the school board or whoever's in charge handle everything that goes wrong. But it's not. Not for me. I've seen it–there are a lot of...gaps in their abilities. And their morals."

Vincent searched his face, feeling as if he were listening to a stranger. Sure, Henry was pushy, but...he was *too nice*. Too good to be true.

I guess I was right about that.

Henry gestured towards the Devil's Maw. "Stuff like this happens all the time. But even more, lately. There's something strange going on in this place."

"Here?" Vincent echoed. *There's no way he knows.*

"Well, not just the Devil's Maw. The school, too. People aren't just falling to their deaths out of nowhere. They're being murdered, Vincent."

Relief found him, but brought with it a new curiosity. Henry seemed to be buying his half-truth...but Vincent could sense he wasn't saying everything on his mind, either.

"You think this was murder?"

Henry nodded. "Most definitely. And this isn't the first time they've killed, either."

They shared a dark, knowing look.

"Percy, too."

"Things like this don't just happen for no reason," Henry said. "Ever since Percy died, I've been keeping an eye out for anything suspicious. People, rumors...I even walk around campus at night when I can't sleep," he admitted.

Seeing Vincent's look, he added, "I know how it sounds, thinking I can police this place all by myself. But it's my school. And I'm stronger than most people. I have martial training, too. My dad has had me in classes ever since I was little."

"Really? Why?" Vincent had no clue why an ordinary mortal would need something like that. Especially one so uncommonly bulky–he couldn't imagine most humans would want to pick a fight with Henry.

"Well..." Henry hesitated. He was searching for an answer.

Vincent's eyes narrowed. *Why?*

Finally Henry said, "My dad learned when he was young, so he wanted me to do it too. It's kind of a family tradition. And I'm glad it is," he added, lifting his chin. "If nobody else will take this situation seriously enough, I'm not gonna just stand by and let it all happen right under my nose."

Vincent nodded slowly. He thought about all those people walking past Mira's body, leaving her there by the water's edge. Then he thought of Melanie and Jake, plotting to stuff her in a shed to avoid blame. All of them averting their gazes, because it was easier.

But Henry...Henry didn't. Henry wasn't going to leave her alone.

"I don't know..." he went on, miserably. "I feel like I could be doing more, still. I was *here*, and all this still happened. We saved Sierra, but..."

Vincent held his breath. *Damn you.*

Then, slowly, he reached out to touch Henry's arm.

Their eyes met. His heart leaped into his throat.

"We can't save everyone," Vincent said quietly. "It's impossible."

"But we can *try*," Henry argued, looking at him desperately.

"You trust me, after what I just did?"

"I *believe* you. You want to help just as much as I do. I can see it in your eyes. You're just like me."

Henry believed Vincent was like him. That he was...*good*.

He stood frozen in the harsh light of Henry's faith, his mind blank and his words dry. Something deep inside him sparked—that little glowing ember he had felt before, where once there had been only shadow.

"Help me keep everyone safe, Vincent. Let's solve this together."

Henry extended a hand towards him.

An image flashed through Vincent's mind—an old painting depicting God reaching a hand out towards Adam. *Creation.* That's what his philosophy professor had said. An offering of life.

And here was his. Henry, the man who dared to reach for Vincent despite everything strange about him, despite barely knowing him at all, despite the darkness that found its home inside him.

He had no idea what Henry saw in him—but it had to be *something*, didn't it? He knew and liked so many people. And yet, something about Vincent stood out to him. It wasn't just Henry being too nice to a stranger down on his luck—not anymore. Henry wanted to trust him.

But should he trust Henry?

He knew he should say no. He didn't have time to go chasing down murderers or helping lost souls move on—no matter how much his instincts bade him to. *No more sympathy*—right? His sixth sense still clawed at his core, dragging him towards the dark woods. That's where he should be. There might still be time to catch Benjamin alone tonight. Finish the job he was sent here to do.

But something else was brewing inside him—a dark storm with the dead girl in its eye, drifting alone in that frigid water.

He wondered if Percy had looked like that, too. Alone, the cold seeping in, empty where he shouldn't be, his bright young face covered in his own blood.

And in that moment, he knew it was more than keeping his promise to Percy, more than righting the natural order. He was going to prove Melanie was involved. He was going to bring her down.

He didn't need Henry for that. He was only human, after all. He didn't understand the true weight of his ambitions. He didn't understand exactly what was at stake–not just life, but death.

And yet...Henry was human. That was one thing Vincent couldn't be, not really. As much as he hated to admit it...without Henry, he wouldn't have gotten this far. And he certainly couldn't have saved Sierra. He might not have even made it out alive.

His father's words echoed in his mind, his heart–a final warning:

Every human is the same at heart. Selfish and treacherous and greedy.

He wouldn't forget it this time.

He took Henry's hand, clasping it firmly. Henry smiled, and that ember inside Vincent became a flame.

"We're gonna fix this," Henry said, and Vincent almost believed him. "I know we will, now that it's you and me."

Vincent moved back, unable to stand in that warmth any longer.

His mind had already begun turning. Melanie had something to do with Percy's murder...but she was nowhere near Mira when she died. Then again, it was her party. He almost asked Henry what he thought, but then realized he had no explanation for why he thought Melanie was involved. He couldn't exactly tell him Percy's ghost had incriminated her. He knew most people here didn't believe in such things.

Henry looked back towards the Devil's Maw. "Is it really important to leave Mira there?" he asked, his tone darkening.

"Someone will find her soon. It's not like anything bad can happen to her now."

Henry grimaced. "We have to find out what happened. I didn't get any useful information from anyone."

"Why would anyone want to murder Mira? Did you know her?"

"Not really." Henry paused thoughtfully. "That's a good point, though. Maybe she was involved in something…"

"Involved in what?"

Henry waited a moment too long before responding. "Beats me."

"Well, did anyone have a reason to murder Percy?"

Henry winced, as if he could hardly bear the thought. "No. I can't even imagine…"

"Maybe he was in the wrong place at the wrong time. You never told me what those wounds on his body were."

Henry hesitated. "He was…found on the side of the road, near the treeline. He had, um…puncture wounds. On his neck."

"An animal, maybe?" Vincent guessed slowly. "Or a knife?"

Henry didn't look at him. "I don't know. I didn't get a chance to see him myself."

Silence persisted between them, heavy with thought.

"We should head back," said Henry, turning. "Will you meet me tomorrow night? We have to come up with a way to pursue this, and soon. Before anything else happens."

"Ah…yeah. Where?"

Henry smiled at him. "How about by the fountain? We can do a little patrol while we're comparing notes."

Vincent found himself wanting to smile back. He didn't. "Alright."

They started back down the slope towards campus. The forest was still shrouded in deep shadow and pale moonlight, but somehow Vincent felt less small among the trees with Henry at his side.

As they walked, his sixth sense gnawed at his ribs, begging him to slip away and *hunt*. But, by some fortune or misfortune, Benjamin's signature had left the woods. Instead it pulled Vincent in the direction of campus, where his prisoner was no doubt safe in his dorm room by now. That tiny window of opportunity had passed.

Guilt roiled in Vincent's stomach. He welcomed it, because he deserved to feel it. There was no way to know if he truly could have cornered Benjamin tonight...but either way, he hoped it was worth it.

I can right more wrongs up here than just one, Father. I can be better.

Vincent and Henry parted ways at their respective rooms with a heavy-hearted goodnight. As soon as Vincent's door was closed, he turned to gaze into the darkness of his room.

"Percy, I think I found your necklace."

CHAPTER 6

THE DEVIL YOU KNOW

That horrible dark presence coalesced just above Vincent. He could hardly see it, but that heavy feeling of dread, like a black hole in his very own bedroom, was unmistakable.

Vincent tapped through his phone until he found the picture he had taken of the turquoise and silver necklace. He held it up, trying to keep his hands from shaking with a great deal of annoyance. He wasn't certain the ghost could see, but then–

"Where...where did you find this?" Like before, the voice seemed to come from everywhere and nowhere all at once.

"The Devil's Maw. Someone–Sierra Pechman–found it deep in the underwater tunnel beneath the swimming hole there. Do you know how it got there?"

"She took it..."

"Who did?"

Vincent felt the silence in the air itself, filled to the brim with confusion. Percy's thoughts were still muddled, it seemed.

"Was it Melanie King?"

"Yes." The syllable nearly crackled with the force of Percy's emotion.

"When did she take it?"

"Just before...before I..."

Vincent nodded grimly. "What else do you remember about that moment?"

"She...she wanted to see it...I believed her..."

"Why?"

"It protects me..."

Vincent looked down at the picture glowing in the darkness. The necklace was certainly beautiful, but it didn't look particularly special.

"Do you mean it...actually protects you? Like some kind of charm? Or was it just for luck?"

"*It's* real," said Percy. The gravity in the room deepened, dragging Vincent's fast-beating heart down with it. "*It's my grandfather's amulet. The spirits protect whoever wears it.*"

Vincent hadn't yet seen Percy with such clarity of mind. A little seed of hope began to sprout in his heart.

"Was it cracked before she took it?"

"*N-no...*"

"Then Melanie must have broken it..." Vincent murmured, half to himself. "But why? I thought she would want its protection..."

"*I-it only protects me,*" Percy said. "*Me and my family. M-my dad always said our ancestors sleep inside it, guiding us.*"

"Really?" said Vincent, intrigued. "So it wouldn't work for anyone who isn't blood-related?"

"*I-I think so...*"

"Then maybe Melanie didn't know that..." And yet, it still didn't add up. Why break it? Percy had already handed it over, so it wasn't protecting him when he died. And as unlikable as Melanie was, she didn't seem the type to throw things around out of frustration.

"Do you remember anything else about that moment? Why would Melanie want you dead?" Vincent pressed. It felt like the clues were beginning to slip through his fingers like sand, none of them fitting together.

"*I-I don't know...I-I don't remember...*" The air in the room began to fizzle with static.

"Nothing at all?" Vincent dared to ask. An awful buzzing was growing in the deepest part of his skull. He gritted his teeth to try and withstand it, but it was too much–

"*I don't remember!*"

Suddenly the shadow disappeared. The pressure faded from Vincent's head. Relief mingled with exasperation as he looked around the room. It seemed somehow brighter despite its lack of light.

"Damn it," Vincent breathed. He realized he had dropped his phone, and bent down to pick it up. The picture still glowed on the screen. He frowned at it. He had been sure seeing the necklace again would jog Percy's memory. But it wasn't enough. If not that, what would?

Frustration mounting, Vincent decided it was best to get some sleep. It had been a very long day, and an even longer night. He might as well take advantage of Percy's relative absence to get some good rest.

He pushed away the prickle of guilt that accompanied that thought. Even in the throes of death, Percy was...kind. He had let Vincent sleep in his bed, even though it was one of the few things he had left to his name.

Then make it easier to help you, damn it.

Vincent hung up his damp towel and got himself ready for bed, by now used to such mundane routines as showering and brushing his teeth. They offered him a very simple kind of satisfaction, like a real human being. Finally, when he settled into his very own sheets in his very own bed, his body sank into the mattress with sudden exhaustion. He hadn't realized just how bad it was until that moment.

He turned the light out, expecting to fade into sleep immediately. Instead, his thoughts bounced around in his head like echoes in a cave. Memories of that crushing water and the tunnel all around him, the eerie stillness of the girl's corpse in his arms, Melanie's insistence on covering it all up, that burning need to bring her to justice...it dogged him with a vengeance. He didn't understand why it all mattered so much, in the face of everything else he had ever endured.

The next evening, Vincent pulled on his leather jacket and set out into the hush of night. He was all too aware of the sound of his footsteps on the pavement. He did his best to soften them, grateful for the fountain's steady crashing as he drew nearer.

He immediately spotted Henry waiting for him there, illuminated only by the streetlamps ringing the plaza.

"Good place to talk about secrets," Vincent greeted him.

Henry smiled. "I'm hoping you have some to talk about?"

Fat chance. "I was thinking...did you hear anything about Mira's body being discovered today?"

Henry's brows knitted together. "Come to think of it...no. I guess nobody found her yet..."

"Really? No one visited a popular attraction like the Devil's Maw all day?"

"I mean, it's not really *popular*...local authorities try to keep people away..."

"Yeah, that's worked so far." Vincent started off with a purpose. "No, that's too convenient. Someone would have found her by now."

Henry followed. After walking in uneasy silence for a bit, Vincent asked, "Where do you usually go, when you do this?"

"I dunno. I just sort of wander, maybe check the perimeter for signs of anything suspicious."

"Do you ever find anything?"

"Not really..."

Now he was almost sure of it–Henry was keeping something from him.

"Then why do you need me?" Vincent pressed.

"Just in case."

"In case what? We run into the murderer having a romantic midnight stroll with their butcher knife?"

"Well–" Henry stopped, his mouth hanging open as he tried to figure out what to say. Vincent's irritation grew. Maybe he shouldn't have agreed to work with Henry after all.

After a moment Henry found his voice. "This killer clearly likes sneaky work. Percy was out on his own when it happened. It's just too risky to go alone."

Vincent narrowed his eyes. "If this is the same person who pushed Mira, they still managed to do it with people around. Do you really think it matters?"

"Yes. Nobody was expecting it at the party. We're on high alert out here, and we've got each other's backs."

Vincent suppressed a sigh. "Fine. But while we're out here, maybe you can at least consider telling me whatever it is you're hiding."

He kept walking, and it took Henry a second to recover. He was silent now, which told Vincent all he needed to know.

He led the way across campus, all the way to the far end behind the football field and the gym. The lights in the field were off, leaving only the sickly yellowish glow of the aging floodlights attached to the building walls. They cast everything into a deep, hazy gloom, mingling with the mist just beginning to roll in from the nearby forest.

Vincent had never been here before, but he didn't need to. Almost as soon as he saw the gym's silhouette, a distinct odor pricked his nose. His lip curled against the scent, both sweet and sour in the worst ways. It reminded him a bit of home.

Henry noticed, and stopped beside him. "What is it?"

Without a word, Vincent skirted the building and crept into the open field behind it. Between the gym and the treeline a lone structure stood.

"Vincent?" Henry hissed, following. "What happened? Did you see something?"

The smell was even stronger here, wafting directly from the little shed. Vincent clamped his arm over his mouth and nose, trying to ward off the worst of it with little success.

"Are you...*smelling* something?" said Henry.

"Are you not?" said Vincent, his voice muffled by his jacket sleeve.

The shed's silhouette was stark against the fogbound sky, looming like a creature about to pounce. It went against every instinct to creep towards it, but he forced himself to. He could hear Henry's footsteps swishing through the grass behind him, and little else. Even the crickets had stopped chirping.

They halted only a few feet from the entrance. It was shut tight, a padlock gleaming faintly in the yellow light carried by the mist.

"This is just an old supply shed," Henry whispered. "Why are we here? I don't smell anything..."

"We need to get it open. I think Mira's body is inside."

Henry looked horrified. "What? Why?"

Vincent shot him a look that invited no argument.

"Okay, I'll–I'll go get some bolt cutters. I'm gonna have to go to Walmart, though–it'll be a few minutes."

"I'll stay here and guard it, then," said Vincent.

Worry and urgency warred on Henry's face, but the latter won. "Are you sure you'll be okay here by yourself?"

"I'll lay low. Don't worry. Just be fast, before someone comes looking for it."

Henry hesitated only a moment more. "Don't do anything rash, okay?"

"You mean, don't be stupid?" Vincent cracked a wry smile. "Yeah, I got that."

Henry offered him one last look of concern. Then he disappeared around the side of the gym, leaving Vincent alone with the stench of rot.

The darkness didn't bother Vincent–he was used to it, and he could see very well in it. If anything, it served him more than hindered him. Most things he would call foe couldn't find him hidden in its depths. He wasn't worried.

Shouldn't be worried.

But, then again, the last time he got too comfortable in darkness, Henry had ambushed him.

Time stretched on, agonizingly so. Vincent waited in the shed's shadow like a predator. But there was no sign of prey. He wondered if that meant *he* was the prey. That would be a first.

He glanced over his shoulder every few moments, just to be sure. He was fairly certain the spine-tingling sensation of being watched was only in his head. He halted the thought in its tracks, telling himself there was nothing to be afraid of. Henry would be back soon.

When he saw a silhouette approaching from around the gym, Vincent almost rose to hail Henry. But something made him wait.

That's when he recognized the scent of peat, the slender form, the furtive silence of its movements. He almost couldn't believe it–but at the same time, it was all too easy.

Suddenly, he was the predator again.

Before Benjamin could even fiddle with the padlock, Vincent stepped out of the shadows. His dark eyes flashed red in the gloom.

Benjamin startled, rounding to face his stalker. His shock quickly fell to scorn.

"So you found me." His voice was cold and quiet.

"You're not hard to find," Vincent growled. He advanced a single step, but Benjamin didn't balk. Even though he was cornered. "What are you doing here?"

He glanced up at the shed that still loomed over them, spewing its stench. A dark realization began to sink in.

"Did *you* steal her body, Benjamin?"

Benjamin smiled. It was a horrible, twisted thing, barely a smile at all. Most people would have missed it, it was so slight. But every detail of his being was carved into Vincent's senses with an otherworldly, searing-hot edge.

"What are you going to do, then?" asked Benjamin.

"You know the answer to that."

Benjamin nodded, his thoughts swimming like minnows in his pale blue eyes.

"Are you sure?"

Vincent slowly bared his teeth. "What do you mean by that? You think you can escape again?"

"I didn't escape. You let me go."

"You tricked me," Vincent snarled.

"Did I?" Benjamin shook his head. "It's not my fault you were too much of a coward to come with me. I don't think that's a trick."

"I told you I wouldn't betray my master. You should have known better than to let that plan slip."

"You're right," Benjamin conceded, bowing his head. His next words came so softly it hurt. "But I believed better of you. I thought you understood the torment of being trapped in the Underworld forever. Witnessed enough of the torture to end it. I trusted you. But I was wrong."

A painful spasm lanced Vincent's heart. It only made him angrier. "*You* didn't deserve to suffer there! *I* didn't–" He stopped, unable to even complete the thought.

"Say it."

"No. *I* was wrong," Vincent growled. "I thought we were different. I thought there had to be some mistake. But we deserved to be there just as much as the rest of those wretched souls. I knew that from the moment you told me you had a plan to save them all. To ruin everything my master built."

Benjamin let out a mirthless laugh. "You mean His prison? His instruments of torture?"

"He saw inside your heart, just like all the others. Everyone in Hell deserves–"

"*You* saw inside my heart. From the moment I was born, I've always lived in Hell. I did everything I could to make the pain stop. The only ways I ever knew how, thanks to my mother. And in the end, I just wanted to escape it. That's all. I had no idea that 'escape' was *worse.* That Hell was real."

Vincent tried to force away the phantom of that pain, the memory of Benjamin's pallid, dead face when he shared it. Flashes of a life Vincent had never lived tearing through his mind, his heart...

"You still had a choice," Vincent growled. "You didn't have to die. You didn't have to sin. Even before that, you chose to, every time you stole and got high and sold yourself, over and over–"

"If *sinning* is trying to put myself out of my misery, do you really think that's fair? Do you really think I deserve to be tortured forever just for that? For *indulgence,* they called it. Gluttony of a different breed. As if I *enjoyed* it. As if I *wanted* to do it. Never mind the circumstances."

Vincent's head swam. "It–it doesn't matter what I think, I just have to trust–"

"And if they think that of me, what about the rest of the damned? What about you?"

"They were right about me!" Vincent snarled, fighting himself, pushing it all down– "It's who I am, Benjamin. I was born for it. I belong to Hell, just like you do."

"So you admit it–our choices don't matter. We were doomed from the start. Playthings for a vengeful god." Benjamin leaned in, flaying Vincent alive with those cold, cold eyes. "And you wanted out. You knew it was wrong. You feel it too."

Vincent's throat tightened. "I was *selfish*." *Treacherous. Greedy.* "I realized what I was doing. What it meant."

"But here you are anyway. Out."

Vincent hesitated. He didn't mean to, but he did.

And Benjamin saw it. "You don't really want to do this, do you?"

Vincent's nails dug deep into his palms. He thought of Percy, Mira, Melanie, Henry...

But the moment had come. If he missed this chance, it would be treason.

"You won't sway me with your lies, Benjamin. Never again. I was wrong– humans are all the same. I swear on Lucifer's name, I *will* keep you in line."

"Will you, now?"

The brush near the treeline rustled. Something was coming–and it wasn't Henry.

Four little points of light, blood-red, appeared in the shadows between the trees. Eyes.

They lunged. And Vincent lunged.

Mid-leap, he was no longer human. In that split second he felt his fragile body give way, his true form bursting through like shedding a skin too small for it. One head split into three, his vision distorting and then resolving, now three times as potent. Night air rushed into his gaping mouths, bringing a depth of scent he had all but forgotten. Power surged through his limbs down to his claws, freed from their illusory prison. Now he was real—a hulking monster, canine but *wrong*.

His fangs met in Benjamin's arm—but no blood surged into his mouth. The wound was dry, the skin thick and spongy.

Then Vincent's teeth ripped away, his body slammed into the ground.

His new claws slashed, but again, no blood spilled from the gash he made in sallow flesh. Panic rose in his throats as the creatures from the trees grasped his massive shoulders, his chest, his legs, each of his three heads.

He snapped his monstrous jaws, flailing and writhing. Any other adversary would have cowered against the fury of the beast that had appeared before them. But not these. Four sets of claws held Vincent so strongly he could barely move at all.

Suddenly teeth plunged into his shoulder, so sharp he felt them scrape on bone. He howled a canine howl, white-hot agony surging through his body. The world was only a blur of shadow and pain and grass and fear. Through the haze fangs flashed, seeking out his life, seconds from his throat—

Something slammed into the creature's head. Its teeth tore from Vincent's shoulder, blood spurting from the holes they left.

Freed, Vincent scrambled away, ears ringing from its shriek, chest heaving as he fought to regain his bearings. When he did, he glimpsed the strangest thing he had ever seen.

Henry stood there in the sick yellow light like an ancient hero. His right hand was encased in a heavy silver gauntlet, raised to strike again.

"You have one chance to back off!" he commanded, once again summoning a sudden intensity that would have quelled any lesser foe.

But these creatures were something else entirely. They looked human, but they certainly weren't. They hunched over, hissing, their eyes flashing red as they fixed on Henry.

"Get back!" Vincent barked. Ignoring the pain coursing through his shoulder, he dove for Henry. Henry's gaze flicked to him.

For a split second, that gauntlet lifted towards Vincent.

He skidded to a halt. At the same moment, Henry's weapon turned back on the monsters. But it was too late.

Creature met gauntlet with a clang. It groped for Henry with monstrous fingers. He staggered, straining against its unnatural weight, his weapon held like a shield in front of his face. It seemed stronger than normal armor, but it wasn't enough. He wouldn't win this contest–and he knew it.

He kicked out sharply, his shoe striking the creature's knee. Something snapped. It snarled, legs buckling–but before it fell, the other creature lunged.

Vincent lurched forward. His fangs snapped shut, crunching on bone. His foe screamed and gurgled, thrashing its limbs and clutching at him with unholy strength. Its hands squeezed around the neck of the jaws that held it.

Another of Vincent's heads lunged. Teeth crushed its arm until the bone cracked. The creature's grip slackened and he saw his chance. With an immense effort he flung it aside.

He rounded on the second enemy. It staggered back, reeling from a blow to the head. Henry was just scrambling back out of its reach when his eyes met Vincent's. Again, they both understood at the same moment.

Vincent turned and ran. He winced against the pain in his shoulder, but he couldn't stop. He barely forced himself not to bound at full pace, knowing he would never forgive himself if he left Henry behind. But to Henry's credit, he ran at Vincent's side with the speed of a seasoned athlete. Perhaps he shouldn't have been surprised.

They dodged around the side of the gym and onto the paths linking the school's courtyards. The pounding of Henry's shoes and clatter of Vincent's claws echoed through the arches of the corridors.

Finally they realized they heard no pursuit, and eased to a stop between the pillars, panting. They looked up and down the hallway, but saw no movement. They were alone.

"Oh my god," Henry panted, leaning against the limestone wall. "We made it. We made it. Those were…"

He stopped. Slowly, he turned. Vincent was almost more afraid of his reaction than the creatures that had attacked them. But he forced himself to look anyway.

Henry's gaze searched each of Vincent's new features, pausing the longest on each of his three heads. Vincent was as tall as Henry now even on all fours, a hulking beast with scruffy dark brown fur and three sets of eyes that burned like embers. Henry kept a wary distance away, but for some reason he didn't seem *afraid*.

Finally Vincent couldn't stand the silence any longer.

"You're taking this well," he said, his voice mostly unchanged despite his transformation. He spoke without moving any of his three mouths, the words echoing from somewhere unknown.

"Um...I'm not...exactly new to these kinds of things," Henry admitted.

The realization jolted through Vincent. *This is what he was hiding.*

"Did you know...?"

"What you are? Well, not exactly...but I had a feeling about you."

So he was *suspicious of me.* Vincent wasn't just being paranoid after all.

"I guess I owe you some answers." Henry glanced behind them. "But not here."

"Do you think they'll follow us this far into campus?"

"They might. Didn't you see them?"

"I didn't get a good look, but..."

"Those were vampires, Vincent." Henry's voice was grave. "Nobody would be able to tell the difference at a glance."

A chill tingled under Vincent's fur. *Vampires...why is Benjamin working with vampires?*

Then, he realized: *they all had no blood.* Did that mean Benjamin was a vampire too?

"Did you recognize them?" he asked carefully.

Henry shook his head. "I couldn't see very well. But I wouldn't discount them being students here."

Good. He didn't see Benjamin. Then again...thinking on it, he only now registered that Benjamin had disappeared as soon as Henry arrived.

Bastard.

But it was just as well—he wasn't sure if they could have fought off *three* vampires. They barely escaped two.

One of his heads sniffed the air, but he couldn't pick out any unusual scents nearby. It was a small comfort. "I think we're safe for now."

But he didn't want to stick around to test that theory. He started down the corridor, grimacing as he tried not to put too much weight on his injured leg. Blood still oozed from the punctures in his shoulder, but it had slowed.

Henry walked beside him, worry etched into his face. "Are you alright, Vinny?"

Again Vincent felt his heart squirm at the affectionate name. He was shocked that any of that fondness remained for the beast that stood before him.

"I will be."

"Are you...stuck in that form, now?"

Instantly his misgivings returned. Henry's question was a confirmation: this form made him uneasy. Of course—what did he expect? A rogue prickle of shame traveled through his body. He hated it. Why should he feel like this about his true self?

"I think I need to calm down before I can change back."

Henry's pace slowed to a halt. Vincent stopped to face him. He stared back at him, a grim shadow darkening his expression.

"What...*are* you, Vincent?"

Vincent met his gaze with his eyes of embers. They betrayed none of the storm roiling inside him, but all of the darkness.

"They call us the Children of Cerberus."

"A hellhound," Henry guessed, with a glimmer of amazement.

The silence stretched between them in the dark corridor, its gravity bearing down on them both until it became too much to withstand. Henry broke first to stride past Vincent, careful not to touch him. He didn't miss that.

"C'mon. I know a good place to rest nearby."

Henry led him through a series of corridors until they stepped out into a much larger courtyard. This one was covered in grass that sloped upward into a tall hill.

"This is the biology building," Henry explained as he began to climb.

Vincent followed, ducking his heads now that he was out in the open. His claws made easy work of the steep hill, and soon they both stood overlooking a stone garden at its summit. The ground was paved with gravel and stepping stones that wound around stately boulders in varying shapes. The only sound came from the rustle of wind against the pronged leaves of several sycamore trees, their tops barely spilling above the crest of the hill. At the center of the garden a thick square window was built into the ground itself. Vincent crept to the edge, peering down to see a large indoor space far below, cast into deep shadow but for a square of light broken by his own monstrous silhouette. He retreated.

"The building's entrance is on the other side of the hill," Henry said, smiling a little at Vincent's curiosity. "Neat, isn't it? Nobody really comes here much, especially at night. And it's the perfect vantage point–no one can sneak up on us from up here."

Vincent settled down in the gravel beside one of the sycamore trees, resting on his side to examine his wound. His dark fur barely showed the blood in the gloom, but the sharp scent still assaulted his noses. He bent the head closest to it to lick it gently. He tried to ignore the metallic tang on his tongue. Another head scanned the courtyard below, ears swiveling, but found nothing.

The middle head watched Henry as he quietly approached. As he knelt beside him, Vincent's other heads turned to look as well, apprehensive.

He knew he was grotesque in Henry's eyes. A multi-headed demon hound, utterly alien, borne from the darkest reaches of the earth where no living soul should ever tread. He was not meant to be seen like this. The gulf between them had cracked open, becoming an abyss, and nothing could ever fill it.

Good, he forced the thought, stubbornly. *Now at least he won't play nice out of pity. Maybe he'll leave me alone, and I can finish my duty and be done with this place.*

But then, slowly, Henry reached a hand towards him.

Panic slammed into Vincent's chest.

No–don't–

Henry froze as the beast before him shifted. The hulking form bubbled and morphed, its bones moving beneath meat and flesh, fur shrinking into skin, two heads melting into the one at the center.

It was all over in a blink. Vincent, human-formed, crouched in the dirt. He clutched his shoulder with one hand, its wound hidden by the leather jacket that remained unmarred from his battle. He shivered as the cold night air found his skin again.

He didn't miss the glint of powerful curiosity in Henry's blue eyes, even in the darkness. He withdrew his hand, even now gazing at Vincent warily like the wounded animal he was.

"We should really wrap that up," Henry said. "We don't want it to get infected."

Vincent couldn't bear the tenderness in his voice. It was too close, too hot, too raw, too forgiving. He didn't understand it.

"Well, do you have a first aid kit in your pocket?" he replied, sounding less nonchalant than he would have liked.

A moment of silence passed. "I guess I should, at this point."

Finally Henry retreated, apparently taking the cue, and busied himself with looking around for enemies. But Vincent didn't feel as relieved as he had expected. Discomfort still seethed under his skin, and nothing he did could quell it. He was quiet for a long moment, stewing in his own awkwardness.

"I, ah…I would have been screwed if you hadn't shown up when you did," he said at last. "Did you get the bolt cutters?"

Henry shook his head. "I was going to, but by the time I got to my car I just...had a bad feeling. I decided to go get you something to defend yourself with, just in case. Good thing I did..."

"And good thing you weren't late," Vincent remarked. He peered at the gauntlet still affixed to Henry's arm. Now that he wasn't busy getting murdered, he could make out a series of runes etched into its silvery plates. "What is that thing, anyway?"

Henry followed his gaze. "This? It's a gauntlet."

"I know that. What are those markings?"

"Oh. Well, it's a special gauntlet. The runes fortify it."

Vincent narrowed his eyes. "Runes have magical properties. So you just happen to have a magic weapon lying around in your room?"

"Not lying around," Henry insisted. "I keep my weapons locked up. Wouldn't want them to get into the wrong hands."

"So...you have *multiple* magic weapons stashed in your room?"

Henry let out a heavy sigh. "I guess I should tell you."

He hesitated.

"I'm...well, there's no easy way to say this. I'm kind of in the business of monster hunting."

Vincent stared at him. "I didn't know that was a thing."

"Yeah, I guess you could say it runs in the family. God, it feels so strange to be talking about it like this," Henry said with a nervous laugh. "It's a secret society type deal. I'm not allowed to talk about it, normally. But you're sort of in on it already."

"I sort of am," Vincent agreed, still clutching his mangled shoulder.

"I know about all different kinds of supernatural creatures, to put it one way. We call them Others, in code. All the things that go bump in the night," Henry added lightly. "I've been training since I was very little. My dad is a prominent member. I imagine you've heard of the Illuminati?"

Vincent quirked an eyebrow. "Isn't that an internet joke?"

"Ha, yeah. I mean, there's a grain of truth to almost everything, isn't there? Anyway, it hasn't been called that for a long time. When the organization dissolved, a sect of it broke off and carried on its traditions. Well...some of them."

Vincent shifted uncomfortably. "Are you going to...*hunt* me?" he said, half incredulous and half afraid of the answer.

Henry snorted. "Of course not, Vincent. We don't just attack every Other we come across. The Illuminati was more that way. Zero tolerance policy. No, the Shadowhand are Wardens, not hunters. We keep the traditions of collecting and preserving knowledge about the Others...that, and stopping them from disrupting the mortal world."

"Disrupting...?"

"We keep tabs on them. Most of them are harmless. Sometimes, we even help them maintain their cover. Anything to keep the peace."

Henry's expression hardened. "But sometimes, if things go south...we have to put a stop to it. That's our vow."

"Well, looks like you have a job to do, then."

Henry nodded, but he didn't seem happy about it. "Now you see why I've been doing all these patrols. Although I didn't know about the vampires...that changes things."

"That's kind of hard to miss."

Henry shrugged. "You'd be surprised. I mean, I'm not a seasoned Warden. I'm only twenty-one. I knew something was wrong, what with the murders and all...but I had to be sure of what I was up against."

"I guess I'm your lucky break."

"Ha. I guess so." Henry gave him a half-smile. "All the same, I'm sorry you got caught up in all this."

"Sure. Guy like me, I always keep my head down."

Henry laughed. But that seemed to pique his interest.

"Yeah...how did you come to be here, anyway? You just wandered out of the woods by yourself. I'm guessing you're not from Greece, after all."

Vincent didn't like the change in direction. He still wasn't fully convinced Henry wouldn't turn that gauntlet on him–if not now, then later.

"What about you?" he deflected. "What's the point of a monster hunter going to a normal college?"

Henry looked away. "Well...I really just wanted to be normal for a while. This school is so out of the way, I thought..." He shook his head. "I guess that was silly. Once you're in, you can't get out again."

"You don't *have* to deal with all this, you know," Vincent told him, albeit reluctantly. He had a better chance of helping Percy and avenging Mira with Henry on his side, knowledgeable as he was. But at the same time, his presence complicated everything. He loathed how muddled Henry made him feel–especially now, when he needed a clear head more than ever.

Henry sighed. "Yeah, I do. I wouldn't be able to live with myself if I didn't."

Of course. Vincent wasn't going to get off that easy.

"You didn't answer my question, by the way," said Henry. "What you're doing here."

Damn it. "I...can't tell you. I'm not allowed to."

Henry opened his mouth as if to protest, but then closed it again. He nodded with a grimace.

"Yeah. Of course."

He suddenly stood. "We should be getting back. I doubt they're gonna come after us now, if they haven't found us already. Can you walk?"

Vincent fought back a new feeling rising hot in his chest–guilt. He couldn't face Henry's gentleness, but more than that, he couldn't bear his resentment. Why did he even care what Henry thought of him?

Stubbornly he pushed himself to his feet as well. "Of course I can walk."

They moved carefully down the hillside. Vincent found it harder than last time by far, with only two legs instead of four. He had to release his grip on his wound to balance, and half-slid all the way down. Henry reached for him on instinct, but Vincent stumbled to right himself on his own.

"Your shape isn't an illusion, then?" Henry asked as they started off. Vincent fought off a pang of annoyance–he just wasn't going to let it go, was he?

"No. It's something I was granted when I came here. I'm surprised you don't know that already."

"We actually don't have much literature on hellhounds. Not every day a creature from Hell makes its way up here. Well...other than demons," Henry chuckled. "They're a dime a dozen. Can't seem to leave humans alone. Do you know any demons?"

"Not really," Vincent lied. "I'm a guard dog, nothing more."

"A guard dog, huh..." Henry murmured. "A Child of Cerberus...who once belonged to Hades, so the legends say. But the Greek gods aren't real...are they?"

"They used to be," said Vincent. He wasn't certain he should answer, but he knew his master would loathe the lack of credit for His exploits. "Long ago, the gods waged war. Hades and his ilk lost. Now Lucifer reigns over the Underworld."

Henry's eyes were round. "Damn. So it's true! Even the Shadowhand didn't know for sure. Wars between gods was one of their theories...but there are so many different stories out there, it's hard to pin down. A lot of humans believe the Christian God is...well, God. That He created everything. But there are so many other gods out there, too, so I *knew* that couldn't be right."

"I don't think anyone knows who created everything." Vincent shrugged. "Not even the gods." He was growing more and more uncomfortable, unsure what he was allowed to divulge. He hoped it wasn't already too much. So he said, "What are we going to do now? We can't take on two vampires by ourselves, clearly."

"Yes, we can. I have all kinds of tools that can give us a leg up."

"What, do you have silver bullets or something?"

Henry gave a little snort. "No. My dad is strictly against guns unless it's absolutely necessary. They make too much noise and they're too much of a liability to transport. *Especially* on a college campus."

"How principled," Vincent said wryly. "Silver arrows, then?"

"Something like that. There are multiple ways to really damage a vampire. I just wish we didn't have to use them."

"Do you think the vampires were just killing to eat? Or...drink, I suppose." Vincent had other theories, but he wanted to see just how skilled Henry was at this monster hunting business.

"Maybe... They're pretty brazen to attack us like that on campus. They can't be affiliated with any of the clans. I doubt the Brethren even know they exist, or else they'd be crawling all over the place..."

"The Brethren?"

Henry blinked, as if only just remembering he was talking aloud. "Oh—um, the ruling council of vampires. There aren't very many vampires left, actually, but the ones that do exist have to be associated with the Brethren. Otherwise, they risk being hunted and exterminated. The Brethren are very careful these days about their exposure, after being nearly eradicated in the Dark Ages by human hunters."

"What's stopping us from reporting these ones to the Brethren and letting them deal with it?"

"We *could*...the Shadowhand have a pact with the Brethren. If I asked my dad..." Henry broke off, shaking his head. "No. I don't want him to get involved in this."

"Why not? It sounds like this Shadowhand could fix everything."

Henry let out a frustrated exhale. "I just...wanted to do something on my own for once."

"And that's worth people dying?"

"No...but that's not the point. It's just..." Henry's shoulders sagged. "Listen...if I called my dad, and the Brethren hunted those two down...they would probably kill them."

Vincent stared at him. "You care about the vampires?"

"You don't?" Henry looked appalled. "They're still *people*, Vincent. Even with their...affliction. We're no better than that murderer if we hand them over to die."

"What if they *are* the murderer? What if they've been killing people to sustain themselves?" It *was* possible...but something told Vincent it was more complicated than that, if Benjamin was involved. He wanted something bigger—something that would disrupt the reign of Hell and Heaven altogether. *Maybe he's feeding the others, to get them on his side...*

"More death is more death. I'm not here for that—I'm here to *stop* it. To help them."

Henry looked so deadly serious, Vincent couldn't bring himself to challenge him any further. If he did, he was sure he would lose any alliance between them. He wasn't sure what he had expected—after all, this was Henry Wellfellow. Principled to the last. Vincent just hadn't realized how far it would go.

And with that realization came another: Henry couldn't know about his duty to hunt Benjamin. If he did...he would never allow Vincent to drag him back to Hell. To eternal torment. It was a fate even worse than death.

If he knew...he would never forgive Vincent.

But then, it was already too late for forgiveness. All of this was his fault. If Benjamin really was behind the murders, and he himself was behind Benjamin...

Percy's face, Mira's face—both flashed through his mind, the way he had last seen them. One of them lively but frozen, only a memory captured in ink, forever faceless in the darkest corner of their shared room. The other unthinkably still, spattered with blood, her eyes open like nothing was wrong at all, a mockery of who she had been.

It all fermented into guilt in an instant, more powerful than anything he had yet felt. Both of their lives were snuffed out because of him. He had done that. If he had just done what he was supposed to from the start, none of this would have happened.

He knew what that meant. He had to find a way to corner Benjamin—alone. No other vampires. No Henry. No witnesses. The only trouble was, Benjamin knew he was onto him now.

He would be ready.

CHAPTER 7

THE WITCH IN WALDEN HALL

W alden Hall was only half-lit, the overhead lights switched off in an alternating pattern. Still, it felt like a safe haven as Vincent stepped over the threshold, the now-familiar scents of old wood and musty carpet greeting him.

They followed the hallway to Henry's room quietly, wary of waking anyone else in the dorm. The bright decor and solitude inside were an instant comfort.

"Sit on my bed and let me see your shoulder."

Vincent awkwardly did as he asked. He waited there while Henry exchanged his gauntlet for a first aid kit from a drawer under the sink. He sifted through it as he sat next to Vincent on the bed. After a moment he glanced up at him.

"I uh, can't get to it unless you take your shirt off."

Vincent cleared his throat, shifting slightly away from Henry. "Right." He tried to shrug off his jacket without moving his injured arm. His hand ended up stuck halfway down his sleeve, flapping about uselessly as he struggled with it.

"Oh, shit...hold still." Henry carefully slipped the jacket off one side of Vincent's body, then the other. It was now obvious that his shirt sleeve was thoroughly bloodsoaked, and both of them gritted their teeth as they looked at it.

"May I...?" Henry said.

Vincent's heartbeat was loud in his ears. "Ah...are you sure I shouldn't go to a hospital or something?"

"It's okay–I'm trained to deal with injuries like this. Besides...do *you* wanna explain to some overworked night nurse how you got fang marks all over you?"

Vincent gave an amused snort. "Point taken."

He sucked in a breath as he lifted his arms. Now that the adrenaline had faded, it hurt even more to move his shoulder. He had no idea how he had run on it earlier. Maybe it was easier in his true form, strong as it was.

He looked away, trying to ignore the warmth crawling up his neck as Henry's gentle hands slid the shirt up over his head and arms. The congealed blood stuck for a moment before the sleeve peeled off. He bit his tongue to staunch a gasp.

Now there was nothing to hide his scars—not even the evening gloom of the forest. His greatest shame was on full display.

He was convinced he could feel Henry's eyes burning over them. But he couldn't bring himself to check. He had the same feeling from before he had changed back into a human in the hillside garden.

He was going to touch me...why?

"This is gonna hurt," Henry warned. Vincent glanced over just long enough to glimpse disinfecting wipes in his hand.

Vincent nodded, tensing. "Just do it."

The first touch felt like fire. He couldn't help the growl that tore from his throat, and he gripped the blankets underneath him until his knuckles went white. Henry swiped the area as gently as he could, but didn't hold back on being thorough.

Shut up, Vincent—you've had worse. He's not trying to hurt you.

He needed a distraction. He looked around the room for one, desperate.

"Is that one of those video game machines?" he asked, gesturing towards a plastic box next to Henry's TV.

Henry followed his gaze, his smile returning at last. "Yeah! You've never played, have you?"

Vincent snorted. "Oh, yeah, in Hell they make these special controllers for dogs. When I go on breaks I get all the game time I want."

Henry giggled so hard he had to stop disinfecting for a second. "Okay, okay! I get it. I just thought maybe, since you've been here for a bit..."

"Really? Who would I be playing video games with, Henry?"

Henry's smile faded. A moment too late, Vincent realized he had invited the pity back in.

So he quickly said, "Do monster hunters have time for video games?"

Henry was gracious enough to follow the cue. "Yeah, actually. I mean, every so often. Between football and class and, y'know, everything else." He fastened a square of thick gauze and tape against Vincent's shoulder, earning a wince.

Vincent peered at him closely. "If you're doing all that, and you're out at night patrolling all the time...don't you get tired? It seems like a lot for one person."

"No, no," Henry said swiftly. A little too swiftly. "I make it work. I'm used to it."

Vincent frowned. "You're used to it?"

Henry shrugged. "It's all the same kind of stuff my Shadowhand training had me doing."

"I thought you went to college to get away from all the Shadowhand business."

"Well...yeah, I did," he sighed. "But for the most part, I have. I mean, all of this stuff is on my terms now. The patrols were my idea. And I love football and theater! I get to hang out with a bunch of people now, too. It's really much better than training at home."

Vincent looked at him curiously. "You only trained at home?"

"Yeah. I was homeschooled before college. It's tradition for Shadowhand trainees, so we can focus on the important stuff. This is...kinda the first time I've gotten to do anything on my own," he admitted.

"Really? But you seem so..." Vincent wasn't sure what word could encompass what Henry Wellfellow was. He gave up. "Aren't homeschool kids like...shut-ins, or something?"

Henry snickered. "No...I mean, maybe some of them. I did get out sometimes. I had joint training and tutoring with kids from other Shadowhand families. But everyone was always traveling all over the States for jobs, so it was a toss-up when you'd get to see anyone you know."

"No wonder you're such a kiss-ass," Vincent mused. "Had to make friends wherever you could get them."

Henry blinked at him, caught off guard. "I am not a kiss-ass!"

"You're a *regular* kiss-ass," Vincent insisted, a wry smile creeping onto his face.

Henry broke into a grin. "You're lucky you're all wrapped up, Vinny."

"What are you going to do, kiss my ass?"

"You wish! I'm the reigning pillow fight champion on this campus. Oh yeah, be jealous."

"Is that the best thing drunk college kids can come up with? Pillow fights?"

"You should've seen the time we lined up mattresses all the way down the hall and set 'em off like dominoes. It was *glorious*."

Henry laughed, and before Vincent knew it, he was laughing too. It took a moment to realize how much he was unused to the sound. He stopped short when he did, but the feeling of tiny bright bubbles in his chest lingered. It was almost enough to drown out the guilt–almost.

When Henry had finished patching him up, Vincent said, "So, where are these special vampire-killing tools?"

Henry stood, snapping the lid of the first aid kit shut. He stashed it back in his drawer, then picked up his gauntlet.

"We're not gonna be using any of those," he said, with a note of triumph.

Vincent's face fell. "What? We just–"

"We don't need them." Henry knelt at the foot of his bed and reached underneath, pulling out a large, squat plastic bin. At first it looked like a normal storage container for clothes or other personal effects, but when he opened it the only thing inside was a very large metal briefcase with a complex combination lock. He began rotating the mechanisms, which made a series of satisfying clicks as he worked.

"If we're gonna do this without the Shadowhand, we're gonna do it our way. Like I said, we're not killing anybody."

"They're the ones killing people. They need to face justice." *And once they're off Benjamin...he'll be the only one I have to worry about.* "And we need to prevent them from killing anyone else."

"There are other ways to do that." Henry sounded completely resolute. He turned to face Vincent, who became self-conscious again as he realized he was still shirtless. He grabbed his leather jacket and carefully slipped it on one arm at a time, wincing as it rubbed against his patched wound.

"Are we at least going to carry *some* weapons, just in case?"

"That depends. Are you gonna try and kill them?"

Vincent shot him an annoyed look. "What do you think?"

Henry squared his shoulders. "Personally, I think you're better than that, Vincent. You were more concerned about me than you were about attacking them. I think you put on a show, but you're not as vicious as you pretend to be."

Vincent froze, stupefied. Then he busied himself with buttoning his jacket, concealing the last of his bare chest and the old slash marks that marred it.

Me...better than that...

Henry seemed satisfied with his silence, and turned back to the case. He finally got it open and stashed his gauntlet inside. Then he began rifling through its contents. "Let's see...not that you need weapons, but do you have any training or preferences? You aren't just gonna turn into a hellhound every time you feel threatened, are you?"

"Of course not." Vincent craned his neck to try and see into the case properly. "I don't know...I've never had to use weapons before."

Henry pondered a moment before pulling out a pair of what looked to be knife handles fashioned from dark rosewood.

"How about these? They're pretty self-explanatory."

He held them out and pressed a button on each of them. Blades as long as Vincent's hand flicked out of the handles, glinting in the lamplight.

"A secret knife?" Vincent took them from Henry and inspected them.

"It's called a switchblade, but essentially, yeah. They're illegal to carry, though, so don't let anyone see them."

"And your father is worried about guns?"

Henry shrugged. "A switchblade isn't gonna bring any crowds flocking to see where the big bang came from."

He showed Vincent how to stow the blades back in the handles. He hid them in the inner pockets of his jacket.

"What are you going to use?" Vincent asked.

"I have all kinds of tricks up my sleeve." Henry winked at him. "Some of them literally. I like my gauntlet the best, though."

He kept the rest of his weapons in the case and locked it again, stowing it in its plastic bin under his bed.

"So since we're doing this your way, what's your big plan?" Vincent prompted, skeptical.

"Well...I haven't gotten too far on that, yet," Henry admitted. "But we definitely need to find out who these vampires are, and why they're operating here. The best answer is that they're students, so of course they would feed on campus." He frowned thoughtfully. "But what I don't get is where they came from. One vampire, maybe. But two in the same place is strange."

"Maybe one turned the other?" Vincent suggested. "Vampires do that, don't they? Make humans into more vampires?" *Is Benjamin turning them? He needed backup, for his big plan...*

"I don't see why they would. That's just more competition for feeding. And it's not like it only takes a bite. It's almost a ritual–the vampire has to drink human blood, and once they're saturated with it they offer it back to a human to drink."

A memory flashed through Vincent's mind. "Those vampires hadn't drunk anything in a while. They didn't bleed when I attacked them." *Neither did Benjamin.*

"Interesting..." Henry murmured. "Then I wonder what they were doing with Mira's body...if that's really what was in the shed. Are you sure that was what you smelled? Could you tell it was her?"

Vincent screwed up his face as he recalled the stench. "It's hard to say...it mostly smelled like death."

"I hate to say it, but I hope it *was* her...rather than someone else we haven't found yet." Henry looked deeply troubled.

Vincent fell silent, pulling at his tie. He had more information than he was letting on...but even though he was taking advantage of Henry's help, he couldn't risk him getting too close to the heart of his affairs with Benjamin. He decided not to mention anything about that. But he did have something else.

"I do have one lead..."

"You do?"

"Percy."

Henry stared at him blankly. "What do you mean?"

"He's...well, he's still here, Henry. In his room."

Henry's eyes widened. They immediately began to glisten with tears. Startled, Vincent looked away.

"Are you serious? Is he...a ghost?"

Vincent nodded. "I've been talking to him all semester. The issue is...he's confused. He can't remember much about how he died. But if he did..."

"He could help us," Henry finished eagerly. But then, his face fell. "I guess it makes sense you can talk to him. I don't think I can. I've been in that room so many times...unless he doesn't want to talk to me?"

"He does," Vincent assured him. "He told me so. He says I'm the first person who's been able to hear him."

Henry sighed. "That's what I get for being an ordinary human..."

That gave Vincent an idea.

"Wait—there might be one more person who could help."

"Who?"

"Ava."

"Ava? Is she...?"

"She gave me a very accurate tarot reading just before the party–a little *too* accurate. I think she might genuinely have the Sight. And I bet that means she can communicate with spirits. Maybe better than I can."

"I assume you didn't ask her at the time?"

"Of course not. 'Hey Ava, I know you just met me, but tell me, can you see dead people?'"

Henry snorted a laugh. "Okay, okay. But...what would she know that you don't? Aren't you like, a gatekeeper of Hell?"

Vincent's innards squirmed. He brushed past the question.

"How am I supposed to know what I don't know? That's why we have to ask her."

Henry seemed to accept this. "Well, let's ask her tomorrow then. You're practically dead on your feet yourself," he added as Vincent failed to suppress a huge yawn. He couldn't argue with that.

The next day Vincent woke feeling refreshed, despite the ache in his shoulder. His sixth sense gnawed at him afresh, hungry for the hunt. He pushed it down long enough to shower, covering his gauze with an empty chip bag he managed to tape around his arm so it didn't get wet. It was a good excuse to eat chips for breakfast–as if he needed one.

Afterwards he met up with Henry at his room, making sure his jacket covered any view of his injury. They went to knock on Ava and Melanie's door, praying that Ava would answer. Their hopes were promptly dashed.

"What is it, boys?" Melanie lilted, peering out at them through the crack. The aroma of coconut wafted out after her. She looked as stunningly pretty as usual, but drowsy and pale–even more so than usual.

"Oh, hi, Melanie!" Vincent could tell Henry was trying too hard to be friendly. He was fairly sure Melanie could tell, too. "Sorry to bother you. We were hoping Ava was home."

"She's asleep," Melanie answered mildly.

"Still? It's nearly noon."

Melanie shrugged. "It's Ava. She'll probably be asleep 'till two."

"Seriously?" said Vincent.

"That's alright," said Henry. "I'll text her later. Thanks, Melanie!"

"Mhm." Her gaze flicked to Vincent, and she put on a sly little smile. "Is that all you wanted? I am free Friday night, if you were wondering."

It took Vincent a moment to realize what she meant. An unpleasant warmth crawled up his neck.

"Ah...I'm not. I've got somewhere to be."

Her smile twitched. "How about the weekend?"

"Also busy." He thought he answered a little too quickly. Melanie apparently agreed; her full lips pressed back into a disapproving line.

"Hm. When are you free, then?"

Vincent groaned internally. "I'll ah, let you know."

Melanie's eyes narrowed slightly. "Alright," she finally said, sounding suitably nonchalant despite her obvious annoyance. Instead of saying goodbye, she immediately shut the door.

"Well, she's in rare form today," Henry remarked as they started down the hall.

"She must be in rare form every day, then." Vincent didn't know why she had to be so persistent.

Henry snickered. "But she's not usually so grumpy. I didn't think she was *that* into you..."

Vincent fought back that creeping, prickly warmth at the idea and shrugged. "Yeah, she seemed tired. Maybe the party thing is getting to her. At least she isn't sleeping 'till *two*. Does Ava always do that?"

"I have no idea. I don't actually know her that well," Henry admitted. "She's usually kinda standoffish."

Vincent could believe it. "Well...if we're not going to barge in and wake her up, I want to go back and look at the shed."

Henry frowned. "I don't know if that's a good idea."

"Do you really think they'll be out there in broad daylight?"

"Good point...vampires aren't exactly keen on sunlight."

"Well, I meant in full view of the public. But that too. Do they actually burn in the sun?"

"Sort of? It's not enough to kill them, but it's hard on them. They prefer to avoid it."

"I'd say we should just keep an eye out for anyone in an oversized hoodie, but..."

That got a chuckle out of Henry.

But his good mood didn't last. As soon as they stepped out the back door, they found themselves in a rainstorm.

Vincent gazed upwards with wide eyes. The entire sky was a blanket of solid gray. A steady, soothing pattering filled the air. Mist gathered between the buildings, softening the world's edges. It felt like he had stepped out into a dreamscape.

"Well, so much for sunlight... Maybe we should save it for another day?" Then Henry sighed. "No, we should look before anyone has a chance to tamper with it..."

"Now would be a great time for those special vampire tools," Vincent said heavily.

Henry patted his side through his sweatshirt. "Already got it covered." He stepped out into the downpour.

Vincent drew in a deep breath filled with the sweet, dark scent of rain. Then he followed Henry.

The first few drops stung his skin with the shock of cold. They reminded him of his first shower, before he had realized there was a hot water setting. But soon they pattered over his hair, his nose, his forehead, collecting on his eyelashes and leaving cold trails like tears down his cheeks. They felt different in a way he couldn't explain. This was wild water, straight from the lungs of the earth.

Suddenly, frigid water splashed over his pants. He jumped, looking up to find Henry standing ankle-deep in a wide puddle nearby, grinning impishly. His own pant legs were soaked too, but he didn't seem to care.

"Hey–!"

Before Vincent could react, Henry jumped again, sending another wave of dirty water in his direction. He tried to be annoyed about it, but the way Henry was beaming at him, he just couldn't manage it.

A playful growl tore from his throat as he gave in, rushing the puddle. He leaped into it, throwing water towards Henry. He let out a yelp as he jumped back, drenching himself even more. He splashed Vincent again, Vincent retaliated, and soon both of them were laughing, their own attacks doing more to soak them through than the other's.

They finally ran out of breath and continued on, wading through the enormous puddle to reach the far side. As they went Vincent realized that despite the water weighing him down, he felt...light. From his heart to his mind. His sixth sense had dulled to a shadow inside him. The rainsong thrummed with his heartbeat. Everything was cold and crisp and alive. Something that had been long dormant within him stirred.

Eventually Vincent realized Henry was waiting for him at the edge of the puddle, watching. Embarrassment crawled into Vincent's skin. He scowled as he caught up.

"What are you smirking at?"

"I'm not smirking. I was just thinking...you've never seen rain before, have you, Vinny? You did live in the Underworld, right? I can't imagine how dreary it must be..."

"I'm not allowed to talk about it," Vincent said, a bit more harshly than he intended. He fought back the return of his guilt and let his ire carry him onward: "And I don't need your pity, Henry."

Vincent started off in the direction of the shed. He didn't look back, but he could feel Henry's gaze hot on his back. He pulled at his tie, but its pressure on his neck wasn't nearly enough to help.

It was a long and wet journey across campus, the discomfort compounded by silence. Hardly any students were out and about on a rainy Sunday, which for once didn't work in their favor. By the time they reached the gym, both of them were on edge. Vincent kept his hands in his pockets, each one gripping the handle of a switchblade.

They crept around the side of the building, once again approaching the shed standing alone in the field behind it. It was far less ominous during the day, but the memories of what had happened here mingled with the fog. Before they had even stepped into the grass, Vincent could tell something was wrong. He could hardly pick up that awful stench of decay.

As they drew closer, they saw it—the padlock was hanging loose on the door of the shed.

"Damn," Henry hissed. "Looks like someone's already been here."

"Probably the vampires," Vincent guessed, knowing it was only a half-truth. "They'd want to move the body now that we know where it is."

Henry sighed. "Yeah...it was a long shot."

They looked inside the shed, but it was empty save for a few pieces of long-abandoned sports equipment.

Vincent wandered around, trying to pick up any traces. The only real signs were spatters of his own blood on the grass. He caught the faintest remnant of the body's odor, but nothing from the vampires.

That was when he realized: Benjamin didn't have any scent, either. He hadn't even noticed until now, because of his sixth sense.

Benjamin must *be a vampire.* Vincent supposed whatever undeath suffused their bodies preserved them, as if sterilizing their essence. That meant he had no way of keeping track of them. His spine tingled at the thought.

At least he didn't have to track Benjamin. Thinking about him, that mysterious plan of his, their exchange the night before in this very spot, made nearly every fiber of his being vibrate in anticipation of the hunt. His teeth finally sinking into Benjamin's empty flesh, dragging him away, dragging him down...

He wondered if he would find Mira's corpse, too, if he followed that impulse.

But Benjamin had already proven too resourceful. There was no way Vincent was going to manage it in broad daylight. If he tried, and caught too much attention...there would be literal hell to pay. He nearly shuddered at the thought of what his father might do.

"Can you track them?" Henry's voice broke through his thoughts.

"Not in this rain," Vincent lied. If he wanted to keep Benjamin a secret from Henry, this had to be a dead end.

They gave up their investigation, leaving that awful shed standing alone in its field. The drizzle kept steady through the afternoon, leaving a sheen of water on their skin and hair as they trekked back to Walden Hall. Despite Vincent's marvel at the rain, it had worn out its welcome. He was feeling uncomfortably cold and damp by the time they made it back into the warmth of the dorm and dried off.

"Did Melanie say Ava would be awake at two o'clock? It's only one-fifteen."

"I think she was just guessing. Or maybe exaggerating?" Henry added hopefully.

"Well, I'm not waiting any longer." Vincent marched over to Ava and Melanie's door and knocked firmly.

There was no reply. Frustration roiled in his stomach, fueled by his renewed vengeance. Nothing was going to stop him now. He knocked again, more insistent this time.

"Hello? Ava? We need to talk to you!" he called through the door.

He waited, but the silence continued.

"Maybe we should try later in the–Vincent, you're just gonna annoy her," Henry said as Vincent began aggressively knocking the tune of one of his new favorite songs into the door.

Just as he was about to start the chorus, the door swung open. Ava herself stood there in a holey My Chemical Romance T-shirt. She looked almost like a different person without her fastidious makeup. Notably less pale. Only her candy-red hair was a dead giveaway, although it was tangled at the moment.

"*What.*"

"I need another tarot reading," Vincent said bluntly. He could almost feel Henry cringing beside him.

"Right *now?*"

"Is one-fifteen a bad time for a reading?" Vincent asked pointedly.

"Not *necessarily.*"

"Then?"

"I'm not a Zoltar machine."

Vincent turned to Henry. "I swear it's real," he insisted, willing him to catch on to his plan. "She's very good, I promise."

Henry's expression changed. Vincent could tell he understood, although he wasn't particularly happy about it. "If you say so." To Ava he added, "Maybe we can come by later?"

Ava looked wholly unimpressed, but to Vincent's surprise she sighed and stepped back from the doorway.

"I'm the real deal, alright? Just get in here and I'll do the thing."

Vincent and Henry shared a look, then entered.

Melanie was gone now, and the room was darker than the last time Vincent had been here. Ava ran her fingers through her hair fruitlessly a few times as she picked up her tarot deck and its cloth.

"Late night?" Henry asked, trying to be friendly.

Ava gave him a dry look. "I don't get up at the asscrack of dawn like some kind of gym rat."

Henry looked a bit put out. Vincent decided to step in. "Read something for Henry this time. He needs to see this."

Ava looked at him suspiciously. "Is it that exciting?"

Vincent recalled the icy accuracy of his first reading. *The Devil. Ten of Swords. The Tower.* He wondered if he should be dreading the final card's meaning a little more...

"It's pretty crazy," Vincent responded. "Henry here is a skeptic, though."

Ava paused, all but glaring at Henry. Vincent sensed her growing reluctance. "If you're gonna be a bitch about it, why should I waste my time on you?" she asked.

"You're just going to have to give him something so specific, there's no way it could be a trick." Vincent tried to sound as smug as possible.

Ava curled her lip, and Vincent held his breath. Finally, she snorted and began shuffling her cards.

"You'll be a heathen by the end of this, altar boy, if I have anything to say about it," she told Henry.

"Altar boy?" Henry repeated, offended. Vincent nudged him lightly with his elbow.

"What did you want to know about?" Ava asked Henry when the cards were ready.

Henry thought for a moment. "Tell me what I'm most worried about right now."

Ava picked a card out of the deck. It depicted three dogs howling at the full moon above them; a river flowed between them, laden with crawdads.

"The Moon," said Ava. "This is an anxiety card, so that much is obvious. But it also tells of illusions. Things look different than they seem in the light of the moon." She looked directly at Henry, her blue eyes suddenly piercing. "You have something specific in mind? You're afraid of a monster. Something that hides in plain sight and thrives in darkness."

Henry's gaze was trained on the card as if he was trying very hard not to look at Vincent. Something inside Vincent churned almost painfully. He wondered how specific the card was–if it was a metaphor, or if it actually had anything to do with dogs. Seeing Henry's expression, he was afraid of the answer.

"Have you always been able to do this sort of thing?" Henry asked Ava, suddenly serious.

She shrugged, looking very pleased with herself. "I guess so. I've had these cards since I was little. My grandmother gave them to me."

"Did your grandmother use them too?"

A little smile played across Ava's face. Vincent felt she was keeping something important just behind her lips. "She taught me how, so yeah."

"Did she ever use any other kind of tool for divination?"

"You're being awfully forward," Ava replied. "You might as well just ask me if I'm a witch."

Henry paused. "Well, are you?"

Ava grinned. "Sure, I am. My grandmother is only the best witch in Oregon."

Henry and Vincent exchanged a stunned glance.

"What's her name, by chance?"

"Magdalena Mistral."

Henry nodded, a smile spreading over his face. "Of course. My father is a personal friend of hers. Do you know a Nathan Wellfellow?"

"No, sorry," Ava said, disinterested. She began putting away her cards with a delicate care. "Is he a witch, too?"

Vincent rolled his eyes, but Henry kept his friendly facade. "That's okay. He's not very high profile outside the Shadowhand. Her grandmother is more of a consultant than an actual member," he added to Vincent. "It's so nice to know you're one of us, Ava! Things are pretty rough around here right now, so we're glad we can count on you."

Ava stared at him blankly. "One of who?"

"I'm a member of the Shadowhand," Henry explained. "Well...junior member. Vincent is...he's one of us, too."

"And?"

"Well...we were hoping you might lend us some help. What with all the...the recent murders," he said more quietly, as if mentioning them gave them power.

"You think they have anything to do with magic?" Ava asked skeptically.

"Probably. Based on what we've gathered so far."

"Which would be...?"

"Are you going to help us?" Vincent cut in, his gaze hard.

Ava returned his stare evenly. "Maybe. Depends."

"Depends on *what?*" Vincent suppressed a growl. "People are dying here. What if you're next?"

"I wouldn't be next," Ava scoffed. "They'd have to have some serious luck to get through me."

"If they're Others too, they may not have as much trouble as you'd think," Henry warned.

"You never answered me. Why do you think they're Others?"

"Because we saw them," Henry said, before Vincent could ward her off. "Vampires."

"*Vampires?* You can't be serious."

"They attacked us. Vincent, show her your arm."

"I'm not taking the bandage off for *her*," Vincent hissed.

Henry gave him a hard look. "This is for Percy, remember?"

Vincent hesitated, but in the end he couldn't win against Henry's resolve. He sighed and pulled his bad arm out of his jacket laboriously. He peeled back the gauze on his shoulder, letting Ava see the two puncture wounds–the perfect imprint of fangs.

"Wonderful. Now it's bleeding again," Vincent grumbled. He barely let her get a look before he replaced the bandage.

Ava stared at the spot even after it was covered. For a moment, even she looked horrified. "Shit...well, I guess that's pretty convincing." Ava shifted her gaze to the two boys dubiously. "But...you guys fought them off by yourselves? What do you need me for?"

"Well, we didn't exactly win," Henry admitted.

"And we don't know how they're involved in this," Vincent added. "Not directly. We found them..."

Vincent didn't see the point in delaying the information now. He and Henry described what they had learned together so far, leaving very little out apart from Vincent's true form. Ava stared at them quizzically until they finished.

"So...what, you need me like some kind of magical bodyguard?"

"No," Henry said.

"Why not," Vincent said at the same time. They looked at each other.

Ava didn't seem pleased. "If you're gonna beg, you two should at least get your stories straight."

"Look," sighed Henry, "we plan on going out every night to do patrols around campus."

"How's that gonna help anything?"

"They obviously operate primarily at night," Henry said. "And two people have died in the last month already. Odds are, having more people on the lookout, we're bound to catch something eventually. We might even be able to save someone's life."

"Or at least figure out why this is happening," Vincent added.

Ava frowned. "Just sounds like a lot of lost sleep to me."

"As if you're not awake 'till four A.M.," Vincent retorted. Henry put a warning hand on his good arm.

"We could really use an extra pair of eyes," said Henry. "Especially from someone as gifted as you are."

Ava was silent for a long moment. To the irritated Vincent, it felt as if she were savoring their anticipation. Finally, she shook her head.

"I'm not gonna go wandering around campus in the middle of the night chasing some half-baked Scooby-Doo plot. Sorry, not sorry. If you find anything worth my skills, feel free to come knocking." She stood, replacing the tarot deck on her desk. "Now will you please leave me alone? I literally just woke up."

"Wait—please," said Henry, rising as well. "We just need—"

"Fine. I have something worth your skills," Vincent cut in.

Ava turned back to him. "Well?"

"A seance."

"A seance," Ava repeated mildly. "You already asked me about that."

"I didn't ask you to perform one. But you said you had, before. Well, we need to talk to someone."

"Who?"

"Percy Quailheart."

Ava looked dumbstruck.

"He's still here. In my room."

"How do you know?"

"I can sense him. Even hear him, sometimes. But he has trouble pulling his thoughts together," Vincent added before Ava could question him. "He can't remember anything about his death. Which of course is what we really need him to do."

"You don't have to come on patrols with us," Henry put in. Vincent could sense his desperation. "We just really need your help with this, if nothing else. Do you know how to...I don't know, pull him together, somehow? Enough for him to remember what happened to him?"

Ava let them dangle for another moment. Then: "I know how to do regular seances, of course. You know, summoning spirits. But I have no idea how to restore his memories, or his essence, or what-have-you."

Vincent's patience finally ran out. "Great," he growled, turning back towards the door. "This was a gigantic waste of time. Thanks for being such a help, Ava."

"Now hold on," Henry said, and Vincent did. He would have paused for no one else. "Ava, do you think your grandma would know a way to help?"

"You don't think she's just as useless?" Vincent said spitefully.

Henry shot him another warning glance.

"Of course she would know," Ava snapped.

"Could you please ask her for us? It might be the difference between life or death for someone."

"Or multiple someones, if this keeps up," Vincent muttered.

Ava sighed. "Alright, fine. I'll ask her."

Both Vincent and Henry let out a breath of relief. The air in the room lightened considerably.

"Thank you *so* much, Ava!" Henry beamed at her. "Welcome to the team!"

She only grimaced. "I told you, I don't want to do your weird little patrols."

"You don't have to, I promise," Henry said quickly. "But you're helping us out. You're still a part of the team."

Vincent had to wonder when it became a *team*. But he didn't protest. Instead, he moved for the door. He had had enough of playing nice with Ava. He had the distinct feeling she was now the main thing standing in the way of his vengeance, if she wouldn't help.

Henry followed him. "Please let us know when you hear back, okay?"

"Yeah, yeah." She waved them off.

The door closed behind them, and they looked at each other.

"Well, that was pleasant," Vincent remarked.

"You could stand to be more welcoming," Henry told him, frowning.

"Sure. If she'd let me."

Henry sighed. "Still, she's a witch. They're incredibly powerful allies to have, if they know what they're doing."

"Does she *look* like she knows what she's doing?"

"I guess we'll find out."

"I don't think we will. We'll be lucky to hear back from her grandmother. She made it perfectly clear she doesn't want to help us."

"Well, I believe she'll keep her word on this. She's not the type to agree to something she doesn't want to do."

Vincent couldn't argue with that. But he was still annoyed. "Then I guess I'll see you tonight," he said shortly. "For more very useful endeavors."

Henry stopped to fix him with a very serious look. Vincent's skin crawled under the intensity of those clear blue eyes.

"I need you to be with me on this. We need all the help we can get."

Vincent's unease grew, and he resented it. "So what, are we supposed to just wander around campus aimlessly every night until she decides to get off her ass?"

"No," said Henry, for once with a hint of annoyance. "We have other things to do in the meantime. In fact, I was thinking—would you be able to track the vampires at all, if we got you a scent to follow?"

"Not for vampires. It's odd, but...they didn't leave any real scent behind."

"Huh? But you told me it was because of the rain..."

Shit. Right. "The rain was washing out the other trails. Not the vampires'."

"Other trails?"

Vincent stopped. He had screwed up.

"Ah...yeah. Mira's body didn't leave much of one. I assume they carried it..."

"That's *one*–you said *other trails*. Plural. Did you find something else there?"

"No," said Vincent, a little too quickly. He glanced back at Henry, offering him his best puzzled look. "I just meant those two."

Henry's eyes narrowed. "No, you didn't. You're lying to me."

Vincent opened his mouth, but any defense he had died in his throat.

Henry, stone-faced, held his gaze captive. "Vincent, I've had it up to here with your bullshit. You keep saying you're 'not allowed' to tell me anything. And now you're keeping something important from me. Why? I thought we were in this together."

Vincent gritted his teeth. "I wasn't lying. I'm not allowed to tell you some things."

"But you keep *everything* from me. You have from the moment I met you. And I get why you'd want to, believe me."

Surprise coursed through Vincent.

"But now, I...I know what you are. That you're a hellhound. And I trusted you with who I am, too. Don't you think you owe me a little more trust back?"

Henry was so sincere that Vincent was taken aback. That guilt began to gnaw at him again; this time, though, it came with a deep dismay.

"I'm sorry that's such a burden for you," Vincent growled.

"That's not what I–"

"I shouldn't have even shown you my true form. I could get in huge trouble for that. I–" He winced, suddenly wondering if there was any way for his father to find out.

"So could I!" Henry argued. "I'm not supposed to tell anyone about the Shadowhand, either!"

Vincent shook his head, baring his teeth. He could feel them sharpening unnaturally in his mouth. "I'm a monster to you. That carries a lot more weight than your stupid Shadowhand."

"You're not a *monster*, Vincent! Why would you–"

"*Don't lie to me!*" Vincent spat. Something far more painful than his injuries had lanced his heart. He turned away from Henry and his pretty words. "I already saved your damn life. I don't owe you anything."

"And I saved yours."

Vincent bit his tongue, hard. He knew Henry was right. Benjamin and his vampires would have killed him, surely, if Henry hadn't arrived in time to even the odds. All of this was his own fault. He shouldn't have underestimated the situation–or Benjamin.

Again. Why am I so stupid?

But admitting that to Henry was more than he could bear. He couldn't stand his pity anymore. He couldn't bring himself to let loose any of the words clamoring behind his teeth. He didn't even know where to begin.

Seeing Vincent's obstinance holding firm, Henry tossed up his hands helplessly. "Fine! Don't trust me! I obviously can't do anything about it. If saving each other's lives means nothing to you, I don't know what could. Maybe I was wrong about you."

Henry paused, as if waiting for Vincent to argue against this judgment. But he didn't. He had nothing to prove Henry wrong. He was foolish for thinking someone like Henry would see anything in him.

"If even you won't help me, I guess it's all up to me again. Just like always. I don't know why I ever thought things could be different."

Henry turned away, leaving Vincent where he stood in the empty hallway.

CHAPTER 8

THINGS THAT GO BUMP IN THE NIGHT

That night, Vincent did not meet Henry for their patrol. He got the distinct impression he had been excused from his duties. He didn't want to go, anyway–the storm in his head was far too turbulent. In the end, he found himself alone in the dark of his room, broken only by the faint yellow light between the blinds and the fainter presence of Percy's ghost haunting the corner. They didn't speak.

It took a long time to fall asleep. His thoughts kept wandering towards the night outside his little room. Henry was there, surely. He was patrolling the campus on his own, hoping to find some clue to stop these murders. He was brave. This was his calling. He was meant to be the hero. Every story Vincent had read so far had one, and they weren't supposed to die. Henry had to be safe–didn't he?

The thought plagued him all the next day. But not all of that night's wounds lingered. By the evening Vincent's injured shoulder had fully scabbed over, the skin around the punctures already fresh and pink. Time was always his friend, at least when it came to physical injuries.

So why was it so hard to get over the rest of it?

When night fell his restlessness became too much to bear, and he decided to go out by himself. He kept his nose out for Henry, carefully avoiding him as he followed his sixth sense. That sick exhilaration urged him on across campus–the hunt. His instincts were pleased with him for following their call.

But this feeling warred with a new apprehension for the darkness that hovered between lampposts. He now knew he couldn't smell his enemy. He only prayed his night vision and his hearing would make up for it.

He made it to Benjamin's dorm window. The blinds were closed. No light leaked from within. All was quiet.

He waited there, his heartbeat loud and hungry in his ears. He was so close. But he couldn't do anything about it. Benjamin had stacked all the odds against him—even more than he knew before.

This is hopeless. He tried to keep the thought at bay, but it lingered at the edges of his mind, taunting him. His father knew this would happen, didn't he? He wanted Vincent to fail.

Benjamin will slip up sometime. He has to. He's only human.

Except he wasn't—not anymore.

Vincent stayed for a long time, unsure of the hour. Finally he grew weary, and returned to his bed.

Every night he did the same, and every night Benjamin eluded him easily. During the day, he let himself slip into the busy routine of an ordinary college student. At the end of the week, he found himself in his favorite spot draped across the arm of the couch in Walden Hall's common area, grazing on his leftovers from dinner. He had begun the night studying for his classes, but soon so many people had filled the lobby that it was impossible to focus.

At first it had annoyed him, but as the days passed he found their presence almost comforting. Sometimes he would retire to work on his own in his room, realizing he would never get anything done otherwise. But other times, like tonight, he let himself fade into the energy of the people around him as he watched YouTube videos on his phone.

Their chatter mingled with the distinctive *clack* of the ping-pong table and the drone of the TV. He found it best to use the earphones Percy had lent him, allowing the din to settle into the background as he listened to his usual thinkpieces or whatever cat video happened to cross his recommended list. He had never before had the ability to simply choose whatever struck his fancy. He had trouble saying no to the snappy video titles and colorful thumbnails.

As some of his acquaintances wandered in, Vincent glanced up to offer them a wave, as he often did.

"Hi, Vincent!" Sierra called to him, hanging off Jake's arm. She had already made a beeline for the large whiteboard hanging on the nearest wall.

Even Jake gave Vincent a "Hey, man," as he extricated himself from her grasp, flopping down in one of the tattered armchairs. Ava was quietly reading on the couch across from him, and didn't look up.

"Jaaaake, aren't you gonna doodle with me?" Sierra pouted. Vincent could tell she was hamming it up–she wasn't the type to whine.

"I told you, I'm not a drawer," Jake grunted.

"You're not a piece of furniture? Could have fooled me," Vincent said with a little smirk. Sierra grinned.

Jake shrugged. "Okay, what? An *artist*, is that better?"

"You *could* be!" Sierra insisted, beaming at him.

"Now now, is that any way to treat your girlfriend?" Melanie chided him, sauntering in to settle on an empty sofa. As always, her presence sent a thrill of anger through Vincent's core, but he didn't let it show. "You should be careful, or someone else might snap her up."

"Yeah, Jake!" Sierra laughed.

Jake scowled at Melanie. He heaved himself out of his seat and snatched one of the markers from its shelf beneath the whiteboard. He immediately set to work scrawling a crude image beneath an announcement about the date for the next floor meeting. Sierra let out a hearty laugh that ended in a graceless snort. It was so infectious, even Vincent couldn't help but smile.

"There. Michelangelo in the house." Jake tossed the marker back onto the shelf with a clatter and slumped back in his chair.

"Y'know, you're not wrong!" Sierra giggled. "The man loved his dicks!"

"How original," Melanie remarked, with a note of disdain.

"Sorry, m'lady." Jake bowed to her, tipping an invisible hat. Sierra snorted another laugh, and Melanie rolled her eyes.

"You're no fun," Sierra told her. She picked up a marker and began drawing a horse with a zany expression. It was apparent she had some genuine talent, and somehow the detail she included made it even funnier.

"At least I have some dignity," Melanie huffed.

"There!" said Sierra when she finished her work, stepping back to admire it.

He liked the feeling that now lingered in his chest, outshining his hatred for Melanie. It was a steady glow, something warm and light and easy. He was a part of something. These people liked him—or, at least, he thought they did. Maybe it was pointless; he would be gone soon, and none of it would matter. But in that moment, in spite of everything, it was...nice. For one moment, he was just an ordinary human being.

Of course, there was still one person missing. He felt it like a black hole in the room, a void that desperately needed to be filled.

A hopeful flutter found his heart as he noticed a message notification on his phone. Then he saw the title.

The others' chatter faded into the background as he read. Finally, a voice broke into his thoughts: "Vincent? Hello? What's wrong?"

Vincent looked up. Sierra and Jake were staring at him, puzzled. But Melanie and Ava both wore grim expressions, staring down at their own phones.

"I guess they finally noticed that girl is missing," Melanie said, her tone unreadable.

"That girl?" Sierra echoed, looking alarmed. "You mean Mira Walker?"

"Yeah."

"They sent out a missing person bulletin email," Ava said. "Didn't you guys get it?"

"No, they were too busy dicking around," Melanie said.

"I thought they were supposed to find the body in the pool..." said Sierra. "Why is she missing?"

"Maybe it sank." Melanie shrugged.

"God...we should talk to the police," Sierra insisted, sounding more distraught by the second. "They need to find—"

"She's dead," Melanie interjected. "It won't do anyone any good to say something. It'll just get a whole lot of people in trouble for nothing."

"But one of them killed her!" Sierra protested.

"Keep your voice down!" Jake growled. Sierra looked at him as if he had hit her.

"Melanie's right." Everyone turned to Vincent, Sierra with the most surprise. "It's over already."

"But it's the right thing to do," Sierra pleaded, although she sounded less sure now. Her warm brown eyes locked with his, and for an instant he saw a glimmer of Henry in them. His skin prickled. "What if the police find who did it because of us?"

"What if they take us in instead?" Jake countered. "What if we can't graduate because of court proceedings? Is that worth it to you, Sierra?"

Vincent shook his head solemnly. "It's too risky. I could get...deported."

The crease of worry on Sierra's face deepened. "I guess you're right..." She sighed. "I just hate it. She deserves justice."

And she'll get it, thought Vincent. He wished he could tell her–but he knew he never would.

When the others said their goodnights, Vincent found his thoughts elsewhere. His sixth sense was gnawing at him again, its appetite piqued by thoughts of Mira. Knowing he wouldn't be able to sleep, he settled into his bed to read.

Only a few minutes had passed when he felt Percy's presence drifting closer. It coalesced just above his shoulder, radiating a powerful curiosity. Vincent glanced up instinctively, only to avert his eyes at the last second.

"What is it, Percy?"

"*What are you reading?*"

"*Paradise Lost.*" Vincent held up the book's cover without knowing if Percy could truly see it.

"*I-isn't that really hard to understand? I've heard that, anyway...*"

"Sort of. Mostly because it's an epic poem. That, and it's from the seventeenth century. The language makes it more difficult. For mortals, anyway. Not for me."

"*But you've been reading it for a while now...*"

"It's a long read. And it's for class, so I have to do it either way."

"*Oh, right...you're a philosophy major.*" Percy was silent for a moment. "*Why did you choose that?*"

"I didn't," Vincent answered without thinking.

"*You didn't?*" Percy echoed. "*Then who did?*"

Vincent silently cursed himself. He was becoming far too loose with the information he kept.

"My father," he said with a sigh. He turned back to his book dismissively. "I don't want to talk about it."

"*Oh...*"

At first, Vincent thought that was the end of it. But his relief drained away as Percy went on:

"*My parents chose for me, too. But I didn't mind. I always wanted to be a doctor and help people, if I could.*" Percy's ghostly voice sounded almost wistful. "*They were very upset when I ended up at this school, though...*"

Vincent couldn't help a flicker of curiosity. "Why's that?"

The air in the room seemed to grow more oppressive. "*It's...it's not the most prestigious place...it's so far out here, after all...th-they wanted me to go to Johns Hopkins, or Duke...or anything with a real name...*"

Vincent shrugged. "This is a nice school, though. I'm liking it so far. Is that why you wanted to come here instead?"

"*I wasn't smart enough to go to the other schools,*" came the reply, its tone suddenly dark. Even the room itself seemed to dim.

"Ah," Vincent said awkwardly. He retreated to his book again, fiddling with his tie. That feeling was creeping in again...

No more sympathy, he reminded himself. The words sounded hollow in his head.

But Percy wasn't done with him yet. "*Why did your dad choose philosophy for you? I've only ever heard people say it's a useless major in the real world...n-not that I think it is!*" he added swiftly. "*I think it's great, if you love it! A-and important, for the world to–*"

"I don't know," Vincent interrupted, his voice sharp. "I don't know why my father does anything. That's just how it is."

Percy's presence began to slowly circle above him, angling itself towards Vincent's front. It made his skin crawl, and he kept his eyes deliberately on the words in his book, not reading a single one of them.

"*But you're different, aren't you?*" Percy pressed, with an intensity Vincent hadn't felt from him before. Even his stutter vanished. "*You're...not human. You said so yourself. But what are you? You never answered me...*"

Vincent's words dried up in his throat. What was he supposed to tell him? It was hard enough revealing himself to Henry, and that was under dire circumstances...but what was the point of hiding it all from a ghost, anyway?

"Does it matter?" Vincent said eventually, trying to sound disinterested.

"*You said you'd help me.*" Percy's whisper came close to Vincent's ear. The specter was drawing closer and closer to him. Its gravity pressed on Vincent's psyche until he began hearing a faint ringing from somewhere in his own skull. He glued his gaze to the pages in front of him, gripping the edges tighter and tighter until his knuckles went white.

"*What if you can't?*"

Not for the first time, Vincent wished he hadn't made that stupid promise. But then...

"Did you *just* remember all that?" Vincent said suddenly.

The specter paused. "*Remember what...?*"

"Your family. Being a medical student. You said you were having trouble remembering your life, before..."

Percy hesitated. "*I'm...not sure. It just...came to me. Like it had always been there...*"

Vincent suddenly wondered if talking to Percy about Melanie and the amulet had restored some of his memories. A tiny flame of hope flared in his chest.

"Percy...do you remember anything about vampires?"

"*V-vampires?*"

"Yes." Vincent faced Percy, but avoided looking at him directly. "Have you ever met one before?"

A chill passed through the room.

"*...No...I-I can't say I have... A-are they actually real? Are you one?*"

Vincent let out the breath he had been holding. "No, I'm not."

"*Th-then why...?*"

"Never mind," Vincent interrupted him, turning away and setting his book down on his nightstand.

"*W...well then what are you? You keep avoiding the question...*"

"It *really* doesn't matter," Vincent said through gritted teeth. "I've had enough of the prying, alright?"

To his surprise, Percy's presence receded instantly. He hadn't expected the force of his words to affect the ghost that much. Then again, Percy was sensitive. He just wanted to be friends. To not feel so alone.

Even after turning out the light, Vincent ended up lying awake for a while after that. He could feel those invisible eyes on him still, crawling up his back. He was beginning to understand more and more why he hated being in his room so much. It almost felt like home.

He tried to imagine what it would feel like to have an empty room all to himself, with no eyes on him at all, judging him and guilting him and waiting for him. It felt like everyone wanted something from him, and even in his own bed he found no relief.

Exasperated, he went to the window, pulling the blinds aside to gaze out at the night beyond. The days had been rainy lately, but today's storm had stopped by nightfall, leaving behind a cloying mist that melded shadow and yellow streetlight. On the horizon, the great black silhouettes of treetops stood against the sky, ever so slightly paler from its cloud cover. All around his little room, his only haven, the world was filled with dark things.

He wanted to stay inside tonight. He was tired–tired of staying out late, tired of that constant nagging sixth sense, tired of missing Henry, tired of hating himself for being so useless. It was already later than usual, anyway. *One night wouldn't hurt...*

But then, he stopped dead. His sixth sense tugged at him from a new direction.

Benjamin was in the woods.

The hairs on the back of his neck prickled. What was he doing out there? Was he with the other vampires? Did he still have Mira's body?

There was no way Benjamin was alone out there. Vincent would surely be walking into a trap. His best hope of discovering anything useful was still Percy regaining his memories...but Vincent hadn't heard anything from Ava about her grandmother all week, as he had predicted.

He wondered if she had given any information to Henry instead. He should have asked her. Maybe he should have done a lot of things.

One thing he couldn't do was stay here. He could at least spy.

I'm a Child of Cerberus. I can outwit a couple vampires.

He grabbed his knives. He pulled on his leather jacket, grateful that his wound had healed enough to not make it difficult this time. Then he left before Percy could question him.

Just when he reached the back door, a familiar voice called out, "Vincent!"

He halted, suppressing a groan. He forced himself to turn around. "Melanie. What is it?"

"Done with your homework?" she asked sweetly. There was something a little too sly in her smile. "Where are you off to? I could come with you, and we could make it into an evening."

"No, I–" He needed an excuse–and fast. "I'm meeting a friend. I'm late already. Maybe some other time."

Melanie's smile faded, and she sniffed. "I thought you were going to tell me when you were free."

"I will when I am." He knew he was terrible at evading her, but what else was he supposed to say?

Henry would know, he thought bitterly.

Melanie held his gaze suspiciously for a moment more, then huffed. "Fine. Have fun with your *friend.* But you'd better text me later."

Vincent didn't have time to wonder if she was just jealous, or suspected something else. As soon as she retreated down the hall, he spun around and emerged into the night.

Outside he shivered, keeping his hands warm in his pockets and curled around his knives. He meandered along paved paths and corridors, consciously muffling the splashes his shoes made in the plentiful puddles.

Vincent felt even more exposed tonight. This time he was sure of what could be lurking just out of sight somewhere out there, just as comfortable in shadow as he was. If only he could smell them. He wondered suddenly, with a prickle of unease, if *they* could smell *him*.

But then a scent did find him—one that was all too familiar. Clove and jasmine.

His heart lurched.

He began following the scent, but it didn't change his course. Both it and Benjamin moved in the same direction. With every step he prayed they would split, but they never did. And with every step, icy dread grew in his stomach.

Soon he reached the edge of the forest. It felt like a monster all on its own, a black, hulking beast waiting patiently for him to step into its maw.

Vincent bared his teeth at it. Then he stepped forward and let it swallow him.

He weaved through the trees, all too aware of every noise he made in the undergrowth. The scent trail kept to a natural path between the trees, making things slightly easier. All the while, he clung with a quiet desperation to the rhythmic chirping of crickets in the night. As long as that was present, he was safe.

But it was too small a comfort.

Suddenly, Vincent paused. Benjamin's gravity was dead ahead, still a ways off to the east. But the scent trail veered away, heading south. Relief flooded him—his prayers had been answered.

Then a horrible snarl tore through the trees.

Bushes crashing and a shout of alarm chased it. Vincent spun around, his heart slamming into his throat. He ran south, whipping out his knives with a sharp click. He didn't care how much noise he made now.

He burst out into a clearing illuminated by shreds of moonlight between the clouds. As his eyes adjusted, they widened.

A monstrous wolf stood outlined in silver, balancing on hind legs far too long for its body. Its torso hunched in a C-shape, the dark fur along its back and neck longer than the sparse coat covering the rest of its form. Its arms bulged with wiry muscle. Its front paws twisted into something resembling hands, each digit tipped with a curved claw. It was beautiful and terrible in equal measure, a perfect fusion of man and beast.

Its tail bristled as it swung its wolf's head around to face its new adversary, lips peeling back in a snarl filled with gleaming fangs. Its eyes flashed yellow-green in the gloom, freezing Vincent where he stood.

He caught his breath. He finally noticed two shapes moving at its feet. One of them crouched over the other. A low groan emanated from the second, and the sharp tang of their blood reached his nose–along with a familiar scent.

Hunter. The guy Vincent had taken down at the Commons.

And Henry was protecting him.

Vincent moved before the wolf could even blink. He skirted it and planted himself between it and Henry, brandishing his knives, locking eyes with his enemy. Instinct urged him on, a powerful need to dominate this canine threat. He willed every ember that glowed dormant within him to burn behind his eyes, showing the beast the power he could summon if it forced his hand.

"Vincent?" Henry's voice rose in shock from behind him.

"Did it touch you?" Vincent growled, keeping his gaze fixed on his opponent.

"N–no, but–"

"Then you have to get away from here, Henry. You can't let it hurt you."

"I know what it is, Vincent–but I'm not leaving you here!"

Vincent's heart panged. *He still cares? Or is he just too noble?*

Either way, it didn't matter to him. He bared his teeth.

"I'll follow you. Just go."

"*No*–it got Hunter! I'm not leaving him here either!"

"He's already *lost*, Henry, look at him!" Vincent snarled.

Henry staggered forward. He brandished his gauntlet at the beast, his face carved into fierce resolve. For all his mortality, Vincent was humbled by the force of his presence.

"Do you recognize me?" Henry challenged the wolf. "Do you know who I am?"

Shock gripped Vincent. "What are you doing?"

In answer the wolf stretched up to its full height, dwarfing even Henry. It bared its long white fangs, a terrible growl tearing from its throat.

Henry's fist relaxed, his gauntlet opening into an outstretched hand. "I can help you! Please, try to remember!"

The wolf took a lumbering step closer, pinning its ears back. The fur along its spine rose. Vincent's blood ran cold.

"Henry!" he warned.

"You're not a monster, are you?" Henry cried. "You're a *person!* You know you are!"

The beast lunged.

Vincent crashed into it head-on, abandoning his knives for teeth and claws.

The werewolf's jaws clamped down on one of the hellhound's three necks. That head yelped as pain shot through Vincent's body. But at the same moment another head's fangs met their mark, tearing into the wolf's arm just below the shoulder. He wrenched his head sideways, jerking the arm with it, and the wolf was forced to let go of his neck with a howl of pain.

Bone crunched as Vincent flung the beast aside. It slammed into the ground, scattering dead leaves and peat. It scrambled to right itself, crouching there with its teeth bared and bloody, glaring up at Vincent with glowing eyes. That split second between them felt like a lifetime.

The wolf surged upward. Vincent ducked, feeling the rush of air and the shockwave of its teeth snapping shut inches from his face. But the satisfaction was short-lived. A weight fell on his back, and before he could react he was face-down in the dirt.

Vincent reared back with all his strength, but his adversary was stronger. The beast crushed him beneath its body. Claws tore into his back, ripping out fur in clumps. He snarled and twisted, kicking up earth and leaves, but he just couldn't free himself. Cold panic began to overwhelm him.

"You're still in there, aren't you?"

Henry's voice shouted from somewhere nearby, fraught with a desperation Vincent hadn't heard from him before.

"*Please*, stop this! You're hurting my friend! *You're killing him!*"

Vincent felt the prick of fangs at the back of his neck. He tensed as panic flooded his senses, unready for the fire and darkness to overtake him.

But they didn't. The teeth stayed there, holding him down, barely piercing his neck.

"Please! Let him go!"

"Henry, kill it!" Vincent choked out. His body heaved beneath the beast. He twisted his heads, trying to free himself, to see, to do *anything*. Why wasn't Henry attacking? He saved Vincent from the vampires before, but now–

"Why are you doing this?"

"H–Henry–" Vincent pleaded.

"What's your name?"

Suddenly the teeth drew away from his neck.

Vincent tried to roll aside, but those great claws clamped down on him again, keeping him pinned. Now he could see the beast looming above him. It gazed across the clearing at Henry, its teeth still bared in a silent warning.

But then, to Vincent's shock, the wolf's maw contorted, slowly, forming words. A deep, garbled voice emerged.

"*He hunts me.*"

Henry's gaze flicked to Hunter's crumpled form at his feet.

"Do you know him?" Henry demanded.

"*Stalking me here,*" the beast answered. It stood tall, just as fearsome, but with each moment the tension behind its stance faded ever so slightly.

"Did he see you like this?" Henry asked, trying to piece things together. He took a tentative step forward. "You don't need to get rid of him just for that, I promise. There are better ways to handle this. I can help."

Slowly the wolf's lip curled again, frustrated. It dropped from its intimidating height. Vincent flinched. But it didn't attack. Instead, it tipped its great head down to look at Hunter, so very small in Henry's shadow. It growled low in its throat.

"*Before I changed,*" it said.

Something seemed to click in Henry's mind. "We won't let him do anything to you. Please, don't hurt him anymore. It's not worth it."

Silence. Then, at last, the wolf stepped aside.

The weight lifted from Vincent's body and he scrambled to his paws. Hot blood dripped freely from his neck. The forest spun around him as he regained his balance. He staggered over to stand between his companions and the beast again, a pitiful but stalwart guardian. He growled, flashing his teeth.

Hunter suddenly coughed and sputtered. His limbs scrabbled in the leaf litter to right himself. At least, Vincent thought that was his goal—he didn't achieve it. Henry immediately crouched to prop up Hunter's back.

"Please be careful. Don't move around too much. You're in pretty rough shape. We need to get you home."

The whites of Hunter's eyes were bright in the gloom, darting around frantically as the fear returned to him. "What—where is she? She—it—"

Henry hushed him, looking up at Vincent anxiously. "Vincent—are you alright? Can you walk?"

Vincent forced away the heartache that ripped through him unbidden. *Do you really care?* His leftmost head glanced back at Henry with a short nod. The pain throbbed through his body, radiating from his neck and back, and he could feel the blood leaving him with every pump of his heart. But it wasn't enough to kill him—he was sure of that.

"Can you carry him?" Vincent growled.

"*Carry* me? There's no way I'm gonna let–"

"I–I don't think so," Henry said. "I'm gonna need your help." He bent closer to Hunter, murmuring something to him, then rose to stand at Vincent's side. A hand settled on his shoulder, a familiar warmth radiating from the spot. The gesture almost hurt as much as his wounds.

"You never answered me," Henry said to the wolf. "Who are you? What's your name? Can you remember?"

The beast paused. Despite its decision to back off, Vincent didn't trust a hair on its pelt.

It drew in a breath. But instead of answering, its body began to warp. Skin bubbled, fur sank into flesh, teeth shrank and flattened, bones twisted and cracked. It fell to the earth, arching its back against the force of its own body breaking apart and reforming. It was horrible to behold, punctuated by groans and growls that turned to softer cries of agony.

And as the scent slowly changed from wolf to human, it became more and more familiar...

At last a human lay before them, naked and caked in soil, hunched against the forest floor like a child curling up to cry. Dark blood dripped down her left arm, much of it shredded by Vincent's teeth. She lifted her trembling head, dirty black hair falling in her face, her narrow, dark eyes finding Vincent's.

His stomach lurched. It was Casey Helliker.

CHAPTER 9

THE WOLF & THE HOUND

66 "Casey?" Henry's eyes widened when he, too, recognized her.

She flinched when she heard her name. Her eyes darted around as she tried to regain her bearings. She curled tighter inwards, covering herself as if only just realizing she had no clothes. Vincent recognized the barely-suppressed impulse to bare her teeth.

"What happened here?" Vincent demanded. Casey looked around in surprise as his voice seemed to resonate from somewhere outside his body. Even she couldn't help a glimmer of fear, which was sobering for him.

"I told you." Her voice was hoarse, but human again.

"Was Hunter...following you?" Vincent guessed.

"Wasn't doing *anything*," Hunter mumbled.

"He's losing too much blood, Vincent," Henry murmured close to his ear. "We have to get him out of here. Now."

"What are we going to do with *her* then?"

Henry glanced between Casey and Hunter, troubled. "We'll have to bring her with us."

Instinct finally won over, and Casey snarled at them with human teeth.

"Blame *him* for this, not me! I'm not going anywhere with you!"

Before Henry could protest, Vincent took a menacing step forward. He peeled his lips back, showing three sets of gleaming fangs.

"You're in no position to argue. Even if he deserved it, you have no restraint. You're dangerous. So you'll be under our care until we sort this out."

To her credit, Casey didn't balk. Instead, she narrowed her eyes. "Just who do you think you are, the werewolf police?"

"Close enough," Vincent growled.

"Listen, Casey," said Henry, holding up a placating hand. "We're just trying to help. Believe it or not, I'm...sorta trained for this. My family deals with these kinds of situations. And Vincent...well, he's my backup." Vincent grimaced.

"What? *Vincent?*" Casey's gaze snapped back to the massive three-headed dog in front of her.

"Didn't recognize me?" Vincent said dryly.

"Can we do this later?" Henry said, almost pleading.

Both Vincent and Casey stopped, looking back to Hunter's bloodied form. He was breathing hard, but otherwise dazed. He clearly had very little idea what was going on around him anymore.

"He needs a hospital," Henry said, gritting his teeth. "I don't see any way around it." He pulled out his phone and started to dial.

"Wait–are you sure?" said Vincent.

"First aid isn't going to cut it." Henry was so worried that Vincent wondered if he was on the verge of panic. Before he could respond, Henry turned away with his phone at his ear.

"Hi, yes, we need an ambulance at the University of Alderwood. A student was attacked by a wild animal. ...Um, the parking lot closest to the gym. Do they know where that is? ...Okay. No, I can't stay on with you, I'm sorry. He's in the woods, I have to move him so they can reach him. Sorry."

The operator's protest was cut short as Henry swiftly hung up. He shrugged off his jacket and carried it over to Casey, who was still curled against the bare earth. He held it out to her, not looking directly at her.

She stared at it, then at him. Finally she took it from him with her uninjured arm and wrapped it around herself. It was enormous on her body, and did its job covering her well. She finally pushed herself to her feet, swaying a little.

Meanwhile Henry crouched beside Hunter again with an air of urgency. "Vincent, please help..." He hooked his arms under Hunter's armpits and hoisted him up with great effort.

"Ughh...put me down, stupid jockhead...think you're better'n everyone..."

Vincent crouched by Henry's side. He hauled Hunter's bulk onto Vincent's back, fixing any limbs that had fallen askew until he was mostly balanced. He kept his hold until Vincent lifted him up. Pain shot through his body from his many wounds, and he took a moment to steel himself.

"Where'm I...? What's all this...?" Hunter bleated, his voice fading as his weakness caught up with him. His hands scrabbled against Vincent's back, brushing roughly through his shaggy fur, and Vincent growled low in his throat. He hated every second of this, but he knew he didn't have a choice in the matter. Not with Henry here.

"I'll lead you back," Henry said close to Vincent's ear, his voice surprisingly soft. He felt that burning hand on the side of his neck, guiding him forward. He let it.

Surprisingly, Casey's footsteps followed behind them without further complaint. They didn't look at her, affording her at least some decency. Even with the jacket covering her, it was painfully awkward.

Henry led them through the forest, and soon they were stepping out into the open again just outside campus.

"Where are they..." he muttered to himself. He led Vincent across the field, then stopped at the edge of the asphalt. "Let's let him down easy."

He reached up to help slide Hunter off Vincent's back. Hunter let out a low groan as he half-fell onto the grass.

"*Fuck*, stop!" Hunter snapped, his words slurred with pain. "Tryin'a kill me! Where's–"

He froze when his bleary eyes fell on Vincent for the first time, mouth hanging open. Then a low wail emerged from it. It resonated through the trees. Vincent pinned his ears back in distaste.

"Hunter, please–" Henry said, exasperated.

"Oh my *god*, will you shut *up*?" Casey snarled at Hunter.

"W-werewolves!" Hunter shrieked. He began rocking his body back and forth, trying to right himself. Each movement forced a cry of pain from his throat, and even from where he stood Vincent could tell he was beginning to bleed even more through his torn clothes. "*Everyone's* a werewolf! Werewolves all over me!"

"I'm not a goddamn werewolf. I just saved your sorry ass from one," Vincent growled. He was beginning to regret it.

"You should go," Henry said to Vincent. "He's already frightened. I'll be okay here with him until the ambulance arrives."

Vincent shot him a dubious glance.

"It's alright," Casey said dryly. "No more werewolves in these woods."

"But there's still–" Vincent caught himself, finishing his sentence with a sound between a cough and a growl. Thankfully no one seemed to notice.

"You think the paramedics want to see a giant three-headed dog?" Casey said. "You realize he told them this asshole got attacked by a wild animal, right? Come on, dumbass, let's go."

She started marching off in the direction of the dorms. Only a moment later, the distant wail of emergency sirens reached Vincent's keen ears.

"Oh–here, take these!" Henry pulled out a set of keys, offering them to Vincent. "Get in my room, it'll be safe there. You know where my first aid stuff is?"

"Yes–okay." Vincent reached out his least injured head, grasping the keys gingerly between his sharp teeth. They barely grazed Henry's fingers, but he jerked back. Vincent winced.

"I'll be back as soon as I can, I promise!" Henry called after him, his words mingling with the shriek of the sirens as flashing lights rounded the corner.

Vincent sped off without a glance back, alarm lending him resolve. He followed Casey's small form across the field, overtaking her easily even with his injuries. He ducked behind the gymnasium with a tingle of relief, trying not to think about that terrible shed just around the corner.

"Where's your dorm?" Vincent asked when Casey joined him. "You need clothes."

"Yarrow Hall. But we're not going back there with you like this. When are you gonna change back?"

"I don't know. Whenever I can relax."

"Oh, good," Casey snorted. "We'll be out here all night at this rate. Let's just get out of here, can we do that?"

Vincent started off again at a slower pace this time, Casey walking beside him as quickly as she could manage. He was grateful for it, despite his urgency. His wounds were deep, and he could feel the blood oozing out and tangling in his neck fur with every step. It made him dizzy just thinking about it.

They skirted the edge of campus, keeping well away from any corridors or paths that would chance them meeting any late-night passersby. Slowly the sirens faded behind them, until they were only a distant whine in the dead of night. Eventually the delicate chirping of crickets resumed to fill the silence, bringing a sense of normalcy that felt utterly fake.

"Calm enough yet?" Casey said wryly.

"What do you think?" Vincent growled.

"Come on. If *I* can relax, you can."

"It's not that simple."

"Seriously? It can't be that hard. I was going completely feral back there, and I still managed to stop."

"Thanks to us," Vincent pointed out sharply. "And unlike you, I know how to control myself. Even when I change. You have no room to talk."

Casey rounded on him. "You have no *idea* what it's like!" she spat. "You're a dog, not a goddamn werewolf!"

After everything that had happened, Vincent's patience finally burnt out. The head closest to Casey slowly drew its lips back, baring its long, pointed teeth. The other two craned their necks, gazing down at her with dark disdain.

"I'm not just a *dog*, you fucking ingrate," he snarled. He loomed over her, his eyes embers in the murk. "I'm a *hellhound*. I was bred and trained by Lucifer Himself. *You* have no idea what it's like. Do you know how many of the wretched I've guarded? The darkness I've been trained to keep? Every moment of my life, I've worked for discipline."

Vincent advanced on her, his fangs only inches from her face. Impressively, she didn't flinch.

"You think you're big and scary because you're a werewolf? Please. You turn into one. I don't turn into a hellhound, Casey. *I* turn into a human."

For a split second he saw something halfway to horror flit across her face. But it was washed away in an instant by her bravado. She took a step back, clutching Henry's jacket tightly with her good arm.

"Whatever. Let's just get back," she growled. But then she looked away. Submission. She spoke his native language.

Vincent let his hackles fall, satisfied with her new wariness. They walked for some time in silence but for the crickets, and by some miracle met no one along the way. Eventually Vincent's thoughts turned to their next move, and he had to break the quiet.

"What time is it?"

"How should I know? I left my phone at home."

"You went out in the woods by yourself at night with no phone?"

Casey shot him a glare. "Werewolf, remember? You think I want to go scouring the forest wherever I drop the damn thing?"

"I thought you were just..." Vincent paused. "Why were you out there, anyway? You said Hunter was following you before you transformed..."

Casey sighed. "Look...sometimes, you just end up feeling the need to get away. I don't know. I guess it's a wolf thing."

It wasn't. The memory of feeling stifled and watched, both in his room and before he had even crawled from the earth, returned fresh to Vincent's mind.

"Well anyway, it has to be late," he said. "No one should be around..."

"It's a college campus. Someone's always awake."

"I guess..."

"I'm not gonna risk being seen with you. You'd better get your act together quick. I'm done freezing my ass off out here."

Vincent grimaced. He had no idea what he was supposed to do about his form. He had only transformed into a human twice before, and the first time he couldn't even take credit for. The second time...

"Come on," Vincent told her. "Follow me."

"What? Where are you going?" Casey demanded.

"It's not far." He turned to head down another path. He only hoped he could remember the way.

"And now you're crossing through the middle of campus? You're gonna get us caught," Casey said, her footsteps close behind.

"I've only ever needed to transform one other time," Vincent said after a moment's reluctance. "So we're going to the place I managed to do it before."

"What, is it a ceremonial bonfire or something?"

Vincent didn't dignify her guess with a reply. Instead he led the way through the corridors, aware every moment how exposed he was even in the dark. Casey followed, although he could tell she wasn't happy about it.

Finally Vincent spotted the grassy hillside just ahead, rising up to the garden surrounded by sycamores. It felt like a lone island on a stormy sea. He bounded forward, only to stumble from the pain that shot through his body. He half-clawed his way up the steep hillside, tearing out tussocks of grass as he went. Casey had about as much trouble as he did with her bare feet, but both of them managed to crest the hill and hide from whoever might pass below them.

"Some goddamn ritual site," Casey panted. She leaned against a boulder, flicking grass from between her toes. "Isn't this the bio building?"

"Yes," said Vincent. He already found the place where he had rested before. One of his heads set Henry's keys between his paws for safekeeping. He forced himself to take a deep, steadying breath.

"Is science just super comforting for you?"

"It's a place Henry took me before to help," he finally admitted. "That's it."

Casey looked at him in surprise. "Oh."

Vincent could practically hear the gears turning in her head. He shot her a glare.

"Will you let me focus?"

Casey was looking at him with something halfway between smugness and sympathy. "I didn't say anything."

Vincent growled to himself, pointedly turning all three of his heads away from her. He could still feel her gaze on his back.

"Can you just leave me alone for a minute? Unless you want to *keep* 'freezing your ass off out here.'"

"I'm not doing anything! What's your deal?"

"You're staring at me. You obviously have something to say. So say it."

Casey stifled a laugh, turning it into a snort. "It's *nothing*, man. I just think it's cute you like him so much."

A rush of warmth flooded Vincent's body, making his wounds feel especially hot. "What?"

"Henry. I didn't think you were *that* close."

Vincent bared his teeth, but it was half-hearted. "I don't know what you mean. We're *not*." *Especially not now.*

"So if I took you to my favorite bike shop will you chill out there, too?"

Vincent fought the strange panic that rose into his throats. He felt oddly exposed, even more than he did in his true form in the middle of campus.

"Okay, okay," Casey said. "Down, boy." She grinned at him and sauntered in the opposite direction, giving him plenty of room to breathe.

Vincent waited until she was out of earshot, then heaved a deep sigh, forcing his fur to lie flat. He bent his heads and closed his eyes, doing his best to block out the uncomfortable warmth under his skin and instead focus on relaxing.

This time, without any external distractions, he could feel himself slipping further and further from his anxiety. Then, an image flashed through his mind–Henry's hand reaching out for him in this very spot, his eyes full of awe.

No. Don't.

Vincent felt his body shift again, just as it had before. Bones rearranged themselves, appendages melted away and conjoined, and then in a blink he was human again.

He was glad Casey didn't see. He stood shakily, feeling far more fragile all of a sudden as his wounds coalesced into this smaller physical form. He made sure he could balance on two legs before he went to collect Casey.

"Oh, come on, that's so not fair...how come *you* get to keep your clothes on?" Casey complained as soon as she saw him.

"I told you, our transformations aren't the same." Vincent didn't wait for her, starting off down the hill again.

Casey followed. "You're such a buzzkill."

Vincent slid the last few feet to the bottom of the hill, then rounded on her. She almost careened straight into him.

"Hey–"

"*You* should be taking this more seriously," Vincent snapped. He wasn't nearly as intimidating in this form, but he still radiated that uncanny sense that something far bigger was hiding behind his burning eyes. "You *mauled* a man tonight. You should be thanking us for intervening before you murdered him."

Casey glared at him, suddenly defensive. "He was stalking me. For all you know *he* could have murdered *me!*"

Vincent snorted. "That man is a coward through and through. He wasn't going to do anything more."

Ferocity sparked in Casey's dark eyes. "Oh, you know that for a fact, do you? Are you a mind-reader?" Vincent opened his mouth to argue, but she interrupted him. "No, don't you preach at me. You have *no* idea what it's like. A lot of men are cowards, and that's why they catch women when they have the advantage. Like being out alone."

"I come from Hell, Casey. My job was guarding the damned. I've seen enough to know what kind of person someone is."

Casey narrowed her eyes. "So what, you think you know my shit better than me?" She let out a fake laugh. "Of course you do. Just like before."

"What?"

"Look, Vincent. I really didn't need you to protect me back in the Commons. Shit like that doesn't deter men like him. It just makes me look weaker."

Vincent blinked at her, incredulous. "You didn't want me to get rid of him?"

"No," she said, but her anger seemed to relent slightly. "I don't need a guard dog, alright? I mean it. I know you think you know everything about judging people or whatever, but trust me, you don't. People are a lot worse than you think they are. Everyone is capable of pretty much anything, if you push them enough."

Selfish and treacherous and greedy. Well, at least they could agree on one thing.

"Too bad. Henry tasked me with guarding you, so that's what I'm going to do."

Casey rolled her eyes. "Right. Whatever *Henry* says goes. I forgot."

Before Vincent could retaliate, Casey brushed past him and started off down the nearest corridor. She left him no choice but to follow.

Soon they found themselves just across from Yarrow Hall at the edge of the trees. Yellow light from the hallway pooled on the ground through the glass of the back door, tantalizing in the deep darkness that surrounded them.

Casey left Vincent there to wait. For a tense few minutes he wasn't sure if she would reappear at all, but to her credit she returned fully clothed, Henry's jacket slung over her arm. They walked back to Walden Hall together in silence.

Vincent unlocked Henry's room with the keys he was given, and the two of them went inside. They were welcomed by the pleasant, clean decor. Again, it was a stark contrast to everything they had just endured–almost insultingly so. The only thought that comforted Vincent was the stash of weapons under the bed.

"Goddamn prep," Casey muttered, sitting on the bed unceremoniously.

Vincent ignored her and went for the drawer where Henry kept his first aid supplies. As he went through them, he shoved away the lament that Henry wasn't there to help him clean up this time. Like hell would he let Casey do it.

"You sure know your way around Henry's room," Casey sneered.

"We're working together," Vincent shot back. "Will you shut up already?"

He stepped up to the mirror, craning his neck to reveal the worst of his wounds. A misshapen gash crossed the side of his neck, blood still oozing from obvious tooth marks. The slashes across his back burned under his clothes.

He had no choice. He shrugged off his jacket and began undoing the buttons on his shirt. Casey's unamused face reflected behind him in the mirror, but as he discarded his shirt her eyes widened.

"Now *that's* a war wound," she said, impressed. He could feel her gaze traveling across the deep scars that slashed along his bare chest. "Where'd you get it?"

"Mind your own business," Vincent grunted, busying himself with unwrapping a packet of antiseptic wipes.

Casey snorted. "As if this isn't my business now. I added to it, so I might as well-" She stopped suddenly, and Vincent was chilled by the horror that crept onto her face.

"What?"

"Can you...y'know...be turned?"

"Turned?"

"Into a werewolf."

"I...don't think so. I'm not human."

Casey's dismay faded to worry, but it wasn't enough. "I hope you're right. For your sake."

"I think you should be more worried about Hunter," Vincent said grimly, turning back to his task.

"...Fuck."

Casey took a deep breath.

"...Fuck! Fuck, fuck, fuck. Ugh!"

She buried her face in her hands, pulling at her hair. Then she stopped with a jolt. She clutched her arm again, reminding Vincent she was seriously injured too. She had tied a hand towel around the spot rather than ruining her shirt, but that was hardly a permanent solution.

"You should take some of this stuff too." Vincent nudged the first aid kit towards her with his foot.

"What does it matter?" Casey said flatly. "I'm fucked. Now he's gonna turn into a werewolf and hunt me down for real."

"We won't let that happen," Vincent said, hoping it was true. He realized he was making yet another promise he wasn't sure he could keep, and silently cursed himself.

He fought off a sudden wish that Henry would come back already. Somehow, it didn't feel so daunting with both of them involved. But he couldn't forget how they had left things last time. He wasn't sure Henry would even want his help now.

"You don't get it." Casey's voice rose in alarm. "You don't fucking get it–Vincent, he's *huge*. Have you seen how huge he is? Just imagine what his wolf form looks like! As soon as he feels his wolf sex drive he's going to hunt me down like a goddamn rabbit! I don't stand a chance! What the fuck have I done..." She groaned, flopping down on Henry's bed and burying her face in his pillow.

That *sympathy* was back, tugging at Vincent like a riptide. He was too tired to fight it. "Henry and I will keep him in line. I swear it."

"As if *you* could do anything!" Casey whipped her head up out of the pillow to glower at him. "You couldn't even beat *me*! And Henry's no better! You think a metal glove is gonna stop a horny werewolf?"

Vincent didn't know what to say. They both fell into a thorny silence. Casey grumbled something and grabbed the first aid kit to start tending to her arm. Vincent made sure his neck wrap was secure before doing his best to dress the lacerations on his back in the mirror. It was a hard angle–the gashes from Casey's claws ran deep along his spine. In the end, he realized he wasn't going to be able to reach properly by himself.

He turned back to Casey. "Can you please help with these?" he asked, hating himself.

Casey took her sweet time finishing up the wrap on her arm before looking up at him coldly. "Sure I'm capable enough?"

"I don't know what you're trying to say. Just help me, would you?"

"Yeah, of course you don't." To Vincent's surprise, she made her way over to him. "Just stand still and don't bitch."

Vincent tried to suppress every reaction he could as Casey worked on his back. The cleanup was horrendous. After seeing how much gauze Casey threw aside, saturated with blood, Vincent realized his shirt was certainly forfeit. He only hoped it wouldn't show too badly on the inside of his leather jacket.

"There. Happy?" Casey grunted as she finished.

"Hardly," Vincent muttered.

Casey tossed the last of the bandage roll onto the floor and flopped back onto Henry's bed. Vincent sighed and began collecting up the remnants of the first aid kit himself. He winced every time he bent over. But he knew better than to expect more help from Casey–as if he would deign to ask.

Finally, just as he was trying to shove the last pack of gauze into the overstuffed kit, the door opened. Both Vincent and Casey flinched, facing it with hackles raised.

Henry looked back at them from the doorway, worry etched onto his features. They relaxed.

"What happened?" Vincent asked.

Henry locked the door before he dared to reply. "They took him in," he said wearily. "He should be okay, they think. They're doing a blood transfusion now."

"Are you gonna just leave him alone there?" Casey demanded.

"Of course not," Henry said with an uncharacteristic note of impatience. "I made sure the hospital will keep me informed on his condition. I'm gonna be there as soon as they discharge him."

"And who's to say he won't escape before then? Or wolf out and mangle all the hospital staff?"

"He's in no condition for that. You nearly killed him."

That seemed to shut Casey up.

"We're fine, by the way," said Vincent. He gingerly pulled his jacket back on.

"Sorry," Henry sighed, his shoulders sagging. "That's a relief."

"So what are we gonna do about Casey?"

"I'm *right here*," said Casey.

Henry began pacing, running a hand through his sandy hair. It wasn't nearly as neat as he usually kept it. "Um...give me a minute."

"I'm surprised you don't have a plan already," Vincent remarked.

"I *will*, okay?" Henry snapped. "I've been a little busy!"

Vincent stared at him in surprise. Henry immediately sighed, rubbing his hand over his dirty face. "Sorry, Vincent. It's just..."

Vincent never found out what was *just*. Instead Henry turned back to Casey. "How long have you been a werewolf for?"

"That's pretty personal, don't you think, pretty boy?"

"I'm not playing," Henry said sternly. "If we hadn't shown up, you would have murdered someone tonight. I need to know everything so we can figure out what to do."

Casey eyed Henry searchingly.

"I've been like this for maybe a year now," she finally said. "I don't know for sure."

"How did you get turned?"

"I don't want to talk about it. Let's just say it wasn't my goddamn choice."

Henry nodded slowly. "So you were attacked, I assume...and you've been through a few transformations?"

"Obviously."

"How did you handle them?"

"About as well as you'd expect. I haven't turned anyone else, if that's what you're asking."

"Did you attack anyone, though?"

Casey hesitated a moment too long. Vincent noticed, and he wondered if Henry did. "I just *said*. They would've turned, wouldn't they?"

Henry paused, too. Then he nodded. "Alright. What do you do when the full moon comes around?"

"Make sure I'm out in the woods far enough. I can feel when it's coming."

"But the moon isn't full tonight. So was this the first time you lost control of it?"

In spite of herself, Casey looked troubled. "Yeah."

"What were you feeling when you did?"

Casey clutched her injured arm tighter. "What does it matter?"

"We need to figure out how to help you. It's good to know what kinds of things trigger you to turn."

"You're not my goddamn therapist."

"He might as well be," said Vincent sharply. "He's the only thing keeping you from being arrested, or worse."

"Look," said Casey, flinging up her good hand in frustration, "I know you're not gonna turn me in. Who's gonna believe you? Just let me go, and I promise I won't do anything like that again."

"No," said Henry, firmly. "You've already proven you're liable to attack people. I need to make certain it won't happen again."

"I promise!" Casey insisted. She broke off with a sigh. "Listen–if nobody gives me a reason to turn, I won't. You have to deal with Hunter, man."

"Trust me, I'll deal with him," Henry said darkly. "But it's not like he's gonna be the only thing to upset you. How will you avoid it happening again, Casey?"

Casey, for all her bravado, found no answer. She was silent for a long moment. In the end, she said, "What are you gonna do with Hunter, then? Huh?"

158

Vincent could tell just by the look on Henry's face that he noticed her deflection. But for some reason, he let it go.

"I'll...I'll keep a close eye on him. I won't give him the chance to hurt anyone until he can control himself."

"I doubt he's gonna care about doing that."

"Why?"

"Um. The stalking, for starters?"

Suddenly Henry softened. "It's okay, Casey. I'll take care of that, too." He took a step towards her, but she shifted away from him defensively. He paused where he was, taking the hint, but went on, "I'll put a stop to it, I promise. Just give me your number, and I'll keep in touch."

Casey eyed him dubiously. "Are...you letting me go?"

"Yeah. Are you gonna be okay walking home on your own, or do you want me to come along?"

"What, you aren't going to chain me up in your bedroom? Make sure I don't go on a rampage while you're sleeping?"

"If you'd prefer that..." muttered Vincent.

"I really don't."

"I believe you when you say it won't be a problem," said Henry. "But we are gonna have to work on controlling your transformations when something upsets you."

"*Upsets*," Casey snorted. "Right. Well, thanks, Your Leniency."

She entered her phone number into Henry's phone, then made for the door. When she reached it, she paused. "What *are* you gonna do, when Hunter gets out? Follow him around all day to keep him off me?"

"No," said Henry, his voice tightening. "Not necessarily, I'll—"

"Aren't you a senior? Don't you have a capstone project? And football practice?"

"*Yes*," Henry said, a bit too forcefully. "I make it work. I *will* make it work. You can rely on me."

Vincent knew that look. He wasn't sure how, but he did. Henry was bluffing—he had no idea what he was going to do. With those nightly patrols of his on top of everything else...

No. You can't help him. He doesn't want your help.

But he wasn't going to be able to do this alone. He had already failed. Vincent recalled that stab of fear when he realized Henry's scent led far too close to Benjamin, seeing him facing down a werewolf on his own...

If I had been there before, he wouldn't have walked straight into danger. Who knew what else would happen to him on his own? He was only human.

And that's why you can't trust him! Vincent's instincts howled at him. *Every human is the same at heart. Selfish and—*

And what? Was there a single selfish impulse in the heart of Henry Wellfellow? The man who nearly gave his life tonight for even someone like Hunter? The man who refused to give up on Casey's humanity even as she almost killed them all?

Who does something like that?

The man who reached out to touch a hellhound.

For the first time, Vincent wished he had allowed it. If only to know what would happen. If only to know why.

He *had* to know why.

Even Casey couldn't seem to find it in her to press Henry further. Instead, she strode off down the hall. The door settled ajar, and Vincent closed it behind her.

Now he was alone with Henry. He sucked in a heavy breath, then faced him squarely.

"Henry...let me help."

CHAPTER 10

CROSSROADS

Henry stared at Vincent, mouth half-open.

"You can't do everything on your own," Vincent insisted, meeting his gaze despite the stammer in his heart. He hated this feeling–like he was standing on the edge of a precipice, swaying, trying not to look down. He shouldn't be doing this...it went against almost every instinct. But here he was.

He had to know what was so special about Henry Wellfellow.

Henry's brow furrowed. Not a good sign. "I don't need your help." He sounded cold.

Vincent fought back his dismay and willed himself onward. Henry was stubborn–he had to take the heat off his pride.

"Look...I think we *need* to work together. Especially now. Between the murders and the vampires and now the werewolves...there's too many problems. Neither of us can do this alone."

It wasn't enough. He could see it in Henry's face.

"I...I need your help, too, Henry."

There. The slightest give. Vincent's heart skipped hopefully–but then:

"But you don't trust me. How am I supposed to work with someone who doesn't trust me?"

The pain was so palpable in Henry's voice, it startled Vincent. He had almost forgotten how strange he was. *Strange* being a word in place of a dozen others that were harder to admit. Henry's *strangeness* had aggravated him before, but now...

No, maybe before now. Maybe it had worn smooth over time, until Vincent no longer recognized its face.

"I wasn't lying, before. I can't tell you everything," he said, allowing his remorse to shine through. This time, it wasn't a complete farce. However *strange* that felt. "I'm bound by laws beyond this world. Promises I made to my masters."

"You promised your masters not to show me clues you find about the murderer?"

Vincent's gut twisted. He couldn't just give up all his secrets. He knew that's what Henry would have preferred–but he didn't understand what he was asking for. His fingers barely even brushed the surface of what lay beneath.

Vincent was going to have to give up *something*. That much he knew. But it also had to be something that led Henry away from Benjamin. For the sake of his mission. For the sake of Henry never knowing how terrible Vincent truly was.

"It was Melanie."

"Melanie?"

"Percy told me Melanie was involved in his murder."

Henry stared at Vincent in shock. "Are you serious? How does he know?"

"He can't remember much, but...I showed him a picture I took of that necklace Sierra found in the caves under the Devil's Maw. I recognized it from the photos he has on his shelves. He remembered Melanie took it from him just before he died. *Right* before."

It took Henry a few moments to put everything together. "You're not saying *she* killed him?"

"I don't know. But she might have. And either way...she most likely meant for it to happen."

He was surprised by how devastated Henry looked. He shook his head helplessly, trying to collect himself. "I just...I never liked her much, but I never thought she'd do something like *that*... What on earth did Percy ever do to her? I don't think he's said a bad word about anyone in his life!"

"You'd be surprised what people are capable of," Vincent said grimly. He only realized a moment later that he was echoing Casey's words.

Henry gave him such a look of dismay it felt as if he was seeing Vincent for the first time—and didn't like what he found there.

"Why did you keep this from me? You can't tell me your masters forced you to. That makes no sense."

Vincent pulled his tie taut around his neck, as if to strangle his guilt. "I know...I know. I'm just...not used to telling people things, alright? It just makes everything more complicated."

He hated every word that left his lips. He hated justifying himself. It felt far too raw, like he was exposing his neck for Henry to sink his teeth into. But he was still teetering on the edge of that precipice. He had made his choice, and there was no going back now.

He hated the relief, too, when Henry's expression softened. Vincent felt his gaze searching him; he wasn't sure what he was looking for, but every instinct wanted whatever it was to remain hidden.

"I'm sorry, Vincent."

What? He wasn't expecting that.

"I didn't realize you were..." Henry trailed off, leaving Vincent with questions that would stay unanswered. He looked gentle again, almost the same as the night they had rested atop the hill overlooking the biology building.

After a long moment, Henry spoke again, his tone darkening. "Vincent...the wounds on Percy's neck. They looked like..."

Puncture wounds. That's what Henry had told him before. "Melanie can't be a vampire," Vincent said, but even as he did, a chill swept through his body. *Why not? She could have done it. I don't know for certain Benjamin did it.* "We would be able to tell...wouldn't we?"

"It's hard to," said Henry grimly. "Like I said before."

"But you *can* tell?"

"It would be small things. Like avoiding sunlight. Unnatural strength. Not eating. Not looking well. Any vampire with half a brain would be careful about hiding the signs."

Vincent's thoughts began to churn. "Have you seen her in the sun lately?"

"Um...I don't think so. But it's been pretty rainy..."

"What about her makeup?"

"Huh?"

"You said 'not looking well' is a sign. Pale, thin, tired, maybe? Wouldn't that be easy to hide with all the makeup she uses?" Something struck him. "The other day, when we called on Ava...Melanie seemed extra tired. Do you remember?"

Henry nodded slowly. "That could be anything, though. Staying up late working on assignments..."

"Or not."

Henry grimaced. "If she did kill Percy...if she drained his blood...then she must've done the same with Mira. And that's why she wanted to hide her body..."

But Benjamin was involved. It wasn't that simple. Unless he was sharing food with her...

The idea of that was laughable. This was Benjamin—it all had to mean something more.

And he couldn't tell Henry that. Not outright.

Then he realized something else: "Melanie has a scent." *Coconut.* "If she was a vampire, she wouldn't have one."

"And she was with us the whole time that night," Henry added, pondering. "She couldn't have killed Mira herself..."

"But then why did she take Percy's necklace?" Vincent pointed out. "Percy told me it's some kind of charm. He said the spirits of his ancestors would protect whoever wore it, so long as they shared the same blood."

Henry paused, nodding. "I've heard of things like that. They're not very common, though. They're usually imbued with magic that draws from blood."

"Actual blood?"

"Yeah. Literally. I mean, something with genetic material. Everything has some kind of life force," Henry explained, sounding suddenly as if he was reciting something from a lesson, "which lends power to magic through ritual. It's just...well, most cultures prefer their dead to move on freely, but I guess some people would rather their family stay behind to help them."

"Does it...actually contain their spirits?"

"So they say."

"Did you notice Percy's is broken?"

Henry's brow furrowed in thought. "I assume Melanie did that..."

"I just can't figure out why. She already got it off him, so it wasn't protecting him when he died." Vincent sighed, frustrated. "I guess at least the spirits inside were released...I hope, anyway."

Henry looked uncertain. "I dunno...maybe they wanted to be in there."

"It's unnatural," Vincent insisted. "I don't like the thought of it."

"Yeah...I guess you know where spirits should be going, huh?" Henry looked at him with an interest that prickled under Vincent's skin. He was getting dangerously close again.

"Yes," Vincent said carefully, avoiding his gaze.

"Does it bother you that they're here instead?"

"Yes," he said again, his discomfort growing. *Why do you keep pushing for things I can't give you?* Every time it only drove more and more wedges between them.

But this time, Henry stopped. He knew he was going too far. But there was a sadness there as well.

"So Melanie broke the amulet and threw it into the Devil's Maw...maybe just to make sure it wasn't gonna curse her, or something. But then why not go after someone else, if she was looking for an easy victim?"

Vincent paused, thinking. "Maybe it had something to do with the amulet."

"You think she targeted him *because* of the amulet?"

Vincent shrugged. "According to him, it was the last thing they talked about before he died."

"Maybe..." Henry sighed deeply, seeming just as lost as Vincent felt. Then he looked up suddenly.

"You said Percy remembered more after he saw the picture?"

"Well, yeah..."

"We should get the amulet back. I'm sure being near it would help him even more."

Vincent nodded thoughtfully. "It's worth a try. We'd just have to convince Sierra to give it up."

Henry broke into a smile. "I guess I'm the best person to do it." Vincent felt a sour pang in the pit of his stomach.

"Other than Jake," he countered.

Henry's smile faded instantly.

"Well...I'll pay her a visit tomorrow."

"What are you going to tell her?"

"I'll figure something out..."

"If she won't give it up, we could always steal it."

Henry immediately glared at Vincent. "What? No way. Why would you say that?"

Vincent blinked at him. "Because we have to get that necklace, period. Do you want someone else to die?"

"Of course not. But there are other ways to do it without stealing from Sierra. Or anyone, for that matter. We're going to do this the right way. We're not thieves."

Vincent suppressed a snort. "Fine..."

"Good."

"What about Casey and Hunter? What's your plan?"

Henry hesitated. Again, Vincent knew instantly–he had no idea what to do. It was so unlike him...

"I can follow them," Vincent offered. "It's easy for me."

"You can't be in two places at once."

"Well, that's where you come in." *If you'll let me help,* he added silently. This was the moment of truth—he noticed Henry hadn't actually agreed to it yet. "Between the both of us, we should be able to handle it."

Henry was quiet for a moment too long. Then he said, "Yeah...yeah. We can handle it. I have an hour after rehearsal on Tuesdays and Thursdays, and mornings on Mondays, if I..."

He wasn't even talking to Vincent anymore. He was trying to convince himself.

"What's rehearsal?" Vincent asked.

Henry avoided his gaze. "Theater. I have a show coming up next month..."

Vincent didn't know how he had missed it before—Henry was working himself to the bone.

"Casey was right, wasn't she? All those things you have to do..."

"It's fine, really. I'm used to it. It's just part of being a Warden."

"But true Wardens don't have to balance college on top of the job, do they?"

Henry sighed. "No, but—"

"I thought you came here to get away from Shadowhand duties for a bit."

Henry finally rounded on him. "Yes, I did, okay? But this is my chance to prove I can handle this case *my* way—without killing anyone!"

Surprise coursed through Vincent's body. Henry's eyes were wild—desperate. He almost looked like a different person entirely, his hair mussed and clothes muddy from the night's events. He was slipping.

Then, just as quickly as it had come, it faded. A softer weariness replaced it, like a cloud passing over the sun. "I just can't do what my dad does, Vincent. I can't."

He looked so miserable and so afraid, Vincent's heart lurched like his sixth sense was tugging at it again. He understood that feeling.

A part of him wanted to go to him, touch him, comfort him in some way he didn't know how to. Instead, he said, "You don't have to. I'm with you. We can still do this."

Henry's gaze flickered over him, searching, yearning for...*something*.

"You're with me?" he said, his voice quiet.

Vincent swallowed the lump that rose in his throat. "I'll...I'll tell you everything I can, Henry. I promise. You can trust me."

Henry held his gaze for a moment longer. Then he softened. "Okay."

It was a half-truth. Vincent knew it was. He was keeping so much from Henry—and not just because his father told him to.

Henry straightened up, squared his shoulders. He looked more like himself again. "Let's keep Casey close," he said. "It'll be easier to keep track of her if she does patrols with us."

Vincent let out a low groan. "Do we have to?"

Henry shot him a sympathetic look, but said, "She's involved now either way. Also, it doesn't hurt to have a little extra muscle, does it?"

Vincent saw the sense in that. But he didn't have to like it. "Fine..."

"And when Hunter gets out, we'll talk to him," Henry went on. "Try to get on his good side. Try to do things the easy way."

"You're not going to offer him a spot on the team, are you?"

"No," said Henry firmly. "We can't trust him. And I don't really want someone like that around all the time, anyway. Especially with Casey. But..." He sighed deeply. "Here's the thing. People like him do bad things because of something bad in their lives. I have a feeling he's terribly lonely, and that's why he fixates on her."

"That doesn't excuse it," Vincent said dubiously.

"Of course not. But like it or not, we have to deal with him somehow. Unless we want to hand him over to the Shadowhand or let him run wild...we have to do *something*. Maybe he'll see reason if we offer him the support he's never had."

Vincent marveled at Henry's optimism. It was like he believed the exact opposite about humankind. Much as he wanted to argue, he couldn't bring himself to. Not with Henry, about this.

Instead, he said, "I'm going to get some rest now. Are we going to meet at the fountain tomorrow night?"

"Yeah...yeah, that's a good idea. I'll text Casey to come, too." But as Vincent turned to leave, Henry added, "You gonna be okay? You look pretty rough..."

"Ah...yeah, I'm fine. I'll heal in a day or two."

"I noticed that. You must have some kind of fast-healing power. I didn't know that about hellhounds. I wonder if anyone does..."

That reminded Vincent...one question still weighed on him. "You don't think I'll...turn, do you?"

"Into a werewolf?" Henry guessed. "No, I don't think it can affect anything that isn't human. Although," he added with a laugh, "you'd make one hell of a superwolf if it did! God, just imagine!"

Vincent couldn't help but smile too at the thought. "A *super mega three-headed* werewolf. Yeah, we wouldn't have to worry about fighting vampires then."

The moment lingered, then faded. It was strange joking with him again, like nothing had ever gone wrong between them. But he knew better than to believe Henry would forget so easily. There were far too many secrets.

The next evening, they met at the fountain as promised. It was almost strangely nostalgic for Vincent; he couldn't deny how pleased he was about working with Henry again.

Except, of course, Casey was going to join them this time.

"Hey, Vinny! You look better," Henry said cheerfully. That was a relief–Vincent had been wondering if his good mood would last. He desperately wanted to forget the tension between them.

"Yeah. I slept most of the day."

"Still, you should come by for new dressings after the patrol tonight."

The warmth in Henry's concern felt just as Vincent remembered, too. It was like the first ray of sun after a long winter.

"Yeah...sure," he said, fighting his awkwardness.

Before he could say anything more, footsteps echoed across the courtyard. They looked up to find Casey sauntering over to join them. She was chewing gum that smelled like cinnamon.

"So what am I doing here?" she said by way of a greeting.

Vincent and Henry shared a look. "Better start at the beginning," Vincent told him.

So he did. It was strange hearing their misadventures all laid out, the past few harrowing weeks–and beyond–compressed into mere words.

"Now hold on," Casey broke in when Henry had all but finished. "You're not seriously roping me into all this, are you?"

"We're certainly not going to let you walk away scot-free," Vincent snapped.

"You're gonna join our team and help us keep the school safe," said Henry with his best attempt at cheer.

Casey shook her head. "You two call yourselves a team? What, the volunteer cop brigade? Security Guards Anonymous?"

"Laugh all you want," Vincent growled. "You're still going to help us."

"And how are you gonna make me?" Casey challenged. "Are you gonna go to the police like 'My classmate is a werewolf and she mauled her stalker, arrest her, officer!'? I don't think so."

"It's not the police you have to worry about," Henry said, with an unusual darkness.

"Yeah, yeah, the *Shadowhand*," said Casey, wiggling her fingers dramatically. But she didn't sound confident. "If they don't know about me already, they can't be that good."

"They only hear about you if you're a problem." Henry held her gaze with a frigid seriousness. "Don't become a problem, Casey. If you're with me, I can grant you immunity from any consequences related to this attack. Even if Hunter turns. Otherwise...I'd imagine it won't take them long."

Even Vincent felt a chill pass through his body. Casey's lip curled, but she faltered.

"Fine. Only if you can promise I'll be safe from them."

Henry nodded. "Yes, of course. I promise. If they find out, I'll hear about it first and let them know you're in my custody."

Casey stared for a moment more, uncertain. Then she resumed chewing her gum, trying to save face. "So what do I have to do, exactly?"

"Well first of all, we do nightly patrols around campus to keep an eye on things," Henry explained. "And outside of that, look out for suspicious activity anywhere."

"Sounds fun. Any tips on what qualifies as 'suspicious activity'? Biting people in the Commons, maybe? Drinking blood from a McDonald's cup?"

"I mean, I guess."

"You'll know it if you see it," Vincent said, unamused. "You're not stupid."

"Just thought it'd help to know what I'm actually looking for." Casey shrugged, blowing a bubble. "You guys are clearly professionals. Loving the onboarding so far."

Henry sighed. "How about, if you notice anything that points to someone being an Other. Keeping track of them can't hurt, in case they're involved."

"*Others.* Right. Good to know I'm being *officially* othered." Casey spat her gum out onto the pavement. "Well, now that I know all the dirty details...don't we have some kind of scavenger hunt to do?"

"It's a patrol," Henry said dejectedly.

"Might as well," Vincent put in. "It's early still."

"Alright...let's go, then. But will you *please* throw your gum away next time?"

"I'll think about it," Casey lied.

They started off down the path. As they crossed into the shelter of a corridor, the night seemed to close in on them, the pillars and walls casting deep shadows that swallowed any light offered by the sconces along the wall. Their footsteps echoed far too loudly in the hush, mingling only with the steady chirp of crickets. It was eerie, but at least it wasn't lonely.

All the while, Vincent's sixth sense growled deep inside him, urging him to veer off and *hunt*. This time, though, it annoyed him more than anything. He did his best to stifle it, letting his other senses take over.

"Where are we even going?" Casey asked. "Don't tell me we're gonna cover every fucking inch of this place before we can go to bed."

"Of course not," said Henry. "We're just gonna wander for a bit to make sure everything's quiet."

"Well I don't hear anyone getting dismembered. Can we go home now?"

"We haven't gone nearly far enough yet."

"What's the point, if we don't even go everywhere?"

"It's good enough," Henry insisted. "After all, if I hadn't been out yesterday, I wouldn't have found you."

That seemed to shut Casey up–for now. Vincent, tired of bickering, took out his phone to check for texts while they walked. He frowned at his empty screen.

"Bored of us already?" said Casey.

"Yes," said Vincent.

"Everything okay?" Henry asked.

Vincent sighed. "I was checking to see if Ava texted me back yet. I asked her earlier if she had talked to her grandmother."

"If she's dragging her ass this much, don't you think that's suspicious?" Casey asked.

Henry shook his head firmly. "She's part of our team, too. We talked to her at length about everything, and she wants to help."

"Well then, where is she?" Casey asked, gesturing vaguely around. "Why doesn't *she* have to go on 'patrols'?"

"She's...difficult to deal with," Henry admitted. "And she wasn't super keen on this part. We really need her help, so I didn't want to scare her off."

"So you say she 'wants to help,' but she actually doesn't care."

"That's not what I'm saying."

"Honestly...she has a point."

Both Henry and Casey turned to stare at Vincent. "Why?" asked Henry.

"Ava *is* Melanie's roommate," Vincent said. "She could be working with her. And she's obviously not motivated to help us. She hasn't given us anything useful yet other than tarot readings. And those barely say anything."

"We did tell Ava almost everything..." Henry murmured.

"Wow, you did?" said Casey. "Oh, excellent work, everyone. You really know how to pick 'em."

Henry glared at her. "I still don't think she's working against us."

"Nah, we're fucked," Casey said with fake cheer. "We're probably walking right into a vampire trap as we speak."

"Come on," Henry groaned.

"Vincent couldn't take those vampires–how am I supposed to do it?"

"You managed to overpower him," Henry pointed out. Vincent grimaced.

"So? That's not hard," Casey scoffed.

"Maybe not for a homicidal werewolf!" Vincent snapped.

"I'm not homicidal!" Casey snarled.

"No? Well let me just go ask Hunter what he thinks."

Henry pushed himself between them. "This isn't helping!"

"Tell him to stop being such a sore loser then," Casey huffed, turning away.

"If we can avoid fighting the vampires, we will," Henry insisted. "We just need to find out what the heart of the situation is, so we can dismantle their plans."

"Then why bother with me?" Casey growled. "Aren't I just a meat shield for you dumbasses?"

"Of course not," said Henry, vehemently. "Why would you think that?"

Casey gestured broadly to herself, her eyebrows lifted. "You aren't keeping me around for the team spirit."

"That's for sure," Vincent muttered.

"We're in this together," Henry asserted. "I don't want you to feel like a bodyguard."

"Then why are you forcing me to be in your stupid little club?"

Henry blinked in surprise. "Don't you care about the murders?"

"From what you've told me, this is way above our pay grade. Considering we're, you know, not getting paid. We're *students*. It's the college's job to keep us safe. And your fancy secret society. I have enough problems on my own without playing mall cop for the whole school."

"And what if you were next on the chopping block?" Vincent said. "Would you care then? What if no one was there to save you?"

"I'm a werewolf. I don't need saving."

"You're not invincible," Vincent argued. "Even you can't take on two or more vampires on your own."

"I'd have a better chance of avoiding them by lying low rather than hanging out with you losers. Y'know—who are apparently *searching for them?*"

"Yeah, we are," said Henry, "because *I'm* not gonna sit around waiting for the next student to die when I can do something about it." There was a harsh edge to his tone that was very unlike him. "We're some of the only people who know about all this. It's our responsibility to help."

"And what if *you* die trying to help? And then there's more people dead?"

"Then at least I tried."

Vincent gazed at Henry, taking in the blaze of determination in his sky blue eyes, in his balled fists and his set jaw and his strong shoulders. He believed every word he spoke. He still believed everything could go his way.

Casey shook her head helplessly. "You're crazy."

"Say what you want. You don't get a choice in this," Vincent stepped in, his tone dark. "You lost that right when you became part of the problem."

"Part of the problem?" Casey said incredulously. "I'm not going around murdering people!"

"You almost did. In fact, you're living proof that our intervention matters."

Casey opened her mouth to argue, but something must have struck her. Instead she turned away with a scoff. "Whatever. Are you gonna figure out how to cure me, then, if I'm that much of a liability?"

"You can't *cure* a werewolf," Henry told her. Then he paused, thoughtful. "But there might be a way to lessen the symptoms... That would help us with Hunter, too. I've never worked with werewolves before, but–"

"If you don't know anything about werewolves, how do you know you can't cure them?" Casey asked, with an air of smugness.

"I know the *basics* about werewolves!" said Henry.

"Oh, you do now? Got it–so number one, human turns into big scary wolf monster during the full moon. Number two, if a werewolf bites you, you turn into one. Number three, it's incurable. Anything else I'm missing?"

"Well, that's not entirely–"

"'Cause I'm pretty sure that's like, *the* most common knowledge about werewolves."

"*Please* keep your voice down..." Henry groaned, exasperated.

"If we're just going to go off fucking urban legends," she went on, ignoring him, "why don't we just Google werewolf shit? Since, you know, everything is just common knowledge now except to us, because we're gargantuan idiots."

"Does Google have that kind of information just lying around?" Vincent asked.

"Maybe...it's just hard, 'cause there's no real way to know if what you're reading is true."

He stopped in his tracks. "Actually..." He pulled out his phone and began tapping on the screen.

"What?" said Casey, shuffling closer to look at his phone. He lifted it away from her, using his height to his advantage. She let out a growl of protest.

"My sister is super into internet cults and stuff like that," Henry explained. "If anyone knows where to look, she will."

"I didn't know you had a sister," said Vincent.

"I guess it didn't come up."

"Will she even help, though?" Casey asked. "I mean, your dad didn't seem keen on leaking you any secrets."

"Serena's not a bigwig like he is. She's only a couple years older than me. Unless she's feeling especially sisterly today, she'll probably throw me a bone..." Henry finished his text and returned his phone to his pocket.

"Is she going to answer right away?" Vincent asked. "It's pretty late..."

"Oh, she'll be awake. She stays up all night sometimes," Henry said, with an obvious note of judgment.

"Not like everyone's favorite football star," Casey snarked.

"Who, me?" Henry snorted. "Come on. I mean, it's good for you to get up early! Working out first thing prepares you for the rest of the day, and energizes–"

"Don't care," Casey cut him off, turning away.

Just then, Henry's phone vibrated. He looked at it, the screen's glow painting his face in bright blue and deep shadow.

"Hey, guys...Serena's got something for us."

CHAPTER 11

THE THIEVES' AMULET

66 **S** erena linked me some kind of forum for werewolves..." said Henry, still tapping at his phone.

"Are you sure it's legit?" Casey asked.

"My sister researches her sources," Henry insisted. "She wouldn't send me something that wasn't real."

He waved them over, holding his phone so they could see. It was a website with white text on a dark background, and little else. Henry scrolled through the page, pausing on photos of various plants and unknown liquids in bowls or jars.

"What is all this, some sort of potion?" Casey asked, suspicious. "Nightshade, wolfsbane...come on, *wolfsbane?* Are you sure this is real?"

"I guess there's a reason they named it that," Vincent remarked.

"These guys say it's helped them control their urges," said Henry. "Especially close to the full moon."

Casey shook her head. "No way I'm taking this shit. Nightshade is poisonous–even I know that."

Henry frowned as he read on. "Wolfsbane is too. Black tea...witch hazel...they're saying some of these ingredients neutralize aspects of the poisons. It looks like these guys are pharmacists. God...I'm not sure I can pull this off myself. I'm no chemist."

"Well, can we order Werewolf-B-Gone off Amazon?" Casey said snarkily.

Henry continued further down, and eventually let out a scoff. "Of course...they're selling it for three thousand dollars a pop."

"At least shipping is free," said Vincent dryly.

"Great." Casey threw up her hands. "Well, I guess I'll be on surveillance forever."

"Wait a minute," said Vincent. He locked eyes with Henry. "Percy. He was studying to become a doctor. I bet he knows some chemistry."

Henry brightened. "Do you think he'd be able to guide someone through the process?"

"I'm sure he could. As long as he remembers how to do it," said Vincent. "So that means our next step is to get that amulet from Sierra. You need to talk to her."

Henry's face immediately fell. "I um...I already asked her."

"You did? Why didn't you say anything?" Vincent had a feeling he already knew the reason.

Henry avoided his gaze. "I tried to make it casual while we were hanging out. Just wanted to borrow it. She let me look at it, but she didn't want me to actually take it."

"So? That's when you insist!"

"I didn't want to upset her!"

"Even if people die for it?" Vincent pressed.

Henry gritted his teeth. "*She* almost died for it. I get why it's important to her. We'll find some other way to help Percy. There are a lot of other things to try."

"We don't have time to mess around. Even mentioning the amulet to him helped him remember some things about his life."

Henry's gaze hardened to a glare. "We're *not* stealing from Sierra."

"What if she doesn't know it was you?"

"*No.* What part of *no* don't you understand, Vincent?" Henry said sharply. Even Casey looked startled. Vincent's stomach began to churn. *Here we go again...*

"Are you willing to throw away this whole operation just for that?" Vincent dared to ask.

"We'll think of something else." Henry turned away, back towards campus. "Let's finish up here."

Vincent opened his mouth to argue, but thought better of it. Henry was stubborn. And he liked Sierra too much. A darker heat began to incubate in the pit of his stomach as he followed after Henry. Casey fell in step beside him, for once keeping her mouth shut as she glanced between the two of them, practically buzzing with intrigue.

Mercifully, the night was peaceful, and they eventually returned to their dorms. Before Vincent disappeared into his room, Henry stopped him.

"Oh–your dressings. Come over and I'll–"

"It's fine. You don't have to be so noble. Just give me the first aid kit and I'll return it tomorrow."

Henry went quiet. Vincent didn't look at him, only waited in the doorway.

Finally Henry left without a word and brought Vincent what he asked for. All he said was, "Goodnight," before returning to his room.

As soon as Vincent stepped inside his own room, he instantly felt those invisible eyes boring into him.

"Percy, did you take chemistry when you were studying here?"

A long silence persisted. Then:

"*I...think so...*" Vincent felt the air shift as the hole that was Percy moved through space, stopping just in front of the bookshelf on his side of the room. "*Here...*"

Vincent felt a chill course up his body, making every hair stand on end. He hated the idea of moving closer with every instinct he had.

Gritting his teeth, he willed that frustration he had been nursing deep in his gut to flare upwards, filling his body with a new instinct to combat that fear. He took a defiant step forward, and then another. He planted his feet in front of the bookshelf.

His gaze alighted on a textbook. "*Biochemistry,*" Vincent read aloud. "We need to make...a potion, of sorts. We have a recipe, but it involves processing some raw materials. None of us have ever done anything like that before. Do you think you could help us?"

Percy hesitated. Then: "*I–I'm sorry! I-I want to help...but I...I can't remember...I'm so useless, drifting here...*"

The air thickened with the ghost's despair. It permeated Vincent's own emotions until they were sodden with it. It felt...old. Rotten. Like something that had been left out in the open air when Percy was alive, and in his death it was now putrefying.

"*I-I can't even remember myself...my own life...it was all wasted, wasn't it?*" Percy mumbled, his voice distorting and echoing as if shifting between planes of existence no one else could perceive. "*I never did anything worth remembering...and now it's all over...I'm just stuck here, forever, doing nothing still...*"

"You won't be, soon," Vincent promised him, fighting through the muck of those feelings that weren't his. It was harder than he expected to separate himself–they felt a little too familiar. The sympathy was winning. "Just wait. We'll help you move past this place, and then you can help us catch the people that did this to you."

"*Will that even matter? I died...and then I'll move on, somewhere else...and all of it was pointless.*"

How was he supposed to argue with that? Percy had died so young...and Vincent knew where he was going to end up after this. For the first time, he wondered if it was even a kindness to help him pass on from this plane. Just because his instincts bade him to didn't mean he could forget what awaited him. Was this little room truly worse than the Underworld?

He belongs there, Vincent reminded himself sharply. *We* both *do. That's the natural order of things.*

But how was he supposed to convince Percy of that?

What matters to Percy? What would Henry say?

"If you help us, you'll prevent other people from getting murdered as well," Vincent told him. "At the very least, you'll know you saved other people's lives, even after yours ended. Not many people get to say that."

Percy's silence lingered, but this time it softened with each moment that passed. Eventually his voice returned lighter.

"*I...I'd like that...*"

Vincent forced a little smile. That's what Henry would do.

"I'll be able to help you get there soon. I have an idea."

Whether you like it or not, Henry, he thought.

The next day, Vincent waited until sundown before enacting his plan. He hovered outside Yarrow Hall, trying to look as casual as possible, until a small group of girls approached to enter their dorm.

"Sorry–I'm supposed to meet my friend Sierra at her room, but my phone died. Can you let me in?" Vincent said, offering his best friendly facade.

A couple of the girls exchanged an uncertain glance, but a third smiled back at him. "Sure, no problem!" She unlocked the front door and held it open for him.

"Thanks *so* much," Vincent said, trying to channel Henry as he ducked inside with a rueful grin. "You're a lifesaver!"

He hung back in the lobby until the girls had disappeared down the hall. He then followed their path more slowly, making sure the hallway was empty before entering it. He scanned the names affixed to each of the doors he passed. None of them were decorated so cheerfully as the ones Henry had designed in their own dorm.

Finally Vincent happened upon Sierra's name, alongside that of her roommate. Relief mingled with nerves in his gut, and he took a deep breath before knocking on the door.

Sierra opened the door, beaming when she recognized him.

"Vincent! What are you doing here?"

"Hey," Vincent greeted her, trying to shove away his awkwardness. "I was just around, so I figured I'd stop by and see if you want to get some dinner and study for a bit."

Sierra blinked at him. "Oh–yeah, sure! I was just about to go get dinner, actually."

"Great," said Vincent, secretly relieved.

"Let me just get my stuff. You wanna come in for a sec?"

Perfect, thought Vincent as he stepped inside Sierra's room. Her side was a bit cluttered. Clothes were flung in different corners or draped over furniture, her bed unmade, and her school supplies strewn about the desk. But she also had volleyball memorabilia, personal photos, stuffed animals, and other trinkets arranged nicely on shelves and walls, giving the place a cozy feeling.

Then he spotted it. Hanging from a small volleyball trophy on her desk was Percy's amulet.

"Damn it, where's my jacket..." Sierra grumbled, crouching down to look under her bed. She began rifling through the clothes there, and Vincent made his way over to her desk as casually as possible.

"What's it look like?" Vincent said, keeping one eye on her. He lifted the amulet off the trophy and swiftly pocketed it.

"Oh, never mind! Found it." Sierra pulled on a tomato-red hoodie, turning back to him not a moment after the amulet was out of sight. "Y'know, you could have texted me if you wanted to hang out."

"My phone died while I was out," Vincent lied again. "I won't surprise you anymore, if it's that terrible."

Sierra rolled her eyes, grinning. "I didn't say that! Sheesh. Come on, you weirdo."

She led Vincent out of her room and chatted on their way to the Commons. Vincent couldn't help the deep sense of satisfaction in his gut. His plan had been so *easy.* He had what he needed, and she was none the wiser. Any nagging guilt was easy to ignore–after all, this was for the greater good. The amulet didn't even belong to her in the first place.

When they arrived, Sierra split off to get something from the stir fry line. When they eventually settled down in a booth, she stared at Vincent's bowl.

"What did you–wait, are you just having cereal for dinner?"

Vincent, already two spoonfuls deep, looked at her blankly.

"Is that, like...a thing, in Greece?"

"Not really." He took another bite, crunching his cereal with a great deal of satisfaction.

"Yeah, I figured you guys ate like...rice and salads and fish and stuff. Or, uh...couscous? I don't know. Isn't food like, a big deal in the Mediterranean?"

"I guess so."

"What are you even having? I've never seen–" She stopped. "You didn't *mix* a bunch of different cereals, did you?"

Vincent shrugged. "Tastes good to me."

Sierra stared at him a moment more, then let out a laugh. "You're so weird. I love you, man."

"You what?"

Both of them looked up to see Jake striding towards them, holding his own plate of food. His gaze bored into Vincent, pinning him against his booth. Any semblance of budding camaraderie from their hangouts evaporated in an instant.

"Hey, Jake," Sierra said. Her tone was light, but her body was stiff.

Jake practically dropped his plate onto their table. "What are you two doing here?"

"We're on a hot date at the Commons," Sierra replied. "What does it look like?"

Jake's lip curled. "You could have texted me to come along."

"*Please* don't start this again," Sierra sighed, folding her arms. "I'm allowed to have friends that aren't you, okay?"

"Of course you are," Jake snapped. He turned to glower at Vincent again. "But *this?*"

"This *what?* Spit it out if you're gonna," Sierra urged, growing more irate by the moment. "Am I not allowed to get dinner with a friend? Am I not allowed to have *male* friends? What is it, Jake?"

Jake balled his fists, his whole body tensing as if barely holding himself back. Then he grabbed his plate, scattering a few french fries onto the ground. "Whatever," he hissed, and marched off again.

Silence persisted for a moment before Sierra let her shoulders sag. "Sorry about that," She avoided Vincent's gaze. "He can get...testy, sometimes."

"Didn't notice," Vincent grunted, resuming his progress on his bowl of cereal.

"He's just kind of a jealous guy. He's insecure. I get it. It's just annoying sometimes."

"Uh-huh."

Sierra sighed. "I know what you're thinking."

Vincent quirked a brow at her. "Do you?"

She finally looked at him. "Don't give me that face. He's alright, really."

"I can see that."

"It's not funny." Sierra shoved his arm lightly.

"You're the one putting up with it. Why do you even like him?"

"He's a good guy, really!"

"That's not an answer."

Sierra sighed again, quieter this time. "I know."

"You could do a lot better, you know," Vincent told her, and he meant it. "Did you even like him before he asked you to Melanie's party?"

Sierra shrugged. "Well–yeah, of course I did. I mean, he was cool. We hung out sometimes, with other people. Y'know–sports people, we all end up in the same circles usually. I just figured...well, it was nice to be liked. I didn't know he cared about me so much. It's been really fun dating him, so far." She paused. "Most of the time."

Vincent frowned at her. "Surely a lot of other people like you too."

Sierra studied her fork. "Well...I'm pretty weird. I know it. I don't really get asked out much."

Vincent scoffed. "Come on."

"What? I don't!"

"You just *did.*"

"Well–okay, fine. So...that was the first time."

"You have to be kidding me. Jake's not the only one who would jump at the chance."

Sierra stopped, confused. "What? Who?"

"Seriously? You don't know?"

"Um, obviously?"

A little smirk seeped onto Vincent's face. He slid out of his booth and stood up, taking his empty cereal bowl with him.

"Hey, wait! C'mon, you *gotta* tell me now!" Sierra hurried after him.

"It's not my secret to share," Vincent said smoothly.

"You ass. You can't just tell me something like that and then leave me hanging! You're gonna drive me insane!"

"That sounds like a you problem," said Vincent, depositing his dishes and ducking out the main door into the evening air.

"Bro, I need this, okay?" Sierra pleaded as they walked down the path leading back to the dorms. "This could cure *all* my self-esteem issues!"

"All of them, ah?"

"*All* of them! You know, an ego boost? Remind me I'm not just a weirdo worthless failure?"

"You're putting a lot on me."

"So? You can take it." After a moment, she added, "Okay, I know you're not supposed to like...base your self-worth off what other people think of you. But come *on*. Humans are social by nature! It's in our DNA, man! We *have* to take what other people think into account!"

"So I guess being a weirdo worthless failure isn't working out for you?"

"I mean...it's a lot better here than it was in high school." Some of her desperation faded, as if the memories were slowly replacing it. "Everyone just thought I was a class clown back then, and nothing else. Nobody ever took me seriously outside of basketball."

"You played basketball, too?"

Sierra flashed him a smile. "Helps being tall. I guess it was an easy pick. Plus the glory was nice, too. Another ego booster."

"As if you need it."

"Are you even *listening* to my tales of woe?" Sierra asked, with a note of drama.

Vincent hissed a laugh. "Saddest girl in the world, I'm sure. Being a volleyball *and* basketball star, making everyone laugh..."

Sierra shoved him playfully. "You're so mean! Dude, it's not all it's cracked up to be, okay? It's not like I'm the best player on the team or something. And it actually sucks when all you do is make people laugh. *If* you care."

"Then why do it?"

Sierra's expression sobered. "I don't know. I guess I'd rather get that kind of attention than be nobody. It's nice when people like you, even for small things like that."

Vincent paused, thinking. "Isn't it easier to be nobody, though? You stay out of trouble. Nobody expects anything of you. You can just do whatever you want."

A wry, false smile played across Sierra's lips. "No, you can't. You end up spending your whole life maintaining that nothingness, so no one ever looks at you twice. You can't do *anything*. And then you get lonely. *Really* lonely. Like, soul-crushingly lonely." She cast him a sidelong glance. "Don't you ever get lonely?"

Vincent was silent for a long moment.

"Henry wanted to ask you to the party, too. I guess Jake got to you first."

Sierra blinked in shock. "What? Really? Henry?"

Vincent shot her a little smile that didn't reach his eyes. "So don't think Jake's the only one who will have you."

Presently, Yarrow Hall stood in their sights. Before Sierra could reply, Vincent spotted someone opening the front door and hurried to catch it. Just as he grabbed the handle, he froze–face-to-face with Casey.

"What are you doing here?" she asked, looking just as surprised as he was.

"Just hanging out with Sierra," Vincent said, trying to keep the nervous edge out of his voice.

Casey glanced past him at Sierra with narrowed eyes, just as she caught up with him.

"Hi Casey!" Sierra chirped.

Casey's suspicion was palpable, but she offered Sierra a brief lift of one hand in greeting. "Hey." She looked back at Vincent. "I didn't know you two were so...close."

"We're just friends!" Sierra said, taking her tone the wrong way. "I'm still dating Jake, don't worry. You can have him if you want him."

Vincent and Casey's eyes met, an intense current of dislike passing between them.

"I'm good," Casey said flatly.

Sierra shrugged. "Suit yourself! *I* think he's a catch," she said with a wink. She scooted past Casey towards the open door.

Vincent followed Sierra as swiftly as possible without looking too hurried. It apparently didn't work, at least for Casey; she continued staring after him as he waved her off.

"Casey's a piece of work, isn't she?" Sierra said bluntly as they reached her room. "She always makes me feel like she has it out for me whenever I talk to her. Then again, I guess she's like that with everyone, ha."

"Yeah," said Vincent, leaving it at that.

"She's always cutting class, too. It's a wonder she's scraping by. Still, I hear she's been hanging out with Henry lately, so she can't be all bad."

An almost giddy look suddenly crossed her face. Once the door was shut, she said, "So you mean it? About Henry?"

Something heavy and bitter bubbled up from deep inside Vincent, weighing hot on his chest like molten metal.

"Yeah. He told me."

Sierra immediately flopped down on her bed. Some of her scattered clothes sloughed off onto the floor, but she didn't care. She looked wonderstruck.

"You think–? No...I mean, he's *so* nice, but someone like him could never..."

"If you're already questioning your relationship with Jake, there's definitely no point in staying with him."

Sierra rolled her eyes, but kept her grin. "Okay, okay, we get it, you hate Jake. Man, and I thought you were hanging out with him just fine all those times!"

Vincent grimaced. "Well, it's a lot easier when he's not hounding me about stealing his girlfriend."

Sierra laughed. "Okay, fair. Well, I'll talk to him about that later."

"When you break up with him?"

Sierra shook her head helplessly. She fell silent for a moment. Then: "Look, I'll...I'll think about it, okay? That's good enough, isn't it? It's just— well, I've never broken up with anyone before, and I don't even know if I really want to...or if I want to...with Henry..."

She stopped mid-sentence, burying her face in one of the pillows strewn about her bedspread. She mumbled something unintelligible into it.

Vincent sighed. "Don't say I didn't warn you."

Sierra threw her pillow at him, missing him entirely. He snorted a laugh as it flopped harmlessly onto her rug.

"Really bringing your A-game, miss volleyball star."

"I wasn't even looking!"

The two of them spent another couple hours hanging out, foregoing their initial studying idea entirely. It was late into the evening when Vincent finally left.

But just as he was heading out into the lobby, a shadow leaped out at him from a corner. He jumped—but then he recognized a familiar scowl.

"Just hanging out, huh?" Casey said, her words dripping with venom.

"Don't do that," Vincent growled, avoiding her question. He tried to slip past her for the door, but she stepped in his way.

"What were you doing, Vincent?"

Vincent glared at her, but his heart hammered in his chest.

"I told you already. Let me through."

"You're a god-awful liar, Vincent. Did you actually steal it?"

Vincent had half a mind to pull the old "I don't know what you're talking about" routine, but even the thought of it was horribly lame. He hesitated before he said, "Yeah, alright. I did. What are you going to do, tattle to Henry?"

"Hmm...I might." She looked intensely smug. "Maybe our little boy scout will let me off easy if he's busy dealing with you."

Vincent glowered at her. "You don't know him very well, then."

"You're playing a dangerous game, lapdog."

"Don't call me that," Vincent snapped. "What are you even planning to do, huh? You think it won't just make everything worse?"

Instead of answering, Casey took her time pulling out a pack of gum, selecting the perfect piece, and feeding the strip into her mouth in a series of tiny bites. Vincent watched her, his annoyance growing.

"Well?"

"Make me an offer," Casey said, chewing her gum pointedly.

Vincent's nose wrinkled in the beginnings of a snarl. "Okay. Let's see how this goes—you tell Henry I stole the amulet from Sierra, he loses his shit on me, and we descend into some kind of ridiculous moral argument for the next few weeks instead of getting you and Hunter the potion that will help keep you from turning into monsters and killing *more* people. Is that what you'd prefer?"

Casey's smirk disappeared. "I don't need you losers to help me control my 'monster.' I've been doing it just fine on my own, until that stalker showed up. I think I have a right to defend myself. I'm just lucky I have basically a superweapon on my side. Most girls don't."

"Oh yeah? What would you have done if you did end up killing Hunter?"

Casey stopped chewing for a moment.

"This really will help," Vincent insisted, trying to lose some of his anger for the sake of their alliance. "Once we stop whoever is murdering people, everything can go back to normal for you. You don't even have to help us with our patrols anymore, if you can prove you won't lose control again on the potion."

"I really don't care about the murders, Vincent," she said, heaving a sigh. "I just want to go on with my life. As long as Hunter's off my back, that's all

I care about. Maybe I should tell Henry, he'll lose his shit on you, and this whole stupid supernatural P.I. game of his will end."

"You really don't care at all?" His dislike for her was sprouting more and more with each word out of her mouth.

Casey gave an irate, theatrical shrug. "What do you want me to say? Of course I don't want people to die, but I also don't want to be involved. You get me? You and Henry clearly love being swamped in all this supernatural bullshit. You ever stop to consider that not everyone has a hero complex?"

Vincent did stop, this time–for a moment. "I don't have a hero complex," was all he managed to say back.

"Yes, you do."

"No, I don't."

"Really? Then why are you, a *hellhound*, bothering with these Nancy Drew shenanigans?"

Vincent grimaced. He had one task he knew he should be focusing on. Even now that sixth sense was pacing like a caged animal inside him, frustrated with his lack of progress. Maybe all of this was beyond his original orders...maybe his sympathy was involved more than it should be...but this was part of his duty. It had to be.

And if he was enjoying being in this world in the meantime, what did it matter? When the time came, he knew he would have to return home.

"Yes, I am a hellhound. It's my duty to enact justice against those who would upset the balance of life and death. Whoever is behind all this needs to answer for their crimes. And it's not a job just anyone can do, with Others involved."

"See? Hero complex," said Casey, with a satisfied sneer.

Vincent took a deep breath, trying to compose himself.

"And Henry's even worse than you," she went on. "Traipsing around like he's the new sheriff in town. All he's gonna do is get himself killed, too."

"His family are monster hunters," Vincent shot back. "He was raised to do this exact job."

"That's fine, if being a noble sacrifice makes him feel better. I'm sure he grew up being told he's gilded and bulletproof, just like his daddy. Learning all the secret tricks of the trade no other mortals deserve to know." Casey's smirk melted in less than a heartbeat, leaving a darkness in her face. "But *I* know that even werewolves are mortal. None of that pomp and circumstance matters if you're dead."

She stopped suddenly. Vincent followed her gaze to where two students were approaching the front door. Once they had disappeared down the hall, Vincent turned back to her.

"We shouldn't be talking here. We need to meet Henry for the patrol."

"Sure. I have some juicy gossip to share with him."

Vincent let out a rough sigh. "Please don't tell Henry. Look, I'll owe you, okay? You can figure out what later. But right now you *know* this is the best thing for our situation. And I also think you know Henry isn't going to let you off easy, no matter what you tell him."

Casey was silent. Then she headed for the door. At first Vincent thought she was going to leave on her own, but instead she propped it open for him.

"Well come on, then," she said, blowing a bubble in her gum.

Vincent suppressed another sigh and followed after her.

CHAPTER 12

POSSESSIONS

V incent's small dorm room felt even more cramped with three people in it. Or...four, technically. Percy was looming in his favorite corner, little more than a trick of the light. Henry was looking around the room cluelessly as if expecting to see something. Casey on the other hand stood very still, her gaze trained on that corner of the ceiling.

"So why did you want to meet here instead of the fountain?" Henry asked.

"I have the amulet," said Vincent. He slipped it out of his pocket to show him.

Henry peered closely at it, breaking into a grin. "Nice work, Vinny! How did you convince Sierra to give it to you?"

Vincent saw Casey's eyes flick to him pointedly, but he pretended not to notice.

"Magic," Vincent said, trying to sound lighthearted. It was hard when his stomach was so sour with guilt.

Why should I feel guilty? He's being stupid.

Henry's face tightened in confusion, but he kept his smile. "Man, I guess I should send you to do our P.R. from now on."

Eager to move on, Vincent took a step towards Percy, holding out the amulet. The large turquoise stone looked almost amber in the lamplight, but it was still unmistakable.

"Is—is that him?" Casey said warily.

"You can see him?" Henry asked, appalled.

"Not really. It's like...I can sort of *feel* it."

Vincent nodded. "That's him, alright."

"I wonder if Others can all sense each other..." Henry murmured.

After one more step, Percy's essence shuddered. Its shadow began to twist and grow, and the lamp's glow dimmed. The air turned frigid. The shadow floated closer to the amulet with powerful hunger and sorrow, something everyone in the room felt as if it were their own.

"*Where...did you get this?*" Casey jumped, hearing Percy's false voice for the first time.

"D-don't you remember?" Vincent said, hating the tremor in his voice. He took a moment to steel himself. "We found it underwater, in the caves beneath the Devil's Maw. Do you know how it got there?"

"*She took it from me...*" Percy whispered.

Vincent nodded, drawing in a long breath. "Can you take it?"

A tendril of shadow emerged from Percy's void, grasping at the stone with a longing that hung heavy in the air. His touch felt like dry ice scorching Vincent's fingers. He flinched away—

And then the feeling was gone.

The amulet dropped with a muffled *thunk* against the rug.

"Vincent?" Henry's voice came in alarm.

"Where is he?" Casey hissed.

The lamp's strength had returned. Percy's shadow was nowhere to be seen. But Vincent could still feel his essence nearby...

He looked down at the amulet lying at his feet. Its silver chain curled around the cracked oval pendant at its center, as innocent as any necklace could be. But anyone with even a trace of the supernatural could feel the darkness radiating from its core.

"I...I think he's..."

Vincent bent to pick up the amulet, half expecting it to burn him as Percy's touch had. It didn't. The stone and metal were cold against his palm, but nothing remarkable. He turned it over, examining it closely.

"What happened?" Henry urged.

Vincent realized Henry hadn't been able to see it. "I...think he went *into* the amulet."

"Is he...*gone?*" Casey breathed.

Worry creased Henry's face. "You didn't trap him in there, did you?" He looked hard at Vincent.

"No," he said, even as his heart sank into his stomach. "No, there's no way. It's broken."

But stare as they did, nothing changed. Vincent shook the amulet, but it didn't react.

"I...I didn't–I can't have–" Vincent glanced at Henry desperately.

Henry looked aghast.

"What do we do?" Casey pressed. "Can that actually happen?"

"Of course," said Henry. "Ghosts get trapped in objects all the time. And this one was made for that."

"We could try breaking it again," Vincent suggested, fighting the rising tide of alarm in his chest. "If it released the other spirits last time–"

"We don't know if it did," Henry said. "We could lose him forever if we do that." He shook his head sharply. "We need help *now*."

He suddenly moved for the door.

"Wait! Where–" Vincent hurried after him. "You're not going to Ava, are you?"

"What? You can't!" Casey exclaimed. "What if she's–"

"She's *not*," Henry insisted. "She's not like Melanie."

"You didn't think Melanie was capable of this either," Vincent pointed out. "What if you're wrong?"

"Then that's a risk we'll have to take," Henry said, almost coldly. Vincent felt his heart grip with that familiar guilt as they locked eyes. He wasn't sure if he could bear being on Henry's bad side again. "Percy needs our help. Now."

Vincent didn't stop him this time as Henry yanked open the door and crossed the hall. He knocked on Ava and Melanie's door urgently, but still at a polite volume, in a very Henry way.

No one answered. He knocked again. Vincent and Casey exchanged a glance. Finally, on the third try, the door swung open.

"*What*, dude? I'm trying to watch *Saw Five*," Ava snapped. She looked to be in pajamas, but she had her usual full face of makeup, making her eyes look big and shiny and her face extra pale.

"We need your help," Henry said, for once not bothering with pleasantries.

"What? I'm not your on-call medium! I'm *assuming* that's what this is about—"

"Something's happened to Percy," Henry cut her off. "Just help us, *please*."

"Are you serious? He's dead, what could possibly happen to him?"

Instantly even Ava seemed to know she had said the wrong thing. Vincent couldn't see Henry's expression, but it was plain enough.

She finally stepped out of her room. "Alright, alright. What is it?"

Henry led her into Vincent's room before answering. "You see that amulet? Percy's trapped inside it now."

Vincent held it out for Ava to examine.

"For real? How'd you manage that?"

"I don't know," Vincent replied weakly. "I just had him touch it..."

"It's a special amulet," Henry put in. "It's blessed with ancestral magic. It's meant to guard the wearer."

"It just...kind of sucked him in, as soon as he touched it," Vincent added.

Ava bit her lower lip as she studied it. "I'm sure it hasn't hurt him. It's probably just easy for him to occupy, if it's magic. Have you tried asking him to come out?"

"You can't be serious." Vincent was already growing annoyed at the haughty air she gave off.

"Well, can *you* ask him?" Henry said to her, ignoring Vincent. "You do know how to do a seance, right?"

"Yeah, I told you I can. It's just..."

"She probably needs to wait on her grandmother to give her instructions," Vincent said. Casey snorted a laugh.

Ava chewed her lip for a moment more, looking disconcerted. "I can do a seance by myself. It's not *hard*. You guys have any candles?"

Henry did. Soon they were all settled in a circle on the floor, the room dark but for the flickering glow of four candles in the spaces between each of them, keeping the shadows at bay. The amulet lay on the rug in the center.

"Yes, we do have to hold hands," said Ava flatly.

The candles' heat licked Vincent's arms as he reached out to take Henry's and Casey's hands, equally awkward with each of them for entirely different reasons.

"Now half-close your eyes, and focus on the amulet. The more intention we give it together, the more likely he'll be able to hear us."

Vincent gazed intently at the amulet with his eyes half-lidded. The candlelight glittered on its silver chain and danced on the polished surface of its stone, overwhelming the turquoise with orange.

The longer he stared at it, the more the crack at its center felt *abyssal*. Even from here he could sense that intangible darkness lingering, a relic of its former master's spectral presence. It made the hairs on the back of his neck prickle, just as they did when Percy's gravity became too great.

After a silence that could have lasted hours or mere seconds, Ava spoke again, sounding strangely far away: "Repeat what I say...

"Spirits that linger upon this earth..."

The rest of them echoed the words in a murmur.

"I call upon thee...

"Reach through time, part the curtain...

"Between our bright window and our dark mirror...

"Ye who cling to the shadows we cast...

"Enter us, and speak."

Though the room seemed to buzz with the energy of their chorus and the silence between, nothing else happened. They waited for a long, heavy moment.

"Um...someone pick up the amulet."

196

Vincent reached for it first, breaking the chain of hands. The necklace lay frigid in his palms, held out in front of him like an offering.

"Spirits that linger upon this earth..."

Ava began again, and the others repeated each verse.

As the final word fell, a shock of cold spread through Vincent's hands and down his arms, all the way to his chest. He could feel each individual rib like an icy claw clutching his lungs. But their hunger stretched further, deeper, fixated on his very core–something intangible, but very much caged in the form he now took.

A stab of panic–he knew at once what this presence wanted from him, and every instinct surged against it without a moment's thought. Defiance blazed from somewhere deep inside him, striking the invader with a heat far too intense for it to withstand.

He felt the presence forced out again, back through his arms and into the amulet. Still, it left him shaking.

"Vincent?"

He only now realized the others had been calling his name. He tore himself back to the present.

"I felt him."

Everyone but Ava seemed to read his tone. "Are you okay?" Henry started to ask, but she interrupted him.

"What happened? Did he speak to you?"

"He tried to take over my body."

"Tried?"

"I'm not letting him possess me," Vincent growled.

"It's not *possession*." Ava rolled her eyes. "If he's really trapped in that necklace, he has to speak through another vessel. You need to let him in."

"That sounds like possession to me," said Henry worriedly.

"It's only for a minute! Then he gets forced out again."

"That's some *ouija* shit," said Casey.

"Yeah, Ava...I don't think that's safe," Henry put in. "From what I've learned, any kind of possession is–"

"Oh, give it here," Ava sighed, leaning over to snatch the amulet from Vincent's hands. She held it out like he did, and began speaking the incantation again before realizing no one else was reciting it with her.

"Come *on*. It's perfectly safe. My grandma and I have done it tons of times. And Vincent was able to push him out easy–I will too, when I'm ready."

The other three looked at each other dubiously. Then they shrugged.

"No skin off my back," Casey grunted.

"If you're sure..." said Henry.

"Spirits that linger upon this earth..."

Again they recited the words. This time, though, Vincent kept his eyes fully open to watch.

As soon as the final word came, Ava began convulsing–first only slightly, then violently. Henry was on his feet in an instant, knocking over a candle in his haste. Casey cursed and righted it, stamping out the flaming spot on the rug.

"Is this supposed to happen?" Vincent said, alarmed.

"I don't know!" Henry grasped Ava's shoulders and shook her. "Ava? Ava! Can you hear me? What do we do?"

Suddenly Ava's head snapped upright. She fell still, her body stiff and perfectly straight. She gazed at Henry with something that could only be described as a powerful hunger.

Then she blinked, and a glimmer of light returned to her eyes. She looked around, mouth hanging open as if there was something remarkable about the room.

"Henry?"

"I'm right here," Henry said, quieter this time. He had sensed it just as Vincent had–there was something off about her.

Ava's attention flicked back to Henry, and a broad smile split her face, staying there a moment too long before it reached her eyes. Vincent had never seen her look like that before. It was even more eerie in the flickering candlelight. Its deep shadows found every crease on her face to settle.

"Y-you can hear me! You can see me!"

Henry slowly retreated as if trying to keep a wild animal from pouncing.

Vincent peered closely at her. "Percy...?"

Ava's head snapped around to look at him, and he almost flinched.

"Vincent! I-I'm here, now!" said Ava's voice, but it didn't truly sound like her.

"Percy..." Vincent forced himself to approach so he could look at her squarely. "Were you trapped in that amulet?"

"Amulet...? O-oh, right..." Ava shook her head, thinking hard. "I remember a dark place...was that it...? I could barely feel myself at all..."

"Were there any other spirits in there with you?"

"I-I don't think so..."

Henry and Vincent shared a glance.

"We were right," said Vincent. "They must have been released when the amulet was broken..."

Henry stepped closer to rest a hand on Ava's shoulder. Vincent knew exactly how warm it felt.

"Percy...I...I miss you a lot, you know." Henry's face twisted with grief as he spoke. "I'm so sorry I wasn't there to protect you. If I had known what was out there..."

Ava immediately wrapped her arms around Henry's shoulders. "I-it's okay, Henry. No one could expect you to be everywhere at once!"

"But I promised you," Henry pressed. His eyes began to glisten. "Nothing bad would happen to you here. And I couldn't..." He choked up.

Ava squeezed him tighter. "And that got me through that first week, Henry. And after. I-it really did. It was the best thing I could've asked for. *You* were. I've never had a friend like you before."

A weak smile spread across Henry's face. He finally returned the hug, sinking into it with a deep sigh.

"A-and anyway, I'm back now, so it doesn't matter! Everything's okay again."

Henry's smile melted. He carefully retreated from the embrace.

"Percy...you're not back," he said gently. "You're possessing Ava. You need to leave her body."

"W-what? No," said Percy. "I–I just got back! I don't want to go back in that amulet! I-it was so dark, and quiet, a-and empty...!"

"We're going to find another way to get you out of there, Percy," said Vincent firmly. "I promise." And he meant it–he was almost startled to realize how much of a soft spot he had grown for his dove-hearted roommate.

For a moment, Percy-Ava looked terribly hurt. Then he became quiet.

"Percy...come on..." Henry urged softly.

"I–I can't."

"What do you mean, you can't?"

"I-I'm trying..." Percy said feebly, squirming. "W-what am I supposed to do...?"

"Do you remember how you got in there?" Henry asked.

Percy-Ava screwed up his face in thought. "I...I don't know...it was like a window was just opened, and I could taste fresh air for the first time in s-so long...a-and then it sucked me through, and then I was *here*."

"Can you still feel that window, somewhere?"

"It's–it's *there*, but it's dark. A-and it doesn't have any pull to it...like if I climb out, there's just a wall behind it."

"But I forced you out," Vincent said. "What's so different now?"

"I...I don't *feel* like I'm being forced out..."

Henry and Vincent looked at each other. They moved away, leaning their heads close together.

"What happened when you did it?" Henry whispered.

"I...could feel him, like ice moving through my body," Vincent murmured. "I didn't let him get too far in."

Henry grimaced, glancing back at the possessed Ava. She was moving her hands along her body, feeling each limb, her neck, her stomach, marveling at them as if she had forgotten what they were.

"I wonder why she can't come back from this...I thought she had done this before?"

"Maybe she lied." Vincent shrugged. "You know how she likes boasting about her oh-so-famous grandmother. Maybe she wanted the spotlight for a change."

"Then why has she been dragging her feet about getting us her grandma's help?"

"Like I've been saying...I doubt she even wanted to help in the first place. I bet she just wanted to brag, then get us off her back. I guess at least now we know she's not a vampire..."

Henry frowned, dissatisfied with that answer. "Do you think he's really stuck in her, then?"

Vincent gazed at Ava for a long moment. She was now watching him anxiously. He didn't reply to Henry. Instead, he returned to her.

"Can you feel any part of Ava inside you?"

"Um..." Percy hesitated, thinking hard. "It's...I don't know. A little glow inside. Like a candle, almost. I-it doesn't feel like me."

Vincent nodded. "She must be too weak to fight back," he said to Henry.

"But she's still there. I'm sure we can figure out how to get her back..."

An idea flickered across Vincent's mind. "You seem much clearer now, Percy. Do you remember what happened the night you died?"

Percy looked alarmed. "Um..."

Henry nudged Vincent. "Don't say it like *that*..."

Percy seemed to recover, though, and shook his head sadly. "I...I do feel a lot better...I can remember a lot about being alive now, but...that part...it's all just k-kind of a blur..."

"Most people don't remember how they died," Henry said, his voice thick with sympathy. "It's too traumatic."

Vincent fought back a sigh. "Worth a try...what about that potion I mentioned? Do you think you could help us make it?"

"O-oh! I can try–"

"Hold on–you're not telling me you're gonna *leave* him in there, are you?" Casey interrupted. Vincent had almost forgotten she was there–she was hovering at the edge of the room, looking uncharacteristically timid.

"Of course not," said Henry.

"We just need to make that potion," Vincent told her. "After that, we'll focus on getting him out of her."

Casey stared at him as if he had just kicked a baby. "Are you out of your minds? You're just going to use her body like a fuckin' meatbag?"

"It should be fast," Henry said, although he sounded uncertain. "And he's not gonna hurt her or do anything weird. I know him. He's a very sweet guy..."

Casey threw up her hands. "Oh, right, just like Hunter is *so completely* harmless! I forgot!"

"You just don't want to take the damn potion," Vincent growled. "That's what this is about."

Casey scowled at him. "Of course I fucking don't. I've made that pretty goddamn clear. But this isn't about that! You're not even listening, *again*–"

"You want us to make sure Hunter is under control, right?" Henry broke in.

Casey opened her mouth to argue, but seemed to realize his point. "Fine. But while you're doing that, I'm not gonna just sit around with my thumb up my ass."

She lunged for Ava and plunged her hand into her pocket.

"H-hey! What're you doing?" Percy stammered. But Casey already had Ava's phone in her grasp.

"What's the password?" Casey demanded.

"Casey, give it back," Henry said, sounding exhausted.

"No. I need it for something. Tell me the password," Casey said again, glowering at Percy.

"I-I don't know it," Percy said, but his tone didn't convince anybody.

"Yes, you do. You're in her head," Casey growled. She advanced on Percy, fists raised. He cowered.

Both Henry and Vincent started towards her. "Casey, don't–"

"Okay, okay! It's '6669'!"

Henry and Vincent halted, bewildered. Casey immediately relaxed, returning her attention to the phone.

"Ha ha. And she thinks she's better than us...there we go." She began tapping on the screen. Vincent slunk over to look over her shoulder. She noticed a moment too late, snatching it out of his line of sight with a glare.

"Why are you pretending to be Ava?" he asked.

"What?" said Henry with concern.

Casey stopped and made a theatrical shrug. "You said her grandma's some crazy smart witch, right? You don't think she could help us out here?"

Henry thought for a moment. "Yeah, but...you don't have to lie to her, do you?"

"If the poor woman knows we got her granddaughter *possessed*, do you think she'll just sit down and shut up about it?"

"I guess you're right," Henry said gloomily. "But I don't like it."

"Yeah. Of course you don't." Casey went back to typing. "Alright, there it goes. Satisfied?"

"It might take a few days to get a response," Henry warned. "We never did get our answer last time..."

The phone buzzed in Casey's hand. Everyone looked at it in surprise.

Casey swiped on the screen and broke into a wry grin. "Guess who."

"Are you serious?" said Henry in dismay.

"Yyyyep." Casey showed him. He let out a low groan.

"I guess you were right, Vincent," he said. "Ava didn't even ask..."

Vincent grimaced, but couldn't bring himself to gloat. "Are you sure you want to bring her back?"

"Oh, come on, Vincent–"

"Kidding."

Henry sighed again and said, "Well...at least we have an answer now. But...it's not gonna be pretty."

"What? What is it?" Vincent craned his neck to try and see the screen. Casey held it away from him deliberately with a smirk.

"Magdalena says we need to use Percy's real body as a temporary vessel," Henry answered. "He's too...um...*weak*...to manifest on his own properly."

Vincent and Percy both stared at him. "Wait...does that mean we...?"

Henry nodded solemnly.

"You know where it is?"

"Yeah. I was there."

"I-I don't wanna see it..." Percy said shakily. He looked on the verge of tears. "I-I don't wanna know w-what it looks like now..."

"I'm sorry, Percy," Henry said gently. "But this is the only way."

"Let's get going, then," Casey said, clearly the only one enjoying the idea.

"Percy has to show me how to make the potion first," said Henry. "We'll have to go extra late at night...I hope they don't post a guard..."

"Well, then I'll run distraction," Casey said, far too brightly.

"This is serious," Henry said before Vincent could do more than open his mouth to rebuke her. "This is a *federal crime*. If we get caught..." He broke off, shaking his head. "Let's just not get caught."

CHAPTER 13

THE WALKING DEAD

Miles away from the college, glass doors slid open on their own, welcoming a visitor with forbidding white light. Everything in places like this was always far too clean, far too blank, like a dream with its details muted by the limitations of the unconscious.

But the acrid sting of chemicals in the air reminded the visitor that he was very much awake. He approached the front desk that rose before him like a proving ground.

The attendant lifted her eyes from her computer to offer him a momentary smile in greeting. The young man that stood across from her returned only a ghost of it, flitting across his freckled, gaunt face like a shadow.

"Good afternoon. Are you here to visit someone?"

"Yes."

"The patient's name?" she asked, sliding a sign-in sheet across the countertop towards him.

"Hunter Mallory."

When he had written his own name on the form, she took it back and looked at her computer. "Alright, let's see...he's in Room 108."

"Thank you." The visitor offered one last polite nod before starting down the fluorescent hallway.

He found the door and slipped inside. The room was thankfully half-lit, providing some respite. The closest of the two beds was empty, but he could see foot-shaped lumps in the blankets on the bed nearest the window.

The patient's eyes fluttered open when the visitor passed the curtain between the two sections.

"Hello, Hunter."

"Uh...hi." Hunter looked the visitor up and down. "Who are you?"

The visitor offered that same specter of a smile, lowering himself into the chair beneath the window. His blue eyes remained as cold as a winter sky.

"My name is Benjamin."

Hunter stared at him just as blankly as before. "Okay? I still don't know you. Why are you here?"

Benjamin's smile turned more genuine–this time from amusement. "Not feeling too well, I take it?"

Hunter scowled as best he could under the bandages that littered his face. "What do *you* think?"

Benjamin ignored his attitude. He turned his gaze downwards, examining a loose piece of the teal faux leather that upholstered the chair he sat in. He could see the memory foam just beneath.

"Do you remember what happened to you?" he asked, as casually as if he were asking a friend about what happened on a date.

"Most of it." Hunter narrowed his eyes at his visitor, who was now fingering the tear in the upholstery. "What's it to you?"

Benjamin did not look up. "Well? What happened?"

Hunter hesitated. "I was attacked by a wild animal," he finally answered, with obvious disdain.

"But that's just the headline, isn't it?" It didn't sound like a question.

"Headline?" Hunter was growing more annoyed with his visitor's mannerisms by the moment. "Look–they didn't believe me when I told 'em what I *actually* saw. You wouldn't, either. So what's the point? Why are you even here, pestering me about it? Did they, like, send you in as some kind of undercover shrink? Huh? You think I'm crazy?"

Benjamin began pulling at the flap of upholstery, angling it to slowly tear the edge. "Not at all," he said calmly.

"Liar!" Hunter snarled. "Stop taunting me! I know why you're here!"

With a tug the piece came off, leaving a gaping hole filled with foam. Benjamin's cold eyes returned to Hunter.

"I'm here because I was there that night. I know what happened to you."

Hunter stared at him, his brain trying to catch up. "Then–then you saw–"

"Say it. Tell me what happened."

"I-it was...it was a werewolf! I met it in the woods, and it turned on me and started ripping me up–and then Henry Wellfellow and that weirdo he hangs around showed up, a-and then *he* turned into a werewolf–"

Benjamin's face grew stony. "Who have you been telling that, Hunter?"

"Well–whoever asked, really! But none of 'em believed me, until you! I keep telling them, Casey Helliker is gonna come af–"

Benjamin suddenly stood, so sharply that Hunter was startled into silence. He grabbed the curtain separating their part of the room and flung it closed. Grasping the bed's guard railing with both hands, he leaned over Hunter with a dark intensity that spooked even him.

"First of all, stop telling them that. They won't believe you anyway."

Before Hunter could do more than draw a breath, Benjamin went on:

"You're extraordinarily lucky, Hunter. Do you know that? You made it out alive. That's a low statistic, when it comes to werewolves. Especially if you piss them off."

"Yeah, I guess..."

"But you must know what that means for you, now."

"Uh..."

Benjamin's eyes flashed. "You're a werewolf, too."

Hunter's mouth hung open, and his eyes grew wide. But Benjamin could tell that under his bravado, he had guessed already. This was the last thing he wanted to hear.

"No," he said, gripping his bedsheets in his fists. "No, I'm not. I can't be."

"You are."

"*No*," Hunter insisted. "How come they've been hiding all this time, then, huh? How come nobody knows about 'em?"

"You saw for yourself," Benjamin said. "You can't seriously try to deny it now. What could possibly explain it otherwise?"

"...Brain trauma." Hunter crossed his arms as if the matter was settled.

Benjamin shook his head slowly. "Don't insult yourself, Hunter. You know what you saw."

With a long, beleaguered sigh, he returned to his mutilated chair and leaned back in it. "They've hidden it well. They've had a long time to get it right. You know they have people for that? A whole organization dedicated to sweeping things under the rug. Multiple, in fact. And even then, they can't escape their own legends."

Hunter was gazing at him now with mounting dread. "Are you saying everything–all that stuff about werewolves..."

He couldn't seem to finish his sentence. Benjamin didn't need him to.

"I'm sure some details differ," Benjamin answered. "But much of it is true, yes. And not just for werewolves." His eyes gleamed like frost. "*So* much more."

Hunter, on the other hand, was horrified. "What–like–like zombies and ghosts and..."

"And countless others. Like it or not, you're one of them now."

Hunter was pale and silent now as it all began to sink in. "W...what's gonna happen to me? Am I gonna turn into...into that *thing*?"

"Around the full moon, yes, I expect," Benjamin said, with an affected note of sympathy. "You have a while still, fortunately. Plenty of time for you to heal and leave this place before you turn. I think you'll find your recovery won't be as laborious as it would have been, were you still human."

Hunter bristled. "I *am* still human!"

Benjamin gave him a withering look of pity.

"W-what am I supposed to do, then?" Hunter's voice began to rise in desperation. "Run away to live in the woods? Won't someone catch me? What if–" He stopped mid-thought. "Casey Helliker. *She* did this to me. Can't I turn her in to these–whoever they are, the ones sweeping things under the rug? Or maybe if *I* killed her, the curse would break on me–"

"That isn't how it works," Benjamin said. "You're stuck with it, now, I'm afraid. And it's better not to alert any authorities. They'll take you down with her. From what I've heard, they aren't fond of liabilities."

Hunter looked even more hopeless than before. "Well then *what*? What do I do?" He seemed to realize something, and his eyes narrowed at Benjamin. "Wait–how do *you* know–?"

"I can help you. I'll look out for you when you change, prepare you for it. I'll make sure no one finds out about you. You *can* manage it–all you need is a bit of guidance."

"Why? What's in it for you? I don't even *know* you."

"I may not be a werewolf, but I am like you, in a lot of ways." Benjamin smiled ever so slightly. "You have to understand...once you step into the shadows, they consume you. There is no way back. Even if you were to step back into the light...you would only bring the darkness with you."

"What are you even talking about? Quit the metaphors and answer the damn question!"

Benjamin's pity lingered, but hardened. "Let's put it this way. I feel for you. From the point of no return we've both found...we're now marked, in a way. We're different, forever. If we don't hide what we truly are, we'll be hunted. From the moment we crossed over into this place of shadows, we were damned. For the rest of our lives and beyond, we *will* be punished for these things that were out of our control."

He sighed, turning over the piece of torn upholstery in his hand. "Of course, if you like, you can waste your time bargaining for a normal you'll never see again...but you will find, sooner or later, that I'm right."

He suddenly leaned in closer again, fixing Hunter with that cold, solemn gaze, as if the balance of everything rested on his shoulders.

"So right now, I'm offering you my hand. I'd rather help you up now than watch you struggle and writhe like I did."

Hunter held his gaze in spite of the apprehension that shivered through his mangled body, the instincts that had frayed into a tangle of desperation and outrage and fear. He didn't know what was going on anymore–and Benjamin knew it.

Just as he said he would, Benjamin reached out a hand. "Let me help you get back on your feet, Hunter."

The sun had set by the time Benjamin slipped out the hospital doors. He suppressed a shiver; summer had finally relinquished its grip on the night air. He glanced up and down the empty street before retrieving his bike from the nearby rack, each clink of metal sounding far too loud in the hush.

As he rode towards home, he cast every sense out into the darkness closing in around him. It was broken only by the ill yellow light of passing streetlamps. They provided no comfort. All they did was give him the slightest chance to glimpse whatever laid in wait.

But tonight, nothing did. Instead, as he neared the college, the darkness was split by blinding white lights on the horizon. They seemed to pick him out from a distance, like predators spotting their next chase.

As Benjamin approached, he began to make out the shadows of the stands at the edge of the university football field, shielded by a chain-link fence. He trundled along the path at its side, making for campus proper—but something made him stop.

He hardly expected *him* to be here, of all places. But there he was, unmistakable even from this distance, wedged in the stands between two of the people he seemed to hang around lately. One of them, a tall girl with dark features, was on her feet, shouting encouragement to one of the players down below. The other companion, pale and dark-haired, kept her seat but seemed to be enjoying herself as well, apart from looking around every so often as if she wasn't sure she should be there.

And *him?* He was smiling. His eyes were glued to that boy on the field, the one everyone seemed to like. Number "1." The football star.

He had *friends.* Another unexpected turn of events.

His tall friend grabbed his arm, pointing excitedly down below. Number "1" was sprinting down the field, shoving and dodging past anyone unfortunate or foolhardy enough to get in his path. But even he wasn't invincible—a wall of opponents cut him off, and he hurled the football over their heads. But his only teammate in range, number "2," was blocked off by a circle of sturdy defenders–there was no way he was going to be able to catch it.

Benjamin blinked, and suddenly he was watching a different game entirely. All four of the defenders were on the ground, and number "2" was pelting across the last quarter of the field, almost too fast to follow. The crowd swelled into a roar as he slammed the football into the turf at the end zone. They seemed just as shocked as Benjamin was, but they didn't care. Looking at the scoreboard, he saw the game had only just started, and the home team was already way ahead.

Curious, he stayed and watched for a while, leaning against the nearest pole supporting the chain-link fence. It was plain to see the visiting team was in way over their heads. Number "1" was as much of a star as he was known for–but this game, number "2" was pulling far ahead of him. After the third touchdown in twenty minutes, the crowd's uproar coalesced into a single chant:

"JAKE! JAKE! JAKE!"

Benjamin's eyes narrowed.

After the game, people began filing out of the stands, chattering excitedly to one another. Benjamin scanned the crowd until he found who he was searching for. The wolf in sheep's clothing was walking with those friends of his.

But then, someone else came up to him. He stopped, his friends slowing to wait for him. Even from here, Benjamin could tell he wasn't happy about it.

After a moment, Vincent walked away with his visitor, leaving his companions to go on without him. They were approaching Benjamin's vantage point, but nothing in Vincent's face suggested he had sensed his presence. Benjamin decided to hide behind the stands, leaving his bike where it stood.

Their footsteps stopped just around the corner. Their voices, although hushed, reached him clearly.

"What do you want?" That was Vincent, as annoyed as Benjamin had guessed.

"We haven't gotten together in so long." Melanie King's voice was honeyed, as usual, a perfect mix of cute and sultry that would have enchanted any ordinary man. "I was hoping you would take me out for dinner. Let's say this Friday?"

Vincent's pause felt like gravel against Benjamin's ears.

"I'm busy Friday. I have a lot of homework to catch up on."

"Really? Again? But you're always around." Melanie's words were incisive, but her tone remained demure. "Maybe Saturday, then?"

"No good either."

"Then when is?"

Vincent growled a sigh.

"Look...I'm sorry, but I don't want to date you."

"What?" Melanie sounded genuinely surprised–even hurt.

How peculiar, for her... Benjamin thought.

"I'm sorry," Vincent said again, gruffly. He seemed at a loss.

"You're joking. Everyone wants to date me," Melanie said with a scoff.

An awkward silence took over.

"Is it because you're gay? That's it, isn't it? I've seen the way you look at Henry. Y'know, I can still give you perks. I mean, I'm me, after all. You'd be crazy to say no to–"

"No, I'm not–I just don't want–"

"You're *not* gay?"

"I'm not *anything*, I–I don't care about that." Benjamin heard a shuffling of feet in the dirt. "Look, I have to go. I'll–"

A sharper scuffle came now, along with a sharp, shocked exhale.

"You haven't forgotten our little secret, have you, Vincent?"

Another growl, softer this time.

"Which one." It didn't sound like a question.

A quiet, mirthless laugh. "Does it matter? You know what I'll do if you cross me."

"And this is why I don't want to date you."

A dangerous silence followed.

"No one says no to Melanie King."

"I just did."

"Fine—then let me spell this out for you, Vincent. If you do this, I'm going to ruin you. Completely. If your little Commons brawl doesn't get you expelled, that girl's murder will. Do you know how long people go to prison for in America, for murder?"

"I didn't murder her." Vincent sounded indignant.

"Twenty-five years if you're lucky. Zero if you're not. The police always love a scapegoat. And wouldn't it fit just perfectly, an edgy guy like you threatening a poor, innocent damsel like me to keep my mouth shut?"

For a long moment, nothing stirred. Then:

"No."

"No? Wait—"

More shuffling, abruptly cut off.

"Get off me. I'm not playing your games anymore, Melanie. I know what you did to Percy."

That stopped her. It took a good long moment before she found her voice again.

"I didn't do anything to Percy Quailheart. What are you saying? That I killed him? Didn't you hear it was a wild animal attack?"

"Oh, stop it. I know you know what's actually going on."

"And what would that be, hmm?" Melanie was trying to sound collected, but Benjamin caught a fearful edge to her tone. He was sure Vincent had as well.

"You're in league with Benjamin Warwick. You helped him murder Percy, and Mira Walker too. I remember seeing Benjamin at your party that night. You tried to play it off, but I didn't forget. And I won't forget about this, either."

Melanie was silent. Benjamin only wished he could see her face.

You've changed, haven't you, Vincent?

"You were so insistent about moving Mira's body, covering it all up. It was pretty well-played, I admit. With so many witnesses, even if it got out, it would be hard to pin on anyone. Better though to keep it quiet as long as possible. What do you think would happen if I got your police involved? Do you think they'd be able to find traces, if I point them in the right direction? Do you think Benjamin is stupid enough not to make sure you take the fall for him?"

Benjamin smiled. *You still know me so well.*

"You're bluffing," she said icily. "You don't think I'd expose you for what you really are?"

Vincent was quiet for a long moment. "So you know, then," he said, his voice dangerously low.

"Of course I do," Melanie sniffed. "I know everything about everyone."

"How? Are you some kind of psychic?" Vincent didn't sound sarcastic. He was genuinely trying to decipher something about her. For a moment Benjamin considered intervening...but he didn't. His curiosity got the better of him.

Melanie snorted. "I don't need to be. People tell me whatever I want to know."

"Except for me." A silence heavy with thought; then: "Your scent is fainter today. Did you forget to put it on?"

"Oh, my perfume?" The slightest anxious note in her haughty voice. "Must have. Do you like it that much?"

"It didn't make any sense to me, before," said Vincent, ignoring her words. His tone was suddenly dark, slithering. "Your scent is so clean. Nothing but coconut. But now, I can tell. There *is* nothing."

"I–I don't know what you mean. Stop being weird, Vincent."

"I always wondered how you got people to like you so easily. You've never seemed that likable to me. But now I think I know why. It isn't natural."

"That I'm so amazing? Are you that jealous?"

"Stop playing games," Vincent growled. "I know what you are. And you know what I am. There's too much at stake for both of us, and you know that. Neither of us are going to blow this up without everyone getting caught up in it."

Melanie was silent. Then she let out a sharp *tch*. "Then what are we gonna do, hmm?"

"*You're* going to leave me alone."

Benjamin could practically taste Melanie's anger rising. "You–"

"Call her off, Benjamin."

Benjamin started. For a while he said nothing, his thoughts turning carefully.

Then he stood. He stepped around the corner of the stands, facing them in the gloom.

"You're sharp," he said. "I wonder how you..."

"You're easy to find."

Benjamin's lip curled. "Then why not take me now?" He spread his arms wide, an invitation.

Vincent's dark eyes burned. "Because the moment I move, your vampires will tear me apart."

He angled his head towards the trees beyond the football field. A dozen eyes gleamed in the darkness.

"I'd rather avoid the spectacle," Benjamin said smoothly. He could still hear the last murmurings of students leaving the stands. "I guess you worked out what I am now."

Vincent set his jaw. "Clever trick. A way to get your body back, after death. How did you do it? You should have been nothing more than a ghost, when you emerged..."

Benjamin shrugged. "I found a friend."

Vincent's eyes slid to Melanie. Assuming. "Did you really think Melanie would be able to distract me from hunting you?"

"Not really. But it was worth a shot. She really took a shine to beguiling humans, after all."

"Why are you turning so many, then? Are they just your glorified bodyguards? Isn't that a lot of feeding competition?"

Benjamin waved one hand dismissively. He was growing tired of this game. "You're not getting anything useful out of me, and I think you know that. Move along, would you? We're not doing this here."

"Not until you call her off," Vincent insisted, jabbing a hand at Melanie.

"I'm not a dog," Melanie hissed.

"What, don't like dogs? Then why do you like me so much?"

Melanie suddenly let out a shrill, venomous laugh.

"You actually thought I *liked* you? Please! I was just doing my job. Who on earth would want to date someone as weird as you? Even looking like that, everyone can tell there's something wrong with you." Vincent flinched. Maybe he wasn't so different after all. "Why would I want to hitch myself to that? You should've just shut up and taken the chance while you had it."

She turned her back on him, stalking off in the direction of the trees and their skulking guardians. It was supposed to be a final word, but it hung hollow in the air.

Vincent and Benjamin shared one last foreboding look before Benjamin too turned, following her into the forest. There was nothing more to say now.

Whispers filled the air, drowning the rustling of leaves in the night winds. Benjamin ignored them all, striding past those dark, searching eyes as he chased after Melanie. Despite her wrath, she finally slowed to let him catch up, her fists balled at her sides.

"*Don't* fuck with me right now."

"I'm sorry," Benjamin said, keeping his voice even. She cast him a murderous glance, but let him speak. "I did tell you it wasn't worth it to keep him close."

"It would've been a smart move, jackass," Melanie spat, her beautiful hair whipping as she turned to march off again through the trees. Benjamin kept pace with her, consciously dialing down his smugness until he felt suitably sympathetic.

"He's charming, isn't he?"

Melanie didn't answer, but looked even more mutinous.

"I know the feeling," Benjamin sighed. "There's just something about him. Fresh-faced, but so haunted. He...believes in people. He pretends not to, but he does. If you hit the right notes, it's easy to win him over. He'll look at you like you hung the moon in the sky." He offered her a look of remorse. "I just...think you got there a bit too late, I'm afraid."

Melanie rounded on him. "You don't get it, do you? He should have been *mine*. I don't *care* who or what he is, I wanted him."

"Even those fancy new powers of yours can't snag everyone's favor. People are more complicated than that."

"You promised me, when you had me do that stupid ritual," Melanie hissed. "And it's worked so far! Everyone I've tried to win over fucking *adores* me."

"Are you sure about that?"

Melanie's eyes narrowed. "You *promised* me."

Benjamin shook his head. "I didn't promise you it would work flawlessly. I told you the glamor would help you turn your reputation around. People would be more forgiving. You would feel alluring. That doesn't mean everyone wants to worship at your feet. I'd imagine they just want you to like them, to varying degrees. There's no *true* quick-fix for social status."

"I've earned everything I have!" Melanie snarled back. "I make these powers work for *me*. No other vampire wields the glamor like I do. I have it all—and I almost had him, too. But you just *had* to be lurking around out there, didn't you? You can't pass up gloating for a *second*, can you, Benjy?"

Benjamin's expression hardened. "You know you can't blame me for this," he said quietly. "He was never going to be yours, no matter what you did. You're not his type. He's not as impressionable as you might think." *Not anymore.*

"Just because you break all your toys doesn't mean I do," Melanie snapped.

Before she could pull ahead, Benjamin reached out and laid a cold hand on her delicate shoulder. She tried to yank it away from him, but he held firm. She hadn't put her full strength into it. Her wide hazel eyes met his, and it was the closest he had ever seen her to breaking. Maybe the closest anyone had.

"Why?" she asked, her voice cracking. She didn't have to explain what she meant.

Benjamin let his face soften. "Because people aren't toys, Melanie. Each one of us is unique. Sometimes there's nothing we can do to change what we are."

"Well, *I'm* Melanie King, god damn it!" Melanie bared her teeth, her once-beautiful features looking nearly as feral as Vincent's. "And that means I get the *world*."

Benjamin's heart panged in true sympathy. "Then you have to win it. You may not get exactly what you want...but you can still get what you need."

"I *need* what I *want*," Melanie said through gritted teeth. "Stop being cryptic."

"Don't forget why we're doing this," Benjamin pressed. "I did promise you, and I meant it. It's already begun, hasn't it? People admire you now. You're important to them. And even after graduation, you won't have to start over again. You'll know exactly where you belong in the world *we* make. No one will ever forget your name."

He could practically see the progress of his words through her heart. She lifted a slender hand to brush the tears from her eyes, her chin held high. The darkness in her face deepened.

"You're right, Benjy. I'll get what I need. I need Vincent to fall."

CHAPTER 14

GRAVE SIGHTS

The next few days passed by uneventfully, much to Casey's annoyance. Although Henry's friend had come through with the chemistry supplies, the ingredients for the potion needed to be ordered online. It was lucky the moon had been full only days before Casey had attacked Hunter—they needed all the time they could get.

Despite Vincent's general reluctance, he did share what he had confirmed with the others: Melanie was a vampire. Even if she didn't admit it, it was obvious to him. It made too much sense—that one-note scent, her uncanny beauty, her strange influence over others. But even so, there wasn't much they could do about it, short of reporting her to the Shadowhand.

"We'll just have to be extra careful," said Henry. "Until we know her plans. There has to be a reason she's doing this. Some way to convince her to stop."

There has to be a reason Benjamin *is doing this,* Vincent corrected silently. But Henry's diplomacy suited him just fine. It gave him more time to figure out his own side of things. He kept careful attention on his sixth sense, just in case Benjamin made a move—especially at night. But he seemed as cautious as always, never leaving himself vulnerable. Again and again, Vincent wondered if he could be doing more to corner him; and each time he thought of those vampires, or night patrols keeping him busy, or needing sleep so he didn't fail his classes and blow his cover.

He didn't think about how much he loved the fresh scents the wind brought, or the chirp of crickets and the rustle of trees in the night, or the comfort of warm food and soft blankets in his quiet little room. He didn't think about Sierra's jokes, or Percy's kindness, or Casey's snark, or Henry's smile.

Or, at least, he tried not to. Because it was *selfish*, and *treacherous*, and *greedy*.

In the meantime, college life trudged on. Vincent encountered his first written assignment, which was nothing to sneeze at–ten pages on the moral quandaries depicted in John Milton's *Paradise Lost*. As much fun as he had been having with the text, synthesizing it in writing was another matter entirely. On top of that, midterms were approaching fast. He was grateful to have his room to himself at last, after Percy was forced to move into Ava's room.

At first Percy's struggle maintaining Ava's life was apparent. The first couple days, Ava's makeup looked like an attempt to join a circus. After one too many suspicious (and rather cruel) comments from Melanie, Percy abandoned his efforts and decided to play it safe with no makeup at all. This was almost as big a change for Ava, and more than once Vincent heard whispers about it from other students in passing. He had no idea what the words "manic pixie dream girl" meant, but he gathered that they thought she was moving to some new phase in adolescent self-discovery.

However, by the end of the first week, Percy appeared to be managing Ava's life better than she had–sleeping during normal hours, keeping her class schedule, and finishing her assignments. Psychology seemed to agree with him. Whenever he and Henry visited, he told them how much easier this coursework was than his old major. While no one who knew the truth was happy about the situation, Henry and Vincent at least appreciated the irony of Percy's success.

Casey did not find this amusing. She seized every opportunity to remind them how long it had been since Percy had taken over, and how long they had left before the full moon returned.

Unfortunately for them, she had plenty of opportunities. They maintained their nightly patrols, and despite Casey's reputation for ditching classes, she showed up every time. They even added a drive-by hospital check every couple days just to make sure everything stayed quiet.

The brightest spot in Vincent's new routine was Henry's return. Being on the same page about their mission seemed to smooth over whatever uncertainties lingered between them. Between that and the vacancies in their usual friend group, they ended up spending much of their free time together.

"It's funny, I never really found anyone else around here who likes these kinds of games," Henry told him one night as they played an old video game from a series called *Star Wars*. "I guess that's what I get for being on the football team."

Vincent bit his lip as he mashed a button, feverishly swinging his character's lightsaber into an enemy. "Who wouldn't like them? I can't imagine the average human goes on many epic quests."

"No. But I guess not everyone wants to. They fill their time with other things." Henry laughed. "You'd think *we'd* want a break, too, but here we are."

Vincent thought for a moment. "It's nice to do important things without risking our lives for once. Even if they aren't real."

"Hah. Maybe so. Maybe we're just insatiable."

"Casey calls it a hero complex."

Henry grinned. "That sounds like her. Well, I don't think being a hero is a bad thing."

A smile darted across Vincent's face. "Neither do I."

Of course, Vincent wasn't Henry's only frequent companion. One Sunday morning, Vincent had just emerged from his room in search of breakfast when the back door opened, followed by a shout of his name. He turned to see Henry ducking inside, brandishing a package with Sierra at his heels. Both of them were dressed in damp workout clothes.

The sight of them together made Vincent's heart stop for a moment–had she mentioned the missing amulet? The only thing that assuaged him was the obvious delight on Henry's face, and he tried to act normal.

"Guess what's here!" Henry greeted him.

"Yeah, what is it?" Sierra said, with a sharp glance at Henry. "Henry won't tell me!"

"That's because it's a secret," Henry said. He winked at Vincent, who was preoccupied thinking of other secrets at the moment.

"Come onnn, what's the big deal? It isn't a birthday present for me, is it?" Sierra badgered.

"Put it out of your mind," Henry said, holding it out of her reach as if he thought she would make a grab for it. She groaned.

"Sorry, Sierra," Vincent told her, with a fake glare at Henry. "I didn't realize I was going to be lying to you." After a moment, he added, "I ah...didn't know you two were workout buddies."

"Oh, yeah!" said Henry and Sierra, both at the same time. They awkwardly broke off and shared a cute laugh before Sierra continued brightly, "Yeah, we have been for a little while! We both have to train anyway, so why not do it together?"

Vincent's stomach churned. "That's nice," he said, failing to keep the discomfort from his voice. Fortunately, neither of them seemed to notice.

"We should start going every morning at this rate," Henry added with a chuckle. "I have to keep up with Jake somehow. You sure he won't share his workout routine?"

"Nope, I tried," Sierra said. "I still can't believe how many touchdowns he scored last game! But I haven't even seen him training in a while, so I couldn't tell you."

"Well, worth a shot. Hey, I'm happy for him—whatever he's doing, it's definitely working." Henry turned his smile back to Vincent. "Are you coming to Sierra's game this afternoon?"

"I didn't know there was one."

"Oh, I um...I just didn't think you'd be interested." Sierra rubbed her arm awkwardly. "I know you don't like sports much."

"I want to see you play," Vincent insisted, glaring at her. He didn't know the first thing about volleyball, but he could tell just how much it meant to Sierra. "You should have told me! Have there been other games?"

"Well, yeah...they're just not as big a deal as football, y'know?"

"Why wouldn't they be?"

Sierra grimaced sheepishly. "I dunno. They just aren't."

"Well, that's bullshit. Invite me next time."

Sierra's expression eased. "Okay. Well, here's your formal invitation, then! Today at four."

It took a moment before Vincent noticed Henry's gaze on him. He was startled to find it so intensely warm, almost tender. As soon as he met his eyes, Henry looked away again swiftly, although his smile remained.

"We'll come together. You'd better kick some ass today, for Vincent's sake!"

Vincent only hoped it would be more interesting than football. But Sierra's smile was worth it, either way.

And Henry's.

Once Sierra had gone, Vincent turned back to Henry, who had tucked the package under his arm. "Are those the potion supplies?"

"Yep! We'll have to get it going tonight. I'll text everyone to meet in my room after the game."

Vincent nodded. "See you at four."

When Henry had gone, the warmth in Vincent's chest faded back into apprehension. With all that regular time together, would Sierra tell Henry the amulet was missing? Had she even noticed? Henry didn't *look* suspicious of Vincent. Even the memory of that smile set his nerves ablaze again.

But then, maybe he was putting on the best show of his life to hide it. It was difficult to tell, with Henry. He wore his heart on his sleeve so much, it had to be impossible...but maybe it was just that easy to hide, since everyone took him at face value.

Vincent forced himself to relax. If Henry really had been working out with Sierra for a while, surely he would have mentioned the amulet by now. She couldn't have told him.

Near four o'clock he met up with Henry, and together they made their way to the gymnasium. It was nowhere near as packed as football games, just as Sierra had said. Vincent couldn't understand why. As they settled down near the front of the stands to watch, he became immediately gripped by the action.

It was almost comically easy to follow compared to football. He marveled as the players dove after the ball with both a ravenous fervor and precise grace. The two teams worked nearly perfectly in sync with each other, each moving more like one organism than separate people. Just like with football, points scored and impressive maneuvers were met with rousing cheers.

Without the bulky uniforms and helmets it was easy to pick out Sierra. She was one of the tallest players, and loudest. Even from the stands Vincent could hear her shouting encouragement at her teammates, and even the occasional taunt at their opponents. She was smiling the whole time. It was clear she was having the time of her life out there.

Once or twice between plays she picked Vincent and Henry out of the crowd, beaming at them. They grinned back at her, clapping fervently. When Vincent looked, he found Henry's face more radiant than anything he had seen yet.

Despite the lightness in his heart, something colder crept in. Suddenly he felt far away from the people all around him.

Finally the last serve was made. After a long, tense round, Sierra spiked the ball so hard that nothing and no one could save it. The gymnasium erupted into a roar of triumph, so passionate that Vincent had to cringe against it to keep the echo from deafening him.

He watched as the crowd surged into the court, the players disappearing in the tumult. He and Henry stayed in their seats, knowing better than to try fighting their way through the throng to find Sierra. Henry continued clapping regardless, a grin plastered over his face. He looked just as thrilled as when he had won his own games.

Eventually the roar died down into a clamor. Vincent finally spotted Sierra amongst the adoring crowd. She was laughing with a teammate's arm slung over her shoulder, Jake at her other side and looking happier than Vincent had seen him in some time.

For some reason, Sierra's words echoed through his mind, uninvited:

I guess I'd rather get that kind of attention than be nobody. It's nice when people like you, even for small things like that.

And: *Don't you ever get lonely?*

"She's amazing, isn't she?" said Henry.

Vincent did not respond for a long moment, his thoughts slowly drowning in the tide of voices drifting up from below. Then:

"...Are you *still* trying to date her?"

Henry cast him a sidelong glance, a glimmer of surprise crossing his face. "I'm not...trying to *date* her, I know she's with Jake. I just–"

"She isn't one of us, Henry." Vincent finally faced him. "She isn't part of our world. She never will be. Not unless you ruin all this for her." He swept his hand out towards the crowd.

"I wouldn't." Henry's radiance had dimmed, turning him back to soft, steady, cold marble. "You know I wouldn't. I just..."

He turned his gaze back to Sierra far below, surrounded by all the trappings of an ordinary, extraordinary life.

"...I guess I wanted everything to feel normal. Just for a little while."

"You're lying to yourself," Vincent said, perhaps more harshly than he intended. Or maybe not. "*Nothing* is normal. Not for us." He shook his head in frustration, a little growl escaping his throat. "Maybe *you* can get away with pretending, for a while. After all, you're only human. But I–"

"You may not be a human. But you're still a person."

The storm roiling inside Vincent froze.

"And you deserve to be happy. Just like the rest of us."

Vincent felt something within him splinter. It stole his words, and instead he too gazed down at the celebration with such a powerful wave of longing that it ached.

As he fell into Sierra's smile, he wondered: *What would I have to do to feel that way?*

Eventually the crowd dispersed, some of them bound for post-game festivities. Sierra meant to join them, but she stopped to exchange excitement with Henry and Vincent for a few minutes. Even in his turmoil, Vincent summoned his best enthusiasm for her sake.

The two of them walked back to their dorm hall, with only the memory of their words between them. The brief glimmer of normalcy had set with the sun. Now they returned to their own small, dark corner of the world.

Soon their little team was gathered in Henry's room as he unpacked the potion ingredients from their box, stacking bags and vials on his desk next to the chemistry supplies he had borrowed. Most of it was utterly unrecognizable–dried plants and powders in plastic bags, oddly-shaped beakers, some kind of burner setup...

Suddenly, Vincent was glad to be studying philosophy. *I guess I owe you that one, Father.*

"I hope you know what you're doing with all this junk," said Casey, echoing his sentiments. She was busying herself prodding little divots into the bags of powder with her finger. Henry noticed and moved it out of her reach, earning a glare.

"It's all here in the forum post." Henry held up his phone. He looked to Percy. "And we've got our very own Einstein here to put it all together!"

Percy blushed using Ava's pale cheeks. It was still strange seeing her acting so bashful. "W-well, Einstein wasn't doing chemistry..."

He sat at the desk and began working, explaining his process to Henry step by step. Henry hovered over his shoulder, scribbling notes into a composition notebook. Meanwhile Casey wandered around the room, making a game out of touching each one of Henry's personal effects, deciding it wasn't interesting after all, and moving on to the next until she ran out.

Finally Percy said, "A-alright, that should do it!"

Vincent and Casey leaned over the desk to look. A large flask bubbled over the burner, its contents an unappetizing shade of greenish-brown. It looked like someone had scooped up swamp water.

"Looks great," said Casey flatly. "So how much of this shit do I have to drink? Do I at least get a solo cup?"

"Oh—i-it's not actually ready yet," Percy said meekly. "Sorry...i-it's gonna have to simmer here overnight."

Casey glared at him. "Seriously? It's already been so long!"

"Well, don't worry. We do have something else to fill the time," said Henry.

Ava's face fell. Casey grinned.

A few minutes later, everyone piled into Henry's Mini Cooper, armed with flashlights and shovels. Casey had of course called shotgun before anyone could explain what that meant to Vincent. She and Henry bickered about the radio station for a good few minutes before Casey won, and the rest of them were forced to listen to heavy metal. The dissonance between the soundtrack and the task at hand was either amusing or irritating to everyone but her.

Still, there was something...satisfying about the music. It was raucous and guttural and shook the tiny car (as Casey had turned the volume up considerably) with each screech of the instruments. Vincent felt it more than heard it, and for a minute he realized he had slipped away, swept up in that angry catharsis. It was so powerful, it even drowned out his sixth sense for a little while—and he was glad of it. The insatiable hunger of it always lurked inside, nagging and gnawing, and he was sick of it.

At last the car rolled to a stop, and he looked up to see the headlights blaring against a fence just ahead. Beyond he could barely make out rows and rows of dark, angular shapes spreading neatly over the fields. At once his apprehension returned.

The music stopped abruptly with the engine. Everyone climbed out of the car.

"I don't see anyone..." said Henry. "Maybe you can check for a scent, Vincent?"

Vincent paused, tasting the air. His friends' scents were obvious. He tried to ignore the familiar taste of clove and jasmine caressing his senses, pulling him towards a comfort he couldn't indulge in. He also filtered out the acrid smell of gasoline and the tang of rust from the shovels. Beyond that, the night air was still and sweet with the aroma of pine and dewy grass. And underneath it all...

"Nothing recent. Someone passed this way a few hours ago, maybe...an older man, I think. But we should be safe, for now."

"W-what about vampires?" Percy asked, his borrowed eyes wide. "You said before that you can't smell them..."

"I guess we can't be sure..." Vincent admitted, hating his own failings.

"Just keep an eye out," said Henry. "We can't do much more."

Everyone swung their legs over the low fence and landed safely in the long grass on the other side. They began to climb the gentle slope, keeping their flashlight beams low just in case. Ironically the light made it more difficult for Vincent to see, dazzling his eyes and keeping them from adjusting fully to the dark. More than once he jumped when a headstone sprung from the gloom, illuminated by an errant beam.

He could almost taste the profound stillness that spread over this place. There was something sacred to it, cold and heavy and rigid as stone. It was the other side of death, one he had never yet witnessed–countless holes in the very fabric of the world where life once was. Each body once belonged to someone, now arranged in cradles of earth and wood, tucked politely out of sight beneath his feet.

But he *had* seen it before. Mira's empty face flashed through his mind, and a chill coursed through his heart. He could almost feel her limp body in his arms again, dragging him down...

"What was that?" Ava's anxious voice cut through his thoughts.

Vincent stopped, taking in their surroundings. "I can't sense anything."

"I can't either," Casey grunted. "What are you crying about now?"

"I–I thought I saw..."

"Don't worry, Percy," Henry said, patting him on the back. "Vincent will catch anything before it gets too close."

His faith in Vincent warmed him. He only hoped it was true.

"B-but there could be all kinds of things here..." Percy murmured. "I-it's a graveyard..."

"Graveyards aren't that bad," Henry assured him as they started off again. "Most everything you hear is just urban legends that get out of control. Ghosts, zombies, vampires, church grims–"

"Church *what?*" Percy squeaked.

"Oh–um, a big black dog with fiery eyes that guards church graveyards. I don't even think this one has a church, so you're safe," Henry teased. "Actually, that sounds kinda like you, doesn't it, Vincent? Maybe that's where the myth came from."

Vincent found it difficult to believe any other hellhounds would have done something heinous enough to be sent up here–let alone spotted in their true form. Only he was that much of a failure.

"Yeah. Maybe."

"Anyway...none of those things actually have anything to do with graveyards. After all, there's no one to eat or drink or haunt, hah. People just think so, 'cause of course a place filled with dead bodies feels unsettling."

"You're telling me," Casey muttered. "How are these graves ordered?" She cast her flashlight around to check each of the names they passed. "Are we close?"

"I think so," said Henry. "Although it does look different at night..."

"Oh, we'd better not be lost," Casey growled.

"Oh, no..." Percy whimpered.

"We're not lost," Henry asserted, looking around at the nearest graves.

"I swear to god, if someone catches us because *you* got us lost–"

Suddenly, Casey's flashlight passed over a name that made Vincent freeze.

She didn't give it another glance as Henry called out, "Right here!" He began striding up the hill. Bewildered, the others hurried after him. Vincent hesitated a moment more before following.

In the valley below, Henry stopped in front of one of the headstones. It was smooth and polished and brand-new. The earth at its feet was undisturbed, but had not yet grown over with grass. Nothing remained of any tributes that had once laid beneath it, except for a few shriveled flower petals.

The words carved into the granite read:

PERCY QUAILHEART
Beloved Son & Friend to All
1998 - 2017

In spite of their urgency, everyone stopped before it. A heavy silence hung in the air between them, as if to press them down into the earth as well.

"Are...are we really going to...?" Percy said quietly. Vincent could see he was trembling.

Henry nodded grimly. "We have to. I'm so sorry..."

Without a word, Casey set her flashlight down and jabbed her shovel into the earth. Henry followed suit. Vincent and Percy were the most reluctant, but after a moment Vincent rested a hand on Percy's shoulder.

"Come on," he murmured, and moved to join the others. Percy just looked at him with Ava's round blue eyes, wide and distraught. Then he too began to dig, without vigor.

It was harder work than Vincent expected, but between the four of them they made quick progress. They stopped periodically to look out over the fields, but no one appeared to accost them.

While everyone else seemed most concerned about this, Vincent couldn't keep that other gravestone out of his mind. The idea of it buzzed in his chest, the pressure growing and growing, until finally he couldn't take it anymore.

He stopped, making a show of wiping his brow and leaning on his shovel. Percy saw him and took the opportunity to breathe as well–although he seemed genuinely fatigued.

Vincent waited until no one was looking at him before slowly leaning down and picking up his flashlight. He began to wander between the gravestones, gradually moving further and further away from Percy's grave. The others didn't seem to notice, too wrapped up in their task.

When he was far enough away, he flicked his flashlight on and began darting it over the faces of each headstone he passed, searching for that name again. He knew it was somewhere on this hill, but he couldn't recall where they were standing when he spotted it. Every grave looked the same. He grew more and more desperate with each passing moment, his heart burning with every beat.

He suddenly heard faint voices rising from the valley. He couldn't tell what they were saying, only that they were alarmed. Gritting his teeth, he continued his search, reading each headstone as swiftly as he could.

Then, there it was.

BENJAMIN WARWICK

1996 - 2017

Requiescat in Pace

It was crafted of plain stone, without a single embellishment or sign of mourning. The grave itself was similar to Percy's, flat dirt that had not yet been overtaken with grass or recently disturbed.

Vincent stood there for a time that stretched on and yet only lasted a heartbeat. It felt like that heart belonged in the ground with Benjamin. Except...

Vincent turned off his flashlight and knelt in the grass beside the grave. He plunged his hands into the earth and began to dig. He chose a small spot in the center of the plot, aiming for depth. He didn't have time for anything else.

He shouldn't risk it. He *knew* what he would find. But something ravenous inside him urged him on.

Two feet down, three...and then four, and he couldn't reach anymore. The voices were slowly growing louder, but they hadn't found him–yet. An impatient growl rumbled in his chest. Suddenly he was a dog, hurling himself back onto the grave and scraping at the hole with massive feverish paws.

He dug deeper–five feet, six...seven. Too deep.

He began digging out the walls, sifting through the dirt in one last desperate attempt to find any trace, but...nothing. The grave was empty.

Benjamin was truly back in his own body, despite how long it had been decaying while he was in Hell. That vampiric magic had revived him, in its own grotesque way. He hated it thoroughly. It was wrong. How could he want to exist like that?

Because it's better than Hell. The thought came instantly. Guilt chased it, at first...and then, it faded away. Because it was true. He couldn't deny it any longer. *Anything* was better than Hell.

Suddenly, the voices grew louder. Vincent snapped back to the present, his six ears pricking as he turned to see flashlight beams approaching from the hillside.

Shit. He couldn't be seen like this. They couldn't see the grave.

Vincent used his great paws to start pushing the dirt back into the hole as fast as he could. He hoped no one would notice the freshly turned earth in daylight.

He glanced up over and over, watching the beams drawing closer. His friends were calling for him. He could tell they were trying to keep their voices as low as possible, wary of alerting anyone else nearby.

Finally, they were too close. Vincent abandoned the grave, hoping he had filled it enough to avoid notice. He took off, keeping his three heads low as he slunk between the rows of headstones, trying to put some distance between him and the others. He noticed a copse of willow trees on the other side of the hill and made for them, hoping for some shelter beneath their trailing boughs.

He ducked between the trees, relief cooling his thudding heart—

A flashlight beam struck him dead in the face. His middle head flinched away, but the others caught the dim figure of an older man behind the light.

Just as the man cried out in terror, Vincent twisted away from him. A blast assailed his leftmost ears. He felt a rush of air as something whizzed narrowly past.

He took off at top speed. His paws pounded over grass and grave dirt. He heard another bang behind him and the unmistakable whine of a bullet ricocheting off stone.

Just as he passed a large gravestone, something leaped out at him.

Vincent pulled up from a full sprint, skidding in the dirt, but he couldn't stop in time—the figure careened into his side, its limbs wrapping around his chest. Panic shot through his veins like fire—

"Vincent, this way! Come on, quick!"

He recognized the voice and the scent—clove and jasmine.

Henry's hands curled into Vincent's fur as he urged him aside, cutting diagonally through the rows of headstones. He didn't let go all the way down the hill. Finally Vincent spotted the fence and the car up ahead.

When they reached the fence, Henry panted, "Hunker down behind the car, alright? I have to go back for the others."

"Are you serious? That man has a *gun*—Henry, you can't—"

"I'm not leaving them behind!" Henry cried, his desperation bordering on vicious. He finally released his hold on Vincent's fur. "*Hide*, Vincent!"

Vincent watched him disappear over the crest of the hill. A soft whine emanated from one of his throats. He finally tore himself away and leaped the low fence with ease, crouching behind Henry's car. He doubted the old man could see him even if he didn't hide, but something in him bade him to obey. He wasn't doing any good just standing out there, and he certainly wasn't going to go back with Henry and help find the others. The sight of him would only make things worse.

Some hero I am, he thought miserably.

He stayed there behind the car for minutes that stretched on and on. He kept his ears pricked, searching for another gunshot in the night, but none came. Nothing did.

It had been far too long, he finally decided. He couldn't even begin to imagine what might have happened. What was he supposed to do, all alone here? What if–

Suddenly, footsteps shuffled beside him. He whirled around, baring his teeth, but immediately recognized the shape now crouching beside him.

"Where the fuck were you?" Casey growled. "We were looking all over for you."

"I was right there," Vincent said, but he was sure it wasn't convincing. "Where were *you?* Where's Henry and Percy?"

"You tell me," Casey said coldly. "Did I hear gunshots?"

"A man saw me. I guess I spooked him."

"Like that?" Casey looked him up and down. "Yeah, I'll say. What were you gonna do, bite his head off? You could've just run for it without changing. You just made it *way* worse for yourself. And us."

Of course–she assumed he transformed out of panic. He went with it.

"I couldn't help it." He looked away from her.

Casey scoffed. "And you lecture *me* about losing control."

Even if she could accuse him of hypocrisy now, the lie was worth it. No one could know about Benjamin. No one could know the murders were Vincent's fault.

"Where *are* they, damn it," he growled. "Did you lose them out there?"

"We scattered when we heard the gunshots," Casey replied tersely. "Henry shouted something about finding you. Percy must've gotten lost in the dark."

"He's a ghost, for fuck's sake," Vincent grumbled. "How does he get lost in the dark?" He sighed. "Henry *did* find me. He went back to try and find you two."

"Then let's hope he guides Percy back first, before trying to find me. Otherwise..."

Shit.

"I need to go find him."

"Not like that, you don't," Casey snapped. "You're a *way* easier target."

"I can follow his trail."

"Change back first!"

"I can't," Vincent snapped.

"Fucking idiot," Casey spat. "He isn't worth it. He doesn't even like you like that, don't you realize that? He's been trailing after that volleyball girl Sierra for months now!"

Vincent's fur bristled along his spine. "I don't care," he lied. "I won't abandon him."

Before Casey could protest again, he ducked around the side of the car and leaped over the fence. It was easy to follow Henry's scent–clove and jasmine, soured with the tang of fear. It wound between rows of gravestones, wandering in search of Percy.

He kept one head's eyes on the fields, trying to pick out the silhouette of the man pursuing them. It was nearly impossible in the murk, dotted with the shadows of headstones that overwhelmed his split vision. He swallowed the lump rising in his throats, telling himself he didn't need to see the old man–he just needed to see Henry.

And finally, he did–just a shadow up ahead, in the center of his trail–

"Vincent, *no!*"

Vincent skidded in the dirt, but he was too late. The figure spun around, its pistol clearly silhouetted for a horrible moment.

He heard an ominous click and dived behind a headstone–

BANG!

A chunk of rock flew into the air, barely missing one of Vincent's heads. He glanced up to see two other figures bolting in his direction.

"*Go!* Go go go!"

Vincent turned heel and pelted down the slope as fast as he could justify. His leftmost head glanced back to make sure the other two were following—but three silhouettes pursued him.

Headstones passed in a blur as he ran. Then he saw the fence dead ahead.

He leaped over it, rounding back to see Henry and Percy clambering over as fast as they could follow. The man was only a few yards behind them, puffing audibly. Vincent bounded back to help, but Henry made it over just as he arrived.

"Get in!" Henry cried as he made a mad dash for the car. Casey poked her head around it, startled, and yanked the passenger door open.

Vincent nudged Percy's remaining leg over the fence, then ran for the car. It was only when he reached it that he realized he wouldn't fit.

"Just go!" he snarled as Percy hesitated at the door. "I'll catch up!"

Percy shot him a last look of terror before hurling himself into the back seat.

"*Vincent!*" Henry called from the front window. The desperation in his voice set Vincent's blood alight. It only made him more certain—he was doing the right thing. He was making up for his mistakes. He was doing what Henry would do.

Their eyes met for a brief moment, and despite the pain of it, that current of understanding flashed between them. Henry trusted him.

"*Go.*"

Vincent rounded to face the older man, the fur along his back bristling dangerously. Tires squealed as the car flew past down the road.

"Get back here!" the man shouted after them, but it was useless.

Then he turned to Vincent, wheezing, and raised his gun with trembling hands.

Fear pounded against Vincent's ribs.

"Try it," Vincent growled, his eyes flashing red in the gloom. "You know what I am, don't you, old man? What will happen to you?"

The man's eyes widened, but he kept his pistol up, however shakily. "In thirty-three years workin' this graveyard, I–I never seen a grim before. You can't..."

"I can't?" Vincent flashed three sets of ruthless fangs. He forced himself to take a step forward.

The man stepped back. Vincent was winning.

"You–you chasin' those kids?"

Why not? "Trespassers among the dead," Vincent growled, one head licking its teeth.

The pistol lowered slightly, but the man looked just as frightened. "W–what were they doin'? Did they have somethin' to do with those murders?" he said suddenly, seeming to put something together in his head. "That kid, down at the college...and the missin' one..."

Vincent did not reply. The car was long gone. He turned, only his leftmost head keeping its eyes fixed on the man, and began to pad down the road.

"Wait!" the man cried. But Vincent didn't. The night fell silent.

CHAPTER 15

HUNTERS IN THE NIGHT

Vincent finally caught up with the Mini Cooper, idling on the side of the road. As soon as he appeared through the mist, Henry and Percy leaped out to meet him.

"Vincent!"

"Are you okay? How did you get away?" Henry rested a hand on Vincent's furred shoulder as he searched his massive body for bullet wounds.

"I'm fine," Vincent grunted, shaking out his coat and dislodging Henry's hand. "I convinced him I was a church grim. He figured I was on his side."

"Fucking hero," came Casey's voice as she climbed out of the car. She gave Vincent a disapproving glare.

"Did you–wait, were you covering for us?" Percy asked, eyes wide. "Is that where you went?"

"Ah...yeah. I thought I smelled someone, so I went to look. Turns out I was right."

"Well, next time give us a heads-up, would you?" said Casey.

"We were worried about you," Henry said, and again he curled his fingers into Vincent's shoulder fur. It felt far more deliberate this time. Each brush of his fingertips was like embers against his skin, a tangle of heat and comfort, until it began to burn.

When Vincent finally moved away, the spot felt raw. Before he realized it he had transformed back into his human form. Somehow it made him feel both more and less safe.

Henry's eyes lingered on him, filled with a complexity Vincent could hardly begin to unravel. He didn't try.

Instead, he said, "What happened to you guys? Did you find–"

"I'll tell you later," Henry interrupted. "We need to get out of here. It's almost dawn."

He turned back to the car and jumped in the driver's seat, leaving the others to pile in after him.

As they drove back towards town, Vincent began to glimpse the first fingers of milky light reaching up to grasp the horizon. The shadows of exhaustion in everyone's faces only looked darker in daylight.

Eventually, and without any warning, Henry pulled off the main road into a nearly deserted parking lot. The others, only half-awake by this point, began to stir as they noticed.

"What are you doing, Henry?" Casey peered out the window suspiciously. "*Denny's?* We're going to *Denny's?*"

"Yeah," said Henry, with a forced note of cheer. "We deserve it, after the night we've had."

"I just wanna go to bed," Casey grumbled, but she got out when everyone else did.

Vincent peered across the parking lot at the neon "DENNY'S" sign glaring at them from on high. The building itself looked inviting enough, warm yellow light spilling onto the pavement from the wide windows all along its facade. They trudged inside, their eyes screwed up against the sudden brightness.

At first the place looked completely empty, rows of plastic booths and tables and chairs as far as the eye could see. Then a young woman appeared out of thin air with menus tucked under her arm.

"Hi, everyone! First guests of the morning, believe it or not–pick anywhere you like."

"Thanks, Vanessa," Henry said, exuding all his usual charm in spite of his weariness. He led them to a large booth nearby.

Vincent moved to slide into the seat beside Percy, but Casey cut him off with a knowing smirk. He glowered at her and took the remaining spot next to Henry. Fortunately neither Henry nor Percy seemed to notice the exchange, and they soon became preoccupied with their menus.

"I'm paying, get anything you like. *Within reason,*" Henry added, with a pointed look at Casey. Her momentary grin wilted.

"Ohh...I haven't been here in years," Percy said, scanning his menu eagerly. "Their waffles are really good...not as good as my dad's, but still..."

"*I'm* getting bacon," Casey announced. She glanced up at Henry with a scowl. "How much bacon is *within reason*, Mother Dearest?"

"None, at this rate," Henry said pleasantly, without looking up from his menu.

Casey sighed laboriously and fell into a glum silence. Meanwhile the bulk of Vincent's discomfort was swept away by the sheer breadth of menu options. He felt like he couldn't read fast enough. Dozens of egg and pancake combinations, sausages, potatoes, waffles, burgers, even steak...how could he possibly choose?

"You doing alright over there, Vinny?" Henry's amused voice broke into his stupor, and Vincent's awkwardness returned.

"Ah–yeah, *fine...*" Vincent said with feeling. Henry and Percy both laughed, and even Casey cracked a smile. Vincent looked up at them indignantly. "What?"

When the waitress returned, everyone rattled off their meal choices while Vincent sweated. When she finally came around to him, Henry said, "It's okay if you need a couple more minutes to–"

"No, it's fine," Vincent said, already lamenting the paths unchosen. "I'll–I'll have the...yeah, the Lumberjack Slam."

The waitress smiled. "A classic. How do you want your eggs?"

Vincent looked at Henry helplessly. He grinned. "Try over easy. Trust me."

Vincent nodded at the waitress. She nodded back, scribbling on her notepad. "I'll be back in a jiffy."

"Lumberjack Slam, huh?" Casey said when she had gone, gazing at Vincent with rare approval. "Maybe I should've gone with that..."

"The more meat the better, right?" said Vincent.

"You know it," said Casey, grinning toothily.

Percy let out a wistful breath. "It's so nice to eat again..."

"I forgot you liked milkshakes so much," Henry said fondly.

"Oh, I hope it wasn't too much to order...!"

"No, no, no, don't even. I'm just happy we get to eat together again."

Percy gave him a weak smile. It was cut short when a straw wrapper smacked him right between the eyes. He flinched, swiping it off his nose with a hand.

"*Really*, Casey?" Vincent groaned.

Henry laughed. "Good shot!"

She raised a fist in triumph.

"What are you, twelve?" said Vincent.

"You're a buzzkill, Vincent," Casey decided. She snatched the remains of the wrapper from Percy's lap and began scrunching it up on the tabletop in a very deliberate way.

Seeing his chance, Vincent reached his foot over to Percy's and nudged it a couple times. When Percy looked at him in confusion, he grabbed his own unopened straw and passed it to Percy under the table. He seemed to get the idea and shot Vincent a grin before he tore the wrapper open...

Meanwhile Casey had picked up her straw, keeping a finger over the top hole to suction water inside it. She began dripping it onto the wrapper to watch the paper rapidly expand.

"See, you're just jealous of my straw magic," she said loftily. "You act like you've never been to a diner bef–"

A straw wrapper whizzed across the bench and hit her square on the forehead. Henry let out a guffaw. She blinked, stupefied, before she realized what happened and glared at Percy with vengeful delight. "Oh, *that's* it–"

"The last straw?" Henry said gleefully.

Casey flipped him off. Then she lunged for Percy, who gave a mew of fright. She ignored Vincent and Henry's protests and squished Percy against the wall, ruffling Ava's hair as aggressively as humanly possible. He writhed feebly, but was unable to stop her until she seemed satisfied with the unrecognizable mass of hair she had created.

"Punk rock," Casey grinned as she flopped back into her seat, admiring her work.

Percy reached up to assess the damage, letting out a groan. "Why..."

"You deserved it!"

"You started it!" Henry pointed out.

"I'm untouchable," Casey said.

Vincent kicked her under the table.

"Watch it, mutt," she snarled.

Vincent was saved from her wrath by the waitress' return. When he laid eyes on the wealth of meat and carbs set before him, he almost felt like crying. He hadn't realized just how ravenous he was.

Warmth spread through his body with every bite. Salt and meat and butter overtook him, drowning out his surroundings completely.

Suddenly, he realized he could hear his name echoing in his ears. Everyone was staring at him except for Percy, who was preoccupied with trying to untangle Ava's long hair.

"Thought we'd lost you," mumbled Casey through a mouthful of egg.

"Ah–did you say something?"

Henry chuckled. "Never mind. Guess I picked a good one, huh?"

Vincent muttered some kind of assent, embarrassed. Casey took the opportunity to lean across the table, brandishing her fork towards his plate.

"Damn it, I knew I should've got the–alright, shit!" she broke off as Vincent hovered over his plate with a growl.

"You'd better not poke the bear, Casey," Henry warned. "Or...dog, I guess?"

"Can't promise that." Casey turned instead towards Percy's plate. She stole a hunk of waffle before he could free his fingers from the nest of hair he was working on.

"Hey!"

"Too slow," Casey said thickly as she chewed her prize. "Long hair's a bitch, innit? You wanna borrow my brush?"

"Well it's not like he can cut it," Henry pointed out. "It's technically not his hair."

"Then maybe he should try a little harder to give it back," Casey retorted.

Against all odds, the reminder immediately shifted Vincent's thoughts away from his breakfast.

"You never told me what happened back there after I left. Did you finish digging? Did you find...?"

All three of the others shared a look.

"What? What is it?"

Henry's face turned grim.

"The grave was empty."

"*Empty?*"

Vincent's thoughts began to race. Two empty graves.

"I know. So much for all the trouble," Casey growled.

"Henry, didn't you see Percy's body after they found him?" Vincent asked.

Henry nodded glumly. "They had it. It had bite wounds and everything."

"So someone must have dug it up..."

"Midnight snack?" Casey suggested.

Vincent glared at her.

"What? Come on, there are *vampires* around!"

"But someone already drained him," Henry pointed out.

"Well, maybe there were a few dregs left! I don't know."

"I-I don't like this..." Percy said tremulously.

Henry leaned across the tabletop to rest a comforting hand on Percy's borrowed arm. "We'll find your body, Percy, I promise."

"That's a hell of a promise," Casey said. "Where do we even start looking?"

There was a resounding silence.

"That's comforting," she grunted.

"It's too late to think about all this properly now," Henry decided, sounding especially weary. "Or early, I guess... We should get some rest and regroup later. Can we agree on that at least?"

Nods and muttering answered, and Henry returned to his hash browns. Following his lead, Vincent once again lost himself in a haze of meat and potatoes and pancakes.

The rest of their meal was subdued. Casey even managed to leave Percy alone long enough for him to fix his hair and eat his food. Finally they left the diner and made for the lonely Mini Cooper in the parking lot. The silent, foggy morning outside felt surreal, as if it should not have dawned at all.

Henry paused to fish in his pocket, pulling out his keys and his phone. He glanced at the screen, and from a little twitch in his expression Vincent instantly knew something was wrong.

"Henry? What is it?"

Casey and Percy stopped too, looking back at Henry quizzically. He didn't answer, and instead tapped on the phone and held it up to his ear.

"Hi–yes, this is Henry Wellfellow. Sorry I missed you. ...Oh, really? That's great! ...No, sure, I'll be by to pick him up in just a few! Thanks so much for calling me."

When he hung up, he turned to the three pairs of eyes staring at him, and looked far less cheerful than he had sounded on the phone.

"Looks like Hunter is ready to be discharged from the hospital. We're gonna go pick him up."

"Oh *hell* no," Casey growled. "You think I'm gonna be stuck in a car with that creep?"

Henry sighed. Vincent could tell his patience was woefully thin after the night they had. "It'll only be a few minutes. And besides, you know we have to look after him now, after what you did. I'll try to keep you separate, but–"

"That's bullshit!"

"I'm sorry, Casey, really. But we have to–"

"Either you cooperate, or we turn you in to the Shadowhand." Vincent turned on her, his dark eyes burning. He was *so* tired of this. And he didn't want her to push Henry any further. "It's as simple as that. You fucked up, and now we have to clean up your mess."

Casey opened her mouth, but no sound emerged. She closed it again, gritting her teeth. Then she rounded on the Mini Cooper and kicked the back tire, hard. The car alarm blared across the empty parking lot.

Henry glanced uncertainly at Vincent. He didn't look happy, but he seemed unwilling to go against him in front of the others. Patiently, wearily, he clicked a button on his key fob and the car alarm ceased. The ensuing silence was almost louder.

Casey wrenched the rear passenger door open. Before she could climb in, Henry said, "Actually, can you take shotgun again?"

"I wish I had one," she muttered. "Aren't you afraid I'll jerk the wheel or something?"

"No." Henry rolled his eyes. Vincent was impressed she had pushed him that far. "I assumed you wouldn't want to sit next to Hunter."

Casey scowled, but obeyed. Timidly Percy took her place in the back, and Vincent joined him.

The drive was prickly and silent. Casey pressed her head against the window mutinously, leaving a smudge on the glass. Percy and Vincent kept glancing at each other, the former too afraid to speak. A few minutes in, Henry attempted to ease the tension by turning on the radio, but even Phil Collins' dulcet tones weren't up to the task. In fact, they only seemed to make everything more awkward.

Finally they pulled into the hospital parking lot. Vincent immediately spotted a nurse escorting Hunter from the building in a wheelchair. Henry parked close by and hopped out to meet them, leaving the rest of them to wait anxiously. He exchanged a few words with the nurse before Hunter stood up.

Vincent hesitated. Then he jumped out to join them.

"Of *course* it's you guys," Hunter was saying. He glanced warily at Vincent as he approached. "What do you want from me, huh? I don't have to go anywhere with you."

"It's a few miles back to school," Henry said calmly. "You've been in a bad way for a long time now. I don't know how far you'll get on foot. It'd be a lot better if you just let me do you this favor and drive you back."

"Why do you care? You've obviously got something up your sleeve..."

"Hunter, we're not gonna hurt you. We saved your life, remember? We could have left you out there in the woods if we wanted. We just want to get you home. It's the least we can do."

Hunter again eyed Vincent pointedly. He was silent for a moment more. "Alright. Fine."

Henry caught Vincent's eye and subtly jerked his head towards the car. Vincent narrowed his eyes. He gave Henry a little nod and led Hunter over. He waited until he was very close before pulling open the passenger door.

"H-hi!" said Percy through Ava's mouth, giving Hunter a little wave.

Vincent suddenly shoved Hunter, forcing him into the backseat. Vincent got in after, sandwiching Hunter between himself and Percy.

"Hey! Watch it–"

Vincent slammed the door shut just as Hunter and Casey locked eyes.

"HELP!" Hunter cried, flinging himself across Vincent's lap to tug at the door handle. But Henry, now in the driver's seat, had already locked the car.

"Shut up," Vincent growled, hauling Hunter back into his own spot.

Panicking, Hunter turned to Percy's side and tried again in vain, pressing poor Percy against the back of his seat. Vincent grabbed Hunter's shoulders and hefted him off his friend. It was difficult in spite of Hunter's injuries. He was obviously much stronger than before.

"Sorry, Hunter," Henry said. He had already pulled out of the parking lot and away from prying eyes.

"What do you *mean*, 'sorry'?" Hunter sputtered, his wild eyes falling on Casey again. "She fucking gored me! She's a werewolf! You *had* to have seen–"

"Yes, she is," Henry interrupted, and Hunter was so stunned by the admission that he fell silent for a precious moment. "But she's not gonna hurt you again. I promise."

Casey muttered something from the front seat.

"How do *you* know? She's *crazy!*" Hunter stopped dead and then said, "Y–you aren't a werewolf too, are you?"

"No, I'm not," Henry replied placidly.

"Then how are you gonna control the bitch, huh?"

"Don't call her that," Henry said sharply. "And Casey's my friend. I know she won't do anything."

"So what? That doesn't prove anything."

"We'll control her the same way as you," Vincent broke in, growing impatient with Henry's diplomacy. "If she doesn't cooperate, we're turning her in."

"What? What does *that* mean?"

"It means," Vincent said, "You'll be put to death. Or worse, locked up in a containment facility. Even we don't know what they do there."

"*They?*"

Vincent hesitated, unsure how much to share with him. Henry decided to answer. "The Shadowhand. They regulate Others–creatures like werewolves that are hidden from the rest of the mortal world. Creatures like you."

A horrible silence hung heavy between them all.

"So you know, then," Hunter said, almost wearily. Vincent was surprised by his sudden resignation.

Henry glanced back at him. "Yeah. I'm afraid so. It's not like you could have avoided turning, given what happened."

"How do *you* know?" Vincent chimed in, peering closely at Hunter.

Hunter avoided his eyes. "I'm not stupid. If all the legends are true, anyway..."

"Most of them are," Henry said. "Including how the curse is spread, unfortunately."

"So what, then? Are you covering for your buddy the she-devil here?"

"Oh, real creative," Casey spat, swinging her head around to stab him with her gaze. "You know what you did, you little creep! You brought this on yourself!"

"Casey," Henry warned her. She growled and slumped in her seat, but kept shooting glares back at Hunter.

"We're not here to point fingers," Henry went on. "We're here to deal with everything that's happened. We honestly just want to help you, Hunter."

"How are *you* going to help *me*?" Hunter growled.

"Well first of all, we have Casey here. She knows better than anyone how to deal with being a werewolf."

"Yeah, because she's been dealing with it *so* well," Hunter retorted, this time mustering the courage to fire a glare back at her.

"There's nothing more she can do to you. And she's under control now."

"Stop talking like I'm not here!" Casey snarled. "I don't need *controlling*, damn it!"

"Yeah, I can see that," Hunter said with a note of smugness.

"Oh, you're lucky I'm up here..."

"*Secondly*," Henry broke in, "we have a potion that will help you curb your instincts near the full moon. If you take it regularly, you shouldn't have too much trouble with your, uh...condition."

That caught Hunter's attention. "A potion? Does it actually work?"

Henry nodded. "It's brewing right now. It should be ready very soon."

Hunter settled a bit more comfortably into his seat, although his bulk was becoming increasingly awkward. Vincent and Percy both squished themselves against their respective doors rather than against his arms.

"So what...you're going to just give me this potion and let me go?" Hunter said suspiciously.

"Well, we can't just turn you loose. Since we're the only ones who know what you are now, we have a responsibility to keep an eye on you."

"What?" Hunter said, his hackles rising again. "What're you planning to do with me, then?"

"Nothing bad," Henry assured him, although Hunter didn't seem convinced. "Just help you if you need it."

"Bullshit." Hunter sounded remarkably like Casey. Vincent was sure she wasn't fond of that.

"And there's the rub," she said wryly.

Hunter rounded on her. "This is your fault," he hissed. "What are they *actually* gonna do to me?"

"Watch you every hour of every day," Casey said. She turned in her seat to fix him with a menacing look. "Or, at least...when you least expect it. You might as well never be alone again. It's excruciating. But I guess we deserve it, don't we? For what we are."

Vincent fought the urge to roll his eyes. It was probably better for Hunter to believe that, anyway. He looked sufficiently spooked, but equally outraged.

"Bullshit!" he said again. "You can't possibly tail me *everywhere!* And if you're watching her, too–"

"We just want to make sure you don't do anything you'll regret," Henry said. Apparently he didn't feel like going against Casey's words either.

"Yeah, you really kept Casey on the straight and narrow," Hunter said savagely.

"We didn't know what she was until that night," Vincent told him. "If we had, we would have prevented it."

"Oh, come on. You really think you're that good? Against a werewolf?"

"We stopped her from killing you," Vincent growled. "If we had gotten there earlier..."

Hunter stopped. "Yeah...hold on. How did you manage that, anyway? It's hard to remember..."

Before anyone could stop him, he seemed to realize something, his eyes going wide. "You're–you *are* a werewolf! You fucking liar! I remember–you carried me back–"

"He's not," said Henry, just as Vincent said, "I'm not."

"I'm a hellhound," Vincent went on, trying to ignore the uncomfortable twisting in his gut. Much as he hated divulging this to anyone, he hated doing it for Hunter even more. "I don't lose control of myself when I transform."

"A *what*?" Hunter stared at him in disbelief.

Vincent was saved from having to explain any further as they pulled into the school's parking lot. He immediately reached for the door handle, but found it stuck tight.

"Hey—let us out!" Hunter glared at the back of Henry's head.

Henry turned in his seat to look at him sternly. "I want to make sure you're taking this seriously."

"Yeah, okay, I am," Hunter replied sullenly.

"You're going to turn into a werewolf near the next full moon. Sometimes earlier than the night itself. If you don't keep a handle on your emotions, you might lose control like Casey did. I need you to get that potion from us when it's ready. It'll help. And I need you to come to us if you start having trouble. We're not trying to act like parole officers—we're just trying to make this easier for you."

"Alright, I get it," Hunter growled. "But why do you even care?"

"We just don't want anyone else to get hurt." Henry's expression darkened. "Besides, we owe it to you. We should have been there so none of this even happened. I'm so sorry, Hunter."

Hunter seemed stricken by the apology. He was quiet for a long moment.

"Yeah. Well...alright."

Henry brightened a little. "Thanks. I'll give you my number, in case you need anything. Can I have yours?"

Both of them got out their phones, but as soon as Henry looked at his he let out a groan. "Damn...I forgot it's Monday. My first class started fifteen minutes ago!"

"Oh, who gives a shit?" said Casey. "Just skip it. I promise you'll survive. I've missed loads."

"And I bet your grades are in the gutter," Vincent muttered.

"Shut up, lapdog."

"I bet I can still make most of it if I hurry," Henry said, glancing back at Hunter. The two exchanged phone numbers, and then the doors all unlocked with a click. Vincent immediately climbed out, grateful for the rush of fresh, cold air that greeted him.

The day was gray still, but much brighter now—mid-morning, he guessed. His own first class would be starting soon surely, but he had no intention of trying to power through education today. Casey obviously agreed, already stalking off in the direction of the dorms. Vincent hung back until Hunter and Percy had gone, leaving him alone with Henry.

"Thanks for helping," Henry said. "But will you please stop threatening Casey and Hunter?"

"What do you mean?" Vincent's mood soured instantly. "You started it."

"I didn't threaten them."

"Yes, you did. You just implied it instead."

Henry frowned. Vincent could tell he took his point, even if he didn't like it. "I'd just rather keep things civil. I don't like ultimatums. And they've already been through so much."

"Both Casey and Hunter are angry and dangerous. They aren't going to cooperate if we don't make the stakes clear." Vincent's ire faded some, replaced by something more vulnerable, if only for a moment. "I thought you wanted my help."

"I do," Henry said, softening slightly. "I just wish you'd be more...delicate about it. We want to help them, not drive them away."

Vincent grimaced. "I'm not you."

Henry went silent, his expression unreadable.

Vincent sighed. He was too tired for this. "I'm going to bed."

Before he could leave, Henry took his arm. His grasp was gentle, but firm.

"I'm sorry, Vinny. I know you're trying to help. I'm sorry for dragging you into this mess."

"It's my mess, too." *More than you know.* "I agreed to it."

"I've...been thinking about what you said. Back at Sierra's volleyball game."

Vincent wasn't sure he wanted to hear what would come next.

"We do live in a different world than...well, most everyone else. Including Sierra. But...I don't think any of us feel that more than you."

Vincent stared at Henry, frozen.

"I wish you would talk to me. I know you can't, or at least you say you can't... You're bound by things I could probably never understand. But it's...hard not knowing what you're thinking. Sometimes it still feels like I'm walking alone, even when you're with me."

Vincent's insides writhed, as if each emotion had claimed an organ and begun warring with one another.

"I don't know if you'll believe me, but...I care about you. A lot. I think you're the best friend I've ever had."

Each of Henry's words seemed to fit into a perfect place in Vincent's heart, carved out just for them.

"You don't mean that." He barely got the words out. His heartbeat was loud in his ears.

"I–I do. I do mean it. It's just..." Henry shook his head, for once the first to avert his gaze. "I never thought I'd meet anyone like you–"

"A hellhound? An Other?"

"A kindred spirit. Apart from my sister, I've never really had anyone around for long who...gets it. Even the other Shadowhand apprentices, they just...well, they don't think like I do. Like *we* do."

He still thinks I'm like him? Guilt was now winning that visceral war inside Vincent.

"I can't even imagine where you come from, what you've been through...and sometimes I forget that. But really, it's almost like...like looking into a mirror, and seeing a shadow of myself there. Someone who's been mired in all the darkest parts of my life even more than I have. And in that...it's almost like I'm Sierra, and you're Henry."

"Then we're just as different," Vincent broke in, the edges of his voice jagged. "You'll never understand me, just like she'll never understand you."

"I don't want to just give up!" Henry said, with a burst of desperation that stunned Vincent. "You're the closest thing to–" He broke off, grasping for words. "If you'd just give me a chance to know you–"

"You *can't.*"

Vincent turned away from him, unable to bear the rising tide in his chest any longer. Memories of every failure were being carried to the surface– betraying his father, letting Mira die, losing his fight with Benjamin's vampires, being too late to stop Casey from turning Hunter, trapping Percy in his amulet, hiding here in this world and indulging himself rather than fixing his mistake with Benjamin...

Was that what he was doing? Was he not trying hard enough? Because *anything was better than Hell?*

And this world was. It was the best thing he had ever known. But was the desire to stay greater than his duty? Greater than his father's orders? Greater than the chaos Benjamin sowed every day he failed to collect him? Greater than the lives of the people he had killed?

Maybe I do belong here, with the humans. I'm selfish, and treacherous, and greedy. I always was. I still am.

"You're everything I'm not."

"Wait! Vincent–"

"Don't you have a class to get to?"

Henry's response died in his throat, and Vincent didn't stop. He strode to the back door of Walden Hall, desperate for the shadows in his lonely room. He couldn't take this anymore–all he could do was release the chaos of his mind into the soothing darkness of sleep.

The next day, Henry texted everyone that the potion was ready. As soon as they entered, the smell of peat overwhelmed their senses. Percy sat at Henry's desk in Ava's body, funneling what looked like street water into amusingly ordinary beer bottles. The window was open and a fan was blowing the worst of the fumes outside, but there was only so much it could do.

"*Damn*–I'm surprised no one's tried busting you for weed yet, Henry," Casey exclaimed.

"I-it does *not* smell like weed!" Percy protested.

"Yes it does," Casey sneered, flashing her teeth at him. She was clearly itching for a fight.

"Was it like this the whole time?" Vincent asked Henry, testing the waters after their last exchange. Guilt and resentment still swam in his stomach, and he was desperate to forget about them.

"You get used to it after a while," Henry answered with a note of misery. Vincent relaxed slightly; at least he seemed to want things to feel normal.

Percy finished hammering down a cap onto one of the bottles he had filled. Then he handed it to Henry. The open bottle he passed to Casey, his hand trembling. She eyed the potion mutinously.

"What are you gonna do if it fucks me up?"

"I have my sister on standby to help," Henry said. "And some pills that will make it come back up, if we really need them. But I trust Percy." Percy beamed at him.

Casey muttered something, glowering at the bottle in her hand. Vincent could taste her fear souring the heady air. He should have appreciated her being humbled, but strangely he found that he couldn't manage it. Instead, he watched her just as anxiously as the others.

Finally, she tipped her head back and gulped down the potion. She didn't even pause to take a breath, determination and spite emblazoned across her face. Then:

"Yep. That's bong water. Tastes like my mom's *dong quai* soup."

"H-how do you feel?" Percy asked, gripping his chair with white knuckles.

Casey smacked her lips. "Peachy."

"Can you be a bit more...descriptive?" Henry asked.

"Peachy-keen."

"Do you feel any different?"

"Not dying yet, am I? I guess it's fine. Thank fuck," she added with feeling.

Everyone relaxed at once. "Well...let us know if anything changes," Henry said. "And we'll take this one over to Hunter."

"U-um–I-I'll stay here and clean all this up, okay?" Percy piped up.

"Sure. Thanks, Percy."

Casey promptly left, and Henry led Vincent out of his room. He texted Hunter on the way, and to his credit he replied swiftly, arranging to meet outside his own dorm hall. When they arrived he was waiting there. He looked at them dubiously as Henry handed him the bottle.

"Is this it?"

"We thought it best to disguise it," Henry said. "And it's perfectly safe–Casey just had hers a few minutes ago."

Hunter gave in and stashed the bottle inside his jacket. "So what do I do with it?"

"Drink the whole thing," Henry said. "Now would be best. It's almost the full moon. It should be strong enough to last for the rest of this cycle. And we'll bring you another one next month, if everything goes well."

Hunter nodded slowly. "So that's it?"

"Yep. Just let us know if you need anything. We'll be around."

"Yeah, I bet you will," Hunter grumbled. "Tailing me already?"

"You know the answer to that," Vincent said, trying to sound menacing.

"Great," Hunter muttered. He turned to leave without another word.

"I was thinking..." Henry began as they started back on their own. "We should probably keep a closer eye on Casey too. Especially with the full moon coming up. We can't wait for her to show up for patrols to make sure she's okay."

"'Okay' meaning 'not mauling anyone else?'" Vincent dared to say. He wanted to hear Henry admit it.

Henry grimaced, liking it just as much as Vincent guessed he would. "In part."

Satisfied, Vincent said, "I can tail her if you want. How often do I have to keep up with her?"

"Just as much as you can. In between classes, of course. Hopefully hers are at the same time."

"I doubt that will matter, considering how much she apparently cuts class."

Henry frowned. "Well..."

"If anyone's going to skip class to follow her, it should be me," Vincent cut in.

"You shouldn't–"

"I'm a *hellhound,* Henry," Vincent insisted. "Do you think I'm here to get a degree?"

Henry only looked more troubled. "Then what *are* you here for?" he said quietly.

Vincent's heart sank into his gut as he recognized the door he had just reopened. So Henry wasn't over their last conversation, after all. His earlier words echoed through Vincent's mind, torturing him with that tantalizing threat of closeness, that guilt, *always* that guilt...

I don't want to just give up! If you'd just give me a chance to know you–

"Fine. You want to know something about me?"

Henry froze, staring at him.

"I trusted someone like you, once. One other time. And you know what happened? I lost *everything.*"

Vincent turned away from him.

"And *that's* why I'm here."

CHAPTER 16

WOLF TAILS

T ailing Casey, it turned out, was easier said than done.

Vincent followed Casey at a careful distance, knowing she would be keeping a special eye out for anyone stalking her after Hunter's release. He was grateful his own senses were comparable to hers.

They kept to their usual schedule of nighttime patrols, which gave Vincent and Henry time to report their findings briefly when the others' attention was elsewhere. So far all was quiet. The potion didn't appear to affect Casey or Hunter negatively, although its merits were still unknown.

"No news is good news," Henry said more than once, with his usual optimism. But Vincent couldn't help a wriggling feeling of doubt.

That wasn't the only source of it, either. Neither he nor Henry had mentioned their conflict since. It felt like Percy's ghost, hovering almost unseen in the corner of every interaction, with a horrible gravity too intense to fully ignore. They now artfully avoided the hangouts that had become a happy routine. They had plenty of excuses, being so busy following the werewolves.

Despite the allure of normalcy, this made it all the more impossible to ignore the truth. Vincent hardly had to remind himself now that he was not just another student at Alderwood. His mission was much more important, and once it was complete, none of this would matter. All of those things he loved about being here were only temporary–trivial things, tiny pieces. They were nice, but they weren't his to keep. He wasn't made for them. He wasn't worthy of them.

Cutting class became a habit as the full moon drew closer. He didn't like the thrill and the gnawing guilt that came with it, never mind the tribulations of catch-up work. They felt too much like the sixth sense clawing at his insides, never ceasing, compounding. He was hunting–just for the wrong target. But with each passing night he was more sure something bad would happen, and he needed to be there to catch it.

On the very day of the full moon, everything came to an abrupt halt just as his philosophy class was let out. The professor asked him to stay behind. Minutes later he emerged into the hall, his stomach a tangle of uncertainty.

Sierra was waiting for him there, eyes wide. "What was all that about?"

Vincent sighed. "Just my missed classes."

"Yeah...you have been missing a lot lately." She studied him for a moment. "What's going on, anyway? I wasn't gonna ask, but..."

He shrugged. "Nothing, really... Just a lot of catch-up. Hey, I have to go. See you later, Sierra."

He quickly veered off as they reached the door to the building, leaving her staring after him. He tried to leave his guilt behind with her. He wasn't about to tell her the truth.

One more missed class is an automatic failure. He would have to be extra careful from now on. Figure out how to follow Casey outside of class hours, and still make sure it was enough, somehow... *Because nothing can just be easy.*

Evening sun blared orange-gold through the trees, and he screwed up his eyes to keep the silhouette of his target in his sights. As long as Casey remained a silhouette, he knew he was far enough away.

It soon became clear she was only heading back to her dorm. Nothing out of the ordinary. He would tail her until she got there, just in case, and then he would break for dinner...

But as she reached the building, she suddenly skirted it, making for the parking lot. Vincent followed, keeping close to the wall. He peered around the corner to see Casey pulling on a helmet as she mounted a small motorcycle.

The realization hit him a moment too late as the engine roared to life. She skidded out onto the main road and opened the throttle, disappearing behind the buildings.

Vincent darted out into the parking lot, stopping when he reached the street beyond. He shielded his eyes with a hand against the dying sun, picking out the receding form far ahead.

Fine–that's how you want to play it?

He strode off down the sidewalk. It would take him a while, and he may never catch up...but he had to try. He *had* to know where she was going–especially with the threat of the full moon looming just below the horizon. She couldn't be alone tonight.

The better part of an hour had passed before Vincent reached the outskirts of town. By now the sun had dipped below the horizon, leaving the sky a wash of deep blue above his head. He shivered in his day jacket, pulling it tighter around his body. The streetlights were sparse here, pooling in near-useless circles on the sidewalk. Windows glowed gold in the gloom, the only respite for the eyes against the lonesome night creeping in around him.

Vincent's pace slowed to a crawl as he approached the first building, his conviction waning. His gaze wandered between the handful of facades, none of them giving him any sign of where his charge went.

Then he had an idea. He inhaled deeply, welcoming the cold air and the acrid stench of gasoline into his lungs. Although the pavement was already saturated with the smell, a stronger tang overwhelmed the rest–fresh from a motorcycle. He started off again, following its arrogant trail.

Suddenly Vincent spotted movement ahead. He moved closer to the buildings, using their walls as cover until he found a good vantage point behind a corner.

Dark shapes moved about, their edges barely outlined by a neon green sign fizzling above the building's door: "DEXTER'S LABORATORY." The dull thud of music emanated from within.

Then one of the forms heaved open a garage door. Light and sound spilled out onto the street. Vincent finally picked out Casey and her motorcycle, parked on the curb. She was standing beside it, talking with surprising familiarity to a short and lean black man with long, neat dreadlocks. Vincent had never seen her so friendly.

He hovered there, watching Casey and the man chat for a minute, their voices drowned by the music. Then she went to join a couple others milling about in the garage, greeting them with a similar warmth. They were gathered around two other bikes, both of them more impressive than Casey's.

But the man with the dreadlocks stopped short. He stood outside the garage for a moment. Then he turned, his dark eyes scanning the street.

Vincent shrank further behind his corner. He also glanced around, wondering what had spooked the man. He couldn't sense anything...

The man called out to the others, who also stopped and looked up. Casey immediately paced to his side, looking around the empty street.

Then, to his shock, she shouted above the music, "Vincent, Henry, you sneaky fucks! Get out here! I know you're there!"

Vincent balked. There was no way that man had spotted him. He had no idea what to do.

Casey was only getting more irate. She stomped out into the street, whirling around in both directions with her arms spread in indignation.

"Come on! Don't be a little bitch! The game's up!"

Gritting his teeth, Vincent finally stepped out from behind the building. All of them turned to face him with a mixture of surprise and suspicion–apart from Casey, who marched up to him with thunder on her face.

"How *dare* you follow me here!" she snarled, shoving him with both hands. He staggered a couple paces, but kept his balance. He bared his teeth at her.

"You know we've been keeping watch over you," Vincent growled.

"I go to your stupid fucking patrols every night! Isn't that enough for you people?"

"It's the full moon tonight. You think we were going to let you go off on your own? Especially after taking that potion for the first time?"

"I'm *fine!* I've *been* fine! Why can't you just leave me the fuck alone?"

Vincent knew she knew the answer to that question. Instead, he glanced pointedly at her companions. "What are you doing here? Who are these people?"

"None of your *business!*" Casey spat.

Suddenly the man who had first sensed Vincent stepped up to her side, his gaze cool as he studied him.

"We're her friends," the man said, his tone casual but reserved. "Not sure we can say the same for you. You should get out of here, man."

"Like hell!" Casey hissed.

The man shot her a quelling look. "Come on, Casey. Cool off a sec."

To Vincent's surprise, she actually simmered down, although her hackles remained up. He had half expected her to transform right in front of them.

"I'm Dex," the man said, offering a hand to Vincent. His mind caught up after a moment, and he took it to shake awkwardly. Evidently it wasn't what Dex had expected, amusement crossing his face as he returned the handshake. "And you're Vincent, I guess."

"I suppose she's talked about me," Vincent grunted, tossing a glare at Casey. He wondered what else she had shared.

"Yeah." Dex shrugged. "Seems to me like she's got more than her fair share of stalkers. Why don't you give it a rest, ah? She's safe with us tonight."

Vincent glanced instinctively upward, but found no moon–yet. He curled his lip as he looked back at Dex.

"I can't do that."

Casey growled. "You don't get to–"

"She's *safe* here," Dex interrupted. His gaze was so assured and so stony that Vincent's skin prickled. He almost wanted to give in.

"But *you* aren't," Vincent insisted, hating that he couldn't explain why. How was he supposed to convince them without revealing her secret?

Dex blinked calmly. "We're fine. We know what we're gettin' into. You'll have to trust me on this one."

Vincent's throat tightened as his suspicion rose. "Do you *know*...?"

"C'mon, let's just go," Casey said suddenly, grasping Dex's shoulder and pulling him back. He actually let her, starting back towards the garage. She cast Vincent one last glare. "Fuck off, alright? I'm not gonna kill anyone."

Then she spun around and marched after Dex. The others exchanged words with her, and she and Dex disappeared into the building.

Vincent hovered on the driveway, his insides boiling. The moon would rise soon, and there was no telling what would happen then. He hoped the potion would staunch her transformation entirely, but they had no proof of that yet. If it didn't...all these "friends" were trapped with her. But why would she risk that? She was hotheaded, not stupid.

I should have gone after Hunter instead, he growled to himself. *Henry would know what to do.*

His gaze fell upon the stragglers in the garage. *What* would *Henry do?*

He started towards them. Two of them glanced at him nervously and receded deeper into the building, but the biggest of them, a pale, gangly man with a boyish face, took too long to react as he tinkered with his ride. By the time he noticed Vincent approaching, it was too late.

"Uh...hey," the man said, running a hand through his short red hair anxiously. "You better get lost, before Dex sees."

"I'm just worried about Casey," Vincent said, changing tactics. This man looked considerably more pliable than the last. "Has she been acting any different lately?"

The man hesitated, shifting his feet. He glanced back helplessly where his friends had disappeared. "Uh..."

"I'm a friend of hers," Vincent insisted, holding his hand out as Dex had done to him. He forced a smile. "Vincent. I assume you've heard of me."

The man didn't look reassured, but he grasped Vincent's hand and pulled it sharply towards his chest. Vincent recalled the motion from when Casey had greeted her companions earlier. He copied it a second too late, but the other man didn't seem to mind.

"Name's Rolf," he said. "She's talked about you, yeah...she was real pissed at you though, so you better scram."

"I just want to know if she's alright," Vincent said again. "Then I'll go."

Rolf frowned, his thoughts furrowing his freckled face. He finally bent his head closer to the much shorter Vincent.

"Well...yeah, I mean, she's been kinda quiet, lately. At least, I think so. Just real serious. Not really wanting to do much. Thought maybe she was just..." He shrugged. "I dunno. There's a lot goin' on."

Vincent chewed on his lip. That was interesting...if even this guy noticed, maybe there was some weight to it after all. She *had* been unusually sullen, now that he thought about it. He had just blamed it on her annoyance with her forced duties, not to mention Hunter...

All of a sudden, Vincent realized just what he was staring at while lost in thought. Heaped beneath the nearest motorcycle were freshly stained newspapers, clearly being used to protect the floor from oil and other grime. This one's headline came into focus:

ALDERWOOD CEMETERY NIGHT WATCHMAN MISSING

Vincent snatched the newspaper up from the floor and scanned it. Rolf's question about this was little more than white noise as he read:

Cemetery night watchman William "Billy" Usher, age 56, was last seen before heading to work at 11:00 P.M. on Sunday. His wife Martha confirmed that everything was normal leading up to his untimely disappearance. "He's been working the night shift there for 33 years," Mrs. Usher said. "Nothing bad has ever happened there before. So I knew something was wrong when he didn't show up that morning." While initially unconcerned, two patrol officers agreed to go out to the cemetery and check on him, just in case.

They were glad they did. Upon searching the area, police found evidence of a struggle. "There was a substantial amount of blood," Sheriff Tim Simons reports. "We found evidence that someone was dragged through the grass towards the woods. But we didn't find Mr. Usher." The investigation is ongoing, and no new evidence has turned up so far. However, suspicions persist that this may be the work of the mysterious alleged serial murderer that has been plaguing the area for months now. Similar attacks began with University of Alderwood student Percy Quailheart, followed by the recent disappearance of another student, Mira Walker. This however is the first incident since Quailheart's that has left evidence of violence at the scene. Experts speculate that–

Vincent stopped reading. His blood had turned to ice. Rolf's voice began drifting back into his consciousness.

"Uh, Vincent?"

He folded and stashed the newspaper in his jacket. If he had any hesitation about leaving Casey with these people, it was gone now–he *had* to get back to Henry.

"Uh, bye!" called Rolf as Vincent turned on his heels, hurrying down the street the way he had come.

The pitch dark closed in around him. But as soon as he left the buildings behind, the first beam of silvery-white pierced through it. Dread filled his stomach like freezing water.

The full moon was rising.

A growl tore from Vincent's throat, and then he was bounding forward on four huge paws. As he ran the trees all around him seemed to lend their aid, their boughs clawing at the moon to restrain it. But they were no match– soon its light pierced through their defenses, dappling the street with silver.

Just as Vincent's chest began to burn, the first golden glimmer of window lights met his eyes. His heart skipped a beat–he needed to change back, *soon*.

But how? He didn't have time to go to the hill atop the biology building. And he was the furthest thing from calm right now.

I can't let Henry see me like this again.

The thought ripped through Vincent–but to his shock, it carried his form with it. In only moments, without breaking pace, he was human again. His insides throbbed even more now, and he coughed as he slowed to a jog. It was the best he could do–he was nearly there.

As soon as he reached a bench he threw himself into it, chest heaving. He fumbled in his pocket for his phone. When he pressed the call button it rang once, and then Henry's electronic voice said, "Vincent? What is it? Where are you?"

Vincent had to catch his breath for a moment before he managed to reply: "Campus, now! Where are you? I need to meet you!"

"Why? What happened?"

"Tell you later–please!"

"I'm outside Hunter's dorm, but I'll meet you wherever–"

"Don't move!" Vincent interjected. "I'll come there!"

He hung up, hauling himself off the bench. He surged forward again, ignoring the stabbing pains in his side as he pelted down the path towards Hunter's dorm hall.

As he neared, he spotted Henry's silhouette waiting just outside. Vincent almost careened straight into him in his haste. His heart skipped as Henry reached out to steady him.

"Whoa–Vincent! What's going on?"

"Look at this," Vincent breathed. He thrust the newspaper into Henry's hands. He moved towards the nearest lamp to peer at it. His eyes slowly widened as he read, and then he looked up at Vincent in horror.

"But–that's–"

"Our guy," Vincent said, finally catching his breath enough to speak properly. "He's dead."

"But–we don't know that," Henry blustered. "It just says something dragged him off–or, or dragged *something* off..."

"Come on, Henry–you *know* it's him!"

"When was this–" Henry stopped, looking at something on the page. "But–that was the day we were at the cemetery! He was there! Whatever it was, it must've happened right after we left..."

"Someone was following us," Vincent growled. "This was deliberate."

"Were they...trying to cover our tracks? They knew we were searching for them?" Henry began to pace, his thoughts as stark as the shadows on his face under the lamplight. "He was a witness..."

Vincent, however, was thinking something else. "How much blood was there when Percy was killed?"

Henry turned to look at him, confused. "What? Um...none, really. Vampires make clean kills, for obvious reasons. Are you..." The realization dawned on his face. "You think this was something else?"

"I think it left the blood on purpose."

The horror in Henry's expression deepened. "But...why..."

"It's a warning," Vincent said, without a trace of doubt.

"For us..."

And Vincent knew who did it. He could almost picture the sneer on Benjamin's face as he left the evidence all over the cemetery lawns.

Even worse...he could almost hear the message behind it, tumbling so easily from Benjamin's lips: *You did this. This was your fault.*

"They—they must know we won't stop looking for them," Henry said breathlessly.

"Maybe so. And we won't."

"Damn it..." Henry growled. "We were right there...*they* were right there...and we never saw them..."

"Don't worry about that now," Vincent said, his voice softening without his consent. He cleared his throat quietly and tried again. "What we need to do is follow that trail."

"The blood?"

Vincent nodded, his heart quickening as the idea sank in. "The dumbass left a perfect trail with that stunt. I can follow it to wherever they took the body—if we're quick about it. I imagine the police will be trying to clean it up soon, if they haven't already."

Henry's face brightened. "Yes! Alright, Vinny!"

Vincent cracked a smile. He couldn't help it.

But another thought wriggled uneasily inside him: what if that was Benjamin's idea, too? What if it was a trap?

And furthermore...he still couldn't lead Henry, or anyone else, directly to Benjamin. Vampires or no vampires.

But what other choice did he have? This was the third murder, and this one was even more his fault than the others. Benjamin was going to keep killing, and Vincent still had no idea why. Or how to implicate Melanie as well.

There are no bodies... That was the common thread. *Where are they? What are they doing with them?* If they followed that trail and found the night watchman's body...maybe they could discover more clues. *Something.* If they didn't...they were back to stumbling in the dark.

"But we can't go right away." Henry turned back towards the dorm hall with a frown. "I have to stay and watch Hunter..."

The other half of Vincent's worries returned to him in a rush. He scanned each of the windows as if they would show him proof of Hunter's safety. He found nothing.

"Have you seen anything at all?" he asked.

"All quiet. I followed him from his last class to the Commons and back here. He hasn't left his room."

"You're sure?"

Henry nodded. "I've been patrolling between the front and back doors. If he snuck off, he would've had to be either very lucky, or *very* fast."

Vincent grimaced. It was a slim chance, but he still didn't like any odds.

"What about Casey?" Henry asked, and guilt squirmed inside Vincent's stomach yet again. "You left her?"

"I had to," he insisted, although at this point he was beginning to regret the risk. "She wasn't cooperating, anyway. She found out I was following her and confronted me with some friends she was visiting in town."

Henry looked alarmed. "It's the full moon, why would she go all the way there? She knows what could happen!"

Vincent shrugged. "Your guess is as good as mine. She's not *stupid*, she must know that."

"Then why risk it?"

"I don't know why she does anything," Vincent said, shaking his head. "But she went inside some bike shop with her friends, and wouldn't hear a word of it. I couldn't even keep a proper eye on her. That's when I saw the newspaper."

"Shit, Vincent! We have to get out there, or—" Henry didn't finish the thought, already turning on his heels.

"Wait," Vincent said, grabbing his arm to stop him. "It's too late now. By the time we arrived..."

Henry cursed again, but stayed. He searched the empty air for answers that didn't seem to come. "God, what do we do? She's gonna turn them all...fuck, why didn't I get Percy to help? I didn't want Ava to get hurt, but—" He broke off, running a hand through his hair and then grabbing it, messing it up. "Fuck...what am I even *doing*? Every day something new goes sideways! How am I supposed to keep up?"

A jolt of alarm raced through Vincent's chest. He recognized that look—Henry was slipping again.

"Henry," he said, his grip on Henry's arm softening. Ignoring his heart hammering in his ears, he slid his hand around to Henry's back and rested it there, holding fast, bending close. "It's okay. Casey must know what she's doing. She wouldn't put her friends in danger like that."

Henry seemed to freeze beneath his hand, his back muscles firm and tense. "We don't know that," he said through gritted teeth. "And Hunter's probably snuck out when I wasn't looking—god, I can't believe I thought I could handle this by myself! I'm so fucking naive. I'm not even a Warden yet! If all those people couldn't do it peacefully, how did I think I could?"

Vincent pressed harder, steadier against him. "You're not *naive* for wanting something better," he insisted, willing Henry to hear the fervor in his voice.

"I *am*," Henry said, his own voice cracking. It took Vincent's heart with it. "What else could I be? I'm just a kid. I've never dealt with a real monster before this. And if this is how it always goes..."

"You think your father would have given me a chance?"

Henry stopped. He finally looked down at him. Something complex hung just behind his eyes.

"And Casey? Percy? Do you think they would still be around?"

"No," said Henry quietly. "Not after what they've done."

"You really think they deserve that?"

Henry shook his head, slowly.

"You're the only thing standing in the way of that. *You.* They've done bad things, it's true...but you know they didn't want to. Sometimes it's just a bad choice at a bad moment. But they're better than that–they *can* be, if only someone like you gives them that chance."

Vincent was almost surprised by his own words. They had been hovering somewhere in his skull, and somehow they found their way through. Even more surprising–he believed them. He believed that of Henry.

Henry didn't reply. But Vincent knew him well enough to know it had reached him. His mind was turning, sifting through the idea of it.

"I'm still here, Henry," Vincent pressed. "I'm still with you. You're not the only one who believes in this."

"I'm not?"

Vincent froze. "What?"

"You don't believe in second chances. You told me so yourself." Henry's voice was so quiet, his tone unreadable. "You trusted someone. Really trusted them. And now you can't do it again."

Vincent fell silent. What was he supposed to say to that? It was true. He had admitted it.

And yet...

"I...believe in *you*, Henry." Maybe he should have said something else. But he was just too tired to lie. "If anyone can prove it's worth it...you can."

Henry didn't argue. He didn't say a word. Vincent prayed that it meant something. That what he said meant something.

The two of them stood there in silence, watching the dark building. One by one the lit windows winked out as the night wore on, leaving only the yellow glare of lamplight and the silvery sheen of moonlight. All was quiet but for their breaths and the steady drone of insects.

Finally Henry's voice broke the hush. "We'd be stupid to go stumbling around out there in the dark, wouldn't we? If...if he escaped somehow, that is."

A fresh conviction stirred inside Vincent. Henry needed him. This was something he could give him.

He finally let go of Henry and made for the back door of the dorm hall, ignoring the questions tossed after him. As soon as he reached it, he immediately had his answer.

"There's no trace of Hunter's scent here," Vincent reported when he returned. "Not recently, anyway. He hasn't escaped."

Henry's shoulders sagged with relief. "Oh, thank god." He glanced up at the moon again. "The potion must've worked after all...I don't think there's anything more we can do tonight."

"I can follow that blood trail," Vincent pointed out.

Henry shook his head, already turning to leave. "No. It'd be stupid to go out in the dead of night like this. Even with good night vision," he added as Vincent opened his mouth to argue. "It's too dangerous. Our enemies have it too. Besides, the trail will be easier to follow in daylight."

"I can smell just fine at night," Vincent grunted. "And it'll be fainter the longer we wait."

"If we're mounting a whole expedition into the forest to find our killer, we're gonna need a lot more preparation," Henry said. He was returning to himself, slowly. "We need to be rested. And I want everyone there. Even Casey," he added pointedly. "We need every advantage we can get. We already have to face two vampires. Probably. I'd be surprised if there weren't more."

Vincent grimaced, but he saw the sense in Henry's plan. He hoped the trail wouldn't lead directly to Benjamin, or his vampires...but it was dangerously possible. "Alright. But we should leave tomorrow, or we risk losing the trail."

Henry nodded grimly. "You got it."

"What about Hunter? Should we leave him alone?"

"If he hasn't turned tonight, I don't think he'll be a problem. I think we can afford to leave him be for a day or two."

"We've certainly made him paranoid enough," Vincent agreed with a little smirk. "We *could* leave Percy behind to watch him..."

"No...you're right, Vincent." Henry lowered his gaze. "I...can't do this alone. We need as much help as we can get. We should give Percy a chance. And he needs to find his body, too. This is one step closer to that."

Vincent felt something small begin to glow deep in his chest. Henry had listened, after all. It meant something.

He nodded. "Tomorrow, then."

CHAPTER 17

NEVER HAVE I EVER

Skipping class hardly should have been the most pressing thing on Vincent's brain at the moment. But he couldn't ignore what it meant for him: the final nail in the coffin for his education. He was choosing his mission over his cover identity. They couldn't wait for a weekend to make the journey into the forest, or the trail might disappear entirely. This was their best chance.

As he crossed the parking lot, heading for Henry's little blue car, the weight of his own remorse felt heavier than the pack hefted over his shoulder. It surprised him, but it also didn't. That was the strangest thing about it. It belonged there. At some point it had made a home inside his heart, and he hardly even realized it.

As he waited by the car, he tugged his tie tighter around his neck. He hoped it would remind him of the redemption that awaited him back home, very soon now. But instead it felt like a noose.

His stomach churned–when did that change? What was happening to him?

The others' arrival penetrated his thoughts. Henry greeted him with his usual smile, but Vincent recognized that flicker of solemn determination behind his clear blue eyes. Percy looked even paler than Ava normally was. Casey seemed as casual as normal, but there was an air of tension beneath the surface. At least her response to Henry's summons proved she hadn't murdered her friends in town after all.

"Good to see you're taking this seriously," Vincent remarked, noting Casey's lack of supplies.

"What?" Casey said flatly.

Vincent tapped his pack for emphasis. Casey only shrugged.

"You're gonna want a sleeping bag at least," Henry said, frowning at her. "And food, and a water bottle, and a change of socks..."

"I'll be fine."

"No, you won't," Henry insisted. "We have no idea how long this is gonna take, or how far the trail goes. We might be in the forest for days. I have all kinds of essentials," he added with a note of pride, readjusting the pack on his back, "but *you* need some personal items."

"Fine," she grumbled. She started trudging back across the parking lot.

"Hurry up!" Vincent barked. She gave no indication of hearing.

By the time Casey returned, the sun was well above the horizon. Vincent's annoyance had swelled close to bursting, and he finally let it loose when she was within earshot again.

"You'd better have packed your whole dorm in that time! The trail is getting colder every minute!"

"Keep your fur on," Casey grunted. The backpack she brought looked significantly less full than anyone else's. She turned away from him and started pulling on the car door handle repeatedly. Henry sighed and unlocked it for her, then went to pack their things in the tiny trunk.

The bright morning mist had mostly burned off by the time they pulled the car off to the side of the road. They grabbed their supplies from the trunk, then started off down the road towards the cemetery fence.

Soon they had jumped the fence once again and found themselves in what should have been the familiar confines of the graveyard. However, it looked quite different—and less eerie—by day. Although they kept a lookout for guards, the place was deserted. Even Vincent could pick up no traces of recent life.

However, one stale scent stood out to him, familiar and unwelcome. His sixth sense growled deep in his gut.

Benjamin had been here.

I knew it was you.

That meant the risks were real. What would happen if they followed the blood trail? Out in the wilderness, away from prying eyes, nothing could stop Benjamin's forces from tearing them apart.

But if they didn't try...they would lose their only lead.

I'm not leaving Percy and Ava like this. I'm not letting Mira and the watchman die in vain. I'm not letting Melanie get away with it.

Besides, Vincent told himself, maybe it wasn't a trap at all. Maybe they would even get lucky and find Benjamin alone out there. Maybe they could take him by surprise.

And then what? It's all over, just like that, and I go back home?

Vincent stayed silent.

"Spread out and keep an eye out for the crime scene," said Henry, shading his eyes against the glare from the sun-touched fog. "Although they may have cleaned it up by now..."

"Keep your nose out, then," Vincent said to Casey. She only grunted in reply, wandering off in the opposite direction.

For a brief moment Vincent was seized by the impulse to check Benjamin's grave again. But it was too risky in broad daylight. Instead he meandered up the hill, searching for the best vantage point. Before he could reach the top, though, Casey's voice echoed across the field:

"Found it!"

Everyone rushed over to find her at the edge of the trees.

"Next time, *please* yell louder so every guard in a two-mile radius can join us," Vincent growled as he approached. But his quip fell flat as the stench of salt and iron stung his nostrils, and he caught his first look at what she had found.

The newspaper was right–it was a grisly scene. Dark, dried blood spattered the ground. An obvious trail streaked through the grass in the direction of the woods. The area around it was taped off with yellow plastic, wound around the nearest headstones as anchors. The ends followed the blood trail and disappeared into the undergrowth beyond.

"O-oh god..." Percy whimpered. Even Casey looked perturbed.

Wordlessly, Henry began following the tape deeper into the forest. The others fell in step behind him. The tape led them into the canopy for a minute or more, before at last the visible trail ceased at the edge of a burbling stream.

Henry looked to Vincent expectantly. The smell of mud and nettles overtook everything else, but underneath it the unmistakable tang of gore remained.

"I've got it," Vincent assured him. He took a couple steps back, bracing himself, then ran to take a flying leap across the stream. He skidded safely into the leaf mold on the other side.

One by one the others followed with no trouble, apart from a moment of trepidation where Percy had to be encouraged across. In the end he cleared the stream as easily as the others, which seemed to embolden him. They walked on through the forest at a steady pace, following Vincent's lead.

Soon the last of the lingering mist dissipated, replaced by little golden beams of sunlight that dappled the forest floor. The frigid air slowly warmed, bringing gentle, bright birdsong and the hum of insects. Something panged deep in Vincent's heart as he recalled that first taste of the world above, not so far from this very spot. It was almost as wondrous now as it was then, even though so much had changed.

In that moment, traveling through the vibrance of the living world with the warmth of his friends at his side, it was impossible to ignore the truth. All of this wasn't just for his promises, or his vengeance, or his duty, or even his sympathy. He did not want to leave this world behind. He had built so much here. He didn't want to go back into the darkness.

But darkness, as it always did, found him anyway. It soon crept over the forest, turning it deep orange and then dusk-purple and then gray. The shadows grew until they swallowed the trees and the travelers within them. Still the trail went on.

"We should make camp for the night," Henry said as they reached a grassy clearing.

"But the scent is only going to get fainter if we wait," Vincent protested.

"I'm tired," Casey complained.

"Wonder why," Vincent shot back.

Casey glared at him. But, strangely, she had no comeback for him.

"We have no idea how much farther the trail goes," Henry said to Vincent. "And it's dangerous to travel at night. We should rest."

"We have flashlights," Vincent muttered, but he was outnumbered. He slung his bag off his shoulder in defeat.

"I-I bet you'll be able to find the trail just as easy tomorrow," Percy said, coming over to help him unpack his supplies.

"We'll see," Vincent grumbled. Looking for someone to vent on, he noticed Casey leaning against a tree nearby. "Hey–*if* you're not too tired, we could use some firewood!"

Casey offered him a rude gesture, then wandered off. Vincent wasn't sure if she was actually obeying or if she just wanted to stay out of his sights. Either way, he wasn't in the mood to chase her down. Instead he noticed Henry had started setting up the tent he had brought, and in spite of their disagreement Vincent went over to help.

When they finished, Henry looked around worriedly. "Where did Casey go?"

Vincent shrugged. "I've followed her enough in the last twenty-four hours. She can do what she wants."

"B-but what if she's gotten lost?" Percy piped up, his eyes wide. "I-it's getting so dark..."

"She can see just fine." Vincent heaved a sigh. "Fine, I guess *I'll* go get the firewood..."

Just as he was about to step out of the clearing, a shadow appeared in front of him. His heart leaped into his throat–but then he recognized Casey.

"Here's your fucking firewood," she growled, brushing past him to dump an armful of branches on the ground. "Happy? Now can I sleep?"

"Be my guest," Vincent said, quite surprised she had followed through. She immediately trudged over to the tent and ducked inside.

Percy lifted the tent flap slightly. "D-don't you want any dinner, Casey?"

"You should keep your strength up," Henry put in.

"I'll eat later," Casey's gruff voice drifted from the tent.

"Don't bother pestering her," Vincent advised, crouching next to the pile of wood.

He paused, realizing only now that he had no idea how to set up a campfire. He knew there was a special way to do it–he had seen it in Henry's movies. He started trying to prop the sticks up against each other in a cone shape. In moments he had produced a mess of tangled branches that more resembled a bird's nest than anything remotely useful. He looked up at Henry helplessly, who was trying very hard not to laugh. Vincent frowned at him.

"What? Go on then, *you* do it!"

"Oh, I can!" Percy chirped, hurrying over. Vincent crossed his arms, standing back as Percy began arranging the branches against each other in a very apt image of what Vincent was *trying* to make. He sighed.

"Too bad you're too old for boy scouts," Henry said to Vincent, his voice higher-pitched than normal as he fought back his laughter. Vincent elbowed him sharply.

Henry brought out some tinder and matches, and soon they had a crackling fire. Its heat darted across Vincent's face, drawing him closer. The temperature had plummeted as soon as the sunlight faded, numbing his nose and hands. He only now realized just how much he needed the warmth.

And with this recognition came hunger. He tensed to stifle the growl that surged through his belly, overpowering his sixth sense easily. The others seemed to feel it too–Henry wasted no time finding their food supplies and beginning to prepare them over the fire. Soon they had canned chili and crackers to feast on, warming their hands on their bowls. It was nowhere near as good as the Commons' version, but even so Vincent finished his fervently and looked around hopefully for more.

"You've had yours," Henry chided him. "The last bit's for Casey."

"She doesn't want it," said Vincent.

"Didn't you bring any chips with you?" Henry grinned at him.

Vincent smiled wryly. "I ate them all."

"Already?"

"It's been months!"

"That was like, a whole vending machine's worth!"

Vincent threw him the most plaintive look he could muster. Even in his human form, he knew how to beg. "Come on, Henry…"

Apparently it was good enough. Henry relented, shaking his head as he fought back a smile. "Oh, alright…but at least go ask her first, would you?"

Vincent snatched the remaining bowl and marched off to the tent. He stuck his head inside, greeted by darkness. He could only barely make out the lump that was Casey. "Hey–"

"I heard you," Casey grunted. "The whole forest thinks you're offering it chili."

"Well, then?"

"Go for it. I'm not hungry."

Vincent's triumph was short-lived as guilt wormed its way in. "Seriously? We've been hiking all day. Where did your wolf go, ah?"

Casey wasn't amused. "Just eat it yourself, alright? Stop bugging me."

"…You must have had a late night."

"You're psychic."

"What happened, anyway? With your friends…"

"None of your business."

"I just–"

"You just *nothing*. Stay out of it. I didn't gore anyone, okay? I didn't even transform."

"You didn't?" That was a relief. He wasn't sure why Casey didn't share the sentiment.

"No. Satisfied?"

He wasn't. But it was clear he would only antagonize her if he kept pressing. "Fine. I'm going."

He returned to his spot by the fire.

"No luck?" Henry asked.

Vincent shook his head. "I tried, I promise." He gazed down at the bowl of lukewarm chili in his hands. He laid it down in the grass beside him with a sigh.

After only a moment, there was a rustle from the tent. Casey emerged, her expression unreadable. She settled herself in an empty place by the fire, snagging the chili bowl along the way. She began to eat it stolidly, ignoring everyone's stares and instead glaring at the campfire as if it had personally slighted her.

"H-hi, Casey!" Percy said with an attempt at cheer. She didn't reply. Henry looked pleased, but knew better than to provoke her.

After a minute of awkward silence, Percy tried a different tactic: "H-hey, have you guys ever played 'Never Have I Ever'?"

"Of course," said Henry, brightening at the idea. "I don't think Vincent has."

"O-oh! W-well, it's simple! Here...um, l-let me start." Percy cleared his throat, then said, "N-never have I ever gotten detention."

Both he and Henry raised two hands up, fingers splayed. Casey snorted.

"Come on. You're s'posed to take a drink if you have. What kind of weak-ass version is this?"

"That's the last thing we need out here," Henry said.

Casey rolled her eyes. She suddenly stood, leaving her empty bowl on the ground. She ducked into the tent, returning with a small bottle of whiskey. She sat back down and took a short swig.

Henry opened his mouth as if to protest, but decided against it in the end. He looked to Vincent instead. "Do you get the idea?"

Vincent nodded, raising his own hands slightly with his fingers out. "Ah...what's detention?"

Percy giggled. "O-oh, it's like a punishment, w-where you have to stay in a classroom after school hours."

"It's usually only a thing in grade school," Henry added.

"I bet I'd get it otherwise," Vincent muttered.

"Why?" asked Henry.

"Whose turn is it now?" Vincent said quickly, looking to Percy.

"O-oh–um, l-let's go clockwise."

"Okay." Henry paused, thinking. "Never have I ever been in a relationship with someone."

Vincent blinked in surprise, but didn't say anything. Percy kept his fingers up, a bit sheepishly, but Casey took another gulp of whiskey.

"Really?" Henry said, looking at her. "I didn't think..."

"A while back," Casey grunted.

"Not in college, then?"

"Nah. High school summer. It didn't last long."

"I'm sorry," said Henry, with true sympathy.

Casey shrugged. "He turned out to be an asshole, anyway." She took a sudden interest in the label on her bottle. "Besides, at least I'm not a loveless loser like you guys."

"Thanks," said Henry.

"My turn," Casey said, a little brighter now. "Never have I ever been in love."

Nobody moved for a moment.

"W-wait–h-how big are we talking?" Percy piped up. "Like...a crush? O-or *love* love?"

"Whatever your interpretation is," Casey said, gesturing vaguely with her bottle. "I sure wasn't in love with that bastard."

Again, silence. Then Henry crooked one finger slightly downward. "I–I don't know if it counts as love," he said bashfully. "So I'm giving it a half-finger."

Vincent's heart sank into his stomach. Was he still hung up on Sierra, even after their conversation about her?

Then he caught Henry's eye. He was looking at him–why was he looking at him? Did he know what Vincent was thinking? Or...?

No. That was ridiculous. Even if by some remote chance Henry had even entertained the idea, Vincent had made it plain–they were too different. He wasn't going to let someone else destroy what little life he still had left.

But in spite of it, Vincent couldn't bring himself to lie. Without fully registering it, he lowered half of one finger, too.

Everyone else missed Vincent's answer as Percy dropped his entire finger.

"Are you for real? *You're* in love with someone?" Casey pressed.

Percy nodded shyly. "Y...yeah...I-I mean, I think so..."

"Who is it?"

"I-I'm not telling! Th-that's not part of the game!"

"But we wanna know!"

"W-why do you care?"

"Because!"

"Oh, leave him alone," Vincent interjected. As much as he, too, was curious, he didn't want to give them any room to focus on the question longer. "Never have I ever..."

What? He hadn't thought this through. But he had to say something.

"...argued with my father. Ah–I mean, a parent."

Both Henry and Percy lowered a finger. Casey took a long swig of her whiskey.

"How have you not?" she said.

Vincent's neck prickled uncomfortably. He hadn't expected to be so heavily outweighed. "I...I don't know. I just haven't. I wouldn't."

"You *wouldn't?* What, your dad's never been a dick to you?"

Vincent clenched his teeth. "I mean..." The words died in his throat.

"I love my dad," Henry piped up, to Vincent's intense relief. "But...we don't always see eye to eye. I don't think I'd bother arguing with him to his face anymore, but..."

"I wouldn't wanna get cut off either," Casey said with a sneer. "With a rich daddy like that."

"Shut up, Casey."

Everyone fell silent. Henry's usual warmth had frozen over in an instant.

Vincent shot a warning glare at Casey and said, "I can't imagine your parents are thrilled with how you turned out."

She let out a bark of a laugh. She took another swig of her whiskey, this time without a prompt, then lifted it in a toast. "Hear, hear."

"I-I've never heard anything about your family, Casey," Percy said timidly.

Casey shrugged. "What is there to tell? Stepdad keeps us afloat, mom won't *ever* let me forget how she came over from Vietnam, how life is *so* much better here, blah blah blah. Both of them think I should be more grateful and work harder and so on. Sorry we can't all live the American Dream."

Percy shrank back immediately, but Henry finally seemed done playing nice with her. "But your parents helped you get to college, didn't they?"

"Only 'cause my brother made 'em. I owe more to FAFSA. You know—student aid?"

"I know what FAFSA is."

"Yeah, well, it's the only reason I'm here. Well, that, and I wanted to get out of my town. It was crampin' my style."

"I-is that what you argued with your parents about?" Percy asked. "That's what it was for me..."

"Seriously?" Casey snorted. "That's all you ever argued over?"

Percy looked hurt. "I–I guess...I-I mean, I can't remember *every* time, but...mostly..."

Casey shook her head. "You guys are all so goddamn lame. Can't even stand up for yourselves. And here you are dragging my ass out into the wilderness hunting vampires. None of this adds up."

"Not everything has to be solved with a fight," Henry said coolly. He had fully lost whatever remained of his good mood. "That's what *I* used to argue with my dad about."

"At least that's interesting," Casey yawned.

"It's *life or death*," Henry snapped. "For people like you. If I were you, I'd care a little more."

Casey stared at him incredulously. "What do you mean by that?"

"I mean, my dad has a very different view on how much tolerance we should afford the Others."

"*Others,*" Casey echoed in contempt. "I hate that term. I guess if the rest of the Illuminati is just like your dad, I should just give up the ghost now and let 'em take me."

"It's not off the table," Henry growled. "Not if you keep behaving like you have been. Vincent told me where he found you last night."

"I told him before, and I'll tell you too," Casey said, jabbing a hand at Vincent, "I didn't hurt anyone last night. I didn't transform. I didn't do *anything*. Save the lecture, okay?" She stood up swiftly, whiskey in hand.

"Wait–what? You didn't transform?" Henry said, but she didn't stop. She disappeared back inside the tent.

"D-did the potion work, then?" Percy asked quietly after a moment.

"I guess so," Henry replied, visibly relaxing now that Casey was gone. "We couldn't see any signs of Hunter going wolf either."

Percy beamed. "Oh, wow, that's great! I-I'm so glad I could help after all..." He let out a little sigh, looking at ease with the world, as if the night hadn't gone so poorly at all.

"I should be able to make it next month on my own," Henry said, and instantly Percy's smile faded. Vincent noticed, but he wasn't sure Henry did. "You really saved us there, Percy. I can't thank you enough."

"Y–yeah. No problem, Henry."

It was clear that the evening had overstayed its welcome. Soon Vincent was climbing into his sleeping bag, swaddling himself as tightly as he could in its depths. The tent was big, but not big enough. He was sandwiched between Percy and Henry, with Casey on the far end beside Percy. Privately Vincent thought that was a good idea–the further she was from Henry right now, the better.

Still, that left Vincent in the uncomfortable position of deciding whether to encroach more on Henry's space or Percy's. The memory of Casey forcing him to squish in beside Henry in the Denny's booth returned at once, and he suddenly felt too warm in his sleeping bag. He did his best to keep exactly centered, ignoring the pressure of his friends' sleeping bags on either side of him.

But his heartbeat thudded in his ears as he lay there in the dark. Henry was so close, all he had to do was reach out slightly and he would feel his warmth. For a moment he wished he could. A touch was so much simpler than the turbulence in his head.

But it still held the weight of everything unseen behind it. It felt like a gravity stretched between them, as strong as his and Benjamin's, always pulling Vincent towards Henry. Always, he resisted. But he longed for the comfort of it, the satisfaction of finally letting go and closing that abyss between them.

As much as he wanted to think otherwise...he was starting to believe his father was wrong.

Every human is the same at heart. Selfish and treacherous and greedy.

Now he knew for sure. Henry was none of those things. Somehow...he was better than that.

Vincent's exhaustion began to claim him, even as his mind churned beneath the covers. But his troubled heart wasn't finished with him yet. Before he knew it his consciousness was somewhere else entirely, far away from the little tent in the dark woods.

Shadows swam before his mind's eye, coalescing into brief images before darting away again.

He was walking across a dark plain, his footfalls turning gray grass to ash beneath his paws. A line of gaunt figures just as ashen rose before him. Ropes draped loosely over their wrists. They knew there was no escape from this place.

A familiar face with eyes like a winter sky appeared. He was like a sunbeam breaking through a storm. The first smile Vincent had ever seen that meant it. Echoes reached his ears:

You must be one of the guardians here. I'm Benjamin.

Mistrust roiled in the pit of his stomach. He was bred with it.

This place is so bleak...have you ever seen the sky before? Do you know what that is?

But Vincent couldn't help himself. With every word Benjamin spun his web around him, dazzling Vincent's eyes with promises.

I found you again. I'm so glad. This place is beginning to wear on me...I feel like I'm sinking...like the shadows here are swallowing what's left of me... How are you whole, still? How do you do it? Is it because it's all you've ever known? Do you feel His eyes on you always, like I do?

And Vincent had begun to question it, himself. Day by day he began searching for that sunbeam amongst the gray, his eyes picking him out on every patrol route that met. Day by day he lost himself in descriptions of all the things he had never known. He felt them like a hole in his heart—something that should be there but wasn't, whose absence left him slowly bleeding, unaware until he had no blood left to give.

What did you do to deserve this?

Vincent wasn't sure. He wasn't sure what he *deserved*.

I remember. I was led into sin. I can barely withstand the memory. Maybe...can I show you? Can you help me with the weight of it?

Flashes of agony, so like his own but so much worse—hellfire in the deepest crevices of his body, the weight of someone else's body on his back, pressing him into the earth, crushing him, deaf to his cries and his screams—

—a pallid face askew before him, lacerated, strands of gray and auburn hair like thread pulled apart, throat purple, bare legs akimbo, her dark eyes windows into the abyss—his heart ablaze with love and frostbitten with horror, ice-hot inside his mangled body—

Did you see my mother's face? Did you see what that man did to her? I thought he would kill me, too. I almost wished he had, for a long time. Until I decided he should have.

I had to follow in her footsteps to survive on my own. What do you do, when you have nothing to give? You sell. So I sold.

I was so young. I had to be smart. I had to look out for myself. But surviving was just a habit, in that kind of life. It didn't take long to realize the drugs were good for me, too. They forced my broken body to feel something better for once. So I tried anything to alter my reality. My own personal Hell on earth. Until I couldn't take it anymore.

That must be it. Why I'm here. I can't think of any other reason. I never hurt anyone like that man did. No one but myself, in the end. Only once I found myself here did I realize...my life never once belonged to me. Not even after I left it behind.

And when that face sought him again, when he turned that last gleam of hope onto Vincent in the darkness, how could he deny him?

Just let me run. Let me get a head start, if nothing else. Look–I'm not swallowed yet, I shed my ropes. I still have life in me. I understand now what I have to do. I don't deserve this, I don't belong here–I need to go back! I need to make all of this right! Wouldn't you, if you could?

And he would, a thousand times over, he would.

Please...help me.

Vincent woke with a start, that face burned into his mind's eye. For a moment he thought he was back home still, the darkness thick around him. Then he heard the soft breathing of his companions and the rustle of leaves outside the tent.

He sighed deeply, the tension slowly draining from his body. A warm weight against his back seemed to soak it up for him, replacing it with a sensation like featherdown deep in his heart. He closed his eyes again, allowing the presence to lull him...

And then he realized: it was Henry. At some point during the night, Vincent had moved to rest against his back. His comfort was instantly assailed by hot shame, and he nearly pulled himself away.

But he stopped.

Was Henry awake? No, his breathing was deep and rhythmic.

Vincent lay there, hardly daring to breathe, his heart hammering in his ears. Every part of his body felt light and charged, like thunderclouds gathering before the first strike of lightning.

But he couldn't stay there forever. And he couldn't face what Henry might say if he woke.

Vincent let out the breath he was holding and carefully wormed his way out of his sleeping bag. That brief, deep comfort instantly faded away to a familiar chill, both inside and out. He grabbed his jacket, then crawled to the tent flap. He cringed at the zipper's sound as he ducked outside. He listened for a moment, but the breathing from within did not break. He turned away.

The shadows of the forest were stark against the silver moonlight that found its way through the canopy. The chittering of night creatures rose to meet him–a reassurance that no unseen predators stalked the little camp. The air out here was enticing, crisp and laden with the fresh scent of plantlife.

He let it lead him from the campsite and into the trees, desperate to shake the lingering remnants of his dream. They burned like embers in his chest. He didn't want to think about any of that, not now. Maybe not ever.

But that wasn't a luxury he could afford, try as he may. It was the only reason he was even here in the first place. He had been circling the truth for a long time now. And here he was, leading the others straight on the trail to Benjamin.

There was no other way this could end. As he wandered like a ghost between the shivering pines, the truth of it seeped into his very being with the cold night air. It was as if his dream had come to remind him of his destiny. He had been hiding from it for so long–but it was a part of him, as real as his paws, his fangs, his burning eyes, the darkness at his heart. He could not hide forever.

He was a guard dog. Benjamin was his reason for being, his charge; but he was also his reason for being *here*, in more ways than one. He was haunted by those first aromas of the world above, brought to him on Benjamin's honeyed tongue. If he hadn't spent so long dreaming of such things from the depths of Hell...maybe he wouldn't have stayed to find out for himself.

Maybe he wouldn't have even let Benjamin go. Maybe he wouldn't have begged his father to let him come here.

For a moment, Vincent had thought his path led to Henry. He thought he would walk by his side into the rosy horizon, the living world and all of its wonders at his fingertips. Maybe he could be like him, and help Percy and give Mira justice, stop Melanie and stop the murders and prove that people deserved second chances, and no one—especially Henry—would ever have to know that it was all his fault for letting Benjamin go. No one would ever have to know the true darkness inside him. But he had known it from the beginning, somewhere deep inside:

Every road led back to Benjamin. Back to Hell. It always had.

Then, suddenly, a strange silhouette caught his eye.

Vincent stopped. After a breathless moment he determined that it was perfectly still—not alive.

He crept closer. The shadows revealed a mess of things sticking out at odd angles. It almost looked like a tower.

Something deep inside him stirred, prickled, although he did not know why. He stopped short, his gaze flickering over it, desperately trying to piece together what he was seeing.

Then, it all clicked into place: *bones.*

Stacks of bones, propped against one another in weird shapes, trussed up with rope and twine to hold them in place. Some of them were far too small to be human. But others...

Vincent's stomach dropped. The forest swayed around him as the realization trickled in like icy water.

The stench of death around such a gruesome scene was fainter than he expected it to be. These bones had been here for a while. But it wasn't faint enough—after all, Vincent had spent weeks with his friend's scent in his nose as he slept. It was unmistakable.

He had found what remained of Percy's body.

CHAPTER 18

THE TOWER

"**W**hat the *hell* am I looking at?"

All four of them now stood before the tower of bones in the dark woods. The moonlight gleamed eerily on the jagged cacophony of shapes. Vincent had not told them what to expect. Now he watched as the realization dawned on each of their faces.

"Oh, Vincent...that can't be..." Henry said, grief warring with horror.

"I can smell it," Vincent said quietly. "It's Percy's."

Percy began to tremble from Ava's body, his eyes frozen on the tower. He shook his head slowly.

"I-i-it c-can't..."

"What the *fuck* did they do to him?" Casey snarled, although she looked almost as frightened as Percy. "What is all this?"

"I-it has to be some kind of effigy," Henry said, very obviously trying to keep himself steady. "But what's it for?" He took a step forward to examine the tower, but Vincent grabbed his arm.

"Don't get too close," he warned.

"Why?" Henry said, surprised.

"I just have a bad feeling about it."

"Um...*yeah*. It's a fucking Jenga tower of bones!" said Casey.

"Just...let me." Vincent stepped ahead of Henry, finally daring to move close to it. *Better me than him.* All the same, his heart thudded in his ears.

Dirt crunched behind him. Henry had ignored his order and was now at his side. He peered up at the imposing structure, the sweat on his temples glistening in the half-light.

"Henry," Vincent growled. "This thing could be dangerous for mortals to—"

"This is my job, okay, Vincent?" Henry interrupted, startling Vincent with his abruptness. "I can handle it."

Without waiting for a reply, Henry continued around the perimeter of the tower, his eyes moving over it with care. Vincent stayed where he was, realizing he was hardly more likely to make sense of it than someone with Henry's background. But still...he was being sensitive again about doing everything himself.

As Vincent waited in silence, he suddenly realized: there were no animal sounds here. No rustlings in the undergrowth, no drone of insects in the night. A shiver traveled up his spine.

Suddenly, before he could stop him, Henry reached out and laid his palm on the bones.

A surge of energy lanced Vincent's heart. He staggered backwards from the force of it, clutching his chest. Judging from the gasps around him, the others had felt it too. His vision swam with colored static.

A shudder passed through him as the alien sensation slowly melted away and his surroundings returned. Henry was standing in the same spot, grasping one hand with the other. He met Vincent's gaze with wide eyes.

"Why did you do that?" Vincent hissed. "Dumbass!"

"Did you feel that? It deflected me..."

"Y-yeah," Percy said quietly, trembling just behind Vincent. "I-it was like s-something jumped through my...my..."

Casey rounded on him suddenly. "Hey–I wonder what would happen if *you* touched it?"

"W-what?"

"It's *your* bones! Maybe it's waiting for *you* to–"

"I don't think that's it, Casey," Henry interrupted.

He stepped away from the tower, to Vincent's relief. He was still staring at it, as if trying to decipher something written in the arrangement of bones that only he could see.

"I...think it's some kind of ward. Or, at least, *it's* warded..."

"What does that mean?" said Casey.

"You think it's guarding something?" Vincent asked.

Henry nodded, but hesitantly. "I just...I don't get it. What would it be guarding out here?"

"More victims?" Casey suggested, looking around as if she expected to see a corpse tied to a tree nearby.

"Maybe..." Henry muttered. "But I didn't sense any boundaries...I can move all around it just fine."

"Let me try." Reluctantly Vincent stepped forward, following Henry's path around the tower. As soon as he passed one side, he felt something–a little grip at his heart, not unlike that earlier burst of magic.

He stopped, but it had passed already. He stepped back again, and there it was. He paused, gazing out into the shadowed forest.

"What is it?" Henry called softly.

Vincent wandered back to the others. "There *is* a boundary. I felt it. The tower is connected to something out there. And...it's heading the same direction as the watchman's trail. Whoever did this...it's the same person that took him."

"Th-then we'd better get going," Percy said.

"Hold on." Casey suddenly turned to him. "Before we go, we have to get you out of Ava."

"W-what?"

"We found your body," said Casey, gesturing towards the tower. "Technically..."

"I hope it still works," said Henry. "I almost forgot about that, god."

"O-oh," said Percy, startled. "I-it's okay! I forgot too..." He began threading and unthreading his fingers rapidly. "L-let's just keep going, a-and we can come back later, so the trail doesn't go cold..."

"What? No way," said Henry. "We don't know if we'll be able to find it again. This may be your only shot."

"B-but this may be our only shot to f-find the murderer!" Percy protested.

Something wriggled uncomfortably in Vincent's gut. He narrowed his eyes.

"Don't you want to get out of Ava's body, Percy?"

Percy balked, and that split second told Vincent everything he needed to know.

"O–of course I do, b-but–"

"Then do it!" Casey advanced on Percy with sudden fervor–more than she had displayed throughout their journey.

With three sets of eyes boring into him, Percy couldn't muster the gumption to argue. He swallowed hard with Ava's throat. Then he gingerly walked up to the tower, stopping a few feet away and gazing up at its grotesque silhouette.

"I...I still don't know h-how to do this," he said, looking back anxiously.

"That's funny, you possessed Ava just fine!" Casey snapped.

"Should we...do that incantation again?" Henry suggested. "The one that Ava did?"

"Do you remember it?" Casey said. "'Cause I sure don't."

"I wrote it down right after, just in case. Here..." Henry pulled out his phone. The glare of the screen was blinding in the darkness. "Alright, everyone, repeat after me."

"Spirits that linger upon this earth..."

The others echoed the words.

"I call upon thee...

"Reach through time, part the curtain...

"Between our bright window and our dark mirror...

"Ye who cling to the shadows we cast...

"Enter your body, and speak."

Silence.

Everyone looked at Ava's body. It remained where it was before, gazing up at the monstrous tower. After a moment, it looked back at them. Vincent knew before it even opened its mouth–nothing had changed.

"I-I don't think it's working...m-maybe we need candles, like last time?"

"This is *stupid!*" Casey slammed her fist down at her side. "*You* aren't trying hard enough!"

"Casey, lay off, he's–"

"No, she's right."

Everyone stopped to look at Vincent, stunned. His stony gaze stayed fixed on Percy. He shrank back.

"He's not trying at all. Are you, Percy?"

"W-what? I'm–o-of course I'm–"

"Stop lying." Vincent took a threatening step towards him.

Percy stepped back, glancing nervously at the tower looming too close behind him.

"I'm not..."

"You're my *friend*, Percy! I know when you're lying!" Vincent snarled.

Percy's eyes widened in shock at the admission, or at Vincent's aggression–or both. His hands–Ava's hands–squeezed together as if they held the brunt of the pressure closing in around him. Then–

"*Okay!*" he cried, his voice echoing through the trees. "I'm *not* leaving Ava, and I don't care what any of you say! I'm in love with her!"

His words seemed to linger long after his voice ceased to carry. The silence that followed was earsplitting.

"You're..." Henry breathed.

"How?" Casey demanded, recovering first. "You don't even know her!"

"I know her better than *anyone!*" Percy argued. "From the inside out! I've lived her life, I've seen her dreams, I hear her thoughts and feel every feeling..." Vincent saw him flush, even in the gloom.

Casey bristled. "You fucking *creep!*" Percy flinched, but for once did not cave, indignation only rising on his face. "What have you been doing with her?"

"I love her in ways no one else could *ever* love someone!" Percy insisted. "She's me and I'm her! You'd never understand!"

"That's—that's not how this works, Percy," Henry said, finally returning to his senses. His eyes were wide. "You can't take over someone's life and claim something like that..."

"I understand her!" Percy protested, clenching Ava's fists at her sides. "And she understands me! She's with me, always! And I'm with her..."

He trailed off. Such a genuine look crossed his face, something so wistful and soft and raw, that Vincent felt his heart twitch in painful sympathy, and he had to look away in fear of it.

"And I'm never leaving her. We'll never be alone again."

Casey suddenly advanced on Percy, her teeth bared like a wolf. "You could have left that body anytime, huh? But you led us on, didn't you, you little worm?"

The look on Ava's face answered for him.

"You get out of that body right this fucking instant, or I'll tear you apart." Her voice was dangerously low. It was almost worse than her yelling. Vincent wondered if she would even still be human right now if she hadn't taken that potion.

"I-I won't," Percy said, visibly trembling with the effort of standing his ground. "Y-you can't do anything to me, or you'll hurt her."

Casey spun around and yelled "FUCK!" at the top of her lungs. Her voice rang out through the clearing, echoing into the trees beyond.

"*Casey!* Keep your voice down!" Henry hissed.

At that very moment, something yellow flashed in the darkness at the edge of the trees. Vincent turned, but by the time he looked, it was gone. The hair on the back of his neck began to rise.

"Fuck," Vincent echoed, far quieter. He turned to Henry. "We need to leave," he said, willing him to feel the urgency in his tone. "Now. Whatever's out there, they know we're here now."

Henry threw him a desperate look. He seemed to understand instantly, and nodded. "Back to camp," he said, turning on his heels.

"*What?*" Casey cried. "You're just letting him *get away with this?*"

"*Quickly,*" Henry insisted, already ten paces ahead. "I trust Vincent. And so should you. If he says we need to leave, we leave. We can deal with Percy later."

Vincent felt heat rush up his neck. This time, he didn't waste his time trying to fight it off. Instead he tossed Henry a grateful glance as he caught up with him.

"W-what about the th-thing? A-are we just gonna leave it like this?" Percy called as loudly as he dared, hurrying after them.

"We can't touch it anyway," Vincent answered. He tasted the air every few moments, but he couldn't sense anything unfamiliar—the forest, his companions, the blood...

It felt like only moments before they found themselves back at their campsite, their setup miraculously untouched.

"We should set a watch for the rest of the night," Vincent said.

"Good idea," said Henry. "I can go first. I'll wake you up in a bit, Vinny."

Casey wasted no time disappearing into the tent. Percy hesitated outside.

"I...I might just stay out here..."

"No way. It's freezing," said Henry, frowning.

"Casey won't do anything to you," Vincent said, although he couldn't keep the edge out of his voice. "Just get some rest."

Percy looked at him fearfully. Whatever courage he had apparently ran out. He ducked into the tent without another word.

Vincent sighed. His and Henry's eyes met again.

"What are we going to do about him?"

"I don't know. I need to think," Henry said wearily, running a hand through his hair. It was markedly less tidy than usual. "You get some sleep, Vinny. I'll handle things out here."

"You'd better wake me up soon."

"Yeah, yeah. I will, I promise."

Vincent joined the others in the tent. This time Percy had arranged his sleeping bag at the farthest end away from Casey. Vincent couldn't complain.

He set up his own sleeping bag in the middle nearest Casey. She growled softly, but didn't protest.

He turned over, staring at Henry's empty sleeping bag on his other side. His heart burned as the memory of waking up close against his side returned to him. Slowly his eyes began to close.

When Vincent woke again, the tent was empty. Everyone else's sleeping bags were missing too, as were their packs. With a jolt of alarm, he dug himself out of his sleeping bag and thrust his head through the tent flap.

Outside the others were finishing packing their bags, the campfire's remnants already scattered. His heart settled in relief. Henry noticed Vincent first and waved.

"Hey, Vinny! You get enough sleep?"

"Yeah, you never woke me up for my watch," Vincent said indignantly.

"You needed your rest," Henry said gently. "We left some breakfast for you."

Vincent couldn't stay annoyed at him. He stifled a yawn–Henry was right.

"Thanks..."

Henry smiled at him before returning to his packing. "Casey, will you help me take down the tent?"

Casey grunted, trudging over. Vincent ducked back inside to grab his things, then retreated to the clearing. He noticed Percy hovering away from the rest of them, his backpack already over his shoulders. He studied the ground with an empty expression, tracing patterns into the leaf mold with his shoe.

Vincent left him to it. He found a serving of instant oatmeal in a pot nearby. It had lost most of its heat by now, but that didn't bother him. He demolished it before the others had even finished with the tent.

At last they resumed following the blood trail. It was fainter now, much to Vincent's displeasure. It led deeper into the woods in the direction of that boundary he had felt earlier. Some kind of invisible line that connected the tower to...something else.

They trekked for more than an hour before a hideously familiar sight rose between the trees.

Another bone tower stood before them, wreathed in the stench of fresh death.

Vincent's pace faltered before he reached it, overwhelmed. It was even worse in daylight. The bones were stained pink, not yet bleached by the weather, but their stark surfaces still seemed to glare down at them through the bright mist.

Everyone else stopped as well, cringing against the sight. It was Vincent who stepped forward first. He forced himself to let the scents back in. Scuffed earth and bloodstains around the base suggested the leftovers were buried at its center. The bones were trussed up in three flat sides, making a triangle shape.

"Look at this," Henry's voice sounded from the other side of the tower. He was pointing at an extra area of knots partway along one of the walls.

"What is it?" Vincent asked.

"I don't know." Henry squinted harder at the wall of bones, trying to see between the pieces. "I think there must be something tied up in the center, between the walls...can you see it?"

Vincent approached a sturdy-looking oak nearby. He pulled himself up onto its lowest branch, then the next one, and the next, leaving the forest floor far below. His heart gripped as the next branch swayed beneath him. He clutched the trunk with both hands. Then he finally dared to peer down, seeing the bright dots of his friends looking up at him from below...

"It's just another wall, inside the triangle," Vincent said when he was safely back on the ground.

Henry's face tightened in confusion. "A wall? You mean more bones?"

Vincent nodded. He crouched down, brushing aside some dead leaves to draw the configuration in the dirt. "It looked like–"

He froze.

"What?"

Vincent stared down at the image he had drawn. "That's...an elemental symbol."

Henry tilted his head as he peered down at the drawing. "What do you mean?" Casey and Percy came over to see.

Vincent scanned the treetops for the angle of the sun through the fading mist. "If north is that way..." He shifted to the right, until his view of the symbol showed an upside-down triangle with a line crossing just above its lowest point. "This one is Earth. East."

"W-what does that mean?" Percy asked.

"I...I don't know." Vincent bit his tongue, his thoughts churning.

He turned back to his drawing, using his finger to add another symbol down and to the left of the first. This one was a regular upright triangle with no lines inside. "Fire. South."

"Is...is that m-mine?" Percy squeaked out.

Vincent nodded grimly. He then drew two lines extending upward from each symbol, meeting at a midpoint between them. "And this spot should be something important."

Henry's eyes lit up. "You might be onto something, Vinny!"

"But what would it be?" Casey spoke up.

"Let's find out." Vincent stood, scuffing his foot over the symbols to cover them. Couldn't be too careful. "But first..."

He held up a hand, gesturing for the others to wait. He began circling the tower again, trying not to look at it for his own sake. He breathed deep, willing his senses to pick apart the different traces he found here, separating the blood-scent from its captor...

Vincent gritted his teeth. He crouched reluctantly in the shadow of the tower, leaning close to the bloodstained earth. He sat there for a minute or more in silence, drawing in every bit he could, but...

"Damn it," he growled. "I can't find another trail, apart from the blood. It's all stale now, I can't pick out anything else..."

Henry immediately moved to his side, resting a gentle hand on his shoulder. "It's okay, Vinny. You did amazing getting us here. Right, guys?"

"Y-yeah!" Percy said, forcing a smile that couldn't mask his nerves. "W-without you, we'd never have made it!"

"Which would be just fine with you," Casey growled at him. He flinched, creeping further away from her. Then she looked at Vincent, and to his surprise she said, "*You* were great."

Gruff as her tone was, Vincent couldn't help a little smile.

The group began hiking west, following a straight line from the tower. As they trekked the sun traveled across the sky, burning off the lingering mist by noon and providing some much-needed warmth.

Vincent's thoughts stewed. He had lost the trail, sure, but he had found the missing bodies. They were needed for this magic. This was the reason behind the murders.

And he knew he didn't need a trail to find their killer. He knew his direction at all times. Even now they were moving closer, that sixth sense in his heart pulling, dragging, drawing him in.

But he had to know why. His heart still burned with the scars Benjamin had left on it. Whatever lay at the center of these towers was the reason he had deceived Vincent into letting him escape into the world–it had to be.

And he wasn't the only one Benjamin had hurt. Vincent couldn't let them all die in vain–not because of his choice. He had to prove it. He had to do this the right way.

Because if he didn't...even if he somehow caught Benjamin alone, away from mortal witnesses and away from his allies...it would destroy everything. He could already see the look on Henry's face in his mind's eye as he dragged Benjamin back to Hell himself. No proof, no explanation, except that somehow he belonged there...it was too brutal for the man who loved second chances.

Or, if he did explain...

I can't let him know this was all my fault.

No–Vincent had to do what Henry would do. Up until the very end.

Suddenly his senses picked up on something odd, jolting him out of his thoughts. Did these trees look familiar? Or was he just imagining things?

Henry stopped. Vincent accidentally shouldered him as he passed, halting a moment too late. But he didn't have time to question him before he too heard it:

A thundering waterfall.

"What are you–" Casey broke off. "Wait–is that–"

Vincent lurched forward again, hurrying now. The others' footfalls sounded behind him. The slope of the forest floor gradually sharpened, and then rocks rose before them. They clambered over as quickly as they could, climbing higher and higher, helping each other when someone slipped.

Then they were standing at the edge of a precipice overlooking a deep, black chasm below, water roaring down endlessly into the darkness within the Devil's Maw.

A shiver traveled up Vincent's spine. The earth swayed around him–but then a warm hand grasped his shoulder, steadying him.

"This is the midpoint?" Henry said, gazing stone-faced down at the Devil's Maw. "This is what the towers are protecting?"

"There must be two more towers," Vincent said, his own voice sounding far away. "One to the west of here, and one to the north..."

"Mira..." Henry murmured, the name nearly drowned by the crashing water.

Vincent turned to him, his thoughts a blur. *Why would Benjamin be protecting this place?* "What do we do now?"

"I don't know," said Henry, looking back at him helplessly. "I just don't get it. This place must be important, but why?"

Vincent grimaced. He didn't have any answers, either.

After a minute Henry sighed. "Let's head back."

"Back? Back where?" Casey asked.

"Home."

That tiny worm of guilt wriggled again in Vincent's chest. Henry's voice was cold. Numb. He was all but defeated, and it was Vincent's fault.

"What, is that it?" Casey asked as Henry began picking his way down the rocks.

"Do you have any bright ideas, Casey?" he said flatly. Casey blanched at his tone. "We've run out of leads. What other choice do we have?"

"W-well, it's not a total bust," Percy said meekly, climbing down after Henry. "W-we found the towers, a-and figured out about the symbols..."

"And about how much of a filthy little traitor you are," Casey growled just behind him. "That was worth the whole trip. Speaking of which, what are we gonna do with him?"

"D-do with me?" Percy squeaked, eyes wide.

"Nothing," said Henry wearily.

"*Nothing?*" Casey spat, bristling. Vincent braced himself. She skidded down the slope to block Henry's path, glowering up at him. "Are you for real right now, Henry?" She speared a finger in Percy's direction. "This bastard stole a girl's *entire life*–and *you* just want to *let him?*"

Henry met her glare with his own. To Vincent's eyes, that cold, stolid defense warred with the empathy that found cracks to seep through. He hated this. But he had reached his limit. "What do you want me to do? I can't force him out of her."

"Then–then we need to find another way to do it," Casey blustered, her fury unrelenting. "There has to be some kind of ritual! Ask your sister! Ask Magdalena!"

"I don't know, okay?" Henry shot back. His voice echoed down the slope. Casey's eyes widened. He instantly seemed to realize his mistake, his exasperation fading into something more gloomy. "I'll...yeah. I'll ask them. Let's just get back, okay? I'm tired."

For a moment, no one moved. Vincent watched Casey's outrage slowly wane, until finally she sighed and turned away. She forged the path towards home, leaving the rest of them to follow.

CHAPTER 19

THE FOURTH SIN

W hen the group finally reached campus, it was like stepping into another world. The familiar walls and gardens and footpaths seemed to exist in a different time, when everything was still normal.

Immediately Vincent recalled the classes he had missed and the warning his philosophy professor had given him last time. He didn't think his heart could sink any lower into his stomach, but it achieved the impossible. He had no idea where to even begin sorting things out from here.

Casey soon parted ways with them for her own dorm hall, ignoring Percy entirely when she said goodbye. Henry led the way back to Walden Hall, urging the others to rest without even looking at Percy. Vincent had no complaints. All he wanted to do was crawl into his bed and maybe never come out.

He did his best. Every time he awoke, his body seemed to drag him back down into the blankets. He let it, over and over. Finally, though, sleep would no longer take him. He laid there for some time, staring up at the ceiling, his thoughts drifting towards a time when he used to find Percy there in the corner, his presence dark and unnerving and wrong. So much had changed— or maybe it hadn't, and it only appeared to.

All of this is because of me, played over and over in his head. *None of this would have happened if I hadn't let Benjamin go. Ava would be free, Percy would be alive, Mira and the night watchman would be alive...* He searched for a reason for Casey to hate him, but found none—that much at least was her own doing.

Going over that fateful night again, he realized another thing, with a much harder kick to his gut: *If I hadn't been there, she would have killed Hunter. She would have killed Henry.*

He finally extricated himself from the mess of blankets. He was dimly surprised to find the golden light of afternoon filtering in between the blinds. He set to work dressing himself. He needed a shower, he realized.

An hour later he found himself at the Commons, freshly groomed but groggy. He picked at his favorite mix of cereal, feeling both hungry and not at the same time. He eventually got through it and went for a plate of meatballs, continuing his grazing idly.

The clatter of silverware on dishes and the usual echoing chatter all around him only made him feel more alone at his empty booth, as if it were a little island in the middle of an endless, shifting sea. He watched the sun sink towards the horizon through the wide windows, tinging the air deep gold and then orange and then gray-blue.

Nothing felt entirely real anymore. He shouldn't be here. Everything should have ended in that forest. It was like he had already gone home, and was simply watching his old life through someone else's eyes.

A sudden buzzing on the tabletop snapped his attention back. He reached for his phone.

Have you seen Sierra anywhere? The text was from Henry.

Nope, Vincent replied. He tried to push away the bitterness that rose from the pit of his stomach. Was Henry still chasing her, after all?

As soon as Vincent had put down his phone, it vibrated again. His annoyance disappeared in an instant when he read:

Nobody else has either. She missed volleyball practice today and her room is empty.

Vincent's blood ran cold. For a moment he sat there frozen, his thoughts racing to catch up. Then another text came through:

Meet me at her room?

Vincent texted back: *Be right there.* Then he jumped up, leaving his dishes and half-eaten meatballs where they lay.

When he reached Sierra's dorm hall, the front door opened immediately– Henry was already waiting for him.

"Can you track her scent?"

His voice was tight. Vincent could tell he was trying his hardest not to panic, but the shadow of it was there just behind his eyes.

"Y-yeah."

Vincent led the way down the hall to Sierra's room. When they got there, the door was shut.

"I already talked to her roommate," Henry said. "She hasn't seen her since yesterday morning when she left for class."

"She's been missing that long?" Vincent's stomach sank.

Henry didn't meet his gaze. "I looked around her side of the room. She took her keys, laptop...anything she would've needed for class."

Vincent nodded, focusing on the scents near the door. Traces of Sierra's citrus permeated the area, alongside those of her roommate. Vincent moved slowly down the hall, trying to follow Sierra's trail, but it wasn't nearly fresh enough–most of it was so trodden into the carpet from every trip she had ever made to and from her room, it was impossible to make out. He shook his head in frustration.

"I can't get it." He threw Henry a helpless look. "Have you told Casey? Maybe she can track it..." There was no question of asking Percy to help this time. They both knew that.

Henry shook his head sharply. He was slipping again. "No–if you can't get it, no one can." He stood there, fists balled at his sides, his thoughts flickering across his face.

"Jake. Maybe he would know."

Vincent frowned. "Maybe..."

"We have to try. Come on."

As Henry led the way out of Sierra's dorm hall, he suddenly darted behind one of the planters in the front. When he returned, he had his gauntlet and a crossbow with him. Vincent didn't question him–after all, he also had an awful feeling they might need them.

It was a breeze getting someone to let Henry into Jake's dorm hall. He seemed to know everyone he passed. Soon they were hurrying down the hallway, Henry counting off the doors until–

The door with Jake's name on it stood slightly ajar. It was dark inside.

Henry stood rooted to the spot. Vincent recovered first, pushing the door open and flicking on the light. The room could not have been less like Henry's, apart from the football memorabilia. It was cluttered, clothes and papers strewn everywhere.

Vincent moved to Jake's desk, resting his hand on the chair. It was kicked out as if someone had left it in a hurry.

"All his stuff is here, except his phone," he said. "Does he usually leave his room like this?"

"Messy? Yeah. Open, no. He's careless, but not that careless, I think," Henry murmured, half to himself. He was still standing in the doorway, as if he had forgotten how to move.

Vincent tasted the air, bending close to the carpet. The stench of fear was unmistakable.

"I've got his trail," he said, already following it down the hall.

Henry perked up, tailing him closely. They left through the back door and went on across campus, all but blinded by their desperation, until they reached the treeline.

They stopped, staring out at the forest they had only left hours ago. Deep shadows gathered beneath the canopy in the last blue light of dusk. The place felt tainted now. Vincent was sure Henry was thinking the very same thing.

"Please tell me it's not her," Henry said suddenly, his gaze fixed on the trees without seeing them.

Vincent hesitated. Then he reached out and gently curled his fingers around Henry's hand. He was trembling. The first heartbeat after felt like fire, white-hot in Vincent's chest and fingertips, but he didn't let go.

"Call Casey."

They stood there like stone, and the moment felt as if it lasted forever. But it was only a moment, and then Henry took back his hand to call Casey.

When he hung up, he said, "She's on her way. Fast, I hope."

To her credit, this time she was. She arrived in five minutes at most, chest heaving.

"This *better* be a real emergency," she panted.

"I hope to god it isn't," said Henry.

For a moment, Vincent wondered if it was worth it to gather Percy after all. With what they were facing, it might make all the difference. But before he could make up his mind, Henry stepped into the trees. Casey followed.

Vincent hurried after them, and the shadows swallowed them whole.

The deeper they went, the darker it grew. And so did the tugging in Vincent's chest–his sixth sense. At first he denied it, but the truth circled him like a starving wolf, slowly closing in.

Benjamin was out here, too.

This was it. It wasn't exactly how he thought it would go. He thought they would have the upper hand, or a plan–*anything*. But he should have seen the writing on the wall. That feeling that he was sitting apart from the rest of the world while it went on around him, like he had already left it...now it made sense.

Benjamin's gravity reeled him in, closer and closer, pulling at something deep and sick within his heart–

And then, a shout.

Henry leaped forward, but Vincent grabbed his arm and pulled him back. He wasn't strong enough to restrain him, but Henry let him. He looked back at him with wide, questioning eyes. Vincent shook his head sharply.

"They'll be ready for us," he whispered. "We should get a better look before we go charging in."

Henry grimaced, but after a moment's hesitation he nodded. He met Casey's eyes, jerking his head in a gesture to follow. Together they crept through the trees, only stopping when they saw movement ahead.

Two silhouettes faced each other, tense, charged, poised to leap. The rusty tang of blood tainted the air. Behind the further of the two, a shape lay crumpled on the ground. It stirred, the whites of its eyes flashing in the gloom as it watched, terrified.

As his eyes adjusted to the growing moonlight, Vincent suddenly realized: it was Sierra.

A massive dark-furred werewolf towered over her, guarding her like prey it had caught for dinner. Its jaws dripped with blood and saliva, dropping in long ribbons to pool in the dirt below. Its pelt was patchy and ruffled, clearly battered.

Facing it stood Jake–just Jake, human and unremarkable. He too was bloodied, his clothes torn, his back heaving as he fought for breath–but he was standing. He carried no weapon.

"Let her *go*, Hunter!" Jake spat, shifting as if readying himself for another attack. "There are *hundreds* of other people here we can use! It doesn't have to be her!"

"*Short-sighted!*" the wolf snarled. His speech came garbled and wrong like Casey's had on the night she turned him. "*She is filth, like them all! Your collar! Your leash!*" He laughed, spittle stretching between his curved fangs.

Vincent could see Jake's limbs trembling even from here, itching to tear the mad grin off the werewolf's face.

"You're *jealous*, aren't you, you stupid bastard?" he shouted. "'Cause you can't get a girl to save your life? She's *mine*, you dumb mutt, so get the fuck over it! You can't take her from me!"

This time the wolf-Hunter broke into a nasty snarl. "*I deserve this! After everything* she *took from me! Never got* anything*! Now I take what I want!*"

"Take some other girl, then, if you have to!" Jake argued. "If you hate that werewolf bitch, make that work for you. I don't know what she has to do with the *element of air*," he said emphatically, as if parroting the words, "but I'm sure you can bullshit it if you try hard enough."

"Like hell." Vincent caught Casey's hiss from the shadows at his side. "I told you. I knew this would happen. He's gonna kill her."

Vincent's heart sank into his stomach as he realized–she was right. All along. Whatever darkness had been brooding deep inside Hunter finally had an excuse to rear its ugly head–this time, with teeth. Guilt chilled his insides– why hadn't he seen it before? Just like he hadn't, with Benjamin...

He glanced aside at Casey, opening his mouth to speak–but he stopped short. Every muscle in her body was taut, ready to fly at her mortal enemy. He reached out an arm to bar her way.

"Wait," he growled. To his surprise, she did.

When he turned back to the scene, Jake was now approaching the crouching werewolf, circling him slowly with his body hunched low, bargaining with every step.

"*Benjamin's orders,*" Hunter was saying. "*Knew you wouldn't stomach it. Knew I could do it!*"

"You fucking liar!" Jake cried. "He wouldn't do that to me! Melanie wouldn't let him! Let her *go*, damn you! I have *everything* now–I'm not gonna let you take it all away from me!"

"*I get her now,*" Hunter grinned. "*My prize. All mine, 'till she's used up. Then when our plan works, you see her again!*"

The werewolf jerked suddenly, lunging for Sierra at his feet.

"Like *hell* you will!"

At the very same moment, Henry burst out of their hiding place. He launched himself across the clearing, skidding to a halt just paces away to load his crossbow and point it at Hunter's massive head.

Casey ducked past Vincent and came to Henry's side in an instant, although she was as weaponless as Jake. Vincent had no choice but to follow, but he kept back warily, behind Henry's line of fire.

Jake spun around, shock warring with outrage on his face. There was something different about him, but Vincent couldn't put his finger on what it was. Something in his face seemed colder, darker...

"Henry?"

"Get back!" Henry said, keeping his sights fixed on Hunter. He looked pained. "We *helped* you, Hunter! Why are you doing this?"

Hunter's lips peeled back to show bright, jagged teeth. "*Tricked you! Not yours!*" he barked in triumph. "*Never–blame her!*" He brandished a claw at Casey. She bared her teeth right back.

"You gutless fucking traitor," she growled. "Henry helped your sorry ass, and this is how you repay him? Did you even take that stupid potion?"

The werewolf shook his great head. "*No need,*" he gloated. "*Benjamin helped me. Gave me new path. Makes me strong. Now I have what I want.*"

"*Benjamin,*" Henry echoed. "Benjamin Warwick? *He's* behind all this?"

Now there was no going back. Everyone knew.

"That weirdo?" Casey glanced around the clearing warily. "Where's the rest of his posse?"

"If they're not here now, they will be soon," Henry said. "Get back, Jake—we'll handle this." He jabbed his crossbow towards the werewolf. "Hunter, if you don't back down *now*–"

"I'm not going *anywhere*," said Jake.

Henry gritted his teeth, glancing over at him. "I get it, I do–but you can't stand up to this, you don't know what you're dealing with–"

"Shut the *fuck* up."

Jake had turned on Henry, every muscle in his body taut and bulging, his eyes dark–even sinister. They fixed on Henry not like a friend or even a rival, but a predator.

A chill coursed through Vincent. Something was very wrong.

"*You* don't know what you're dealing with. You haven't for a long time now, Henry."

Henry searched Jake's face, utterly baffled. After a moment he seemed to resolve something. "Jake, I don't know what he's promised you, but–"

"*Nothing*, you stupid fuck," Jake snarled. He took a menacing step forward. Vincent tensed, every instinct warning him of what was only a twitch away. "I already have it all. I'm stronger now than you've *ever* been. I'm unstoppable. I can have anything I want now. Even *you* can't take it from me."

Henry's brow furrowed as he tried to piece it all together. "What are you saying?"

"Forget it," Jake scoffed, an ugly sneer creasing his face. "You won't get it. And that's fine. Great, even." He jerked away from his progress towards

Henry, much to Vincent's relief—and instead fixated on Hunter. "I can save *my* girlfriend on my own. Stay out of my way, and I won't kill you."

Vincent barely had time to register the anguish on Henry's face before a snarl tore across the clearing, snatching his attention. There Hunter crouched low over his prey, his matted, bloody fur bristling along his back. Sierra looked so tiny at his feet, barely recognizable at all, caked in dirt and blood. She gazed up at the monsters before her with wide, terrified eyes, so meek compared to her usual fire.

The sight came like a punch to the gut. She didn't belong here. She belonged to a clean, bright world beyond the reach of these horrors Vincent knew so intimately.

Hunter's lupine eyes darted between his adversaries, assessing them with every ounce of brainpower he had left in him. He knew he was outnumbered.

Then he said in his warped voice, *"Jake! Give me the wolf-bitch, I will trade!"*

"What? Fuck you!" Casey spat. "Try it, I dare you!"

"This is crazy, Jake!" Henry broke in before Jake could reply. "You're my friend, man, I–I thought we..." He shook his head desperately. "I've always had your back, and you've always had mine! Are–are you jealous of me? I didn't even know–"

"Bullshit!" Jake hissed, rounding on him again. "Are you fucking serious? Mr. Perfect doesn't even know he's perfect? Can't even spare a second to think about anyone else? Too blinded by the limelight?"

In spite of everything, something twisted into place in Vincent's mind. Seeing Jake standing there, a pale imitation of Henry's talent, his courage, his goodness—he couldn't fully blame him for his resentment. Vincent had felt it before, too, in his own way. He knew he could never be like Henry. But it was pointless raging against it like this, kicking and screaming in fate's grasp.

"I'm–I'm not perfect," Henry protested, thunderstruck. He stood frozen there like his world was cracking apart all around him. "I'm just *me*, I...I'm just trying to help people, damn it! That's all I ever–"

"Keep your excuses," Jake growled. "I don't care about you anymore. I have way more important things to do now that I've Ascended."

He left Henry standing there blankly and faced Hunter, his eyes narrow. "Let her go, then. I'll trade if you leave her alone."

Hunter's maw split into a bloody grin. He stepped over Sierra, leaving her lying there in the dirt, and padded to Jake's side. His eyes flashed yellow in the gloom as he turned his sights on Casey.

"*Air-headed. That works for ritual,*" he rumbled, swiping his tongue over his fangs as if he could already taste her blood.

"I don't care," Jake said with a shrug. He too turned towards Casey with that strange, indescribable darkness radiating from him. "Benjamin can deal with all that magic junk. And if she doesn't work, we'll just find someone else."

Casey took a threatening step towards them, her fists clenched at her sides so hard they were trembling. But something was wrong. She wasn't angry enough. She didn't feel wild or dangerous like she usually did. Vincent's instincts weren't warning him about her the way they were for Jake.

Three things happened all at once. Casey skidded backwards–Jake was in her face–and Henry stood between the two. He had deflected Jake's blow, his gauntlet brandished like a shield in front of him.

Jake blinked in surprise, but it quickly turned to a sneer–half annoyance, half pleasure. "You still don't know you're outmatched, do you? Lemme clue you in, *bud*."

Again Jake lunged, but Henry was ready for him. He loosed a crossbow bolt at the same instant Jake lurched forward. It struck him square in the chest. Jake hissed like a wild animal, stopping dead a foot from him and staggering back as the bolt jutted out just beneath his collarbone.

There was no blood. Instead, the wound began to smoke.

"W-what is this?" Jake grasped the bolt and yanked it out of his flesh, letting out a groan of pain. He threw it to the ground, peering down at the black hole it left in his chest.

"I...I didn't want to believe it." Henry sounded more lost than Vincent had ever heard him. "What happened to you, Jake? Did Benjamin do this to you?"

"*Benjamin?*" Jake cried. "*I* did this, *me!* I don't need goddamn handouts! *I* wanted this—*I* earned this! I knew I could take it—only the strongest can use the Ascension like I can!"

"It's a *curse*, you damned fool!" Vincent spoke at last as he moved to stand at Henry's side. "Now you're stuck like this forever—and you're only as strong as any other vampire! It's not even you, it's all borrowed!"

The last shreds of his sympathy for Jake were ebbing away fast, replaced by a powerful hatred. It felt right, he realized, gazing at this dark reflection of himself and loathing every scrap of what he saw there. It was like dragging the carcass of his own failure into the light—something he could finally face, and fight.

"Oh, Jake..." Henry murmured, so miserably it kicked Jake back into a rage. His terrible eyes bulged as they fixed back on his enemy.

"*Don't you fucking pity me!*"

He lurched forward, but Vincent was ready—he transformed mid-leap, plunging his hellhound jaws into Jake's shoulder before he could so much as touch Henry.

Vincent flung him back with all his might. Jake spun around in midair—but he landed hard, his feet skidding and kicking up clumps of grass and mud.

Vincent stood between Jake and Henry with his hackles raised, growling deep in all three of his throats. He now towered over his adversary, but despite the shift, Jake didn't seem cowed. He answered by revealing knife-sharp fangs that glinted wickedly in the moonlight.

"The fuck are you?" Then he scoffed. "Whatever. I'll kill you, too."

"You don't need to do this!" Vincent's voice echoed from somewhere unseen as he bared three sets of massive teeth. "Benjamin is only using you, don't you realize that? Whatever he's promised you, you've already given up too much for it!"

"The only thing I gave up was *weakness*." Jake had already begun to march forward, his gaze set on his new prey. "And everything that came with it. Stupid, boring, everyday shit. I'm not *everyday* anymore. I'm Jake motherfucking Helmer."

He hurled a punch from nearly a yard away. Vincent caught it in his teeth–but the other fist slammed into his leftmost head. His vision burst into random color. He released his grip on Jake's hand, reeling. The other two heads glimpsed Jake's second strike coming, but he wasn't fast enough to avoid it. It sent him flying back with supernatural strength. He fell on his side, dazed. As he did, one of his heads saw Casey standing just feet away, still human-formed. Grunts and snarls and the clang of metal told him Hunter had seized his opportunity, grappling with Henry close by.

"What are you doing? Help Henry!" he shouted at her, fighting to stand.

He wasn't fast enough. Jake's fist flew again, aiming for his rightmost head. Vincent opened his mouth on instinct to grab it, but Jake was ready this time–he caught Vincent's muzzle in his hand.

Jake's other hand joined in, and suddenly Vincent's jaws were being pried open with superhuman strength.

Panic shot through him. His paws scraped against the earth as he was forced back, inch by inch. He snapped with his other heads, but only the middle head could reach in the first place, and Jake angled his body each time to avoid the bites.

Vincent's jaws began to ache, then burn as Jake pulled and pulled them apart, stretching them beyond where they should be. The pain radiated through his temples to his skull as it took the brunt of the strain. Terror flooded Vincent's chest as he realized it was about to crack–

Suddenly the pressure lifted. Jake fell back onto the ground with a sharp cry. Vincent shook his rightmost head, trying to clear the pain. His other heads fixed on Jake, ready to strike–only to see Henry pulling away from his thrashing body, where a long silver knife jutted from between his shoulder blades.

But Hunter was still after Henry–and had a clear shot to his back. Vincent's stomach lurched as the werewolf lunged–

"*Henry!*"

Vincent leaped. Hunter's weight crashed into him, throwing them both aside into the dirt. The impact drove the breath from his lungs, and in that dazed second Hunter pinned him down. He snapped and fought beneath the massive werewolf, trying to free himself, but it was no use at this angle. His teeth closed on empty air, his vision filled with the blur of trees and a wolfish grin set against moonlight. His blood froze as he realized he was outmatched– the werewolf was stronger.

Then, one set of teeth finally met their mark–Hunter's fangs plunged into Vincent's middle neck.

He howled in agony as his vision went red. His limbs scrabbled feebly in the dirt. His life was leaving him, pouring from his neck. More than the pain, he could feel the growing wetness, the heat of it clogging his fur. Soon he would find out what happened when a hellhound died.

No! he cried out, and he wasn't sure if it was in his head or not. He would *not* give up–he couldn't leave his friends to this grim fate. Without him, they would surely die, along with countless others.

They had given him more than he thought he deserved–even the simplest of things. A laugh, a meal, a promise, a smile, a hand up, an ounce of trust. If he let all of that mean nothing, he would deserve every dark thing anyone had ever thought of him. Especially himself.

Henry's voice echoed through his mind–a conversation they had had long ago, that night when they first made their pact to stop the murders.

We can't save everyone, Vincent had said. *It's impossible.*

But we can try.

Always, Henry tried. That was just who he was.

But Vincent? He wasn't Henry, who despite being so very mortal threw himself between death and the ones he cared about every single time; Henry, who had been the first face Vincent had seen in the light of day–and that face had been kind, despite everything he was or wasn't; Henry, who had shown him the best of humankind.

But if Vincent could be even a shadow of that, he would give everything he had left.

He tore himself out of despair, out of darkness, and let his body go limp beneath Hunter. He held his breath, forcing himself to lie as still as possible.

Instantly Hunter lifted his head and let out a garbled laugh of triumph. He was feral, out of his mind–acting on pure instinct. He didn't see the ruse.

And there was his opening. Vincent's fangs lashed out with cruel precision, and a horrible howl pierced the chaos of battle.

All the weight on Vincent eased. He ripped himself free, staggering back out of reach.

Hunter stood doubled over before him, clutching the left side of his face with both clawed hands, screaming like a dying animal. Blood gushed from between his fingers, dyed black in the gloom.

"What did you do to him, you mangy bastard?" Jake's voice lanced his ears from nearby. Vincent had a split second to catch him pulling himself to his feet, wreathed in smoke, a bloodied Henry crumpled feet away from him.

Vincent's heart caught in his throat, but before he could panic, Henry stirred.

Jake was distracted. He didn't see the crossbow bolt gripped tight in Henry's fist.

A new shriek of agony and fury joined Hunter's. Smoke poured out around the bolt, now jutting from Jake's thigh.

When Vincent looked back to Hunter, the werewolf had begun to back away. He finally lowered his hands from his face, revealing a glistening hole where his left eye had been. His good eye flashed in the shadows, glancing from Vincent to Jake and Henry, still locked in combat. Then he turned his head, picking out another silhouette on the ground nearby.

Vincent realized what was happening a moment too late. Hunter lunged for the injured Sierra. The coward was going to make a break for it.

"*Sierra! Run!*" Vincent howled, lurching after Hunter and knowing he wouldn't make it in time.

But another figure hurled itself between the werewolf and his prey. Hunter barreled into it, snarling as it knocked him off course. Vincent seized his chance–he closed the distance, tearing into each of Hunter's shoulders with his teeth. Hot blood spilled into his left- and rightmost mouths. He flattened his ears against the howl as he pried Hunter off his challenger.

At first he couldn't see who it was. Had Henry somehow beaten Jake on his own? But then he caught a familiar face.

"*Casey?* What are you doing? Transform!" Vincent called, still dragging Hunter back with all his might. The werewolf flailed his limbs, but couldn't reach Vincent–yet.

"I can't!" Casey shouted back.

Before Vincent could reply she dived for Sierra, pulling her up with all her strength. Sierra was dazed, maimed, but alive. Her eyes locked with Vincent's for a single second before Casey tugged her away, limping across the clearing towards the trees beyond.

Suddenly Vincent felt his paws lifting off the ground. His stomach dropped.

In a massive display of strength, Hunter heaved Vincent up over his head. The dark forest spun around him and the ground rose to meet him–*hard*.

His vision went black for a horrible moment. A dull ache throbbed in all three of his skulls.

Gradually his surroundings returned. He scrambled to right himself. He looked around, and after a moment the blurry image resolved into Hunter racing away into the forest.

"Shit!" came Casey's voice from nearby. Vincent turned to see her flash past him, her sights set on Hunter's fleeing form. "Don't let him get away!"

Just then, a desperate cry rose from behind them, snapping their heads back in its direction.

Henry was pinned beneath Jake, struggling mightily but in vain. Even as they watched his thrashing grew weaker. His gauntlet had vanished–his crossbow was the only thing barring the vampire from his head and neck.

"*Henry!*" Vincent cried, leaping for him–but his legs buckled beneath him.

He skidded against the dead leaves, the forest swaying around him. He couldn't even feel the pain anymore, but he knew it was only a matter of time–the damage was done.

He fought to get up, but his body wouldn't obey. It was like he was trying to move through tar. Frustration and fear shot through his nerves.

"Damn it!" Casey snarled at Vincent's side. She had taken a lurching step towards Henry, but faltered, her gaze darting back to Hunter's getaway.

Vincent choked as Jake gripped Henry's crossbow, wrenched it aside–

"*Go!* Help him!"

A new, familiar voice pierced the chaos. Ava–no, *Percy* shot past them in pursuit of the werewolf. Vincent and Casey stared, astonished at his sudden appearance–but Henry's next cry forced their attention back.

Casey bolted for Henry just as the crossbow clattered across the ground, far out of his reach. Jake lunged for his throat–and Casey threw her arms around Jake's neck, wrenching his head back. He choked, twisting madly to throw her off him.

That split second was just enough. Henry jolted up and lanced Jake through the middle with that long silver knife.

Jake fell back on top of Casey, who wrested herself free before he could retaliate. But he didn't get the chance–Henry hurled himself on top of him, pinning him to the ground.

Smoke billowed from Jake's body, tearing across Henry's visage as if to shield the force of his fury from prying eyes. Vincent only glimpsed flashes of something utterly foreign in those clear blue eyes–something monstrous.

Henry had wrenched that knife from Jake's ribs. It glinted in the moonlight as he brought it down again and again, piercing Jake's helpless torso over and over and over–

Vincent dragged himself forward, his limbs trembling as he fought the invisible ichor tugging him back towards the earth. His vision was beginning to fade at the edges, the shadows creeping around him, closing in–

No–

"*Henry! Stop!*"

Vincent thrust himself atop Jake's body, right as the knife flashed again. His bulk knocked Henry back, but he lunged forward again without a thought.

The knife halted just above Vincent. It jerked as if some unseen force compelled the hand that wielded it to finish its wicked work. For a moment Vincent thought it might.

But then, slowly, it retreated.

Henry knelt there, chest heaving madly as he stared at Vincent with eyes as round as the moon above his head. He hardly looked like himself at all, his once-perfect hair muddied and tousled, his marble face marred with blood, scared like a boy and half-wild like the werewolf that had almost claimed his life. But slowly his essence returned, bleeding back into those ice-blue eyes until they saw the scene before them clearly once more.

"What are you *doing*, Henry? Kill him!" Casey's voice seemed to come from far away.

"We need him alive," Vincent insisted, his gaze still locked with Henry's. Both of them knew that wasn't really why Vincent had stopped him.

Henry withdrew, crouching in the mud with haunted eyes. He nodded dimly, returning the knife to its sheath inside his jacket. He pushed himself to his feet, swaying slightly. He had lost a lot of blood.

Casey growled at the verdict, but didn't argue further. Instead she peered into the trees where Hunter and Percy had disappeared. "Percy, he–he actually showed up." She was silent for a moment. "Should we follow him?"

Vincent frowned, unsure. He glanced at Henry, expecting his input, but for once he didn't seem to want to take charge. His gaze was far away, trained on something unseen.

Unsettled by this, Vincent answered. "We don't know what we'd be walking into out there...we're in no shape for another fight."

As he tuned back into his senses, he could feel that unmistakable presence again—Benjamin was out there, too, somewhere in the forest. They were far outmatched now, whatever he had waiting for them.

"What if Percy gets Ava killed out there?" Casey countered.

"I...I think we have to trust him," Vincent said quietly. "He's...well, Percy. He won't fight. If anything, he'll come back with some information." *He has to.*

Casey held his gaze for a long, dubious moment. Then she nodded gruffly. "Alright. But this one's on you." She looked down at Jake, still curled and smoking on the ground at Vincent's feet. "What are we gonna do with *him?*"

Vincent paused, trying to pull his chaotic thoughts back together.

"...The shed behind the gym," he said finally. "We can lock him up there."

"And what, keep him there forever?"

"No. Just...until we get what we need from him."

"Which is?"

"More information," said Vincent, starting to get impatient. The forest was teetering around him again. He had no idea how he was even going to get home in this condition. "And then—and then we can figure something out. Let's just get back, okay?"

Even Casey seemed to sense his urgency, and didn't complain. Both she and Vincent looked around the clearing with a shared helplessness. Sierra still slumped against a tree, Jake was all but unconscious, and Henry and Vincent could barely stand.

"I...I can't carry anyone by myself," Vincent admitted. "You have to go wolf."

"Didn't you hear me? I *can't,*" Casey said roughly.

"What do you mean?"

"The potion, numbnuts!" Casey growled. "It's suppressing me! I–I haven't been able to transform since..." She trailed off, but they both knew what she meant.

It struck him suddenly–how subdued she had been during their trip into the forest, and even before that. It was like the bonfire within her had died down to the dull glow of embers. He had noticed, but he hadn't thought much of it. Yet another thing he had misjudged. Fresh guilt overtook him.

"I...guess I'll do my best."

Vincent heaved himself forward, fighting to steady himself on all four paws. He shoved his rightmost head beneath Jake's body, nudging it halfway onto his back. He felt it slipping–but then Casey was there, tugging Jake back up with an immense effort until he was more secure.

"I'll get Sierra," Casey said, making her way over to where she had left her.

Finally Vincent noticed Henry trudging over. He had found his gauntlet, dented and bloodied, and was carrying it limply in both hands like a dead animal. When he got close he stumbled. Before Vincent could react, Henry grabbed onto him, clinging to his leftmost neck to support himself.

"Sorry," Henry breathed. Vincent hated the quail in his voice. "Can...can I lean on you?"

Vincent's left head nodded, bracing itself against Henry's weight. Casey joined them, lugging Sierra with her. She looked even tinier now, half-falling under Sierra's bulk, but she also looked determined.

"Let's go home."

CHAPTER 20

HEAVEN & HELL

The journey back was long and painful. The trees passed achingly slowly, each step sending a fresh wave of fire through Vincent's insides. Dragging his consciousness back from darkness became his biggest challenge – it wavered every few moments, fighting to rest.

But he couldn't. Who knew what still lurked in the shadows, and how long it would take to catch up?

It was long past midnight when the bedraggled group finally reached the college grounds. It was deserted, thankfully. They skirted the edge of campus until they reached the shed behind the gym.

The door was closed, but the padlock hanging from it was still loose. They found the inside just as they had last seen it–empty and dark but for some spare sports equipment. The stench of death had faded away entirely, as if it had never been.

Henry let go of Vincent's shoulder. He ducked his three heads and stepped partway into the shed, allowing Jake's limp form to slide off onto the wooden floor. He landed with a dull thud. His wounds had stopped smoking, but even in the eerie lamplight Vincent could make out the unnatural black holes marring his body. He wasn't breathing.

"Is...is he...?"

"It would take a little more than that to kill a vampire," Henry said quietly. He avoided Vincent's gaze, leaning heavily on the side of the shed. Vincent got the sense that "a little" wasn't much.

"Are you sure?" Casey asked, still supporting Sierra.

"Their bodies disintegrate when they die," Henry said stiffly, as if forcing the words out.

Suddenly, a rush of footsteps over grass caught Vincent's ear. He spun around, baring his teeth as a desperate fear flashed through him.

No–not now–I don't have any fight left!

But then he caught a familiar scent. Relief flooded his body a moment before Percy burst out around the corner of the gym. When he reached the shed he doubled over, fighting for breath.

"You made it!" Casey exclaimed. It was the happiest she had sounded to see him since Vincent could remember.

"What happened?" Vincent demanded.

"It's–a ritual!" Percy coughed.

"What is?"

"The–the bones!" Percy's eyes were wide and fearful. "I–I followed Hunter, all the way to one of the towers! And–and *Benjamin Warwick* was there," he added breathlessly. "I–I think he's their leader, or something...Hunter was telling him what happened, and then..."

He took an agonizing moment to catch his breath, then choked out, "Benjamin w-was talking about a ritual...th-the towers...there are four of them, one for each element, j-just like you were saying, Vincent!" Vincent nodded urgently, willing him to go on. "A-and there's just one left to build...a-and then..."

"Then *what?* What is the ritual for?"

"I–I don't know!" Percy shrank back. "He was starting to say something, s-something about the Devil's Maw, a-about a portal, and opening it...b-but then Hunter caught my scent, and I had to get away..."

Vincent's stomach dropped. "The portal...?"

"What portal?"

Henry, Casey, and Percy all looked at Vincent. He clenched his teeth. There was no point hiding it now.

"The chasm there. Beneath the waterfall. It's...it's a rift between worlds. It's a portal. The one I came from."

Absolute silence followed his words. Not even the crickets chirped in the forest beyond.

"*That's* where you came from?" Henry breathed. Vincent avoided his gaze, his stomach crawling.

"So the rumors were true, all along..." Casey muttered.

"B-but why is he trying to open it?" Percy asked. "W-why would he want to go to Hell?"

That's what I want to know, Vincent thought. Benjamin had only just *escaped* from Hell, and that was no small feat–there was no reason he would ever want to go back. Let alone going to these lengths for it.

"We need to talk to Jake," Vincent decided, his gaze falling upon the crumpled form in the shed. "He'll know."

"Are you sure he won't die if we leave him here like this?" Casey asked, turning to Henry. "He's not lookin' so hot..."

"You heard him," Henry said, with a note of bitterness. "He's strong, now. He'll be up soon. And then he'll be dangerous."

"Really? Even after all that?"

Henry nodded solemnly. "Vampires heal quickly, just like werewolves."

"Someone needs to guard him, then." Vincent looked towards Casey, and her frown told him she caught the question behind his eyes.

"I *told* you, I can't transform. I'm practically useless if he decides to break out."

"No, you're not." Vincent glanced at Henry. "Do you have any spare weapons on you? The ones that make that smoke?"

Henry nodded, shrugging his crossbow and quiver off his shoulder and handing them to her. "These bolts are dipped in holy water. It's like poison for vampires."

"That's what I'm talkin' about." Casey grinned, weighing the crossbow in her hands. "Alright. But you guys had better come back soon. I'm exhausted."

"We'll take it in shifts," Vincent promised.

"What about Sierra?"

She was still leaning against Casey's shoulder, propped up between her and the wall of the shed. She was conscious, but barely, her eyes half-lidded and unfocused. Dread settled like stone in Vincent's stomach.

"She needs a hospital," he said, trying to keep the tremor out of his voice. Terrible images of Hunter's mangled body after Casey had gotten to him flashed through his mind. There was no telling what Sierra had been through before they arrived–or what would happen to her now.

"How are we gonna explain this one?" Casey said. "This is the second time we've 'found' some poor loser mauled in the woods. They're gonna start asking questions."

Vincent thought for a moment. "Percy can take her. They won't recognize Ava."

Percy's eyes widened, half in trepidation and half in delight. "M-me?"

"Yeah. You did great tonight, Percy." Vincent didn't want to think about what would have happened to Henry if Percy hadn't arrived when he did. "I know we can count on you."

Percy wrung his hands anxiously, but beamed at him. "I-I won't let you down!"

"Why *did* you come out there?" Casey growled suddenly. "How did you even know where to find us?"

Percy ducked his head. "I...p-please don't be mad, a-alright? I just...I've been looking out for you guys, e-ever since we got back...I...I didn't like how we left things..."

"So you thought you'd try and get back in our good graces?" Casey snapped. "You think a little favor like that will make us forget what you're doing with Ava?"

Percy flinched, but Vincent broke in: "It wasn't a 'little favor.' He might as well have saved Henry's life." He fixed Casey with a stern look. "I saw you hesitate, when he needed help. You wanted to go after Hunter. If Percy didn't show up, you might not have made it in time."

Casey scowled, but the glimmer of guilt in her dark eyes was obvious. "That doesn't make up for everything else."

"No, but we can deal with all that later," Vincent argued. "Ava is safe, for now. And we could use his help, anyway," he added. "Ava was a mess. She didn't want to help us, even though she could have made all the difference."

Before Casey could protest further, he turned back to Henry. "Come on...we need to get home."

Henry nodded faintly. He was sinking lower and lower against the wall of the shed, not even realizing he was doing it. Vincent's heart twisted as he took in just how battered he was. He had never seen him this bad before. Every other time Vincent had shielded him from the worst of it, and they managed to deescalate or flee.

If this is what one vampire and werewolf can do... He didn't want to imagine facing Benjamin's other allies. He didn't even know how many there were. If Benjamin was able to seduce Vincent to his side, there was no telling how many other people he now had under his charms. Not to mention Melanie, and her mastery over that power of glamor...

Vincent offered his shoulder to Henry again, but he shook his head. "You should change back," he said weakly. "Someone might see you when we get near the dorms."

"I...I'm not sure I can get you all the way there like that," Vincent admitted, hating his own weakness.

"Percy can help," Henry said, turning to him. "When we get back, I'm gonna give you some more stuff to help with Jake. Think you can run it back here?"

Percy nodded eagerly. "Of course!"

Henry looked back to Vincent, his expression softening like frost at daybreak. Vincent was startled by the sudden shift, in the face of everything that had just happened.

"C'mon, Vincent. You can do it. Just close your eyes."

Vincent's heart fluttered in his chest, but not from the danger they were in. Henry reached out, resting his palm warmly against Vincent's rightmost forehead. He shut his eyes, warring with that exhilaration thrumming in his veins.

He realized that, for the first time, he didn't mind the touch. It was overwhelming, but not in a way that made him recoil. He...wasn't afraid of it anymore. That startled him more than anything. Instead, it was an echo of those few precious minutes in the tent after his nightmare, when he had huddled beside Henry in the dark, stealing what he could of his warmth.

Except this time, Henry was giving it to him. There was nothing stolen, nothing secret. Not in this touch. Not like all the words and feelings he could never untangle.

And the longer he stood basking in that warmth, the farther he felt from the mask he had become so accustomed to. Uncertainty began to creep back in. Why couldn't he change back? He *had* to. Why wasn't it working this time?

But Henry knew him too well. He brushed his hand up Vincent's forehead, around his ear, tangling his fingers in the thicker fur around his cheeks. But he didn't stop there—he looked to the second head beside it, met its eyes, touched its bloodied muzzle gently. And then he moved to the third, just the same. He took in all of their wounds, all of the ways they each defended him. He held each head in turn with a steady tenderness that set Vincent's nerves ablaze, tingling from the tip of his nose to his tail.

Henry looked at him as if he wasn't a monster. Those clear blue eyes trusted him more than anyone ever had, without a shred of doubt. Maybe for the first time.

In that brief moment, Vincent never wanted to change back.

Finally Henry leaned forward, pressing his forehead to Vincent's. He didn't need to say anything. Vincent understood. He didn't have to hide from him—he just had to keep him safe. There was only one way to do that, now.

For a moment more Vincent sank into that heat, letting it nestle into that hollow place in his heart where it belonged. Then, before he knew it, he was human again.

He opened his eyes, finding Henry still gazing at him with that warmth unlike any other. Somehow, though, he caught a glimmer of something new that he couldn't quite place. He felt his heart stutter in his chest.

"That's the way," Henry said softly.

He leaned carefully against Vincent's shoulder. Vincent was grateful, considering his own condition. The pain remained, but had consolidated into his single head and neck. Only his own exhilaration kept the worst of it at bay.

Percy hurried to Henry's other side to help. Their progress across campus was slow. It was almost an hour before they found themselves at the front door of Walden Hall. It felt like such a long time since Vincent was last there, even though it had only been a matter of hours. He realized he had fully thought he would never see it again.

The halls were thankfully empty, and soon they were back in the sanctuary of Henry's colorful room. He laid his dented gauntlet on the floor, abandoning his usual care, and sank down onto his bed with a sigh of relief. Vincent, exhausted, sat beside him.

"The cache is under the bed," Henry told Percy. He hurried to get it, and Henry directed him on how to open it. In the end Percy emerged with a long silver chain, a fresh padlock, and some more silver knives identical to the one Henry had used on Jake.

"Tie Jake up with that chain," Henry said wearily. Vincent could tell he didn't like it, but there was nothing for it. "It'll keep him from breaking out. And the knives are for you and Casey. Just in case."

Percy nodded and stashed the items in his jacket pockets as best he could. He looked worriedly at the both of them.

"A-are you guys gonna be okay?" Without waiting for an answer, he suddenly said, "I–I'm sorry I didn't help sooner, with the fight...I just...I-I thought I'd just get in the way..." He bit his lip. "B-but I...I should've helped anyway...y-you guys almost *died* out there...and I'm...I'm already..."

Henry offered Percy a soft smile, shaking his head. "You did plenty, Percy. You're not a werewolf, or a hellhound, and you didn't have any special weapons. Better you stayed out of harm's way."

"B-but–"

"And Vincent's right, you helped save my life. You were incredibly brave."

"You chased down a *werewolf*," Vincent added. "That's nothing to sneeze at."

Percy smiled at them, fighting back the tears welling at the corners of Ava's eyes.

"Now go help Casey," Vincent insisted, nudging him. "She's out there by herself. We'll be safe here."

Percy's gaze grew determined, and he nodded. "I-I will! Text me if you need me!"

In a moment he was gone, closing the door behind him. Vincent and Henry sat in silence, side by side on the neatly-made bed in that bright little room, as if nothing terrible had ever happened in all the world.

"He's braver than he used to be," said Henry after a while. He shifted on the bed. "You remember where the first aid kit is?"

Vincent nodded. He went to get it from the drawer Henry had shown him.

"I wonder what changed," he murmured as he returned to the bed, opening the kit. His heartbeat was still loud in his ears, despite the peace all around him. After a moment he said, "He has to give her body back, sooner or later."

"He knows that, I think," Henry sighed. He held out an arm for Vincent to start assessing his wounds. He barely even winced when Vincent set to cleaning them. "But we can't force him. He has to decide that on his own."

Vincent was quiet as his thoughts turned. Then: "What was he like, before he died?"

"Oh...not so different," said Henry with a note of fondness. His smile slowly faded. "But...obviously, he felt different. He was alive. He still had his whole future ahead of him. He had room to make mistakes, meet people, change things. Now..."

"He feels empty," Vincent finished. The ensuing silence seemed to agree.

"He's a ghost," Henry said softly. "What do you expect?"

"I know. It's just...I can sense what he used to be. Or...what's missing, I suppose. When he was a proper ghost, on his own, he felt...almost like a hole in the air. In the fabric of the world. Like he was taking something from it."

Henry gazed at him curiously as Vincent continued to bandage his arms. "He...doesn't belong in this world anymore. Maybe that's what you were sensing."

"But he's here anyway," Vincent argued. "It's no wonder he clung to Ava, once he found her. Much as I don't care for her...she was whole, still."

The memory of Percy's desperation flitted across his mind: *I understand her! And she understands me! She's with me, always! And I'm with her... We'll never be alone again.*

"She had a life left to share...and he could finally touch someone again. Maybe in a way he never had before, even when he was alive," Vincent murmured.

After a moment he realized Henry's gaze lingered on him, and warmth crept up his neck. He busied himself with unwrapping more bandages. He didn't look up, but out of the corner of his eye he noticed Henry shifting to pull his bloodstained shirt off. He halted halfway through with a groan.

"H-hey...a little help here, please?"

Vincent finally looked up to find the shirt stuck just over Henry's head, his arms up awkwardly. In spite of himself, in spite of everything, a laugh bounced up from Vincent's chest.

He reached out to help Henry wriggle out of his shirt, his face burning as his eyes grazed the gentle curves of Henry's chest and stomach, down to the starker lines of his hips poking out from his dark jeans. All of it was marred only by the places where his smooth skin was gouged and torn away. The sight made Vincent cringe. He had only seen Henry like this once before, but somehow it felt like something sacred, something he should have been able to safeguard. Now his chest was burning too, hot with shame and vengeance alike.

"Vincent...?"

His name snapped him back to the present. He began tending to the wounds on Henry's torso as gingerly as he could–both for Henry's sake and his own. Touching him like this was almost too much to bear, especially now. Vincent's nerves were so frayed that he could no longer control the tremor in his fingertips. He loathed every wince and twitch of Henry's muscles responding to his touch. He worked in silence, unable to speak, hardly daring to breathe, the hour stretching into eternity.

Finally, Vincent saw no more blood. He moved back with a grateful breath. Henry stood and crossed to his closet, taking out a fresh shirt and handing it to Vincent with an almost shy smile.

"Afraid I'm at your mercy again, O king of shirts..." Henry teased.

Vincent cracked a wry smile, shaking his head. He helped Henry pull it on as best he could. Then Henry said, "Um...my legs...Jake, uh, caught me a couple times..."

Vincent cleared his throat quietly. "I won't look."

Henry grinned. "I guess I can patch up my own legs. And here I was getting used to being pampered."

"Ah–no, I mean, I can–"

"It's fine!" Henry laughed, pulling the first aid kit closer to him with a wince. "I still have to do yours, anyway."

Vincent busied himself with inspecting his own wounds while Henry carefully slipped off his jeans. Vincent's head and neck had suffered the most, and were going to need more tending than he could provide from this angle. However, many smaller injuries dotted the rest of his body in more reachable places. He got a head start on them, biting his tongue to keep from wincing as he gently scrubbed and bandaged them.

By the time he had finished, Henry had patched up the gashes on his legs and was pulling on some loose pajama pants. He chuckled as he turned back to Vincent.

"Guess I won't be fashionable again for a while."

"However will you survive?"

"I've been through worse, somehow." Henry sat down on the bed again at Vincent's side, and it took everything in him not to move away. He could feel the anticipation traveling up his body, prickling like electricity.

Henry lifted his hands slightly. "May I?"

Vincent nodded, twisting so Henry could help him shrug off his jacket first. Then he undid the buttons on his own shirt, his fingers fumbling on every one, to his great annoyance. Still, he was grateful he could do that much for himself.

Henry pulled Vincent's shirt off his shoulders, and then his body was bare in the warm lamplight. He averted his gaze–both from Henry and his own chest. More than his wounds, he didn't want to see those scars again.

Then Henry's fingers brushed his chest, and a shiver passed through him. Vincent was sure Henry could feel his heart hammering in his ribcage.

"Are you okay?" Henry said, his voice barely above a whisper.

Vincent nodded without looking up.

"Does it hurt...?"

With you, it always does. "It's okay...don't worry about me."

Gentle hands lifted Vincent's tie over his head, leaving him feeling truly vulnerable. Then they touched his jaw, carefully tilting his head so Henry could reach the gash on his neck. The scabs at the edges scraped together as they flexed, and Vincent could feel the blood still oozing from the center of each puncture.

"You really got beat up, huh..." Henry murmured.

Vincent didn't answer. He could only sit still, and try to breathe.

"I'm sorry...I...I didn't mean to leave you with the brunt of it..."

"You didn't," said Vincent. "You wouldn't. You were doing the best you could."

Suddenly, he lost his nerve. Without his tie to ground him, in this strange body that wasn't quite his, his awkwardness overtook him. He moved away, just enough to make Henry retreat. The moment froze between them, neither of them seeming to know what to do now.

"...Do you think Sierra will be okay?"

That worked. Henry finally looked away, a deep shadow over his expression. "I hope so. She...didn't look good."

Vincent instantly regretted bringing her up. The memory of her terror pierced his heart.

"Why did we leave her alone?" Henry said through gritted teeth. "We should have known better...the one time we left this place unprotected..."

"...I'm sure Benjamin knew."

Henry looked up at him. "You think?"

Vincent nodded, before realizing his certainty felt too personal. He backed off a little. "He's been one step ahead of us the whole time, after all. First with Mira, the shed, then the night watchman, the towers..."

Henry nodded grimly. He looked haunted again, like he had after Vincent had stopped him from killing Jake.

"You were right all along, Vincent. I should've never gotten involved with her. I wish she'd never even found that stupid amulet."

Guilt stabbed Vincent straight through the middle, sharper than any silver knife. He wondered if the amulet might have protected her, if he had left it with her. If it only worked for Percy's bloodline, maybe it didn't matter...but it didn't stop him from feeling that, somehow, he was responsible for whatever happened to her now.

But Henry seemed to have the same idea. "Maybe if I'd just left her alone, Jake wouldn't have felt so...and then he wouldn't have..."

"What Jake did isn't your fault." Vincent finally met his gaze, his own serious.

"He said so himself! He said I was...perfect. Too perfect. Stealing the limelight. Selfish."

"You're *not*." Vincent's eyes burned into Henry's, willing him to hear the conviction behind his words. "He can blame you all he wants. But he made those choices for himself. You being yourself didn't force him to shirk his humanity." He let out a little snort of disdain, looking away again. "If anything, you just showed him something he didn't want to face about himself. He deserved to know it."

"Do...do you hate me, Vincent?"

Vincent's heart nearly cracked in two, he sounded so small. He had seen Henry hopeless only a handful of times, but never had he witnessed him so unsure, so completely at another's mercy. It stirred something in him that he had buried deep.

He cares what I think of him. He trusts me.

"No. Never. How could I? Henry...everywhere I go, from the moment I met you, I've seen the way people look at you. Like you're the brightest star in the sky. The one they look to, to know which way to go. You're not just good at football, or video games, or monster hunting...you're *good.*"

Vincent pushed through the instinct to shut himself up, to dam the truth deep inside.

"There are all kinds of people in this world. But you...you're different. You always look out for everyone. You don't care who they are, or what they've done. Sometimes to a fault," he added, a crooked smile darting across his lips. "You still think they deserve kindness. Even someone like me. So if anyone else hates you like Jake does...it's only because they wish they could be half as brilliant as you."

He turned away to prepare some more gauze, feeling profoundly exposed—and not just because of his body. But then, suddenly, Henry's fingers alighted on his shoulder.

He froze, his breath caught in his throat. They were light and warm and hesitant, as if waiting for rebuke. None came.

Slowly, gently, Henry's fingertips brushed the edges of the scars across Vincent's chest. Then his palm pressed there, moving up his chest to his collarbone, fingers tracing its ridge to the divot below his neck.

"You...saved me, Vincent."

"I...I didn't. It was Casey, really. And Percy. I couldn't reach you in time, before he..."

"No," said Henry, fixing him with those eyes like a summer sky. "*You* saved me. You stopped me. I...I almost lost myself."

Blinking in surprise, Vincent met his gaze. It flickered over his features, searching them, taking him in. He wanted to break it, but he was frozen there, terrified of what Henry might glimpse in the shadows behind his own eyes.

He hated it, but he loved it. He was laid bare in a way he never had been before, even when Benjamin found him on that desolate plain far beneath the earth. Henry was looking at him to see him. Not to use him. In that tiny moment of connection, he could feel it as if Henry's thoughts were his own.

"Without you...I couldn't do it. I couldn't keep going. I've been alone for so long..."

He was so close now, it felt as if Vincent was falling into that clear sky in his eyes. The earth soared above his head, so far away it didn't even matter anymore. Now the heavens lay before him, so near that he could reach out and touch them.

"But I'm not anymore."

Henry's lips brushed his, softly at first, lighter than a moth's wings. Then they were warm and steady, and Vincent was no longer falling upward, but drowning. Every nerve was suddenly ablaze, his senses static, the weight of this new world bearing down on him and crushing the breath from his lungs.

He let it drag him into its depths. He didn't care anymore. He let his breath run out, consigned himself to death at its hands. It was all worth it for this one moment. He had never felt so alive.

And then, as swiftly as it had come, it was over.

Henry moved back, his eyes still flickering over Vincent's face. He could easily read the worry and the exhilaration and the inexplicable sadness flitting through them. Before he knew it his fingers slipped into Henry's, warm and searching.

"Did you...did you mean to...?"

Henry's fingers closed around his own.

"Y...yeah. I–I hope that was..."

"Of course, I just–I never thought you'd..."

Henry's smile was tender, genuine, ever so slightly tremulous. Vincent had never seen him like this before. "I–I meant what I said, Vincent.

You...remind me who I am. What I'm fighting for. You remind me it's not all hopeless."

His smile slowly faded, replaced by something so weary it was almost somber. Vincent caught his eyes roving down to the scars across his chest.

"I know it's hard for you...I know you can't give me everything I want. Like you said...we live in different worlds. But...you're here, still. You're here for me in a way no one else ever has been."

That familiar guilt rose again in Vincent's chest, but he fought it back viciously. He wouldn't let it destroy this moment. Nothing could.

"I know a lot of people look to me. I'm happy I matter that much. But...I don't know. Sometimes it feels like...it's just expected of me. And outside of that, most people never stop to think twice about me. *Really* think. As long as I keep doing whatever I do for them...that's all that matters."

"Until it doesn't."

Henry nodded, ever so slightly. "I...I really don't care. It won't stop me. But..."

They fell silent for a long moment, the air between them heavy with thought, with feeling.

"...I feel the same way."

Henry looked at Vincent in surprise.

"I'm a Child of Cerberus. I was bred to guard the prisoners of Hell. That's all I've ever been. That's what I was made to do. But now..."

He felt Henry's gaze trying to dig deeper. Frost began forming on his heart again at once. Henry couldn't go any further. He couldn't know Vincent had caused all of this by setting Benjamin free.

"...Now there's so much more."

Mercifully Henry relented, nodding softly. His gaze wandered far away again.

"You know...I do feel like a star. The one you say I am. A hundred thousand miles away from everything, surrounded only by darkness."

A tiny smile crossed Vincent's face. "Then I guess I'm the darkness."

Henry smiled too, his sadness ebbing away. But he still looked ever so tired. It was bone-deep. He had lost too much tonight.

"...I'll stay here tonight," said Vincent.

His words came in lieu of everything else that could have—maybe should have. They could have talked forever, he was sure, tried again and again to untangle everything they had silently woven between them since they had first laid eyes on each other at the edge of the woods. But there wasn't enough time for that now.

He wondered if there ever would be—or if he would ever gather the nerve to do it. But for now...there was one thing he could do.

"All night. I promise. I'll keep watch, and you can sleep in peace."

"I'd like that," Henry murmured. "But only if you promise to rest, too."

"Okay. I will. I can do both."

Heavy and soft with affection and exhaustion alike, they finished dressing their wounds, hardly caring at all about them anymore. There was so much more to be done, and they both knew it—but for now, this moment was theirs, and no one else's.

Henry nestled under his covers with a contented sigh. Vincent turned off the light and settled on the floor, his back resting against the side of the bed. He gazed up at the strips of yellow light pooling on the ceiling through the blinds, listening to the silence and the crickets chirping faintly beyond the walls of their little room. No college students stirred tonight, disturbing the stillness. The night belonged to Vincent's racing heart, the half-formed thoughts swimming in his head, the feelings that had only just caught alight from the embers that had been glowing inside him. He marveled at them, how strange they were and yet how familiar, how long he had known their heat despite everything that had kept him from letting them grow. Everything that told him he did not deserve such happiness, that it was impossible.

But it wasn't. Just like Percy, Vincent was here anyway, even if he shouldn't be. And he was going to seize that chance, no matter what it cost him. None of it mattered anymore—not now that Henry loved him.

Vincent's heart pounded wildly in the dark, his brain overtaken with a buzzing that refused to let him rest. He wanted to change back into his true form, to run across the gardens and over his and Henry's favorite hill, to howl his glee to the whole world outside. But he knew he could do none of those things.

Restless, he reached his hand up, sliding it over the sheets until he found Henry's hand, warm and limp. He grasped it gently, running his fingers over his palm, savoring every line and curve he found there as if to memorize them all. He sat there for a long time in the dark, begging dawn to never come.

But he knew it would. The longer he stayed there, the more his thoughts began to churn. When dawn came, he would have to face the truth at last. Everyone knew it was Benjamin, now. They had proof, witnesses. Vincent was closing in on him, and he had no choice about it anymore.

Then again...maybe he never had. And when it was all over...he would have to go home.

He didn't want to go home. It was horrible to feel, even more horrible to admit. He didn't even want to think about what his father would do if he knew. But tonight he had let the light in, and he couldn't deny it any longer.

He liked being alive. Being a person. And when he went home, he would be nothing but a guard dog again.

He didn't want to go home.

But Benjamin does, he thought. *He wants to open the portal. Why?*

Moreover...couldn't Benjamin just step back inside the chasm? Vincent had just assumed that when he was ready, he could return the same way he had come. Something was missing.

And Jake knows. He's been building those towers.

All of a sudden something inside him reared up, gnashing its teeth, nearly carrying him off his feet. That deep, dark instinct to protect Henry was clawing at his ribcage now that he had fed it its first real meal. It eclipsed his sixth sense, as if it never existed. He couldn't keep the image out of his head– Jake baring his fangs at Henry's neck, only inches from tearing his life away forever. He had almost lost everything before he even truly had it—all because of Jake.

And if Benjamin had his way...he might lose it still. There was no way he would spare Henry now that he was involved in this—and there was no way Henry would stop, either. He would finish this if it was the last thing he ever did.

Vincent carefully slipped his hand out of Henry's, standing up in the dark.

He cast one last glance at Henry's sleeping form, illuminated only by the stripes of light that found their way through the blinds. He looked utterly serene curled up in his blankets, his hair mussed in a way it never was during the daytime. He showed no trace now of the weight of both worlds, which he had shouldered ever since his father had laid the first enchanted weapon in his young hands. For a moment, Vincent couldn't move. He wanted to stay here, to fulfill his promise, to keep him safe.

But he *did* have to keep him safe. There was only one way to ensure that now.

Vincent slipped down the hall and through the back door. He ignored the burning of his wounds, tightening the tie around his neck until it pressed painfully on his bandages—a reminder of what was at stake, a reminder he deserved. He slunk off into the night; but it would be dawn soon.

A menacing growl greeted him when he arrived in the field behind the gym, swiftly staunched when its owner recognized him.

"Vincent?" said Casey. "What are you doing here? Where's Henry?"

"He's safe," Vincent assured her. "Asleep. All quiet here?"

"Yeah. Percy took Sierra. The leech hasn't even woken up, far as I can tell."

Vincent nodded, his gaze falling on the now-padlocked door to the shed. "You're sure he's still out cold?"

Casey followed his gaze suspiciously. "One way to find out."

Vincent took the key from her and unlocked the door. It took a moment for his eyes to adjust to the even deeper darkness inside. When they did, he couldn't help the satisfaction that crawled into his chest.

Jake sat with his back against the far wall, his bulky body trussed up in Henry's silver chains with his arms behind him. He looked up at Vincent with hatred he didn't bother to disguise, his clothes torn and his wounds black. If they were healing, the progress was slow.

"Good morning," said Vincent with a smirk.

"Shove it," Jake spat.

Vincent's eyes met Casey's.

"Want to help me with something?"

A little smile quirked across her face.

Vincent stepped into the tiny shed, Casey at his side. She shut the door behind them, plunging them all into darkness.

"What are you doing?" came Jake's voice. Vincent was pleased to catch a note of alarm.

White light suddenly flooded the room. Casey set her phone down on the floor, its flashlight throwing deep, eerie shadows upward onto the ceiling. Jake pressed hard against the wall, cringing away from the brightness.

Vincent crouched only inches away from his face. Jake glared back at him defiantly, but Vincent didn't miss the flicker of horror when Jake caught the flash of red in his dark eyes.

"You know what Benjamin is doing with those people he killed." Vincent kept his voice low.

Jake flashed his fangs. "You know I'm not telling you shit, fleabag."

Vincent nodded. "I had a feeling," he murmured. "So let's make something clear between us."

He reached around Jake's back, grasping one of his tied hands. A horrific CRACK echoed through the shed.

A strangled cry tore from Jake's throat, swiftly stifled through hard-pressed lips. He hung his head over his chest, his breath coming fast now. As he refocused on Vincent, his eyes rolled wildly with fear and fury both. He looked more human than Vincent expected.

But it wasn't the first time Vincent had seen a human like this. There was something primal in them still, and it always burst monstrous from their flesh at the end of the line.

Maybe they had a true form too, just like he did.

Vincent gazed at Jake coldly, waiting. When it became clear Jake wasn't going to break first, he sighed.

"You're tough, I'll give you that. I'm sure all that football training gave you a high pain tolerance. It sounded pretty rough at times, from what Henry told me."

CRACK. Another yelp followed, piercing Vincent's nerves. But he didn't care. He was steadier than ever. His purpose was so simple now, after everything. This was something he was good at.

For everyone he's helped murder. For Henry.

"Good thing this place is so far out," Vincent mused. "And it's so very early in the morning. And...well, you try getting a college student up early. No one's going to hear you. But we can always try again tomorrow, if you want to drag this out."

CRACK. Jake managed to hold it in this time, clenching his teeth hard enough that his shout only came as an echo behind them.

"Do you really owe Benjamin that much, to keep his secrets for him? I thought you had everything you wanted now. You won't soon, if you keep this up."

"Go to hell." Jake's chest heaved as he wrestled with the pain. "I'm not giving you anything. *You,*" he said with unbridled disgust, "slobbering all over Henry's every move. You're pathetic. You're almost as bad as—"

Then the door burst open, flooding the shed with the gray light of dawn.

"What—what *is* this?"

Vincent spun around, shielding his face against the brightness with his arm. His heart froze over.

340

Henry stood there, a proud silhouette in the light of day. Vincent had never seen such a look of horror on anyone's face, even in the darkest depths of Hell itself. He watched every shimmering drop of hope slowly drain from the eyes of the one he loved most.

"Let him go, Vincent," Henry said, ever so quietly.

Vincent's heart jolted.

"What?" Casey cried, outraged. But Henry only had eyes for Vincent.

"We...we can't." Vincent's voice came so weakly it didn't even sound like him anymore. "He's dangerous. And we need to know what Ben–"

"Let. Him. Go."

Vincent flinched. Blood roared in his ears as his desperation rose. He wished Henry would break, yell at him, do anything but keep him shackled in that horrible, frigid gaze.

For the longest moment, nothing and no one moved. It was as if the whole world had frozen over as well. Like it would never move again.

But then, slowly, Vincent did. He reached for the chains.

"What? *No!*" Casey shouted, but Vincent didn't hear her. He fumbled with the lock, his hands trembling.

Then a new voice broke in, dripping with poison and honey.

"My, my...what an unpleasant scene."

CHAPTER 21

THE RIFT

66 **Y**ou!" Casey snarled as Melanie King appeared in the doorway beside Henry. She wore a sneer befitting her name, as if all the world's riches had suddenly materialized at her feet.

"Me." She tossed her sumptuous dark curls behind her shoulder with a flick of her head.

"What are you doing here?" Casey growled. For a moment Vincent thought she might transform then and there, despite the potion's lingering effects.

Melanie's eyes widened innocently. "Why, I was just having a morning stroll when I heard the most *dreadful* noise! I thought our friend the football star would be just the person to handle whatever nefarious things were going on."

Henry's cold sideways glance told Vincent that he wasn't buying it either, but to his dismay that was all Henry had for her. Instead his glare remained on Vincent, unyielding. He didn't speak, even as the silver chains loosened and fell away from Jake's body, their jingling too loud in the morning hush.

Jake immediately rose, clutching his mangled hand tightly in his good one. Nobody seemed able to look at it. His bedraggled body and clothes were drenched in sweat, and his breath came in heavy huffs as he shouldered his way past Vincent and Casey towards freedom. Casey twitched and nearly lunged, but even she seemed cowed by the force of Henry's ire.

Henry moved aside for Jake to pass. When he reached Melanie she took his arm with both hands, clutching him to her side almost possessively. Both of them glared at Vincent and Casey with an overwhelming malice–and triumph.

"See you around," Melanie lilted. Then she and Jake turned and began crossing the field.

Every instinct shouted at Vincent to protest, to drag them back by force, but he didn't dare. All he could do was watch until they had disappeared around the side of the gym.

After what seemed like forever, Henry finally spoke.

"What were you two thinking?"

His voice was just as hushed as before, dark with an unspoken fury. Vincent forced himself to meet Henry's cold glare.

"It was my idea. We *need* to know more about Benjamin's plans. Otherwise, we're running in blind. We barely have a chance to stop him as it is. Even the forces we've seen are more than a match for us, let alone anything else he has up his sleeve."

The temperature behind Henry's eyes seemed to be dropping with every word out of Vincent's mouth.

"And you thought *torture* was the way to do it?"

His words lanced Vincent's heart. It felt like it stopped altogether. When it started again, it was borne by a rising wave of heat from deep in the pit of his stomach.

"If a few broken fingers is all that stands between us and stopping countless more deaths? Absolutely."

"*No,*" said Henry, with a savagery Vincent had never imagined could come from Henry Wellfellow. "How could you even consider stooping to that level? We are not going to *torture* people to get what we want! That's not how we do things!"

"He's not even alive anymore, Henry!" Vincent snarled, his temper flaring to meet Henry's. "He *killed himself* to become stronger—you heard him! And you think causing him a little pain is—is what, unforgivable?"

"He's still a *person!*" Henry shouted, finally shedding that veil of restraint. "He was at our mercy, he'd given up! There are countless other ways to stop Benjamin!"

"Not without risking so much more! Do you want more people to die because you're too busy scraping together another plan? Is that really worth it to you?"

Henry flinched, but his fury blazed even hotter. "I *know* I don't have all the answers! But I know one thing for sure—the ends do *not* justify the means, Vincent!"

They were nose-to-nose now, but so differently from the last time, only hours before in the tenderness of night. In the harsh light of dawn, everything was gray.

A long, horrible silence passed. Nothing dared to move, the whole world tangled up between the two of them. Then:

"I...I thought you were better than this."

Vincent took in every harrowed line he had carved into that beautiful face of marble.

"But I'm not."

His words fell, the final grain of sand in an hourglass that had been draining since the moment he first saw the color green.

What had he expected? Henry was the brightest star in the sky. True north. He had all of that to uphold, because he was Henry Wellfellow. And because he was Henry Wellfellow, he couldn't do what had to be done. He was never going to finish this alone. Henry had known that all along, but now, Vincent saw it where he couldn't. Vincent was the only one who could save him.

Of course it had to be this way. He was never meant to be happy. If he truly cared about Henry, about goodness itself, about everything he had come to love about this world, the *real* world...he could no longer be a part of it.

"Fine. If you won't do what needs to be done, I will. For you."

Before Henry could react, Vincent burst out of the shed. He bolted across the field, ignoring Henry's and Casey's shouts behind him, finally giving in to that howling, clawing, ravenous sixth sense deep in his heart.

The sky was growing brighter by the minute, but the last shadows of night still clung to the world with desperate claws, staining everything around him gray. He welcomed it. It only showed the world as it was to him now.

Not long, now, he told himself as he ran. *It's almost over.*

He didn't slow even when he reached the dorm hall's entrance, shouldering past the little group of students who had just emerged. They stared after him with shouts of confusion as he forged ahead into the hallway. He didn't even need to look at the names on the rooms as he flashed past. He knew exactly where he was going.

Then he stopped dead. His gaze was pulled by that ceaseless gravity in his heart, down the stretch of hallway, all the way to the end. A single figure stood there, eyes wide and blank with shock.

In that single instant, the flames erupted again from the darkest depths of Vincent's being. His costume burned away and he was a hellhound again, his true self down to his core.

He surged down the hallway. Mortal eyes appeared from open rooms, reviling him and shrieking in fear as his hulking form barreled past.

Benjamin turned, sprinting for the back door—but Vincent reached him in two great bounds. His teeth clamped around Benjamin's leg and he fell, his head cracking on the thin carpet. The glass door shattered as Vincent's weight slammed into it, shards scattering everywhere.

Dark blood streaked over the pavement as Vincent dragged Benjamin across the parking lot and into the grass beyond. They seemed to catch every rock and pothole along the way—but Vincent didn't care anymore. There was no damage that could matter now, no stakes that could stall him, no leverage that could quell his wrath. No more games. No more sympathy. There was only the hellhound, his quarry, and the chasm in his heart that he had filled with flame.

Through the gray forest they traveled, crashing through the undergrowth, the only sound rising through the morning mist. As he ran his heart steadied, forgetting its agony and the abyss at its back, reveling in the thrill of the hunt. His legs pumped and his free heads panted, striding faster and faster as trees darted past, his instincts carrying him forward in the empty ecstasy of freedom—

And then the thunder of water reached his ears, and he burst out into a familiar clearing. He slowed at last, chest heaving, gazing up at the looming might of the Devil's Maw high above him.

I'm coming home, Father. Maybe there was still one person he could avoid disappointing.

Vincent heaved Benjamin through the leaves, making for the rockfall he would have to climb to reach the rift. The roar of the waterfall seemed to draw him in, a choir calling his name in an eldritch language. As his paws carried him up the slope, he heard nothing else—not until color flashed before his eyes, barring his path.

Henry gazed up at him from the ledge just steps away, stone-faced, cold, steadfast. He looked at him as if Vincent was his final adversary to defeat, the last obstacle between him and his destiny as a hunter—a hero. And Vincent realized that somehow, he had always known it would end like this.

"Stand aside." Vincent bared his teeth in a warning.

Slowly Henry shook his head, not breaking his gaze for a single second.

"Drop him." His voice was steady.

"You know I can't do that."

A glimmer of regret shone in Henry's eyes, but it was gone in an instant.

"This isn't the way things should go, Vincent. This isn't justice. You can't just drag him away and call it done."

"This is the way things have to be. Someone has to stop this, by any means necessary."

Suddenly a rasping sound rose from Vincent's jaws. Both he and Henry looked down in surprise, realizing a moment too late that Benjamin was laughing.

"You're already damned, just like me," his hoarse voice drifted up from where he dangled, his bloodied leg between Vincent's teeth. "Why bother with the heroics now? You could just stay here in the mortal world and lie low, and Daddy would never be the wiser."

A low growl began deep in Vincent's chest. "Shut up with your wheedling. Listening to you got me into this mess."

"I gave you the idea, but you went along with it," Benjamin pressed. "You like it here. You deserve better than to spend all your days in Hell being Lucifer's pet. If your dad had any brains at all he wouldn't have sent you up here. Did he really think you'd get a taste of freedom like this and then come crawling back with his prize like a good boy?"

"What's he talking about, Vincent?" Henry looked from him to Benjamin and back again. "You were sent here for *him?*"

Vincent's growl intensified and his lips curled, flashing cruel fangs. "You're not getting out of this, Benjamin. I have a duty and I'm going to fulfill it. My father will honor me when I return, and you'll rot in Hell the way you were supposed to."

Benjamin snorted. "You think he'll praise you when you get back? After all this time you've wasted? You could've had me *months* ago, but you stalled because you wanted to live the good life up here. And not only that–didn't you notice how many people saw you back there, when you caught me? He's going to be *furious.* You're never going to see the sun again. And that'll be the least of your worries."

"*I don't care!*" Vincent snarled, the final thread holding him together snapping. "Don't you get it? There's nothing left for me here! Not anymore." His voice broke at the last moment.

Somehow Vincent managed to hold onto the last scraps of his bravado, but only just. He forced his burning gaze onto Henry again. "I'm taking him. Now. Get out of the way, Henry."

Henry met him with that same stony resolve. He was so much smaller than Vincent now, so fragile compared to the might of a Child of Cerberus, but he stood Herculean there at the edge of the world without a single weapon.

"No, Vincent. I won't let you do this. You'll have to kill me first."

Vincent's heart surged so hard in his chest that he thought his ribs might crack. Henry thought Vincent would kill him?

"HEY!"

A new voice echoed through the clearing, almost drowned by the crashing water. All of them turned, stunned, to see Casey stumbling in from the trees, chest heaving as she fought for breath.

"Don't do this, Henry," she said, a strange desperation carved into her face, only half-filled with the anger Vincent expected from her. "You *know* Vincent would never so much as scratch you. You *must* know that."

Henry blinked, just as surprised as Vincent by her pleading. "He's..."

"He's doing this *for* you, Henry," Casey insisted. "Don't you see that?"

Henry's mouth fell open, but no sound emerged. He looked utterly lost.

"Someone has to," Vincent growled. "It's like Benjamin said. I'm already damned."

"So what?" Casey argued, a trace of her usual fire flaring up again. "You're here now, aren't you?"

For a brief moment, something reached him. Why was she trying so hard for him?

But then the reality of it returned in a terrible tide. All the deceit, everything he had hidden and borrowed just to stay here a little longer, just to pretend he mattered for a little while. But nothing mattered anymore–his friends knew exactly what he was, now.

"No. This is the reason I came to this world. Benjamin was my prisoner, and I let him escape. I was weak–I let him deceive me. The truth is, none of those people would have died if it weren't for me."

It was a savage pleasure, finally releasing those words. Now there was nowhere left to hide. At last he would get what he deserved.

But he didn't get the chance–because suddenly the ground disappeared beneath his paws.

The earth rose up to meet him, slamming into his side and knocking the breath from his lungs. He struggled to scrape his senses back together, but the world was a heaving blur of color and sound.

After a horrible moment his lungs finally inflated. With a gasp he flipped himself upright, his vision spinning. He saw that the others had been knocked over as well. Thankfully Henry had slid down the slope rather than falling off the cliff's edge, but he was far too close to it for comfort. He pushed himself up on his knees with a groan. At the edge of the clearing, Casey too fought to right herself. Both of their eyes were drawn to the waterfall. Vincent turned to look.

A pillar of pure black void rose from the chasm at the Devil's Maw, shooting so high into the sky Vincent couldn't see where it ended. It seemed to suck in all the light around it, warping its immediate surroundings like a dented mirror. Even the sky seemed darker, as if the sun itself had dimmed.

Vincent's heart twitched and throbbed, straining towards the pillar as if it too was being pulled inside. He fought the urge and looked around desperately until he spotted Benjamin a few yards away, crawling through the dirt towards the edge of the clearing. But his mangled leg dragged uselessly behind him, a bloody anchor. In two bounds Vincent crossed the gap between them and laid a heavy paw on his back.

However, Benjamin didn't seem too disappointed to be stopped. Instead he twisted his head around to grin at him. His freckled face was smudged with grime and blood trickled from his crown, but he looked as triumphant as he could muster.

"It's done," he breathed.

"*What's* done?" Vincent demanded, icy dread trickling into his stomach. "What did you do?"

A low chuckle escaped Benjamin's throat, ending in a cough.

"The portal's broken. Now no one can control who goes in or out."

Vincent froze. "You *broke...*"

A new figure appeared at the edge of the trees. Startled, Vincent looked up and saw Melanie wandering into the clearing as if sleepwalking, her gaze fixed in awe upon the pillar of darkness.

"So there it is." Satisfaction spread across her face. She turned to Benjamin, still pinned beneath Vincent's paw, apparently unconcerned with his plight. "You were right about that amulet."

"What?" said Vincent, numb with shock.

"You didn't figure it out?" said Benjamin. "We studied its power. Worked out how to break it. Now it can't imprison spirits anymore. Magnify that impact…" He gestured towards the pillar of darkness. "Genius bit of magic, really. Hats off to Percy's family. Using the life force of the recently-deceased as a conduit…"

Thunderstruck, Vincent's racing thoughts began to fall in line piece by piece. The amulet was broken, and there were no more spirits inside…he already knew Percy had lied about not being able to return to it. That meant…Percy was *never* trapped inside. Why hadn't he put the pieces together before?

"The totem we made from Percy's body was enough to break the amulet, and then some. His bloodline was the anchor for that piece of magic. But we had to go bigger for a portal to the Underworld. Appeal to some of the oldest entities in the universe." Benjamin lifted four bloodstained fingers, one after the other. "Fire. Earth. Water. Air."

"You…you finished the ritual, didn't you?"

"Duh," said Melanie. "You let us go, remember? All we needed to do was find the right sacrifice. Or, rather, *I* did," she added smugly. "I always pick the perfect sacrifices, don't I, Benjy? And *you* found the perfect distraction."

Vincent's stomach plunged. *Percy. Mira. The watchman. Sierra, nearly…* It was Melanie who had been choosing them. Even Sierra, despite what she meant to Jake. And now…

"Who did you kill?" His own voice sounded very far away.

"It doesn't matter, anyway," Benjamin told him with a smile. "You'll see her again soon. Death is dead. Now no one will ever cross over to that wretched place. Our souls belong to us, now. Thank her for the amulet for me, will you?"

The icy liquid in his core spilled over, and numbness spread through Vincent's body. He stared down at Benjamin's face without seeing it.

"No. Please. Not her."

"Vincent!"

Casey's warning made him look up to see several others entering the clearing–students and townspeople of different ages, all of them fully outfitted with hooded jackets, all of them paler than they should be. And at their head was Hunter, human-formed this time, heavily bandaged with a jeering snarl on his face.

Just as Vincent suspected. At least he was right about one thing.

His instincts kicked in, driving back his shock. For a moment everything stood frozen as the air shifted in the clearing–each side gazing at the other, assessing their odds, weighing their options.

Vincent moved first.

"*Stop him!*" Melanie shrieked. But Vincent had already grabbed Benjamin, his massive jaws clamping around his collarbone, his shoulder, everything both heads could reach. The last head remained free, its eyes locked on his goal, blind to every threat rapidly closing in on him.

"Vincent, *no!*"

Henry's cry alone pierced the veil, but Vincent fought back the pain of it. He bounded up the rocks, climbing towards the thundering falls. His claws slipped on wet stone over and over, but each time he forged ahead with a haggard determination. To him, this was all that mattered now. The only thing that would make up for every single evil Vincent had caused in this world by being such a fool.

And then he was standing at the precipice, gazing down into that bottomless abyss. Its dark center surged upward still, greedily, endlessly into the sky. It gripped Vincent's heart so powerfully it seemed to have grown teeth, gnawing and tearing and gnashing and devouring every last scrap of warmth that still lived inside. For a moment he teetered there, his claws scrabbling against the stone, grit showering down into the blackness.

Just as the first shoes found purchase at the top of the rockfall, he let go.

Benjamin fell. Down, down, his limbs splayed, his hair flying over his face, covering those winter eyes.

And then he was gone.

The footsteps ceased. Dimly Vincent registered the figures gathering all around him, staring down into the chasm in horror.

The silence that fell seemed to echo louder than the waterfall. How long it lasted, no one could be certain—mere moments stretching into eons as again the world and its fate shifted on its axis.

Finally, Melanie was the one to break it.

"You moron," she hissed at Vincent. "Didn't you hear what he said? He's just going to come back—the portal is broken."

Vincent stood there, frozen still. Her words echoed in his three skulls.

"You're right."

He jumped.

The onlookers' cries were consumed by the crashing water as he sailed down, down, down... The wind rushed through his fur, the abyss reached out with its hungry claws, dragging him back where he truly belonged...

He braced, but there was no need. Solid ground met his paws, sudden but without impact. When he opened his eyes, a familiar sight welcomed him.

Gray, so much deeper and darker than anything the surface could produce. Plains stretched endlessly before him, grass whipping violently in shimmering waves, assailed by a hot and merciless wind. Great fissures scarred the earth in every direction, vivisecting the hills and leaving their edges crumbling into even deeper darkness.

The sky was black, because it wasn't a sky at all. It was a ceiling, so high above it couldn't be seen. This meant that the Underworld itself produced its own light—not so much light as simply a thinner darkness. On the farthest horizon a great stronghold loomed, its countless black spires piercing the not-sky like fangs.

And winding backwards, all across the landscape, from the distant hills to steps away, legions of human figures trudged single-file. Each one seemed to follow the next blindly, as if taking comfort in their presence. Each time one of them dared to glance up, to take in their gruesome surroundings, they seized with fear and quickly lowered their heads, returning to their grim march. Some of them seemed to materialize from thin air; others walked from somewhere far beyond.

None of them seemed to notice the pillar of light striking the earth, as if sunlight was leaking down from the surface. Vincent had never seen anything like it–it was not there before.

But he wasn't here to marvel, or even to lament his return. He was here for one thing only.

Benjamin had only just scrambled to his feet, scanning the steadily marching line of souls with a fervor.

"Where are you going? I've made a way out–look!" he cried, pointing up to the bright pillar. "Step into the light, all of you! You can escape this place now!"

Slowly some of the line looked up at him with wide, frightened eyes. One or two followed his finger to the light, the realization dawning on their sallow faces. They began to wander away from the line, leaving gaps like wounds in their ranks. Some of the others following behind them continued doing so, only realizing what was happening when the light struck them full in the face.

Vincent wasn't sure why he kept watching. He knew he should stop them–stop Benjamin. But he hesitated.

The first of the phantoms paused before the great pillar shining down, gazing at it fearfully.

"Touch it!" Benjamin urged. "Don't let these cruel gods decide the weight of your soul! Take it back, damn it! Go back to the world!"

The lost soul reached out. The moment their fingers brushed the light, it swallowed their gray form whole. A cool breeze like a sigh swept over the watchers. It passed in an instant, but sent a ripple through those who were left.

As if waking from a deep slumber, they began clambering forward, each of them reaching out for the light with eager hands. One by one they disappeared into it—more and more by the minute, a great tide, no longer a serpent slithering eternally along the plains to its doom.

Something strange stirred within Vincent as he saw this. He stood there, his paws rooted to the blasted earth, his gaze lingering on that pillar of light with more hunger than he had ever felt.

"Do you see now, Vincent?" Benjamin's voice broke through his reverie. He gazed straight through him, his ice-blue eyes shining with that beautiful light, a hideous dichotomy. "They don't belong here. None of us do—not even you. You knew that from the beginning, didn't you? When we first met on these plains?"

Vincent's lips twitched around his fangs.

"You didn't even get a chance to live. And the rest of us," he said, sweeping his arm towards the tide of souls, "were *broken* by the one we had. We couldn't rise above the agony we were dealt—and the gods blame *us*, despite all the good fortunes others were gifted from the start. How is that fair?"

Vincent stared into those cold, cold eyes. Then, finally, he spoke.

"You're setting them free?"

"Do we deserve to burn forever here for circumstances beyond our control? For not lying there and taking that cruelty with a smile?"

"Where are they going?"

"Back to the world," Benjamin said with glee. "Their spirits can go wherever they wish."

"What about the ones meant for Heaven? Will they..."

Benjamin's smile twitched into an ugly, vengeful scowl. "They don't deserve anything better than the rest of us. We *all* try our hardest to make it through this life—what makes *them* so much more deserving of eternal happiness? Because they were dealt a better hand from the start? Because it was easier for them to live a 'moral' life?"

"What gives *you* the right to judge and condemn everyone any more than the gods?" Vincent growled. "You decided all those people deserved death, just because it would serve you best. They could have kept living their lives peacefully before you got involved. Before you *ruined* them."

"Ruined them? I'm *helping* them! Death means nothing now! And most of them aren't even truly dead–they've Ascended, and now they–"

"Don't you *dare* say that to me!" Vincent snarled. "Death means *everything!* It strips you down to a *shadow!* I've seen what it turns people into, their desperation for living again–" He saw flashes of Percy's empty presence in the dark of their room, his madness as he clung to the last dredges of life through Ava–

He stopped dead. Something floated to the surface of his mind–something he hadn't considered before. His memories of Percy transformed into Benjamin himself: that lonely figure on the endless gray plains, begging, clawing at Vincent to understand even a scrap of what he had been through during his short, hideous life, to share even a mote of his warmth with him.

"You're dead," Vincent murmured, staring at Benjamin as if seeing him for the first time.

Benjamin's eyes narrowed. He was as canny as ever; he seemed to catch Vincent's thought as it flashed past. "No, I'm not. Not in the way you think. Not anymore. I was restored."

"Being a vampire isn't *restored*," Vincent argued. "You're still dead. Do you even remember what it felt like to be alive?"

"What does it matter?" Benjamin shrugged, but a shadow haunted his expression. "I think what you're talking about, dear Vincent, isn't feeling *alive,* it's feeling *good.* The only time I ever felt *good* was when the pills forced all the shit away for half a second. Being *alive* was just a cycle of being hungry and scared and sick, and waiting for my mom to come home. Sometimes she'd make things better for a bit. And then she was dead, and it was up to me to do it all myself."

Vincent was quiet as the idea of it sank in. "You...didn't like being alive?"

"Don't misunderstand me–it was better than Hell. Funny...giving it up was supposed to solve everything for me. And now I'd give anything to have it back." Benjamin snorted, but it was a humorless sound. "Everything changed after this place. I decided to stop running, because I realized there's nowhere left to run to. And I realized just how *fucked* this whole game of life and death really is. All the way to the top. To its makers."

"And that's why you started plotting against Lucifer..." Vincent shook his heads. "You know humans have free will, don't you? You could've changed things..."

"So could you, Vincent."

Vincent froze.

Benjamin offered him an empty smile. "But it's not that easy, is it? You were born to this," he said, gesturing to the bleak landscape surrounding them. "To your father, your master, your duty. All your life, you were told you were only good for one thing. And that'll follow you forever, everywhere you go. Even if you muster the courage to walk away."

A chill traveled all through Vincent's body, to the very tips of his claws. A thousand thoughts scattered across his mind, warring with one another. He desperately tried to scrape them together. "I'm–I'm a *hellhound*, Benjamin. I don't get free will."

"And yet, all those choices you made brought us right here, right now."

He was right–however much Vincent wanted to deny it. Henry's words returned to him: *You may not be a human. But you're still a person.* All of this was proof enough.

And that made everything so much worse. Suddenly a dizzying universe of possibilities opened before him, where once there had only been orders.

"I started talking to people, down here–people like you," Benjamin said, a gleam in his eyes. "Death gave me the opportunity to learn so much I never knew about the world before. There are so many strange and wonderful forces out there. Powers us little mortals never get. Powers that could interrupt the cycle of judgment–breathe new strength into those I saw straying down the path that would lead them *here*."

"I...wasn't the only one you were talking to?" Vincent's heart clenched.

Benjamin seemed to read his thoughts. His expression softened into something far too close to pity. "I wasn't just using you, Vincent. Befriending a guard was part of the plan, yes...but I could tell you were like me from the start. Another sorry soul trapped in this miserable circle. I wanted to help you as much as anyone."

"But you *were* using me," said Vincent through gritted teeth. "If I didn't let you go, you couldn't have gone back to the mortal world. Couldn't have killed all those people." It was all rushing back to him–how stupid and naive he was, how all of this was his fault...

"That's the thing, Vincent–this is so much bigger than any one of us. One person's feelings, one person's life, compared to the suffering of countless *millions*–"

"What did you do? Find a vampire to turn you? Start turning people who could build your little army? I bet Melanie was a great addition," Vincent growled, his claws grinding into the dirt.

"Oh, Melanie..." Benjamin gave a rueful smile. "She's been so helpful since she Ascended. She really was the most bitter, miserable person when I met her. Barely spoke a word. I guess college isn't much of a fresh start when high school's already beaten everything out of you." He sighed. "I think she picked up a thing or two from her bullies. I do worry all of this is more of a revenge quest than anything, for her...but I had to motivate her somehow. I haven't had much luck yet with guiding her on a better path."

That didn't surprise Vincent in the slightest. Whatever twinge of shock or sympathy that found him was eclipsed by the knowledge of everything she had done. "A *better path*? You really think making people into vampires is saving them? You think *you're* capable of changing them?"

"It's the first step," said Benjamin. "And it's better than death. Thanks to how your masters run this place. I can give the people who need it most the power they never got. Uplift them. And together we will wield the strength to challenge the *gods*."

Vincent's eyes narrowed. "What do you mean?"

"Revolution, Vincent."

For a horrible moment, up was down and down was up. "How? You can't–"

"I can!" Benjamin insisted. "Now that we've broken the portal, the whole world will know the truth! What it's been missing all this time! What it should be fighting against—and for! Do you even know what's been going on under the surface, Vincent? What your master has been working towards? What he's been making you do, without even knowing it?"

At this, an invisible wall of iron surged up inside Vincent. He saw Benjamin again for what he was. *Liar. Traitor.* Using Vincent for his plans. Working with people like Melanie and Jake and Hunter. Sacrificing people on his own terms.

"No," he said, and Benjamin drew a breath as if to tell him—but Vincent didn't let him. "Not another word of your poison."

Suddenly, Vincent threw all three heads back. Three howls pierced the darkness, echoing across the desolate plains of Hell in eerie harmony.

And then, rising from far, far in the distance, another triad of howls answered.

CHAPTER 22

DUST TO DUST

"**W**hat did you do?" Panic flashed across Benjamin's face for the first time.

"I'm sick of your lies, Benjamin," Vincent said as he lowered his heads, wearing a cold determination. "I won't let you continue wreaking your havoc on the world. You should have known better than to betray me."

"Betray *you?*" Benjamin cried. "Is that what this is about? Is that *all* you care about? I told you, I wasn't just using you! *You* betrayed *me*, Vincent! You promised to escape with me! And then, at the very last moment, when both of us could see the light of the world above–"

"I still let you go!" Vincent snarled. "I went against *everything* for you! Because I believed in you, damn it! I felt your pain, and I–I couldn't–"

"But it wasn't enough, was it?" Benjamin spat. "You'd rather be crushed under your master's heel, just like your father. You refuse to rise above it. You'd betray anyone for it."

Vincent's heart lurched. "You left me, at the portal."

"You turned me in! You stalled, spouting your bullshit about second thoughts–all so Cerberus and that sister of yours could make their move."

Vincent flinched. "I didn't tell them! I just..."

"Let them take me," Benjamin finished for him. "They almost had me. And you did *nothing*. I barely escaped." He looked out across the dark plains, where that howl had answered from. "But this time...you *did* call them, didn't you?"

His eyes flashed wildly, and Vincent realized his intentions a moment before he bolted. He made it a single step towards the portal before Vincent caught him, slamming him to the ground with a heavy paw.

"Do you have any idea what you cost me?" Vincent snarled. One of his heads jerked its muzzle towards the scars across his own chest. "I was lucky my father took mercy on me! I almost *died* because of you! I'm not letting you wage wars and kill good people and ruin the rest with your false promises. I thought you cared about me–but it was just your vendetta, all dressed up like some kind of hero's gambit–"

"It's not a *vendetta*, god damn it!" Benjamin hissed, thrashing vainly beneath him. "The world doesn't have to work like this, Vincent! Do you really think we deserve *this?*"

He jammed his palm against Vincent's chest–against his scars.

Vincent froze, inside and out. Everything turned to ice.

The words spilled out before he could catch them. "*I* deserve it."

Benjamin shook his head. His eyes were...sad. "Nobody deserves that."

At that moment, they both spotted it–a dark dot on the horizon, streaking across the plains towards them. Fast.

"You *know* this is wrong, Vincent," Benjamin pleaded, his desperation rising. "You've changed–I saw it! You love the mortal world! What would your friends think if they saw this? What would *Henry* think? Don't all those 'good' people believe in second chances?"

Vincent's heart jolted painfully. "I–I'm not like them, Benjamin. I never have been. Just like you said."

"So what, then? You really want to go back to everything you suffered here?" Benjamin demanded. "Back to your father? You think you can just forget everything you saw and felt and loved in the mortal world?"

"I have to!" Vincent burst out. "I'm a *monster*, Benjamin! They hate me! I was born to be hated! I was born to do my duty, not to–to rewrite the world's rules!"

The figure was coming closer every moment. He could see its silhouette now, four paws racing over the grass, leaping over fissures with a vicious grace, three sleek heads with their burning eyes fixed on their quarry.

"Who do you think wrote those rules, Vincent?" Benjamin snarled. "Your masters! God and Lucifer, locked in their own damned vendetta, using all of us–humans *and* monsters–as pawns in their little game! You think you can just watch when one of your friends makes it here for some stupid choice they made in life, and you'll have to guard them and make sure they suffer for the rest of eternity? You think anyone, *anyone* can be perfect?"

Henry shot into Vincent's mind–Henry, silver knife plunging over and over into Jake's smoking chest, moments away from something he could never undo. Something that surely would have landed him here.

Henry, his light extinguished, gray and listless and afraid, for eternity...everything that made him who he was, gone forever.

Vincent had saved him from that. But there was still a whole life ahead of him, so much time to slip up–

The drumming of paws reached his ears. She was closing in.

"Vincent, *please!* Help me!"

Vincent broke. He released his hold on Benjamin, lunging for the pillar of light. He heard Benjamin's desperate footsteps pelting behind him–but the thunder of pawsteps drowned them in an instant. He felt his sister's hot breath at his back, her teeth snapping at his tail as he leaped, squeezing his eyes shut hard against the blinding light–

A massive paw clawed the damp stone at the edge of a deep, black chasm. Dirty limbs shook as they hauled a great beast from the depths of the earth itself. He crouched on the precipice, gulping breath, his brown fur dark with water and clinging to his hulking form. Only feet away a waterfall thundered down into the abyss. It spat on the monster that stood on its lip, daring him to venture too close so it could swallow him again. From its center a pillar of darkness speared the sky, bending the light around it as if to devour it, too.

Green. For a moment, it felt too good to be true. Sunlight struggled through the layer of clouds high above. The air was cold and damp and still, the last fingers of mist swirling at the forest's edge. All was silent but for the roar of the falls. The earth seemed to hold its breath. Something had changed.

This once-stranger to the world stood at the edge of it, taking it in. He was back. He never thought he would feel this way again.

But then the guilt began to crawl back inside. He turned, gazing back into the pillar of void.

But nothing emerged.

She took him.

He could still feel that sixth sense, urging him back into the darkness. He wasn't sure if it was Benjamin, or the void itself. But it didn't matter. It was too late to go back now.

Vincent's keen nose led him through the woods, ever more silent as the roar of the waterfall slowly faded away. It seemed so much darker, somehow, as if a shadow had fallen upon the entire world. He half-expected Benjamin's vampires to emerge from the canopy and challenge him, but nothing did. He didn't even see any ghosts, despite their exodus from the depths of Hell. Nothing but this strange darkness.

Finally he picked out figures up ahead, gathered around a familiar, grotesque image: a tower made of bones. The stench of death was so fresh here, it took all of his strength to come any closer.

Beneath it, another scent was obvious. His stomach clenched as he recognized it. It wasn't who he had expected.

When the others heard his footfalls they spun around, ready to fight–

"*Vincent?*"

Casey bolted to his side, surprising him as she threw her arms around his middle neck. His wounds from the day before ached as she did so, but now the pain hardly meant a thing.

"We thought you were–" She struggled to find the words, finally going for: "*gone*, for good! What happened?"

Vincent's gaze settled on Henry, still standing in the shadow of the tower. Henry stared back at him, his expression shifting constantly like ripples in sunlit water. There was a war going on behind his eyes. And Vincent didn't want to know which side would win.

Casey took his muzzle in both hands, fixing him with her own scrutinizing gaze. "You went to Hell, didn't you? How are you here right now?"

Vincent shook one of the heads unburdened by her grasp. "I left him there." His tone was as numb as he felt. "I let them take him. And...I decided to come back."

Casey's eyes widened. "You–they let you do that?" She didn't need an answer–his expression told her everything. A disbelieving smile spread across her face. "You *ran?*"

Vincent didn't share her triumph. He could hardly believe he had done it. He wasn't ready to think about what might happen because of his decision. To him, or Benjamin.

Apparently Henry wasn't about to give Vincent the luxury. "They're going to come after you." His tone was unreadable.

Vincent gritted his teeth. "They have bigger things to worry about right now, thanks to Benjamin."

"Well, what are you gonna do, then?" Casey asked. "You can't go back to school."

"No," Vincent agreed, remorse thick in his voice. "I've already failed my classes, anyway. I don't have a choice."

"Not because of that, moron," Casey snorted. "They'll know where to find you now, right?"

Vincent grimaced.

Then Henry spoke again, quietly. "Why did you come back?"

Vincent tried to look at him, but he couldn't. As if Henry was a ghost, too impossible to witness.

"I...don't want to go home."

It was real now. He had said it aloud.

Benjamin was right. Maybe about everything. And that made everything so much worse.

"I fulfilled my promise. My duty. I brought Benjamin back. If my father wants me dead...then I'll be dead to him. I don't want to be a part of that world anymore."

He could feel their shock without looking. Then Casey punched the air. "Fuck yeah!"

He was surprised by her eager support. *Her*, of all people. Something must have changed after all, somewhere he didn't expect. But it wasn't unwelcome. It was a strange comfort.

But Henry remained silent. Vincent finally forced himself to look–but he still couldn't see anything. Henry's expression was just...blank. He was staring at the tower.

"You know who it is, don't you?" Vincent said quietly.

Henry slowly nodded.

"I thought she was safe, when I sent Percy away to help Sierra...I-I thought..." Casey stopped, shaking her head sharply, her fists clenching at her sides. "This is all Percy's fault. Ava wouldn't have even been involved if he had just left her body. And now she's..."

"Where is he now?" Vincent glanced around as if expecting to glimpse his phantom drifting about the trees.

"Haven't seen him," said Henry darkly. "Back in your room, I expect. Now that Ava's dead, he's only a ghost again."

His words were so plain and so brutal, it didn't even sound like him anymore.

"Henry," Vincent said, the name spilling from deep inside his chest, filled with more feeling than he could staunch. More than he could say, in any other words.

Henry finally looked at him, and a single shadow hung on his face: remorse.

"You need to get out of here, Vincent."

Vincent's heart missed a beat. "What?"

"You and Casey. The Shadowhand are coming."

"What?" Casey echoed, suddenly furious. "You called them here?"

Henry's eyes squeezed shut. "I'm sorry. I didn't know what else to do."

"Fuck, Henry!" Casey snarled. "You're blaming *us* for this? If it weren't for you and your stupid fucking line in the sand, none of this portal-breaking bullshit would have happened!"

"It's not just about you, Casey!" Henry burst out. "I can't fix the portal to Hell! Ava's dead, Sierra's in the hospital, Melanie and Jake and Hunter and all those vampires are still out there... This is so far beyond all of us–beyond *me*. I should have known that from the start."

Vincent had never seen Henry like this before–so utterly and completely defeated. He had finally slipped away. A star extinguished.

"I'm *sorry*. I should've..." He stopped. Then he fixed his gaze directly on Vincent. "I'm sorry. For everything."

Before Vincent could even begin to piece together what he meant, Henry turned away. "Go–both of you. Hide, somewhere far away. I can't undo it now. But I'll try my best to head them off."

"Henry–wait!" Vincent called after him, his heart seizing up. "What will they do to you? What if they–"

"I don't know," he said, without looking back. "But whatever it is...I deserve it."

"Don't do this!"

But Henry didn't falter. Vincent took the first step after him, but Casey's hand grasped his neck fur, stopping him.

He didn't fight her. He couldn't bring himself to. Everything inside him was just too turbulent–he couldn't think, couldn't feel any one thing strong enough to tell him what to do. Instead he watched as Henry strode off into the shadow of the trees, until his silhouette disappeared into the fading mist.

"You heard him, Vincent," Casey said when he had gone, almost gently. Shockingly so. "We have to get away from here. Far away, where they won't find us. Otherwise, they'll take us both, and..."

Recalling the look on Henry's face, Vincent didn't even want to imagine what the Shadowhand would do to them.

Casey tugged at his fur. "C'mon. I know just the place."

He found his voice. "Are you sure?"

She tossed him a wry, empty smile. "Don't you trust me?"

He didn't answer.

She snorted. "Well, you'd better start. We're in this together, now. Besides, you still owe me for not ratting you out to Henry for stealing that amulet. Remember?"

It felt like a lifetime ago. Such petty things. But something in Casey's face was so earnest, so uncharacteristically kind, that he couldn't help but trust her. After all, they were outcasts now, in a way no one else was.

The two of them traveled through the forest, leaving that horrible tower and everything it stood for to its silent vigil. Vincent even managed to assume his human form again, after a time. They emerged at the edge of campus, but did not cut through it. Instead they skirted the outside, leaving Vincent only distant views of the place he had come to call home. He could see the garden paths from here, dotted with benches and streetlamps, the outdoor hallways and their sculpted archways, corridors into paved squares ringed by classrooms.

He even caught a glimpse of the grassy hillside atop the biology building, guarded by sycamore trees. His throat tightened, as if he had swallowed a stone. All he could do was look away, look ahead to the path they carved for themselves, far beyond the college's manicured boundaries.

Finally they found themselves on the main road heading into town. Before he really realized it, they were standing in front of the neon sign that read "DEXTER'S LABORATORY," no longer glowing in the daylight. The garage was closed now, although the thump of music still emanated from within.

Casey went up to the shop's front door and knocked loudly. In only a few moments it swung open, revealing a curious Dex staring back at them.

"We're in some shit," Casey said hastily. "We need a place to crash."

Surprisingly, Dex nodded immediately. His gaze flicked to Vincent with a glimmer of uncertainty, but he moved back from the doorway to let them both in.

The inside of the shop was overall unremarkable, with concrete floors and displays along the walls sporting all kinds of motorcycle paraphernalia, from keychains to visors to leather jackets. Casey led Vincent behind the counter and through a door, Dex in tow.

They found themselves in what appeared to be a proper residence, with couches, armchairs, tables, a TV, and other furnishings. Vincent could see part of a kitchen around a corner, and stairs leading up to presumably more living space. Two of Dex and Casey's other friends were lounging on the couches watching a TV show apparently called "The Crocodile Hunter." They looked up in surprise as their new guests entered, lingering on Vincent.

"Hey–give us some room, will ya?" Dex said, and the two men scrambled to sit up. One of them hurriedly turned off the TV; Vincent recognized Rolf, his confidant from their last meeting. They seemed to sense the tension in the room, waiting silently for something to happen with wide eyes.

Dex threw himself into the nearest armchair and leaned back, kicking up the footrest. Casey wasted no time claiming one of the couches for herself, muscling in on Rolf's seat until he scurried away to join his companion on the couch across from it. Vincent sat beside her warily.

"Looks like we're about to have some company," Casey growled. "All of us are gonna have to lie low for a bit."

Dex's eyes narrowed. "*All* of us?"

Casey nodded. "Yeah. These guys aren't playing. They know about people like us–what to look for."

Vincent's brow furrowed as he caught a strange undercurrent in their exchange.

"Casey, what kinda shit did you get yourself into?" Dex sighed.

"It's not my fault, this time!" she insisted. "This is serious!"

"Okay, okay. But you better explain."

"I told you about them already." Casey glanced at the nearest window nervously as if she thought someone might come crashing through it to ambush them. "The Shadowhand."

"Wait–you *told* them about the Shadowhand?" Vincent said, thunderstruck.

Dex let out a low chuckle. "I guess the wolf's gettin' out of the bag, huh? You want me to tell him?"

"They're werewolves, Vincent," Casey said bluntly.

Vincent stared at her in shock. "You *turned them?*"

"Fuck no!" Casey growled. "I found 'em!"

"Told ya you didn't have to worry about us, man," Dex smirked, leaning back in his armchair casually.

Vincent could hardly believe it. "But...there are so many of you!"

"Yeah, that's the idea," said Casey, rolling her eyes. "We found each other online. Why do you think I chose *this* college, way out in the boonies? I grew up in SoCal."

Gazing around at this ragtag bunch, the pieces finally began to fit together in Vincent's head. At the same time, a strange flame of hope sparked in his chest.

"You're in hiding?" he guessed.

"Kinda," said Dex with a shrug. "I mean, the werewolf part is. But we're just out here tryin' to live our lives, y'know? Nobody bothers us, we don't bother them."

"We look out for each other!" Rolf piped up, grinning.

"We can trust them, Vincent," Casey said.

Vincent stared back at her, gathering his scattered thoughts. "You...think we're all safe here?" he said, gesturing to the other werewolves as well.

"We know how to keep outta the spotlight," said Dex with a sly smile. "Promise." Then he turned back to Casey, some of his bravado fading. "So...what exactly are we goin' up against here?"

And Casey told them. Vincent waited silently, letting her take the lead, thanking her inwardly for all the messier details she left out. But mostly he let himself tune out, not wanting to relive the past few hours. Before he knew it her story was over, and Dex's voice snapped him back to the present.

"Shit," he said with feeling, running a hand through his dreadlocks.

"What're we gonna do?" said Rolf, alarmed.

"What Casey said," Dex replied with a grimace. "Lay low. We gotta round up the pack, get 'em all back here. And we'll all stay here 'till it's over. We'll set watches, do some perimeters around the place. And keep a good eye on our cousins in the hot seat," he added with a jerk of his head towards Casey and Vincent. Then he snapped his fingers at the two on the couch. "Hey, let's get 'em set up in a spare room, yeah? The good one."

"Aw, c'mon…" the man Vincent didn't know groaned. "I just got here!"

"Good, then you won't mind re-packing your shit." Dex gave him a wry grin. "Take 'em up on your way, will ya, Terry?"

Vincent found himself grateful for Dex's strangely good humor. Maybe this arrangement wouldn't be so bad after all.

He stood when Casey did, and the disgruntled Terry led them up the stairs. Gray light shone in from the windows overlooking the forest behind the shop. It was almost peaceful here, despite the dull thud of the music still reverberating through the floor.

"It's this one," Terry pouted, swinging open one of the various doors along the hallway. Inside was a cozy room with a loft bed on either wall.

When everything had been cleared away and Terry left them to their own devices, Vincent heaved himself up onto the now-empty bed. For a long moment he sat there in the half-light of the little room, surveying his new home.

It almost didn't feel real. Although he had to admit this was nicer than his well-worn dorm room, he had grown so comfortable with where he had been. He found himself missing his belongings especially–everything he had chosen for himself, by himself. Maybe he could convince Casey to help him go back and snag them later. All he had now was the clothes on his back, his phone, and…

Slowly he reached into his pocket. When he drew his hand out, it held Percy's amulet. It lay innocently on his palm in a heap of turquoise and silver chain, as if it had never caused a single trouble in all its days.

Could you have saved Sierra? Vincent asked it silently. He had no idea what would happen to her now–if she would become a werewolf, if the Shadowhand would imprison her, if she was even safe. Then, he realized–

Could you have saved Ava? Percy? Ava was dead. Percy...he didn't know. Maybe he would never see him again, either, now that his host was gone. If only Vincent had been able to convince him to take his amulet back...maybe he could have stopped that, too.

Maybe he could have stopped all of it.

But somehow, he couldn't fully come to terms with everything. His guilt and his grief felt foreign to him, as if he were standing on the other side of that window beside him, watching his own life through the glass.

He turned to it, half expecting to see himself, but instead found a view of the forest beyond. It looked so serene from inside, completely silent, only a picture to his eyes. He wondered what might emerge from it soon to shatter the safety of this werewolf haven. Who else might find their lives gutted and flipped inside-out thanks to him. Did these people know who exactly they were sticking their necks out for? What it might cost them?

And Henry...was he really sorry?

For everything, he had said.

For meeting me? For loving me? For betraying me?

Suddenly footsteps thudded from the hallway. Vincent turned to see Dex entering the room with fresh bedsheets and pillows heaped in his arms. He dropped some on each of their beds. "Lemme know if you need anything else."

Vincent returned the smallest smile. "Same here. I'm all yours, whatever you need me to do while I'm here. I...really can't thank you enough for this."

"No big, man." Dex flashed him an easy grin. "But you bet we're gonna put you to work–that's how all this goes, y'know. Like Rolf said, we look out for each other. If you're gonna stay with us, you're part of the pack, Vince."

Vincent blinked. He wasn't sure what to think of this new nickname. But all the same, the idea of a pack...it stirred something deep and familiar within him. For an odd moment the image of his sister tearing across the desolate plains of the Underworld flashed across his mind.

He nodded.

"Cool," said Dex, turning on his heels. "After dinner, you better take first watch with us."

When Dex had gone, Vincent found himself settling into the silence he left without really meaning to. Even Casey seemed unusually subdued. She didn't break it or even look at him as she began arranging her sheets on her bed. But unspoken words hung heavy between them, too many to count.

Come nightfall, Vincent met Dex and Casey in the small yard behind the building. The leaf-polluted lawn bordered the treeline, and if he tilted his head up he could see his bedroom window from here. Dusk painted the forest purple-gray, with deeper shadows gathering under its canopy.

Vincent's anxiety also deepened as they entered the trees. He could smell no trace of strangers, but he knew that wasn't entirely reliable. Not with vampires. And, worse still...he only now realized that he could no longer feel the sixth sense that tied him to Benjamin. He could tell, now, with an odd certainty.

It felt like he was walking blind. Completely alone, for the first time. The thought nearly rooted him to the spot.

But he could still feel the pull of the Devil's Maw itself, however much it had faded with distance. It was like a wound in the flesh of the world, whose nerves somehow connected to Vincent's very being. It wanted him back. He could feel it.

Suddenly, Dex broke into a run. Alarmed, Vincent snapped his gaze up just in time to see his body twisting and morphing and tearing itself apart and together again—until a great earth-colored wolf burst from his bones, bounding into the waiting forest.

"Dex?" Vincent called. But he was already gone.

He looked over to Casey. She was gazing out to where Dex had disappeared, an obvious longing hovering on her face. Vincent's heart twisted.

"I...didn't know you could transform whenever you want," he said quietly.

Casey didn't even afford him a glance. "Only close to the full moon. When you're not hopped up on werewolf poison."

Guilt swept over him again like a great, heavy tide, and this time it was too much. Finally he let the words rise like smoke from where they festered in his chest, mingling with every other regret.

"Casey, I'm...I'm sorry. About Hunter. About Ava."

Casey stayed silent.

"Henry and I, we..."

"I know."

Those two little words, spoken so quiet and solemn, tore through his heart like lightning. "I was wrong. About so many things. And now...*everything's* wrong. I should have—"

"I *know*, Vincent. Just listen to me next time, would you?"

The flood of his words died halfway out of his throat. But even so, his heart felt horribly, strangely lighter. He wasn't sure how Casey, for all her belligerence, found it in herself to forgive him. To trust him, even. Maybe he would never know.

"Then tell me now. What should I do? Henry's out there, taking the fall for us..."

"He'll be fine," Casey insisted, without a trace of doubt. It was almost enough for him to believe her—almost. "His dad's a bigwig. They won't hurt him." She suddenly sighed, and then her words came softer. "Whatever you think of him now...whatever he thinks of you...he still gives a shit."

Vincent's heart thudded painfully in his chest. "You're sure? After all that?"

Casey allowed a half-smile to sneak onto her face. "Yeah. He's still got that hero complex, after all. He proved that much. If he didn't care...if he hated you...he wouldn't have done what he did."

Surely, she was right... Even if Henry couldn't face what Vincent had done, this was his answer to it. His own moral sacrifice. For nothing and no one but Vincent.

But did he want Henry to do that for him? Did that mean he had corrupted the one person that had proven humans could be good, after all?

But then, he looked at Casey. Rough and standoffish and combative as she was...she had defended him. Supported him. Even let him in, just enough. He had given her little reason to do any of that, and yet...

"Casey...do you remember what you said, before? About how anyone can be pushed into doing horrible things?"

Casey finally met his gaze. "Yeah. And I stand by that."

"Do you think...Henry's worse, because of me?"

He sounded so weak, so pitiful, he felt that hatred creeping back in. But this time he held fast against it. Of all people, Casey wouldn't pity him. If she thought he was weak, she would jump on him in an instant. For once, he simply let himself be at her mercy.

What he didn't expect was for her to crack a smile.

"Yeah. And thank god for that. It's about time he stopped being so damn insufferable."

Vincent had no idea what to do with that. He just stood there dumbly until she added, "Honestly, Vincent...nothing is that simple. Being worse or better depends on who you ask, and when. I think he's starting to get that."

"Do you really believe that?" Vincent asked quietly, miserably. "Do you think he'll ever want to see me again?"

"I *hope* that stupid meathead knows you were trying to do the right thing!" Casey growled. "But right now...we can't let his sacrifice go to waste. We'll lay low until this blows over, and then we'll figure out what to do. We'll find him. Yeah?"

It struck him just then, how confident she sounded. Offering him a shoulder to lean on. Telling him how things would go. Lending him optimism. Believing in him. She almost sounded like Henry.

He smiled to himself. If Henry could get to even Casey...maybe he had given Vincent something, too.

Or maybe Henry wasn't the only good one after all. Maybe his father was completely wrong about humans, and Benjamin was right. Maybe if they could be pushed to do worse...they could also be pushed to do better.

And maybe Vincent could, too. Maybe he already had.

"C'mon, Vincent. Let's go finish this damn patrol. We're never gonna get away from this shit, are we?"

He snorted a little laugh. "Never."

So he slipped into his hellhound form and started into the forest, side-by-side with Casey. As he did, instinct rushed back to him, dimming his tangled thoughts and sharpening his senses. He welcomed it. The dark pull of the chasm seemed to blur into the shadows beneath the trees, taking his fears with it.

In spite of everything that had happened, everything he didn't understand and everything else he had lost...*he* wasn't lost. It gripped him fully, now–that inkling that had reached him earlier, that feeling of being a part of something more. In that moment the forest belonged to them and they to the wild, and crickets were singing in the undergrowth, and their hearts beat together in the darkness. Somewhere out there, Henry's did too–still fighting for everything good in this world. Still fighting for him.

He wasn't alone anymore. He knew this world, now–he had become a part of it. And he also knew that he would do anything to stay.

Thank you so much for reading!
If you liked this story, please rate and review on Amazon/Goodreads!
It helps other readers find my work, so I can keep making more.

COMING SOON

Find out what happens next in

BOOK 2: OUR BRIGHT WINDOW

Because we all know Vincent's gonna go after Henry...

ACKNOWLEDGEMENTS

First and foremost, there would be no story without the imagination and heart my two favorite people share. Thank you Darla, for creating something truly magical—and for your grace in allowing me to smash it around like Play-Doh until it fit my purposes. You have always encouraged me to pursue the things I care about, no matter what anyone else thinks. And thank you Pierce, for much of the same. In many ways this story is a love letter to you, and also to the similarly smashed-up pieces inside both of us that may not have always fit together.

Second, an endless amount of appreciation and love for the most incredible alpha reader in the universe. Thank you so much, Sketch, for your infinite patience and dedication towards every draft you had to slog through. Without your expertise I doubt this project would have come to fruition.

Third, the most ardent thank-you to my wonderful beta readers, Sarah and Elle, and all the detailed and passionate feedback that really polished this hunk of rock into something special. And a special shoutout to Moss, to whom I owe any success I ever see thanks to your advice and generosity. If more people were like you, the world would be a much kinder place.

Finally, all my love to my family and friends, of course. To my mom for always encouraging me to chase my passions, creative or otherwise, and for loving me through so many things much of the world doesn't. To my dad for showing me how to afford all people the respect they deserve, and modeling the worldviews I treasure and try to emulate. To my buddies Fro and Zack for all the laughs and for inspiring this story—thanks for baring your souls a little, for the sake of our shenanigans. And lastly to my fur babies, both past and present, for that special unconditional love that heals all wounds.

Last but not least...thank YOU, dearest reader, for taking a chance (hehe) on me. As my debut novel, I can only hope making it this far means you found something worth loving in here somewhere. And that means the world to me. All I really want is for my ideas to matter a little bit in the grand scheme of things.

If you like my stories, please share with someone you think would like them too! Making a living as an author has been my dream since I was a little bullied middle-schooler drowning my loneliness in books, and readers like you make that dream real. So thank you, from the depths of my weird little heart.

ABOUT THE AUTHOR

James Chance has always been haunted by monsters. Everyone has some kind of creature inside them. Everyone is a little dark and strange. His stories explore how our monsters make us human—and what we should do about it. Drawing from a background in nonprofit finance and sociology, he strives to forge understanding between people in an increasingly weird world. He lives in Southern California with his family of rescues (animals included).

Find me on social media!

Instagram:	instagram.com/aferalchance
Threads:	threads.net/@aferalchance
Bluesky:	aferalchance.bsky.social
YouTube:	youtube.com/@feralchance
Tumblr:	a-feral-chance.tumblr.com
Ko-Fi:	ko-fi.com/jameschance

**Sign up for my newsletter and receive
a free short story prequel to *Our Dark Mirror*!**

 **aferalchance.com**

www.ingramcontent.com/pod-product-compliance
Lightning Source LLC
Chambersburg PA
CBHW030044130726
47901CB00007BA/1881